NEW LIFE

NEW LIFE

Laura Greenway

To Leda,
Enjoy the books!
Best Wishes
Laura Greenway
11-23-18

NORTH STAR PRESS OF ST. CLOUD, INC.
St. Cloud, Minnesota

ACKNOWLEDGEMENTS

My friends: Sandra Morris, Kathy Strege, Penny Griffiths, Susan McPherson, Linda Vanswol and more, for always believing in me.

I would also like to thank my sons Alex and Joseph Greco for loving me and while they may not have fully believed the importance of this event to me, they supported me in the effort.

I would like to thank my granddaughters Kahlan and Anna Greco for just being alive to make me want to be an inspiration for them. Hi Kahlan! I promised you I would put your name in my book!

I would like to thank my sister, Cindy Siefert-Raw for her "reach for the moon" idealism. If you want it bad enough, you CAN do it. Thanks Cindy, for the motivation.

I would like to thank my mother, I. Helen Siefert for listening to my chapters as I wrote them and finally saying, "Enough! I want to see the final product in print!" That helped me want to finish this book.

I would certainly like to thank my father Henry Siefert for his stories about wood nymphs, hodags and other mythical creatures of Wisconsin that were the inspiration behind this book.

Thank you Seal! This would have never happened if not for your belief in me and in New Life.

But most of all, I would like to thank my husband Bill, for his constant encouragement. No matter what I wanted to do in life, he supported me completely. Without his support and love, this book would have never been attempted, nonetheless completed. Thank you my wonderful husband.

CHAPTER 1
MOVING

Mom did it. She actually did it. She had been talking about this move for years, but now she had finally done something about it. When my mother, Valerie, made up her mind about something, it took an act of Congress to change it.

My name is Laurel. My dad, Ben, who wasn't my real dad in the biological sense, was in the Army and had just been mobilized to Iraq. Mom had said she wasn't going to stay in the D.C. area without him. I called Ben my dad to his face and to mom, but otherwise I thought of and called him Ben.

Mom had wanted to move back to Wisconsin for a long time, but the Army kept us moving to every place but Wisconsin. She was always commenting on how she couldn't wait for the day Ben would retire so we could move back to Wisconsin. But, now that he was mobilized to Iraq for the next year and would be retiring when he got back, she decided that she and I were moving back to Wisconsin now. There was nothing holding us in Washington, D.C., anymore. Ben wasn't there. We really had no good reason to stay, but I was loathed to move again just the same.

Mom had knocked on my door, walked in after I invited her in and dropped the bomb on me. "The moving company will be here in two days," she said calmly while she looked around my room.

I had two days to pack, and my room was a mess! It would have been nice to get more notice. It's not like we had to sell the house or give notice at the apartment complex or anything. We lived in military housing, and when orders for Ben came through transferring him somewhere else, there was no real notice to give, except to the military housing office. They were always real cool with the whole moving thing at the drop of a hat, as the lady at the housing office probably dealt with this kind of thing on a daily basis. This was the first time that we weren't going to a new duty station. This time we were going to the home we all had wanted for a long time.

While it was nice that the Army paid a moving company to move us to our next duty station, or in this case being the last move, to our home of record, the pain of getting ready for the move—any move—was something I hated . . . every time.

"What does dad think about this move? Can't we discuss this?" I asked as I looked around my room. Everything would need to be pitched out or ready for the

1

moving people to box up. It was a lot of annoying work, so I was trying to stall for time.

Mom smiled and said that we would be fine, that there were empty boxes in the hallway for the stuff I wanted to give to the thrift shop. Every military post that we lived on or near had a thrift shop for the service members and their families to buy used items at a fraction of the cost of what new would be.

My mother looked at me and smiled and said, "Your dad agreed that this was what was best for us, for all of us. You and I will have a year to get the north woods house ready for your dad when he gets there."

She looked so calm about this whole thing. "But Dad's only been gone for a week!" I cried. "How'll he get mail to us? How'll he be able to get in touch with us? Will he get my text messages?" I knew I was complaining, but I couldn't help it. Why did we have to leave so soon? I knew the answer. Mom was a school counselor who had always wanted to be a therapist. However, she had to have a license to be a therapist, not just the Master's degree in Community Counseling that she had already received. The degree was good enough to be a school counselor without the license. She wanted to wait until we had moved to Wisconsin to take the licensing exam, and we were in the middle of summer. There was no school now, so it was the perfect time to move.

"We have our cell phones. He'll call us through the Army com link, as usual. Once we have Internet service, he'll send us emails. He'll text you, don't worry!" She said as she walked out of my bedroom and shut the door behind her. She opened the door back up, gave me a big smile and said, "Your dad has the address of the north woods house. He'll send you snail-mail letters, too. You know we have been waiting for this for a long time." She had a wistful look as she exited my door the second time. I wish I could be that excited about this move.

Mom and Ben had been planning their retirement for the last seven years. Both of them loved the Wisconsin north woods and had talked about retiring there when Ben retired from the Army. I liked what I'd seen when I'd been up there the few times we were able to go to the north woods house. When Ben inherited some land in the north woods of Wisconsin, he and mom had built a house on the river for their retirement home. They would laugh and call it the Forever House. It was going to be our forever house. Of course, some day I would move out when I went to college or when I got married, but being an only child, eventually the house would be mine.

The house was a two-story log cabin. At least, it looked like a log cabin. The neat thing about the house was it was made out of recycled materials processed to look like real wood, with wood pulp mixed in to give it the right color. The texture, color—everything about the logs looked like real lumber. It was cool to know that we didn't kill any trees to build our house. There was a screened in porch in the front of the house, which faced the river. The back of the house faced the parking area and driveway. We had four bedrooms and three full baths. At the times when Ben was stationed at an Army post near the house, we would open it up for vacations. Right now, the house was mothballed. At least that was what I called it. There were no actual mothballs, but the exterminator did have a contract with my mom and Ben to come through a couple of times a year to make sure that the bugs and mice didn't make permanent homes in our house. The pipes had been winterized with antifreeze and all of the furniture and lamps had been covered with sheets to reduce dust. I wondered now if my mom had talked to a plumbing company about getting the well water turned on and pressurized and the electric company about getting the electricity and gas turned on. Knowing my mom, she had arranged for that before even telling me that we were moving. I wondered if George was going to go to the house and get it ready for our arrival.

George Loon was my mom's childhood friend from the Lac Du Flambeau Indian reservation. He would occasionally drive down from the reservation and check on the house. He was distantly related to my mother, as my grandfather on my mom's side was part Ojibwa Indian. Mom's aunt Susan, my grandfather's sister—now deceased —used to live near the reservation and do volunteer work there. Sometimes when my mom and her dad would go up north, they would go to the reservation with Susan. Susan and my grandfather did work with the tribal council, helping the residents of the reservation, while my mom used to hang out with the Ojibwa Indian kids, which I suppose are correctly called Ojibwa Native American kids. "The adults would get together to do important grown up stuff!" Mom would laugh and say. "George and I just wanted to hang out together with the other kids our age."

As I reflected on things my mom had told me, I wondered if our house in Tomahawk was too far from the reservation to go to school with the reservation kids. I wondered if the natives had their own school. Even though at that moment I wasn't currently in school, it would have been nice to finish my senior year with kids that I knew. I didn't know any of the kids at the reservation, but because my mom knew George and he lived on the reservation, it would have been easy enough to meet some of them. I had just finished my junior year. I was seventeen years old and as far as I was concerned, I was not going to finish high school with anyone I knew. I was going to a new school in a new place, and I would miss all of my friends. Well, as much as they were friends. I guessed truthfully, I'd miss the familiarity of the last five years of being in D.C. more than my so-called friends.

My friends weren't all that terribly close to me. I thought of who could be considered my best friend, Jennifer, who was selfish and knew she was beautiful. She never made me feel like an ugly duckling next to her, just that I wasn't as good looking as she was. Then again, no one was. Jennifer was gorgeous in the fashion-model sense, with perfect curves and long blond hair. She was beautiful and vain, and she thought that I agreed with her most of the time. She liked it when people agreed with her. Not that I actually did agree with what she was saying all the time, it just seemed easier than arguing or having her mad at me. She got angry real easy. I also didn't make demands on her, so I think that was why she liked me. She wanted to be the center of attention. Since she was the most popular girl in the school, she only hung around with kids who were good looking. I was no fashion model, but I knew I wasn't ugly. I looked at myself in the mirror on my closet door and appraised myself critically. I didn't look too bad.

I had long hair, about half way down my back. It was thick, but not so thick that it poofed out at the bottom. It hung stick straight, and it was a light brown. I wished it had some natural curl to it. Mom had naturally wavy hair, and she complained about it, but mine was straight as straw. It was a pretty color though, a natural color that I had never seen on anyone else. To me, my hair appeared to be just a shade different from normal light-brown hair. To me it looked kind of like a dye job that was a mistake but turned out surprisingly nice. Maybe I just hadn't seen that many people with this shade of light-brown. I usually saw a lot of blonds or brunettes, or kids with black hair, but none with hair the same color as mine. As I was studying my reflection in the mirror, I looked at my green eyes. Mom has green eyes too, but side by side, people said I looked like I had bright-green contact lenses. They were similar to Mom's eyes but a much deeper and brighter green. Mom always smiled and told me that I had emerald eyes. I was always a little self-conscious about them, because when people looked into my eyes, occasionally they would do a double take. Once in a while people would ask me if I was wearing contacts. When I said no, they sometimes looked like they didn't believe me. But, hey, didn't blue eyes come in different shades? What was the big deal with having green eyes that were so bright? As far as I was concerned, I was lucky. I didn't need glasses or contacts. I had 20/20 vision. It didn't matter what color my eyes were, did it?

I was fairly tall, at least compared to my mom. I was five-foot-eight, and she was five-three. I was also probably too thin, although I didn't have an eating disorder. At least I didn't think I did. Funny to have a teenager say she didn't have an eating disorder. Weren't all psychologists saying that most teenagers had some kind of eating disorder? Mom insisted that we all eat a healthy diet, and she tried to make a variety of foods, although vegetables were always the biggest portion of the meal, at least for dinner. Breakfast was usually a bowl of cereal with some one-percent milk. Lunch was a sandwich, either peanut butter or a lean cold cut with fat free mayonnaise on whole wheat. Either way, there wasn't a lot of fat in our diet. Mom had an average build and so did

Ben. While my mom was not obese, it wouldn't have hurt her to lose a couple of pounds. I think she snuck chocolate into her diet. I laughed at the thought. Maybe she snuck chocolate a little too often. I wasn't into chocolate or desserts or sweet things like that. I didn't even like candy. It was another way I felt different from other people. All of my friends loved Halloween and candy. I enjoyed the parties and social activities. I'd give away my candy. I liked being with people even if I didn't feel like I fully fit in.

I looked around my room at the pile of neatly folded clean clothes my mom had placed on my dresser. I looked at the pile of books on the floor and the overloaded bookshelves. I loved to read. I looked at my school note books tossed on the desk last June, and here it was the end of July. I thought of school books. Yeah, I was starting a new school this fall. Starting over—yuck. I sat on my bed and contemplated my future. I didn't relish the idea of going to a new school for senior year. I tried to convince myself that it'd have been harder to move during the school year.

At least now I didn't have a boyfriend I would miss when I left. Mark and I broke up at prom. He was a senior I had dated for the last six months of school. He was taller than I was and quite good looking in a high-school-jock kind of way. I caught him kissing some skank in the hallway on prom night. What a way to remember prom. Some boyfriend he'd turned out to be. Mark had been my first real boyfriend, too. Good thing we hadn't gone very far in our relationship, or I think I would have been devastated by his kissing this other girl. I had contemplated more than hand holding or kissing with him, and I knew he was certainly interested in pursuing other activities in our relationship, but the opportunity never presented itself to go any farther. Mom was big on group activities and chaperones, so while I was allowed to date, there always had to be someone else around. The girl Mark was kissing at prom, Melissa, was also a senior and didn't have the restrictions on her activities I did. She was known around school as easy. I guess my boyfriend decided that she was better than waiting for a chance with me. While the betrayal had stung my pride, I wasn't in love with him. I'd thought I was, but after that night when I saw him kissing Melissa, I saw him as a testosterone controlled idiot and not worth my time. It was easy to avoid him after that.

I went into the hallway and grabbed a box to start the whole thrift-store box-packaging activity. While holding the box, I looked around for where to start. I had books on the floor, clothes on my dresser, a collection of horse bone-china figurines, including some winged Pegasus horses. I always wished that they were real. Horses were really neat, but a winged horse! How exciting would that be? At night I'd fantasize about a winged horse coming to my room and taking me out into the night sky.

I sat on the edge of my bed with the box on my lap. It wasn't like I was totally against living in Wisconsin. It was just the whole packing up and moving part I hated. I hated new schools and trying to make new friends. I hated trying to fit in when I never really seemed to fit in anywhere. Each move we made, each new house brought the hopes that this would be the perfect place for me. I had these high expectations that I'd be around other kids who liked what I liked and were maybe, just maybe, like me.

In this last move to the D.C. area, at the new school, Jennifer and I got along when we first met. I knew her type, and I knew how to play the game. I knew how to get her to like me. I could see right off that she was part of the "in crowd" and that was always a good place to start in a new school. I was friendly without being too friendly. I let her do the talking and pretty much kept my thoughts to myself. I'd learned early in life that no one was interested in my thoughts other than my mom and Ben.

I was really interested in nature. I had an obsession with knowing all the different types of trees, birds, animals, and foliage wherever we lived. The girls my age in all the places I'd lived had absolutely no interest in these things. They only thought about My Space, Facebook, texting, Internet sites, boys, hair, clothes, and makeup. At least, since we had reached our teen years. It was Barbie dolls before that.

When I was younger, I'd pick and sniff the leaves on the trees and bushes and try to talk to my new friends about the different textures and scents of leaves, but other kids had no interest. If I tried to push the subject on them, they'd stare at me like I was nuts, so I let it go and went on the Internet with them or experimented with makeup so I'd fit in. I had my own Facebook site. However, when I was with Ben, he was always interested in what I wanted to talk about. We bought books on the different trees in the different states where we had lived. We bought bird books and sometimes would go to a local park to bird watch. I could never understand how the other kids couldn't be interested in the natural world around them. I guess I was a naturalist or a botanist at heart. Mom and Ben didn't try to force me to be interested in nature. If anything, I pushed it on them. Sometimes Mom would give me a weird look if I became too interested in the woods. Like there was something wrong with wanting to know each tree, bird, and shrub. But Ben thought my interest in the natural order of things was great and encouraged me. Ben was a great guy. I would have expected more encouragement from my mother, as she herself had had an obsession with the woods when she was younger. She loved being in the Wisconsin north woods. However, she was not interested in the name of each living plant there. I was born in Wisconsin, and conceived in the north woods.

I don't know much about my biological dad. Truth is, I don't know anything at all. I don't know what he looked like. I've never seen a photo, and I don't even know what color his eyes or hair were. I imagined his hair must be the same as mine, and just as straight. I figured he must have been tall, too. I wondered what his personality had been like. Sometimes I wished he'd just show up one day, knock at the door and tell me he had been searching for me all of these years. Mom wouldn't talk about that time in her life. She kept telling me that someday—when she was more comfortable with it—she'd tell me all about the short time she knew my father.

I know Mom grew up in lower Wisconsin. She told me lots of stories about the cottage her father owned in the north woods and that she went there a lot while growing up. My grandfather's cottage had been about an hour's drive from where our house was. Grandfather would take my mother up to his cottage any chance that they had to escape the hustle and bustle of city life. Racine, the town where Mom was born was not the biggest town in Wisconsin. But it was a large city with noise and telephones and no peace and quiet. Mom would tell me it was not unusual for her dad and her to go up for a weekend. It was a six-hour drive from Racine to the north woods cottage by Presque Isle. Just the anticipation of knowing in a few hours they would be in the north woods would make Mom and Grandpa happy on the drive up. Mom said Grandpa would laugh during the long drive to the cottage and say half of the fun of being at the cottage was seeing the wood nymphs frolic in the trees. Mom said she would laugh with him, knowing there was no such thing. All legends and jokes. Mom and her dad would have a nice weekend at the cottage, then drive back to the city house in Racine on Sunday. Mom said that, while they enjoyed the long ride up to the cottage, not so much the long drive back.

On one trip up to the cottage my mom told me about when she was first old enough to take these long trips with just her father. Her dad told her about the Rhinelander Hodag. The Hodag was a mythical creature, a cross between a cow and a dinosaur. It was a really unfriendly beast but had the best tasting milk. The legend said that during the height of the logging camps in northern Wisconsin at the end of the nineteenth century and the beginning of the twentieth, the real manly lumberjacks would dare each other to go out into the woods at night to milk a Hodag. The stories said the biggest, strongest lumberjacks thought it would be great fun to come back with a bucket of Hodag milk. However, many of them never returned to the camp after venturing out into the woods at night to find the legendary beast. The Hodag only came out at night. No one knew where they stayed during the day. The stories said that, once you heard the cry of the Hodag, you never forgot it. The sound made the skin feel like it wanted to peel right off of your bones because it made the skin crawl so horribly. Almost no one ever saw a Hodag. The exceptions were the rare lumberjack who went out into the woods and came back with the milk. However, the minds of these men were never right again. The man's mind would regress to some part deep inside. They'd scream blood-curdling screams in their sleep. Some of the men who returned would be able to talk, but what came out of their mouths would be some kind of babbling. Complete gibberish. Occasionally one would describe the Hodag with its spikes and huge teeth, but was this what he actually saw or delusions and hallucinations? The lumberjacks that survived the experience with the Hodag would forever after have the mind of a child, able to do easy tasks but ruined forever. Eventually the logging camps disbursed, and no one heard of Hodags again. Now and again, there would be talk of a child or an adult who ventured into the woods at night and never was seen again. Was that because they were lost, or did the Hodag or some other animal eat them? I guess the lesson of the story was—do not go out into the woods at night, especially alone. I didn't want to go out into the woods at night. Not that I was afraid of Hodags. I was afraid of real things like bears and wolves.

Mom said Grandmother didn't enjoy the north woods cottage very much as she had more work to do there than at the city house in the southern part of the state. There were no bathrooms, no running water, no modern appliances, no air conditioning, or any other modern conveniences in the cottage. Grandma avoided the north woods, preferring the comforts of the city house. The way Mom described it, it was evident that Grandma didn't like to rough it. However, my mom said that she and her father had found it great fun with no modern amenities. They enjoyed making do with what they had, and living sparsely was most of the fun.

Mom said the cottage was up the hill from a large lake and had lots of acreage. There was no civilization for miles. It wasn't unusual to see a bear or timber wolf walk past the cottage. It was rustic and seemed to almost blend in with the woods. There was the main cabin with two additions built on. The main building had a huge white cedar bunk bed set in the corner, a six-chair table next to it, a pot belly stove, a desk, and a cabinet. There was a small hallway that led to a tiny bedroom with a curtain for a door, and at the end of the hall was a wood-burning cooking stove next to an old fashioned original ice box that was used to store dishes. The first addition was the kitchen. It had a kitchen sink, where a large basin was set for washing dishes and dish water would run out of a pipe into the woods. There was a refrigerator. There was also a propane gas range, but my mom said that was never used. She'd laugh and tell me that the mice probably lived in there. The second addition was an enclosed porch that had a larger curtained-off area for a bedroom. That bedroom had a full-size bed, dresser, and a large closet. There was a large table at the other end of the porch by the front door. Another large sliding-door closet held fishing gear and coats by the front door. The cabin had a generator—rarely used as kerosene lanterns worked fine for lighting. The refrigerator was run by propane from a tank, and food was cooked on a wood stove. Heat was provided by a pot-belly stove in the middle of the living room. Drinking water was brought in gallon-sized washed-out milk jugs. The outhouse was the toilet facilities.

Bath and wash water was obtained from runoff in a rain barrel and heated in big pots on the wood stove in the fall, winter, and spring. The lake provided the bathing and washing water in the summer. I thought that was kind of gross, but Mom said she and her dad did it all of the time at the cottage. Grandfather taught my mother how to live off of the woods. She knows how to tap maple trees and boil the sap for syrup. As an adult, she'd go to the cabin alone or with her father. As her dad got older, they went there less. Mom would go up there for the weekend by herself. After Mom married Ben, she stopped going up to the cottage. Both my grandparents are deceased now. I didn't know them very well. They died while I was quite young. I wished I could have experienced the times when Mom and Grandpa went to the cabin enjoying the fresh air and isolation from humanity and telephones.

Mom wasn't shy and got along great with people. But, there were times she enjoyed being alone. When she went to the cottage before she met Ben, she said the cell phone was left in the car. It was while she was staying at her father's cottage that she met my biological father. I don't know how they met. Mom said she hadn't dated much before she met him and said she fell in love with my dad at first sight. My mother still has high morals, so I believe she told me the truth. Mom and my real dad had a great weekend together, and then she never saw him again. She walked away from that weekend pregnant with me. That's all she'd tell me about my bio dad. She'd only tell me not to judge her for having a weekend adventure. She'd tell me how she loved me enough for two parents. Then when Ben came into our lives when I was still really little, she told me we were now a complete family. Who my bio dad was didn't matter.

Sitting on my bed with the box in my hands, I thought about how I hated the idea that I wouldn't be able to talk to Ben. I knew I'd be able to talk to him on the phone and text him, but that wasn't the same as in person. He wasn't my real dad, but in every way that counted, he was. He was kind to me, listened to me, and I knew he loved me. Not just because I was his wife's daughter, but because he was genuinely fond of me. I loved him too. I really hated it when he was gone. Usually the Army only kept him away for a few weeks at a time. But sometimes he left for longer periods. I guess overall we were lucky though. He had only been deployed overseas once before. Ben had just left for a twelve-month deployment. Mom hated it. After his return, we expected he'd be able to retire, and we were all going to live in the north woods of Wisconsin. Only now we weren't waiting for him to come back. Mom and I were moving by ourselves.

CHAPTER 2
WISCONSIN

I was ready when the moving van arrived. All of the stuff I didn't want had been boxed up and dropped off at the thrift store with Mom's old stuff. She and I stayed out of the way while the movers packed all of our belongings into the moving van. Mom was drinking her coffee—her custom when the moving men came. Every time we had to move, the coffee maker and cup were the last things to be packed. Should I start my own moving traditions? Did most people do such things? I guessed when a person moved often enough, it wouldn't be unusual to have a tradition or two about moving. That was one good thing about moving to the forever house. I wouldn't be moving so often anymore.

"Did you pack all of the things you can't live without for the next week or so in your suitcase and put them in the truck?" Mom asked.

"Yeah. I only need clothes and a couple of books," I said distractedly looking around our home and seeing it filling with moving boxes while all of the things that made it our home were packed up carefully. All of the photos from the hallway, our family gallery, were off of the wall and waiting to be wrapped in bubble wrap and placed in a box. Mom and Ben's favorite pictures from the living room were already on the van. Some guy was taking my bed apart so that the mattress, box spring, and frame could fit in the van. Another guy was packing up kitchen stuff. Each time we moved, I couldn't get over how much stuff we had in the kitchen. I truly believed that Mom had every kitchen gadget there was, old and new. Every new product on the market supposed to make cooking easier, food taste better or preparation quicker, Mom bought.

Mom and I sat on the last piece of living room furniture. I thought about Karen.

Mom's girlfriend Karen had flown out to D.C. to drive our car to Wisconsin while Mom drove Ben's pickup. Karen left a couple of days before we did so she could meet the electrician at the north woods house. By the time Mom and I arrived, the water, electric, and gas would be turned on, and we could just move in. Mom had some great friends from her childhood. I wished I could make friends as easily and keep them as long as she did.

As we sat there, I thought about what had happened a couple of days ago— right after I had packed my first thrift store box. I had called Jennifer. When I told her that I was leaving, she just paused, then asked when. I told her in a couple of days.

She said, "Huh, no kidding?" We talked for a minute. Then after another pause, she just said, "Well, see ya." Then she hung up.

I thought that having a friend for almost five years would warrant more than a "huh" and a "bye." I had asked her if she was going to miss me, not really caring I guess, whether she would or wouldn't. But in a kind of masochistic way, I wanted her answer. I knew what she was going to say, or at least the meaning behind the words. She said in an uninterested kind of way, "Uh, yeah, sure, I guess."

I didn't ask if she would write me. I knew she wouldn't. It was the same every move. There had been times when I'd think I'd made a decent friend, but when it was time to leave, it was no big deal. The fact that it was no big deal on my part either didn't improve my thoughts on the matter. Was I just a military brat that didn't make close friends because subconsciously I knew I would be leaving and there could be sad feelings? I felt sadder that I hadn't had better and closer friendships. It was more a feeling of something missing. There was more to life than I was getting, more to friendships, and there was a hole in my life. I didn't understand the hole, but I knew it was there. I kept wishing and hoping that each move would be different, that the next move would find me one friend like my mother had. Only my mother didn't have just one friend. She had lot them and kept them. Mom made friends so easily. Why was it so hard for me? What was wrong with me?

I was sitting deep in thought when Mom waved her hand in front of my face, saying, "Hello, are you in there? You seem so lost in thought." She took my hand and gently raised me to my feet. She sighed. "I have to wash my coffee cup now. They're almost finished. We have to let them do the last bit of packing and take the love seat out to the truck." Less than an hour later, we were on our way.

I knew we were getting close to our house when we drove past Stevens Point in central Wisconsin. The quality of the air started to change. It had a cleaner taste, and the pine scent was perfect, the kind of scent home fragrance companies were always trying to copy. My lungs felt they could handle more air, it seemed so fresh. I took lots of full breaths and started to relax. I liked the smell and feel of the north woods. We were getting close now. Another hour. After almost two days. I was tired and my mom was even more exhausted. She let me drive a little, but since I had only had my license for six months, not for long stretches. She didn't want to test my highway driving skills, especially with Ben's big Dodge Ram pickup.

We were just outside of Tomahawk, Wisconsin. Really close. Our gravel driveway was a mile long. This was going to be a pain in the winter, I thought, with all the twisting turns. There were no tree branches in the road. Wow, that was a first. There were always tree branches to be cleared when we got there. I wondered which of us was going to plow the driveway in winter? Me? Mom? Was she going to hire somebody to do it? Maybe a miracle would happen and Ben would be able to come home before winter. Even as I thought that, I knew it wasn't going to happen. Not unless he was wounded or dead. Neither was acceptable. I sighed. We would just have to wait and deal with it. Mom would figure out what to do. She always figured everything out.

We pulled up in back of the house to unload. Karen waved from the back porch. Mom's car and Karen's car were there. At the end of the driveway, we could fit four cars easily. We also had a four-car garage with a work room.

The lawn was mowed, the bushes were trimmed and the debris, if there had been any from the previous winter had been cleared away. It didn't look like there would be a lot of exterior work to get the house presentable. On closer inspection, it didn't look like the yard needed any work at all. Karen trotted down the stairs of the porch with a big grin. "Glad to see you finally made it!" she said.

"It was a long drive and, boy, am I glad we're here. It looks great! Did you find many branches in the driveway? How did you get the lawn mowed and the exterior so cleaned up? Who brought your car up?" Mom asked Karen.

"Wow, lots of questions. It sure is nice to see you, too. I didn't do the clean up, though. I thought you hired it out." Karen replied. "Inside is all cleaned up, too. All the dust covers are washed and put away, and there's no dust on any countertops. I wouldn't mind hiring whoever it was you hired to clean up my house. Oh, and my son and a friend of his followed me up from Racine in the friend's car and then went back. That's how I have a car to go home in." Karen said, smiling

"I didn't hire anybody," Mom said thoughtfully. "I don't know who did this."

Karen looked confused. "Maybe George did it. Did he know you were coming?"

"Yes," my mom replied. "That must be it. Hey, I am really glad to see you, you know! I really appreciate not having to wait for plumbers and utility guys!" Mom said to Karen and asked how her drive from D.C. was. She asked if the car handled well and a lot of other mundane things. Karen and my mom walked into the house, but I decided to go around the house to the river.

There was a pier now. There hadn't been one the last time I was there. Was it called a pier or a dock? I wasn't sure. Was there a difference? I would call it a pier. I walked out onto it and sat at the end and took off my tennis shoes and socks and put my feet in the water. The water was cool and felt good on my feet after the long drive. I leaned my head back and looked up at the tree branches that reached out over the water over my head. The sky was blue with almost no clouds. The weather was warm. For the first time—even though I'd been here before—I felt like I'd come home. I thought about that for a while. Home. What a concept. I'd been here all of ten minutes, and I felt as if I'd come home. In all of the other moves in my life, we ended up on some other military base. All had the same things—gate guards checking for ID cards and automobile authorization stickers on post vehicles. There was a commissary and an exchange. Outside the post were always pawn shops, second-hand stores, and a variety of restaurants.

This spot reminded me of a campground. But with big differences. There were no people around. This wasn't a man made or preserved area. This was the real deal. I was in the middle of the north woods of the Wisconsin forest. I was sitting on a pier by a house in the middle of a natural wilderness. I could imagine a time when the Native Americans would walk along this river, spearing fish. Bears and deer walked around here. Still did. I thought about it. Porcupines, foxes, beavers, badgers, and raccoons all lived in these woods. I thought that was unbelievably cool. Even though I liked people—and I wanted to be liked by them—I never felt as if I really fit in. I was more comfortable alone. I liked the idea of living with nature. I liked this place. I felt I could really be myself here.

I didn't have to put on a front to be accepted, and I didn't have neighbors watching every move I made. Okay, when we lived on military bases the neighbors probably weren't staring out particularly for me, but there was always some neighbor in a nearby yard or a neighbor standing in front of his house watching the world go by. Worse yet, other teenagers up the block would be doing stuff without inviting me. Then as I sat there knowing no one would see me and realizing I felt at home, I laughed. A real laugh. A deep down from the bottom of my gut kind of laugh. I laughed and laughed until I cried, and I was at peace. Was this a cathartic experience? Was that the right word? Was it just a release from the stress of moving, or was I really comfortable. Truth was, I felt good. I couldn't get over how much I liked this place. I wondered why I had never felt that before when I was here, and I thought the reason was because it had always been a vacation before. A vacation with work involved. We would come here for a week or two at the most. Ben and I would usually spent the first few days clearing out bushes that blocked the view of the water, mowing the lawn, clearing the driveway of fallen branches, and doing repairs. Mom cleaned up the dust and washed dust covers, just to put them back when it was time to leave.

The pier was new. I had never seen one like it. I honestly hadn't seen that many piers in my life, and I couldn't remember ever concentrating on their details, but I couldn't see any hardware holding it together. It looked like it was made of wood, but the boards were like nothing I'd seen before. They were smooth, but they were cut in a way different from any boards I had seen before. They looked like they were branches. They appeared almost naturally grown to look like boards and not cut into boards. *Huh*, I thought. In fact, the whole pier looked like it came from one piece of wood or one tree. It was cool looking. I liked it. There were even benches on each side. They weren't big enough to block a boat being docked there, but wide enough for two people to sit on each. They, too, looked like they were made out of the same piece of wood as the rest of the pier. I wondered who my mom had found to do this kind of work. I wondered why she didn't tell me about it. Maybe she didn't think I'd be interested, but with my interest in botany and the sciences, why wouldn't she think I'd be interested? Maybe it was a surprise. If that was the idea, it worked. She knew I liked to fish. Maybe it was a surprise for me so that I had a place to do that. I rarely caught anything. Ben tried to teach me techniques, but to be honest, neither he nor my mom were very good at fishing. But, I did like to try. They did too, and we all got excited when anyone caught anything.

Peace and tranquility. That was what it was called, wasn't it? I didn't remember having had a truly peaceful moment before, not like this. Don't get me wrong, I'd been happy. I'd had lots of times when I was happy. I enjoy my time with Mom and Ben. I loved them and they loved me. We did fun things together. I even enjoyed my various schools. I especially liked science. But here, in this spot, I felt blissfully happy, and it made no sense. I was just a seventeen-year-old girl sitting on a pier with her feet in a river enjoying a summer day. What was so special about that? There was no phone, no computer, no video games, no books, no conversations with other girls, and no boys. There was just me on the pier, having a moment with nature, and I liked it. I must have sat in my state of unreasonable bliss for an hour or more, when I noticed my mom calling for me to help unload the pickup.

After unpacking the truck, I walked around the house to see if there were any other changes. Mom and Karen were still discussing how wonderfully clean the house was, and what was mom going to give George as a thank you gift for getting the house ready for us. "I only just called him a couple of days ago" Mom explained, "I don't know how he had the time to get all the dust out of all of the crevices and all the dust covers washed and put away. I'm really impressed with the yard work and the clearing of broken branches from the driveway."

"Amazing." Karen, agreed. I heard them talking through the kitchen window. I could smell Italian food cooking. I went in to investigate.

After dinner, the temperature started dropping. In the Wisconsin north woods it could get cool at night even in the summer. After living on the edge of the Mason Dixon line, my mom and I weren't used to summers with cool evenings. It had been hot in D.C. Mom asked me to carry in some wood from the pile for a fire in the fireplace. As I walked out behind the shed to our wood pile, I saw another interesting thing. The wood pile had been filled. Ben taught me how to find wood old enough to burn well, but not so old that it would go up in flames too quickly. That was no good. It was important to know the difference between rotted wood and well-seasoned wood. Well-seasoned wood burned best, and all of the firewood in our wood pile was well seasoned. There was at least a cord of wood here. Who would have done that? I wasn't completely sure how much wood was in a cord, but it was a lot, and this was a whole lot of wood. I was guessing that there was enough wood stacked that, if we lit the fireplace every day for a year, we wouldn't run out. Did George do this, too? Where'd he find the time in less than a week? Wow, Mom had some nice friends. Did she know about this? I gathered up an armload of wood and went back into the house.

"Mom, did you see the stack of wood in the wood pile out back?" I asked as I brought the wood into the living room and put it by the fireplace.

"Hmm, dear?" Mom replied sleepily. She was falling asleep on the couch, completely tired out. I had slept a lot more on the trip than she had. Karen had helped her with dinner. We had spaghetti with a jarred sauce, and Pillsbury biscuits. Karen and I had cleaned up and loaded the dishwasher. Mom had pretty much stayed awake the entire trip across from Washington, D.C., to Tomahawk and lay on the couch after dinner. I didn't think that the wood pile was important enough to discuss at that moment. I figured it was another thing that George did. I put some wood in the fireplace and added a starter log. I pulled out a long fireplace match and lit the starter log. Mom and Ben loved the fireplace but hated dealing with paper and kindling. She didn't mind cleaning out the ashes. That was always her job when we were packing to leave after a vacation in this house. She'd clean the fireplace and do the vacuuming. Ben and I would load the suitcases into the car. But we weren't leaving this time. I thought it funny that my mom liked roughing it and camping as a kid, but now liked modern conveniences.

I'd pulled the starter log—made from wood pulp and saturated with something flammable—from a box next to the fireplace. I wondered if they lost potency after a couple years. It'd been that long since the last time we'd been here. But the starter log caught when I touched the match to it. I checked to make sure the damper was open. It was a good thing I used the really long matches, or I would have burned my fingers.

Yup, Mom loved the north woods and nature but also indoor plumbing, a dishwasher, electric refrigerator, central air, and a furnace. This house was very different from the cottage my mom and her dad went to when she was younger. I thought it funny how people and things changed as they aged. I bet Mom and Grandpa didn't have starter logs up at the old cottage.

That old cottage had been torn down years ago. Mom showed me where it had stood on Grandpa's land. Trees and bushes were retaking the clearing where the cottage had been. The road into the place, too. Mom had trouble finding it. It was overgrown. The land was now in some kind of trust or some legal thing where it had to go back to its natural state after my dad didn't want it anymore. I wasn't even sure who owned it now.

I watched the fire for a while, then glanced at my mother. She was asleep. She looked so young. It was hard to believe that she was thirty-seven years old. Ben was thirty-six years. He had been seventeen when he joined the Army. I wondered how he would like being out of the military.

Karen was holding a glass of scotch in her hand and swirling the ice around. I thought she was looking at me, but when I really looked at her, I saw she was looking into the flames deep in thought. I wondered what she was thinking about. I went into the kitchen and got myself a glass of milk.

I sure liked it that we were not living out of a cooler, that we had electricity. If not for Karen, we would've had to wait at least a day or two before the utility truck and plumber would have been able to come out here and get everything operational. I liked having indoor plumbing. I laughed to think of Karen using the woods as an outhouse before the plumber got here. If not for Karen, we would have been living out of a cooler and using candles for light.

When I went back into the living room, I thanked Karen for helping us out by driving my mom's car and getting the utilities turned on. She smiled at me over her glass of scotch, toasted me and said she was glad to do it. Knowing how my mom's friends felt about her, I totally believed her. Mom had that kind of personality. She genuinely liked people, and people responded to her in kind. Mom was always the first one to help a friend in need. We sat in silence for a while watching the flames until they died down. When the fire was down to coals, we said good night to each other and went upstairs to our beds.

THE NEXT DAY I GOT UP EARLY. Mom and Karen were still asleep. The first thing I noticed was that Mom had gotten up during the night and gone to bed. She was no longer on the couch. I smiled. She was starting to get some arthritis, and sleeping on the couch sometimes made her back ache. So I was glad she was in her own bed. That was another good thing we found when we arrived. We didn't have to make beds. They were made with freshly aired out sheets and blankets. I had smelled my pillow when I had first walked into my room. I was glad it didn't have a musty smell from laying on the bed for so long. But no, it was like the sheets and blankets had been freshly taken off of the clothes line. They smelled of sun.

No one else was up yet, so I set up a pot of coffee for Mom so all she had to do was push the start button. Ben would always bring her coffee in the morning. He'd wake her up with a kiss and coffee, and she'd say that was the best way to have a great day. With Ben in Iraq, if I set up the coffee for her, maybe I could help her have a great day. Not that she needed a lot of help. She was naturally happy and had a positive attitude. But I knew she might feel bad that Ben wasn't there. I got myself a bowl of cereal out of one of the boxes Mom had brought with us, put the cereal box in the cabinet and poured milk on my cereal. As I ate, I looked outside at another beautiful sunny day. Finished, I put my dish and spoon in the dishwasher and went outside.

I wondered what to do. Usually on the first full day here, Ben and I would begin the cleanup of the yard. There was always raking and mowing. But not today. I went back inside and wrote my mom a note, telling her I was going for a walk and put it on the table in the kitchen. I would've liked to have done some fishing on the new pier, but, with my luck, the DNR would show up, and I didn't have a fishing license. I think in Wisconsin after the age of sixteen, a person needed a license. It'd ruin my first full day to get a ticket for fishing illegally. Hence the walk. And I figured if I stayed near the water, I wouldn't get lost. That was another thing about me. I got lost easily. A path followed the river. I walked along it. I thought it might be a deer trail.

I noticed the bark had been chewed off trees way above where the deer could reach, and I thought porcupines had fed on the bark. I could hear small animals running through the leaves. Birds filled the trees. I wasn't alone. Wildlife was all around me. But, I felt that there was more than little animals watching me. It felt as if *someone* was watching me. I didn't feel threatened, though. I thought about that. I'd heard horror stories of murderers being anywhere, even in remote places like this. If I screamed no one would hear me, except maybe Mom and Karen, and I didn't think they'd hear me this far from the house.

So, why wasn't I afraid? I had been camping before, but never as far from civilization as this place. Plus, there were always other campers nearby. There was always some barking dog at someone's campsite. But here, other than birds in the trees and some rustling in the dead leaves, there was no sound. Bears roamed these woods and wolves, too. What would I do if I came across one of them? Then, as long as I was fantasizing about wild animals, I thought of the Hodag, but they only came out at night, didn't they? I chuckled about my musings. Maybe I was being watched by Mother Nature.

I kept thinking I was being watched, but I was absolutely not afraid. Actually, it was more than not scary, it was comforting. I was glad that I had this feeling of being watched and also in a strange kind of way, it creeped me out. Why was I not afraid?

As I walked along, I thought of a song my mother used to hum to me when I was a baby. I don't remember hearing her hum that song in a really long time, but for some reason, it seemed appropriate to hum it now. I didn't even consciously think about the tune, I just hummed as I walked. And, I remembered it all. I never knew any words to it, or if it ever had any words. It was something I'd only ever heard from my mother.

After an hour or so of walking, the path ended. There was this huge thick wall of foliage in front of me, but the path did not go around it. The wall of bushes seemed to stretch to the water and deep into the woods for a really long way. I couldn't see the end of it. I had never seen that kind of shrub. I was curious about it. It actually looked almost solid. The path just stopped at this leafy wall. I would have thought the path might follow the edge of the wall, but it didn't. When I tried to follow the wall away from the river, I encountered some bushes with sharp needles that would have torn my clothes and skin if I tried to push my way through. They kind of looked like rose bushes, but I didn't see any kind of flower on them. Even with all of my science classes, I realized that there were lots of kinds of plants I didn't know. Maybe I'd learn them in college.

I tried to push my way through some less thorny bushes, but I couldn't get the plants to move apart. It was like they were braided or something, and they were tough. I wondered if an ax would get through it. But, then I thought, why would I want to ruin a neat plant arrangement? I decided that whatever wildlife was able to find its way into that dense part of the woods had a right to its privacy. I turned around and went back to the house. I had walked a couple of miles. I wondered how much land we owned, and how far I'd have to walk to find people. It didn't appear that I could follow the river to find anyone, at least not this way. About one hundred feet or so from the house, I no longer felt the eyes watching me. The feeling was simply gone. Just like that. It wasn't until I got back to the house that I wondered why there would be a clear trail to the green wall. Maybe deer walked into the river to get to the other side. The bush wall did not extend into the water. That must be it. Or, maybe there was a secret way into and through it. I sighed. I stopped thinking about it when I went into the house.

Mom and Karen were up, sitting at the dining room table drinking coffee. "Hey, thanks for setting up the coffee" Mom called over to me as I walked in the door.

"No problem. Glad to do it," I said with a smile and joined them at the table.

After Mom and Karen finished their breakfast and coffee, Karen said she had to head back to Racine. Her daughter and son-in-law were coming from Green Bay, and she wanted to be home when they got there. Mom and I stood on the front porch waving good-bye. We spent the day unpacking and putting away the stuff from the boxes that we brought in the pickup. I had forgotten about these boxes. The movers wouldn't pack candles, liquids, or batteries, so we had plenty of those things to put away.

The next day, the moving van came and brought in all our stuff from Washington, D.C. We spent the next couple of days unpacking and putting away essential stuff and then Mom said it was time to go and see George.

CHAPTER 3
GEORGE AND THE RESERVATION

It had only rained once since we arrived and that was last night. Just before the rain came, I was lying in bed with my windows open, listening to the coyotes. I was glad I was on a second story of a house as I listened to their yapping. They sounded like wolves, only their voices had a higher pitch. As the rain started tapping on my window sill, I thought I heard a real wolf in the distance. It had a deeper voice than the pack of coyotes. It sounded kind of mournful, but that could have been my imagination. As it rained harder, it started coming in. I got up and closed my bedroom windows. I could only hear the rain tapping on the roof after that, and I fell asleep.

I got up in the morning to another beautiful day. The rain had stopped during the night. I opened my windows and noticed that the pine scent was sharper after the rain. Everything smelled clean and fresh. Downstairs, Mom said she had called George and had asked him if it was a good day to come up to the reservation. He had said it was. It was the beginning of August and the sun was shining brightly. I was ready to see the reservation. It had been a couple of years since the last time I had gone up there. Almost every other time we had come up to this house in the past, we always tried to take at least one day to go and see George.

As I ate my breakfast, I thought about the day before. A charity truck had come. We got rid of furniture we weren't going to use anymore, stuff just taking up space. They hauled away a dining room set with six chairs, two beds, a couch with a loveseat and some miscellaneous side tables. I helped carry out the lighter stuff, and mom directed which things were to be removed. Now we had more room for the stuff we were going to keep.

This morning, I sat at the table and ate my cereal. The kitchen table was like a bistro high-top table with the two chairs. As I sat there, I was thinking about the last week or so of my life. I liked the north woods, at least what I had seen and experienced so far. Mom and I have not seen a lot of people since we got here unless we ran into town for milk and stuff, and we had stayed pretty much close to home. It'd be nice to see someone familiar. I didn't know George well, but he liked Mom a lot, and he liked Ben, too. He seemed to like me. It would be fun to see George.

It took us over an hour to drive to the reservation. Now that Mom had her car back, she preferred to drive it. It was a Jeep Liberty. This was her third one. She liked the way the Liberty handled, she loved the four wheel drive, and she liked the amount of stuff it could hold. She even had a roof rack. The only thing she didn't like was the mileage. But, lack of gas conservation didn't stop her from buying a new one when she was ready.

Mom knew how to get to George's house. As we got out of the car, she called out. "Hey, George! How are you doing?" George had been watching for us and met us by the curb.

George was a big man, taller than Ben. He towered over Mom. George had thick long black hair he held back with a hair tie. I thought it was longer than the usual cut for a man his age. Maybe it was an Indian thing. At least he didn't wear a head band. He had to be at least thirty-seven. I figured he had to be about same age as Mom. He had wrinkles around his eyes that crinkled when he smiled, and he was smiling now. It looked like he spent a lot of time in the sun. He had massive arms. Whatever he did had to involve lifting heavy stuff. He had the dark reddish-brown complexion that most of the members of his tribe had.

He gave Mom a bear hug. "Easy George, don't squish me," she complained. "I break easy." He kept smiling and set her back down on her feet and came over to me.

"Gently, gently" I mumbled to him and he got an even bigger grin on his face. He picked me up and hugged me, too, just not as hard as the one he gave my mother.

"I'm so glad to see you, two" he said, still grinning widely. "I've missed you!"

"I missed you, too." Mom said with a big smile. "I love it that we are here to stay. We aren't moving again. We can get together much more often now."

"That sounds great!" George responded still smiling.

Mom looked up at George and said, "How are you doing? Have you found someone new, yet?"

The smile left his face. George had been married once, to his high-school sweetheart. According to Mom, they'd been madly in love. Iris had been a little petite thing. Mom said she had beautiful waist-length black hair that fell in natural waves. I know I had seen Iris, but I really didn't remember her. I'd seen pictures of Iris and George together. He looked like he could crush her. But, even though George was as big as a bear, he seemed a fairly gentle giant. The pictures of George and Iris looked very happy. Iris had died five years ago of cancer. As far as Mom and I knew, he hadn't dated anyone since Iris's death.

"No," George said softly. "And I'm not looking either." Then he perked up, and said, "Tell me about you! How was the place when you got up here?"

Mom punched George softly in the arm. "You know how it was. It was perfect. Thanks for cleaning up the yard, and getting the inside of the house ready for us."

"I didn't do anything," George said, looking at Mom seriously. The smile was no longer on his face.

"What do you mean you didn't do anything? Didn't you clean the driveway and the yard?" Mom said in astonishment, "Then who did?"

George shrugged. "I have no idea. Weren't the doors locked when you got there?"

"Karen opened the house up to allow the utility people in to turn on the gas and electric before we got there. I'm sure she would have said something about the doors being unlocked. Karen didn't do the cleaning, either," Mom said with a wry smile.

That's creepy I thought. Totally weird. A lot of work had been done to the place to get it ready for our arrival. Everything had been cleaned inside and out. Even the windows had sparkled. There hadn't been a speck of dust in the whole house. Mom was a good housekeeper, but it was never as completely dust free as the house was, and it had been vacant for a couple of years. Who would do that if not George? Nothing had been stolen. The television sets were still there. The stereo that was there, and it was a good one, a Bose system. That would have been something someone might want to take. Plus, Ben's gun case was still there. I had a piggy bank full of state quarters on my dresser, and it'd still been there. The last time we left, we just covered up the furniture, probably with dust all over it. So, who cleaned up the house and yard? Who stacked all of that wood by the shed?

George said, "The last time I was down to your place was two months ago to let the bug guy in to spray." The exterminator. Yeah, it was important to keep the bugs and critters out of the house. "Is there anyone else up here with a key?" he asked.

"No," Mom said softly.

"Maybe it was the wood nymphs." George said.

I thought he was kidding until I saw the look on his face. *Yeah, wood nymphs or gremlins that did it, no doubt,* I thought sarcastically.

Mom hadn't seen the look on his face as she was looking away from George when he spoke. She looked back at him and said, "Wood nymphs? You've got to be kidding me, George."

"Well, somebody cleaned your place up, didn't they?" George said seriously.

Mom said, "Well, nothing was stolen. I mean, there is no sign of a break in. The house is spotless inside and out. There was definitely someone in and around the house, but it doesn't appear that whoever it was wished us harm. I don't see any real danger here. Do you? I mean, other than considering that persons unknown were in the house."

George thought about it for a minute and then said, "Maybe you should make a report to the sheriff's department just the same or at least put in an alarm system."

Mom laughed and said, "We're so far from anywhere, it'd take at least twenty minutes for a sheriff's car to get here. If whoever did this was hostile, Laurel and I wouldn't have a chance."

A thought occurred to me. "Hey, maybe it was Dad. Maybe he arranged this as a big surprise."

Both Mom and George seemed to consider that. "Well," George finally said, "At least have the keys to your car near you. You can push the panic button. The noise the Jeep makes may scare anyone trying to break in away. That'd maybe give you enough time for you to call the authorities."

"Yeah, I'll do that." Mom agreed and then asked, "I hear you have new additions to the museum. What new things do you have?"

"Well, we found a previously unknown effigy mound. Some hikers found it. A lot of artifacts were found—old arrow heads and stuff. Would you like to see them?" George asked, looking from my mom to me.

"George, are there any other teenagers around here?" I asked. It wasn't as if I didn't like the museum. I did. It might have been interesting to see whatever was in there, old or new. But, I was ready to find people my own age.

"Oh, yeah," George said. "Go one block north. There is a clubhouse for teenagers with video games, a pool table, foosball table, and pinball machines. It's called the Abinoojiiyag Center. On a Saturday afternoon, there are always a few kids there. Here's five bucks," he said as he reached into his wallet and pulled out the five and handed it to me. I looked at Mom. She smiled. I took the money.

"Thanks" I said politely. If it had been anyone but George, Mom probably would have frowned about my taking the money. Obviously mom trusted George and his decision to give me the cash.

"Don't worry, honey." Mom said. "If we finish at the museum before you're ready to come, we'll be having coffee at the diner. I'll see you later."

Yeah, that was cool, I thought. I knew where the diner was. We had driven past it on the way here. I headed for the teen hangout, Abee something or other. George said.

As I walked toward the youth center, I looked around. The houses were all neat and clean, and the yards were well maintained. There was money here, and I could see it was making a difference. Money from the casino at the other end of town benefited the reservation. The casino was a huge building with an attached hotel and a couple of upscale restaurants. It even had an auditorium for live bands. I had read the marquee as we drove. I knew some of the acts, and they were popular bands. *Yup*, I thought, *It's nice to see that the casino was a benefit for the whole community.*

Mom had shown me pictures of the reservation when she was a kid. This was before the casino had been built. Most of the houses were rundown shacks then. There was no grass in the yards. Cars were on blocks. Sometimes a deer skin stretched on a rack between the houses. It looked like a ghetto back then. The people in the pictures didn't look happy, either. All of the photos showed serious faces and frowns. I never saw a happy face, except for George and my mom. I didn't see photos of other kids. I wondered if my mom and George noticed the poverty of the area.

The houses here were nice and new. The streets were well maintained. There were curbs and sidewalks now. Years ago the reservation leaders had no money to improve the living conditions. Their lives and homes were strictly low budget before the casino. What a difference between the old reservation and this nice clean reservation. I was glad I didn't have to see the reservation when it was rundown.

It only took me a couple of minutes to get to the clubhouse. There were five teenagers there, four guys and one girl. I walked in, and they stared at me. "What do we have here, a wood nymph?" one of the guys asked, and they all laughed.

Whatever, I thought and started walking back out. Then the same guy said, "Hey, I'm sorry. Come on back. I didn't mean anything by it. Come in! My name's Adam Whitestone. This is Jason Redhawk, Jeremy Coyote, and Jason's sister Melody. Who are you?" He said looking at me and waving to his friends.

"Um," I mumbled, "my name is Laurel Redmond.

"Hey!" Adam said, "We have three people here with the word red in their names. That's kind of cool, isn't it?" And then he laughed. I got the feeling that he laughed a lot. It wasn't a mean laugh. It sounded welcoming—the kind of laugh that didn't make me uncomfortable. I smiled. Then, I started to laugh with him. It wasn't having three people with red in their names that was so funny. It was that his laugh that was contagious.

"What brings you to Lac du Flambeau, Laurel?" Adam asked. I looked at the group of them. Adam was the largest of them. Not older, just bigger. He was taller and looked stronger than the other guys. Jeremy, next in size, was probably the best looking guy in the group. Cuddled up next to him was Melody. She was really pretty with dark eyes and dark hair. She seemed to be studying me, and found me interesting. Jason had a great smile and was really good looking too, just not quite as good looking as Jeremy. But Adam drew my attention. He had a charismatic way about him and was really good looking in a dark-haired, dark-eyed Native American way. It was evident that he was the leader.

"Mom and I just moved to Tomahawk. Mom is friends with George Loon. We came up to visit George." I explained.

There were some couches and chairs along the wall, and we all sat down. "George? Is Valerie your mom's name?" Adam asked leaning toward me.

I felt like I was being scrutinized. "Yes," I replied. "Do you know her?"

"I don't know her personally. I just know of her." He glanced at me and then looked at his friends. "Maybe the wood nymph joke wasn't so far off of the mark," he said with a smile.

"What's that supposed to mean?" I said, again uncomfortable.

"Hey, I'm sorry. We hear stories though. Us Ojibwa Native Americans love our stories and legends!" He said. "Plus," he said, "George is my uncle."

He had me curious, and he seemed sincere. I had heard more about wood nymphs in the last couple of weeks than I had ever heard of them in my life. "I don't know much about wood nymphs." I said. "I only know my mom told me her dad liked to watch them frolic in the woods. She said she never saw one. Mom never believed they were real. I don't think they're real, either."

"Really." Adam replied slowly, shaking his head. He looked like he wanted to say something, then changed his mind. Instead, he asked if I wanted to play pool.

"Sure!" I said, glad at the change of subject. "I like pool, but I'm not very good."

We all got up and headed to the pool table room. While Adam was setting up the game, he asked me. "Have you ever heard the stories about the wood nymphs?"

"Other than some goofy stories my mom would tell me about her dad watching them in the forest. No, I haven't heard any good stories." I replied.

As he racked up the balls, he stopped and said. "We have lot of folks on the reservation that swear they're real. They're supposed to be tall, thin and have straight hair."

I ran my hand through my hair and laughed. "Ah, now I see why you mentioned wood nymphs when I walked in. What else do you know about them?" I asked as I sat on one of the chairs by the pool table. "I like legends and stories."

He told me lots about the legends of wood nymphs that afternoon. He said that there were different kinds of nymphs. Some were forest or wood nymphs, and some were water nymphs. They lived near springs and rivers. Adam said that they were identified with the gods, and had special powers or abilities. Some could control animals, some could control the weather, and others could foresee the future. All of them could move faster than the speed of sound without creating a sonic boom. Wood nymphs could also get through the smallest of spaces. As a rule, they lived a really long time. They lived much longer than a human. The legends said that they were supposed to keep the forests and streams healthy.

I laughed at that. "Good luck with that! The pollution that people are inflicting on this planet is going to make that difficult."

Adam didn't laugh. Instead, he said, "I heard that the wood nymphs might be dying off because of that."

"You talk as if you believe this stuff," I said, grinning. "Have you ever seen one?"

"Maybe." He said with a wink. "We have other legends, too. We have legends about us, the Ojibwa people. We have a story about how people came to be on the earth. Do you want to hear about that?"

"Yeah, that'd be cool." I said. I leaned back in the chair to hear his story.

Jeremy and Melody started a game of pool. "The world started with the mother earth." Adam said as he sat next to me. "She came from a spirit in the sky. She was pregnant when she came to the earth, and she had a baby girl. The baby girl grew up and fell in love with the wind. They got married, and the wind and the girl had four children with different personalities, and they ended up being the four seasons. As each child grew, his and her temperament was displayed in the seasons. The girls were even tempered and became spring and fall, and the boys ran hot and cold. The hot one had a temper, but could also be real friendly. He had a generous nature. That one became summer. The other boy was cold and distant and not friendly at all. He became winter.

"While the world was being created, the gods in the sky world realized that even though the earth was developing, it needed more to it. So the gods threw some spirits towards the earth through a hole in the sky to see what would happen. As the spirits entered the sky around the earth, they changed into different animals depending on where they came into contact with the earth.

"The spirits that landed in water turned into fish, beavers and otters, as well as other sea creatures. The spirits that landed near the mountains and flatlands turned into bears, wolves, goats, and other land animals. Some spirits didn't wait to get to the earth. They became birds. The gods saw the animals inhabiting the earth and that was good. But, it wasn't enough. Some of the animals seemed smarter than others. They were clever and had bright minds. These animals were given the gift of being able to get even smarter and were able to turn into humans. Some of the animals really liked being human and using their hands and minds. Our tribe believes that each person born in our tribe has a spirit animal attached to them. The person is both human and the animal that the person in a prior life originated from. Couldn't you just see me as a magnificent bald eagle?" He finished his story with a wink and a smile.

"Actually, I can picture you more as a bear." I said smiling back at him and getting up from my chair. We all laughed.

"Yeah, bears are cool," Adam said laughing while he got up from his chair.

We went back to the pool table. We played all afternoon. When we got hungry and thirsty, there were vending machines. The cool thing about these particular vending machines was that they were free. We just pushed the button for a Coke and down the can would come, ice cold and ready to drink. A bag of chips was available at the touch of a button. I asked how they were able to have free snacks and drinks, and Adam shrugged and said the casino paid for it all. Playing pool was free, too. The only games that cost any money were the video games and pinball machines. While we were playing pool, sometimes we would play one on one, and other times we would play teams.

Adam was the best pool player. I was the worst, but Adam would always pick me for his partner when we would play doubles. Adam was seventeen, the same age I was. Jeremy and Jason were also seventeen. Melody was sixteen.

I asked where they went to school. Adam told me the kids went to school on the reservation. He said that it was a good school, too. The tribal counsel only hired good teachers and could afford to pay them good wages with the proceeds from the casino. The casino really was a good thing for the reservation. I wondered if all reservations with casinos benefited like this one did. It would be nice, I thought. Kind of fair play, in a way. All the Northern European Americans could come to the casinos and spend their money to benefit the Native Americans. I mean, didn't the Northern European Americans steal their land in the first place? No one forced anyone to go to the casinos. But hey, if people wanted to spend their money at the casinos and the tribe benefited, it was all to the good. I would've liked to have gone to school here with them, and I probably had enough residual Indian blood to be allowed. But, we lived too far away. I'd be going to the high school in Tomahawk.

"What do you plan to do after high school" I asked the group at large. This was while I was watching Jeremy and Adam play a game one on one.

Adam said he wanted to go to UWM for botany. Jeremy took his shot and said he wanted to go to UWM or another college for agriculture. Jason laughed at Jeremy when he missed his shot and said he had no idea which college he wanted to go to or for what. He wasn't even sure he wanted to go to college.

"If I could go to California for college, I might like that. Not that I want to stay away forever, I just want to see a bit of the world before settling down. I want to go someplace warm." Jason smiled as he said it, and we all laughed a little.

Northern Wisconsin had nice summers, but tended to be really cold in the winter. Melody said she wasn't sure if she wanted to go to college, but if she did, she would like to be at the same college as Jeremy. When she said that, Jeremy smiled at her. They looked really happy together, and I wondered if they had the real deal, as in real love. I wondered how long they had been going out together.

They looked like they were in love. At our age, was there real love, or was it just the puppy love that the grown-ups talked about? I had never been in love. I wasn't in any hurry to fall in love either. I mean, when all guys wanted to do was slobber on me and try to get into my pants, where was the love in that? But after looking at Jeremy and Melody, I thought maybe they had hope for true love. He wasn't slobbering. He seemed to really like just being with her. My old boyfriend never treated me like this.

We had been there together for hours and I was having a great time. I was amazed. These kids were really nice. They were smart and funny and I liked them. They welcomed me like I belonged. I didn't feel like a freak. I had a little bit of Indian blood in me. Did that count? Did they know that? I thought they must. Jeremy and Adam had just finished their game, when Mom and George walked in. Mom asked me if I was having a good time and making new friends. I was honestly able to say yes on both counts.

George greeted everyone and introduced my mom to the group. George said to Adam. "Are you being nice to Laurel?"

Adam said that he was trying, but mentioned that the talk of wood nymphs made me uncomfortable.

"Adam, let's not go into old legends and stories, okay?" George said giving Adam a stern look.

"Okay," Adam said and winked at me. I was thinking he had already told me most of what he knew about the mythical wood nymphs. Later, I realized he had hardly told me anything.

"Valerie, would you and Laurel like to go to dinner with me tonight? There is a nice steak house next to the casino. As a resident of the reservation I get a discount. Whoever I bring with as a guest also gets a discount. I would really like it if you would allow this to be my treat." George said.

"Can I come, Uncle George?" Adam asked. He was standing right next to me.

Mom looked at me to gauge my opinion. I nodded. I liked to go out to eat.

"Sure!" Mom said. "That'd be great! Thanks!"

"Yeah, you can come too." George said to Adam.

I said good-bye to my new friends, and George, Mom, Adam, and I walked back to George's house. We drove in separate cars to the restaurant. This way, Mom and I could go right home after dinner.

It really was a nice restaurant. I wondered if I was going to be allowed in with jeans on. I looked around as we went in and I saw other people casually dressed, too. The tables had white cloth tablecloths, and white cloth napkins.

"This is really a nice place, George," Mom stated as she sat down "Is the food as good as the atmosphere?"

"Better." George replied. We had a server right away, and our food was served quickly. Portions were large, and they were delicious. I noticed that there wasn't a whole lot of conversation while we ate. I had a broiled walleye dinner cooked to perfection. George and Adam had sirloin steaks, and Mom had stuffed shrimp. After dinner, we sat there with our full stomachs, and George commented, "You know my brother and I are descended from the original tribal chief, Chief Keeshkemun, right?"

Mom nodded, and he continued. "Yeah, my brother still sits on the tribal council. Does Laurel know how Lac du Flambeau got its name?"

I shook my head

"In the 1700s, the tribe would hunt at night in canoes, using torches held over the water. The fish would come to the surface, to the light, and one tribal member in the canoe would spear the fish. When the early traders and trappers came to the area, many of them were of French descent, and at night as they would walk by a lake. They thought the lake was on fire. They could see the flames out on the water, but not the canoes. They gave the area the name of Lac Du Flambeau, or Lake of Flames. Neat, huh?" George finished.

Yeah, I thought. That was neat. After dinner, Mom thanked George for dinner, and we headed home. On the way home, I looked out of the Liberty's side window and thought about wood nymphs and animals that became human.

CHAPTER 4
FISHING AND
ACTUALLY CATCHING FISH

On Monday morning at breakfast, Mom said she had to go to on Tuesday to Wausau to take the licensing exam to be a counselor in Wisconsin. The test was in the early afternoon and would take a couple of hours. I had the choice of going to Wausau and waiting while she took the test or staying home. She said we could go school shopping after the test. But if I chose not to go on this trip, we would just go another day to shop for school clothes. I said I'd like to stay home. I asked if we could we run into Tomahawk before she left so that I could have a fishing license and do some fishing while she was gone. She agreed. We needed some groceries anyway.

Tomahawk was about ten miles from our house. The one bad thing about living in the middle of the north woods, it wasn't just a quick walk to the corner store for a gallon of milk. It wasn't quite a Broadway production to get anywhere, but it wasn't convenient, either. After breakfast, we got dressed and headed into town. Tomahawk was a nice town, but I didn't know where the teenagers hung out, if they hung out anywhere. It wasn't like they had a mall or anything, at least as far as I knew. I figured I'd find out about such things when I started school.

We stopped at the bait shop and bought licenses. We also picked up a couple of cartons of worms for bait. Then we went to the grocery store. On the way home, I had that feeling of being watched again. It was so strong. Where was this coming from? I looked around, and all I saw was road and trees. There were some wild turkeys by the side of the road, but they didn't give me that feeling. As we drove down our driveway to the house, the feeling got stronger. I swore I should be seeing someone staring at me. I didn't see anyone. We pulled up in front of the house and unloaded our groceries. Mom said she wanted to check out some things on the Internet, as we just had our Internet hooked up. One of the bedrooms was set up as an office. There were quite a few unopened boxes from the move but we weren't in a huge hurry to un-pack everything. Everything would get done in its own time Mom had said.

I went to the shed and pulled out a folding chair, card table, tackle box, net, and fishing rod. At the end of the pier, I set myself up, picking a spot for my chair with the table next to me. I put my tackle box on the table and put a red-and-white bobber on my line with some lead weights and a small hook for pan fish. I was hoping to catch some blue gill or crappies. I put a worm on my hook, and then reached over the pier to rinse my hand in the water. The water was brown from the tannin from the trees up river. It wasn't polluted, but it didn't look real good with the brown tint. I looked in the water as I rinsed off the worm stuff from my hand. The water was about four feet deep at the end of the pier. I thought I saw a face in the water. I swear I saw a woman's face with swirling dark-green hair. It vanished almost as soon as I saw it, fading to black. Must be the light filtering through the water.

I had all day to fish. I cast out my line and heard the little *kerplunk* as my worm and bobber hit the water. It was a nice day, and I settled in to wait for a bite. I thought about how clean the air was here. All I could smell was pine and an earthy smell. It was very peaceful. I didn't have the uncomfortable feeling of being watched today either.

The face I'd imagined in the water hadn't looked friendly. Why couldn't I have imagined a happy face in the water? *Strange thing to imagine,* I thought to myself. In this happy place and on this bright day, I should have imagined a smiling face.

As I sat there fishing, I saw a bald eagle circling way up high. When I first saw it, it was just close enough so I could make out the white head to determine what kind of bird it was. I glanced at my bobber to make sure it hadn't gone under. I thought I would feel a tug on the line or something, so I watched the eagle. It circled lower and lower. Such a magnificent bird. I could see why it was the symbol for the United States. As it neared, I realized that this was a really huge bird. I was not used to seeing bald eagles and had never seen a live one before. I had only seen them on TV or in books. The bird gracefully caught a branch with its talons at the top of a pine tree about 100 feet away from me. It tucked its wings in and settled onto the tree. I could see it clearly. It was so beautiful, so majestic surveying the world. It appeared to look right at me. I thought of yelling hello to the bird, but figured I would scare it off and I didn't want to do that. I thought of Adam telling me about the history of his tribe and how the people originally came from animals. I waved at the bird, feeling silly. I wanted to acknowledge its presence in the tree near me. It dipped its head as if to acknowledge me back, and I smiled. I knew it was stupid, but I felt I had actually communicated with the bird.

I looked back at my bobber. It was slowly being pulled by the river current. I reeled the line in to check on my bait, and the worm was still there. Not even a nibble. I readjusted the length of the hook from the bobber and cast the line back into the water. "Here fishy, fishy, fishy," I said out loud. Nothing.

After another ten minutes, I pulled in my line to check the bait. The worm was still there. It was drowned and lifeless but still on the hook. I pulled off the dead worm and threw it on the bank of the river. I put a fresh worm on the hook. I rinsed my hand in the water. No imaginary face in the water this time. I cast the line out and the worm hit the water about twenty feet in front of me.

"Come on fish!" I said to out loud to myself. I really wanted to catch enough fish for dinner tonight. After another half hour of just sitting there without a nibble, I brought the line back in and replaced the worm again. I cast out the line in a different direction. I wanted to see some bobbing action with the bobber. I was getting bored and I didn't want to be bored. I wanted to catch some fish. Why wasn't I any good at this? What was I doing wrong? I was getting frustrated with this whole endeavor. I knew I wasn't very good at catching fish, but usually I caught at least one! Today, there wasn't even a nibble. I had listened to the radio at breakfast, and the announcer said this was a good day to fish! I was fishing during prime time. Nothing. Not a nibble. At this point, I would have gotten excited about a snagged line. That at least would have been some kind of action going on. Getting the line unsnagged would have given me something to do.

I jerked the line a bit in my impatience and said, "Come on fish, bite my hook!"

Not ten seconds later, my bobber dropped like there was a stone attached, and I felt the tell-tale tug of a fish on my line. It felt like a nice-sized one, too. I could feel the fish trying to pull the line out of the reel, and I had the drag set kind of tight. I still heard the *whir* as the line was pulled by the fish. As I wrestled with and reeled the fish in, I grabbed the net and put it under the fish and hauled it up onto the pier. It was a crappie and at least a pound. It was a keeper! I held up my fish to the eagle, and he opened his huge wings and flapped them at me while letting off an eagle screech. I thought he was congratulating me. I wondered if he thought I should give it to him.

This time I did yell up at him, "I'm catching dinner for me and my mom!" The eagle bobbed his head once at me as if to acknowledge me. I laughed at my silliness, but the eagle stayed in his tree watching me. I put my fish on the stringer that I kept in the tackle box for the rare instance that I did catch fish and attached one end of the stringer to the table leg and set the fish in the water to keep fresh. I rebaited my hook and cast my line into the same place in the water where I had caught the crappie. I thought that this was it. I had found the spot. The eagle leaned over as if to be the first one to see the bobber go down. I swear that eagle looked like he was anticipating the next fish as much as I was. As the minutes ticked by, nothing happened. I pulled up my line to make sure I didn't accidently knock the worm off of the hook when it hit the water which had happened in the past. Nope, the worm was still there.

Again, I was getting frustrated. Catching one fish was worse then catching no fish. One fish almost wasn't worth the bother of filleting it. I knew I would though. Not that I was the greatest conservationist, but I wouldn't waste the fish. I would fillet it and put it in a freezer bag and freeze it. I would keep freezing fish I caught until there was enough for a meal. I looked at the tannin river and thought, *If there's one fish in there, there has to be more.*

"Come on fish!" I yelled at the water. "Don't fail me now! I need dinner tonight! Bite that hook!" I felt stupid, but, again, not ten seconds later, the bobber dropped out of sight. I reeled in another fish, a nice sized bluegill. I placed it on my stringer with the first fish and looked up at the eagle. He screeched at me and flapped his wings. I yelled at him that he had to catch his own fish. With that, he opened his wings and flew down to the water. He skimmed the water not ten feet from where I sat on the pier. He was huge! I had no idea that bald eagles got that big. As he went past me, he looked at me and screeched again. I swear he winked at me, but can birds wink? Then he was gone, around a bend in the river a couple of hundred feet away from where I sat.

I sat there for a few minutes thinking that I couldn't wait to tell Mom about the bird. She might think the bird was dangerous. I'd never heard of a bald eagle attacking anyone. I wasn't afraid. But it did have huge talons and a big curved beak, and I was quite sure that it could do some real damage if it wanted to. I'd enjoyed its company.

I caught four more fish. It seemed I had to get anxious before a fish would take the bait. I'd sit there getting bored, really wanting to catch a fish, but only when I demanded a fish did I catch one. I knew that made no sense, but it was fun to fantasize that I had control over the fish. In the end, I had three crappies, two bluegills, and a sunfish. All were keepers. I saw the sun heading to the western horizon, and I put my fishing stuff away in the shed. I took my catch into the house and filleted the fish. I scooped the skin and bones into a bucket and took it out into the forest to bury.

When Mom got home, I had the fish in ice water in the refrigerator waiting to be breaded and fried. I asked how she did on her test. She said because it was electronic, she already knew. She passed! Now she just had to find a job. She asked me what I'd done that day, and I proudly showed her my catch. She was very impressed.

She fried the fish up and made hush puppies and French fries. It was a great fish dinner. It wouldn't have tasted better in a restaurant. Perhaps I had a bit of a bias since I caught the fish.

As we enjoyed our dinner, Mom said, "This is wonderful! How did you catch the fish? What did you use for bait?"

I told her, "Worms. And I ordered the fish to bite the hook."

She laughed and said, "Of course, you did. It was silly of me to think it was the bait that made the fish bite the hook."

We laughed and cleaned up. I worked in my room for the rest of the evening, unpacking some more boxes and putting things away.

CHAPTER 5
HIGH SCHOOL

I t was my first day at the new high school. The weather was overcast when I hiked the mile to the bus stop at the end of the drive. As I walked up the drive I thought I really needed my own transportation. It started to rain right after I got on the bus. Mom said that she'd pick me up from school that day and I was glad. I didn't look forward to the long hike to the house when the school bus dropped me off after school, especially if it was still raining.

When I had registered a few days ago, we didn't wait for the office staff to get me into the system. I was told I could pick up my schedule on the first day of school. I waited at the office counter for the secretary to find my file and pull my class schedule. I noticed a tall boy walk in and speak to another member of the office staff.

He was dressed casually, but the clothes were expensive, all brand name. I saw the name on the back of his jeans. I had tried to get Mom to buy me a pair of those jeans, and she'd laughed. Those jeans cost more than a week's worth of groceries. As I tried to look at him out of the corner of my eye, I wondered if he was what the girls back in D.C. would call a player. He looked like one. I'd met the type before. Players could talk really smooth and get girls to do whatever they wanted. Then they'd dump them. My old boyfriend was a player, but I never fell for his smooth talk.

He looked like a rich kid with more money than sense. He had good looks and obviously had money. Girls fell all over themselves trying to get noticed by guys like that. I wondered how many hearts he'd broken.

"Good morning, Mr. Woodson!" the school secretary said, smiling at him. "So, it appears you're going to be joining us and not going to be home schooled this year?"

"No," he said. "I decided I wanted at least one year of public school."

Oh, that voice. I had never heard such a beautiful speaking voice on a teenage guy. Not too deep, or too high. It was perfect. His intonation was so smooth. His words were clear and soft. If melted chocolate had a sound, that would be this voice. Radio announcers would kill for this voice.

"Oh, I understand, Ash. Your family has always been very generous to our school. We're very happy to have you here!" The office person gushed up to him.

He had straight hair the exact same color of my hair. That really startled me. I stared at him. His hair wasn't anywhere near as long as mine, but longer than the fashion for guys at my old high school. It looked good on him. I wanted to know if anything else about him was similar to me. He left the office, not even glancing in my direction.

The secretary called for my attention. "Miss Redmond? Hello? Miss Redmond? Here's your schedule. You'd better hurry. Class starts in two minutes and your first hour is almost on the other side of the school."

I wondered how long she had been trying to get my attention. I was wondering what his eyes looked like. Were they green, too?

I took the schedule and thanked the secretary. When I got out in the hallway, the boy named Woodson was nowhere to be seen. I thought about him as I counted room numbers heading for my class. He said he was going to college next year. That meant he was a senior like me, so maybe I'd have some classes with him. I figured that would probably be likely since this wasn't a huge school. I got to my first class, chemistry. I liked chemistry. After the teacher passed out books, I put Ash Woodson out of my head and paid attention.

When the class ended and I got up to leave, the boy who had been sitting next to me introduced himself. "Hi, my name's Rodney Johnson. You must be new. I know everyone here, and I don't recognize you. Are you related to the Woodsons? You kind of look like you could be." I looked at Rodney. We were the exact same height. Rodney had dark brown hair worn in a popular style, kind of wavy, like it was mussed up with hair gel.

"Yes, I'm new, but I'm not related to the Woodson family. Not that I know anyway. My name's Laurel. Mom and I just moved here from D.C."

He looked closer at me. "I swear you look like you could be Ash's sister."

"Huh, yeah, I saw him in the office this morning when I was getting my schedule." We walked down the hall. "Are there other . . . Woodson kids?"

"Not really. However, the whole Woodson family looks the same. They're cousins. Ash is the first one to attend public school. They're real big on home schooling or private schools. They are a pretty big family, though. They're also rich. I mean, no one sees them much unless they need something in town. The Woodsons own a lot of property on the edge of town, and their cousins or whatever, live on adjacent properties next to the forest. I think Ash Woodson is the youngest of the whole family. He is an only child. What's your next class?" Rodney said as he looked at his schedule.

"I've got physics next." I said looking for the room number.

"I got math. I'll see you later, okay?" He said and headed in the opposite direction.

He yelled back, "Hey, I have lunch sixth hour. Do you?" I looked at my schedule and nodded. "I'll see you at lunch." he said as he walked backwards down the hall.

"Yeah, sure," I called back. Rodney seemed nice enough. It looked like I made my first friend in my new school.

When I got to the physics class, I saw Ash Woodson sitting in the back row. By the time I got there, the only available seat was in the front row. I took it. The teacher handed out books, and we spent the next hour discussing vectors and angles to see what level the overall class was with the dynamics of physics. Grades meant a lot to me. Even though I wanted to get distracted thinking about Ash, I firmly focused on what the teacher was talking about.

After class I looked for Ash. One of the girls in the class asked me a question just as he walked by and I didn't get a chance to talk to him.

By the time I got to lunch, I realized that even though the Tomahawk High School wasn't in a big community, it was a pretty good school. I learned that the football team was called the Hatchets. Yeah, that made sense. The Tomahawk Hatchets. Rodney was waiting by the cafeteria door.

"Come meet some of my friends!" he said, leading me to a table full of people. All the guys at the table were involved in some kind of sport. They all had letter jackets on. Though it was a bit warm for the jackets, I guessed they wanted the freshmen to know who were Hatchets.

"Hey! This is Laurel! She just moved here from DC." Rodney told the group.

I got various forms of greetings. Then one guy asked, "Why ever would you want to come here?" and everyone laughed.

"I would give anything to just visit D.C. It sounds so interesting, being the capital of the country and all." A tiny blond girl said. "I'm Mary Peterson," she said. I looked at Mary, and while she wasn't beautiful in the classic sense like my old friend Jennifer, she had a pretty smile and didn't seem as cold as kids at other schools.

While I looked at her, the other kids around the table were all stating their names. They went through them so fast, I knew I wasn't going to remember everyone's name and said as much. Rodney told me not to worry. I'd get to know everyone as the year went on. I said hi to everyone and got in the cafeteria line. I ordered a fish sandwich, fries and a Coke for lunch. It wasn't bad for cafeteria food. I didn't see Ash.

My next class was an art class. We found out that we would be working with copper or brass. We had a choice of making either a pin or a ring. I chose the ring.

I had Drama for my last class of the day, and Ash was in that class, too. Again, I did not sit near him, but I thought I felt his eyes on my back as I sat in the front row again. I thought of the feeling of being watched at home by the river.

The Drama teacher's name was Miss Becker. She told us that seniors were expected to participate in the school play. The play was going to be *Pride and Prejudice* by Jane Austen. There were a lot of groans as the class realized it was a romance. Miss Becker said that not everyone had to be actors, although each of us had to try out for a part. The students who didn't make the cast had to do something else with the play. There were plenty of stage positions that needed filling. This included lighting, curtain handling, makeup, and sets among others.

In the hallway after class, I saw Ash look at me. He did have green eyes. He didn't look happy. I thought he was going to talk to me when Rodney came up to ask me which bus I was on. Ash turned and walked away. I told Rodney my mom was picking me up. He said that was cool, and that I would see him tomorrow. When he left, I looked around for Ash, but he was gone.

I saw the Jeep Liberty immediately when I came out of the front door of school. "How was your first day?" Mom asked as I threw my book bag in the back seat and climbed in.

"Not bad," I said. "There's a boy here who has hair the same color as mine" I said.

"Really?" Mom asked as she pulled away from the curb. "Did you talk to him?"

"Didn't get a chance. I met another guy in my chemistry class. Rodney introduced me to some nice kids at lunch." I replied.

Mom laughed, "Ah, honey, I'm glad. I want you to feel welcome and at home here. Hey, I got you something! Wait until you see it. You're going to love it!"

When we got to the house, there in our parking area by the garage was a Jeep Wrangler. It wasn't new, but it looked in good shape. It was a black two-door model with a removable hard top. "Is that for me?" I whispered. We got out of the Liberty and walked to the Wrangler.

"Yes. Do you like it?" Mom replied watching my reaction.

"Oh, yeah, I sure do. It's way too cool! Is it a four wheel drive, too?" I asked enthusiastically. I couldn't wait to try it out.

"Yup." She said and handed me the keys. "The owner's manual is in the glove box. Get to know your new car. Okay, *older* car."

But not real old, I thought.

"Take it for a drive and be back in two hours for dinner," she said.

I got into my new car. I had my own vehicle now. I didn't have to walk down that long driveway and wait for a bus ever again!

I took the Jeep for a long drive. I played with the four-wheel drive, but I didn't do any off-road stuff. At first I just practiced stopping and starting along the driveway. I put it back into two wheel drive and drove down the highway with the windows open. I tried out the windshield wipers, air conditioning, and heater. By the time I got back home, I thought I knew my little Jeep pretty well.

When I walked in the door, I could smell fried chicken. "How do you like it?" my mom asked from the kitchen.

"Great! I love it! Where did you get it? Does Dad know about it?" I gushed as I walked into the kitchen.

"Yes, your dad knows about the Jeep. Now listen, it only has liability insurance, so if you hit anything, the car's gone. Also, you're going to have to get a job to continue the insurance. I'm giving you the car, but you're going to have to get a job to keep it up and pay for gas," she said as she put the chicken onto plates.

"I'll start looking for a job tomorrow," I promised as we sat down to eat.

After dinner and clean up, I went to the office upstairs to do my homework. That was the nice thing about having a four-bedroom house. We had space for an office and a library. Both the office and library had day beds in case of overnight company, but I had a place for homework. It didn't take me long to finish, so I went downstairs to the enclosed porch facing the river. It was dark outside as I listened to the sounds of the forest. An owl hooted in a nearby tree. A loon called out on the river. The pack of coyotes sounded far away tonight. I heard a huge splash by our pier, but I couldn't see anything in the dark. It was a big splash, but then nothing. I wondered if a bear had fallen in. While I was sitting there, the phone rang and I answered it. It was Ben! He had gotten the email about the Jeep.

"Hi, honey!" he said. It was a poor connection. He sounded far away, and the phone line had a lot of static. "How do you like the Jeep?" There was a nine-hour time difference between us and Iraq, so it was morning for him.

"Oh, Dad, it's awesome! I took it for a drive and it runs great." I enthused and gushed some more about the Jeep. "How are you doing? Thanks for the emails. I really miss you!" I talked fast, worrying that we might get cut off, which had happened before. We talked about my first day at school and then Mom heard me on the phone and came downstairs. "Wanna talk to Mom?" I asked. He did. I said, "Bye, talk to you soon!" as I handed the phone to her.

She took the phone and sat on the couch to fill him in on all of her activities since the last time they talked.

I went upstairs to clean up for bed while Mom talked to Ben in a low voice. While I couldn't hear the words, I could hear her tone. She missed him. When I went to bed, I wondered if I would ever be in love like Mom and Ben. Then, as I was going to sleep, I found I was thinking of a boy with straight hair the color of mine. Mom had met my biological dad only an hour's drive away, was it possible that Ash was related to my real dad? I thought of my green eyes in a guy's face as I fell asleep.

I decided I should talk to Ash. I saw him getting out of his car when I pulled in to the lot. He had a black Toyota SUV. It looked new. I wondered if it was his or his parents' car. I hurried out of my car to catch up to him. "Hey, Ash!" I called.

He stopped and turned. He didn't look happy. "What?" he said almost angrily.

This kind of stopped me in my tracks. I wasn't expecting hostility. "Um, I just wanted to meet you," I said, feeling stupid.

"Well," he said. "I don't want to meet you. You don't belong here." He turned and started walking away.

I couldn't believe this. I didn't even know him! "And you do, I suppose!" I yelled at his back. I held my purse tightly in front of me to keep from hitting him with it.

He stopped and turned just his head back. "Yes," he said. I saw the smirk. Then he strode away.

Rodney had seen the whole thing and came up to me and said, "Wow, what he said was really lame. You didn't deserve that. What a prick."

We watched Ash's back as he strode into the school. "Don't let him get you down." Rodney continued. "I think you belong here!" He said with a smile. "His family owns a lot of property. Maybe they believe that they're better than everyone else. I heard that his family's been here forever. I think they might be one of the first settlers in this area. Whatever. I don't care what he thinks, and I think he is an idiot." Rodney finished. He put his arm around my shoulder.

I smiled weakly. I know my face had gone red. I was doing everything I could to hold back the tears. As Rodney and I walked toward the school, I couldn't believe a stranger would talk to me like that. I couldn't believe I'd let Ash get to me like that. I didn't even know him! Who was he to talk to me like that? Why would I care whether he liked me or not? I kept wondering, what did I do to deserve this treatment? No matter how I tried to tell myself that it didn't matter what Ash thought, I still felt bad. Of all of the people I'd met, he was the one that I wanted to get to know the most.

"Don't worry about it. I'm fine! I don't care what he thinks!" I said to Rodney as I started running to the class. As I ran, I knew I was lying to myself.

At lunch time, Rodney told everyone at the table what Ash had said to me. The shocked looks around the table were comforting. "We like you and are glad you're here." Mary stated firmly.

I smiled back at her and at the rest. "Thanks!" I said, and I meant it.

In drama, we were all given a copy of *Pride and Prejudice*. "I want all of you to go home and study the first act tonight. Tomorrow, we'll do tryouts for the character parts."

When I got home, I saw Mom wasn't there. I unlocked the door and let myself in. A note on the table let me know that Mom had a job interview at a clinic just outside town. I grabbed a Coke and went upstairs to get my homework done. I saved drama for last. As I read the first act of *Pride and Prejudice*, my mind drifted to Ash Woodson. What was his deal? Why did he dislike me? Why did he think I didn't belong there? I couldn't concentrate on the play and gave up. Why was I letting this one guy get to me so much?

I went downstairs just as Mom walked in. "I got the job!" she shouted. "I passed the licensing exam on the first attempt, and I got a therapist job at my first interview! It is in a small clinic, but I'll have my own office and waiting area . . ."

"That's great!" I said with as much enthusiasm that I could muster. She looked at me and saw the tears that had been threatening to flow all day slide down my face. I didn't mean to burst her bubble. It just happened. I didn't want to cry.

"Oh, honey!" she whispered. She came over and hugged me. "What's wrong?"

"Do you remember yesterday when I told you about a boy who looks kind of like me?" I asked, trying not to hiccup through my tears. "Well, today I went up to say hi, and he told me I didn't belong there. He had a really ugly look on his face when he said it. Why would he say something like that to me? He doesn't even know me!" I wailed. That was it. The tears were really coming down now. My eyes had decided to open up the water works. What a horrible time for me to lose my cool. Mom had great news, and I was spoiling it for her. It made me feel even worse.

Mom hugged me tight and asked, "What about that other boy you told me about? Wasn't Rodney his name? How did he treat you today?"

"Fine," I mumbled. "He's nice to me. I think he likes me."

"What about the other kids? Were they nice to you?"

"Yeah, they were nice to me." I sighed. I tried to focus on what she was saying, but I was still hurt by Ash Woodson not even giving me a chance to even talk to him.

"The world is filled with unthinking and uncaring people. We all try to avoid them as best we can. Think of the nice people you met and try to put this one boy out of your mind. Don't let him get you down," Mom said gently.

"Yeah, okay," I said. She was right. I was letting Ash get to me. I knew I was giving him control over me by crying over what he had said. He had no right to that, and I told myself that I wouldn't think of him or allow him to hurt me anymore. But, that night, as I went to sleep, I thought of his intense green eyes glaring at me.

The next day, I ignored Ash and he ignored me. I continued to sit in the front row of the classes that we had together, and he continued to sit in the back row. I enjoyed my time with Rodney, Mary, and the rest of the group at our cafeteria table during lunch. When I got to Drama, I found that Miss Becker was dividing the class with boys on one side and girls on the other. She had each student read a line from the play. We could pick which character we wanted to read for the first reading. If too many girls tried out for Jane Bennett or Elizabeth Bennett and too many boys for Mr. Darcy or Mr. Bingley, then Miss Becker said she'd have to delegate the parts.

She asked the boys trying out for Mr. Darcy to read the part where Mr. Darcy and his friend Mr. Bingley are at the ball and Mr. Darcy was stating that the only good-looking girl at the ball is Miss Jane Bennett. A few of the boys tried out for the part, including Ash. For the girls trying out for Elizabeth Bennett, of which I was one, we had to read the line where Elizabeth spoke to her friend Charlotte after she had just heard the remark by Mr. Darcy stating that she was the only good-looking girl. My feelings were still pretty sensitive over Ash's comment, and I felt a kinship with Elizabeth Bennett. I knew how it felt to feel unwanted and shot down.

Without intention, I put real feeling into the lines as I read them. I was the last one to read for the part, and Miss Becker said she would tell us next week who would get which character. There would be an open casting call after school for any other students who wanted to try out for the play. Students were also needed for stage hand positions.

A week later, when I got to the drama class, the cast roster sheet was tacked up outside of the classroom door. I found out that a really pretty girl in the class, Noreen Jensen got the part of Jane Bennett. I was cast as Elizabeth Bennett. Rodney, who wasn't in the class, but wanted to be part of the play, had tried out during the open casting call and got the part of Mr. Bingley. Mary got a part as one of the other Bennett sisters, and Ash got the part of Mr. Darcy. I had been really excited about getting a lead part until I saw that he'd be Mr. Darcy. *Great*, I thought. Now, I'd have to see him during rehearsal and have him hate me then, too. I looked up from the sheet. Ash was standing right next to me reading the names as well. He looked at me briefly with a strange look on his face and went into the classroom and took his regular seat in the back. I considered for a few minutes about whether I should pull out of the play, and then decided that this was too cool an experience to let Ash Woodson ruin for me. If he had issues, that was his problem. I'd be the best Elizabeth Bennett, ever. I couldn't wait to tell Mom that I got a lead part in the school play.

After class, Rodney was waiting outside the classroom. "Did you see?" He exclaimed. "I got one of the main parts, and so did you! How cool is that?"

"Yeah," I said, trying to match his excitement, "So cool! It would've been better if someone else got the part of Mr. Darcy, though." Rodney agreed as he walked me to my Jeep. We talked about how fun it was going to be to rehearse together. The play was scheduled for the end of October. There would be a lot of rehearsals between now and then.

I got home and told Mom. She was excited for me. I told her that Rodney and Mary got parts in the play, too. I didn't tell her Ash would be Mr. Darcy. Then I went online and sent an email to Ben.

As I was booting up my computer, I felt I should have been happier than I was. I was still giving Ash Woodson control over my feelings. This should have been one of the happiest moments of my life! No one helped me get the part. I did that all by myself. I was liked for myself by lots of the kids and I felt I belonged, even though the one guy I wanted to like me didn't. Why was I letting him bother me so much?

I told myself to shake it off and go with the good feeling of being a main character in the play. Mom and I celebrated by going to the Silver Bird Supper Club for dinner. On the way there, she showed me her clinic. We celebrated my part in the play and her new job as a therapist.

On Friday, I went to the school library after my last class. I wanted to get a couple of books by Jane Austen to review over the weekend. I wanted to get an idea of what her other characters were like in her other books. I saw that the library was really big for a small school. Apparently, Mr. and Mrs. Woodson had donated a lot of money to build the library when the school was built. The plaque in the front of the library stated that they felt education was important. And then they home-schooled Ash? I was wondering what kind of parents would spend this kind of money in a school and not have their kids go to that school.

The library had rows of books about six feet in height. I went to the computer in the corner to find out where the Jane Austen books were. I got to their row and was scanning the titles when I heard voices one aisle over. I couldn't mistake Ash's smooth voice.

"I can't stand her." I heard him say. I forgot all about Jane Austen. "She's an abomination. She shouldn't exist!" Ash continued to growl.

Then, I heard another voice, a soft, clear, gentle adult male voice say, "Oh, Ash, she does exist and you have to deal with it. I don't think she was an intentional mistake. Other than looking a lot like us, she doesn't seem to have anything special about her. She's just a girl. She seems kind of nice. I have seen her in the hallways. Leif Oakton of Copper Clan didn't mean for this to happen, but it did. I'm surprised that he had anything to do with the mother. Before anyone knew what he had done, Leif was in that accident and died less than a week after meeting the girl's mother. I heard that he had told his brother that it was foretold by Olivia that a daughter would be conceived and born of their union. He asked his brother to watch out for the mother and daughter. After his death, Leif's older brother Forrest took his words to heart and decided to take responsibility for Leif's actions and watch over the mother and daughter. The mother didn't need any help, and so he didn't approach her. Even though they don't know he exists, he's been watching over them for years. The mother was made to forget Leif, in the most elemental way, you understand. As I understand it, she married a decent human being. Good thing for the new husband that he is kind, or I think Forrest would have killed him. I think that Forrest takes his responsibilities a little too seriously, especially in this situation." The guy with the soft voice chuckled softly.

"Anyway, keep in mind, that no one foresaw this happening. No one could stop it. So, the girl lives, and we have to deal with it. I wouldn't worry that they live here now. While nobody knew she would move to the Wisconsin north woods, the girl will probably not be here that long. She's a senior. College is next. Then she's gone.

"Forrest is head of the Copper Clan. We don't need to create a rift between ours and the lead clan. So, take it easy. She may be of mixed blood, but don't hold that against her. She doesn't seem to have abilities, so keep your peace. She never need learn the truth."

They had started to walk away, so I could barely hear the last part or if anything came after that. I might have followed except that I seemed frozen in place, vibrating with confusion. Were they talking about me? Ash and the unknown man didn't say my name, but what other mother and daughter who recently moved here could they be talking about? I would never forget the man's voice. It was soft like I'd imagine a down pillow it if could talk. Who was Forrest Oakton? My uncle? Was Leif Oakton my real dad? I had to know the answers to these questions. I forgot all about what I was in the library for and went home. Mom and I needed to have a serious talk.

CHAPTER 6
ANSWERS

Mom wasn't home when I got there. I paced. I couldn't sit still, couldn't do my homework. I felt as if I had to know the answers about my real dad, immediately. I couldn't wait any longer.

Mom finally got home a couple of hours later. I was wound up pretty tight when she walked in with department store bags in hand. She took one look at my face, put down the bags and asked me what the matter was.

"I need to know about my real dad, and I need to know now!" I was shouting.

"Wow. Okay, let me get a drink. I think I need a drink for this one," Mom said. She had turned very pale and her hand shook when she reached to pour herself some scotch. She seemed to be taking an extraordinarily long time to get a drink and sit down. She gestured for me to sit next to her. She looked at me intently. "To be honest, I don't remember a lot. It's not like we were drinking, either, because I don't drink very much," she said as she took a little sip of her scotch and looked at me.

"My car stalled about two miles from the cottage while I was driving up one Friday night."

"I was alone, and it was late. There are no street lights in the north woods." She smiled ruefully. "I had been sitting there with my cell phone in my hand, but I had no signal to make a call. I hadn't started panicking, but I could imagine some car rounding the curve behind me and plowing into the rear of my car. Just when I started getting really nervous, I saw headlights coming towards me. The car pulled over, and this tall, very handsome man stepped out. He looked a lot like you. Your hair is just like his. I remember that much," Mom mused.

"He used my flashlight to look under the hood, did something with some wires and told me to try to start the car. I turned the key and it started immediately. I can't tell you how relieved I was. I asked if he wanted to stop by for a drink or something. He thought about it a minute, then said yes. He followed me to the cottage, and we talked until dawn. It's funny. I'd been so tired, then all wound up. Then he came, and I was great.

"The next day he said he had to leave for a while. I asked if he could come back later, and he said he would. It was after he got back where my memory gets kind of blurry. I know we went somewhere together, but it seems like a dream now. We spent the rest of the weekend together. I was supposed to go back to Racine on Sunday but put it off until Monday. I told him I'd be back again the following weekend, and he said he would come see me. But, he never did. I never saw him after that one weekend."

"What was his name?" I asked.

"I don't remember." Mom said softly. "I remember what he looked like, and I certainly remember the emotions of the weekend. I remember feeling a love so strong I thought I would explode with the intensity of it. I know it sounds stupid, but I really believe it was love at first sight. I remember looking into green eyes like yours and feeling as if I was looking into the soul of everything good and kind in the world. That's what I remember. The way I feel now, it's like I was drugged to keep me from remembering. I also think that, if the love wasn't so strong and you weren't here, I'd believe the whole weekend was nothing but a dream."

"If I told you a name, would that help you remember?" I asked softly. "Was his name Leif Oakton?"

Mom jumped as if hit with an electric cattle prod. "Oh, my God!" She exclaimed. "It was! I remember! How would you know that?"

Then shuddering, I told her about the conversation I heard in the library. "They hate me because I am illegitimate, and if they were talking about me, my real dad is dead. For some reason, the Woodson family thinks that I'm an embarrassment to their family. They think I'm some kind of mixed breed, and the way I feel right now, I wish we had never moved here," I said flatly.

"Oh, honey!" Mom said softly and reached over to hug me. "I'm so sorry you had to hear that. I can't change the past, and you're well-loved. You know that. Ben and I love you. Also, just maybe, they weren't talking about you." But we both knew the answer. "If they were," she continued softly, "I wonder if I could get some answers to some questions. I wonder if they would talk to me."

"Oh, Mom!" I cried. "You can't go asking that family questions. They're reclusive. They'll make you feel like I feel now. They'd be mean to you and say horrible things. I just know it. Maybe we can find out more about the Copper Clan if we knew where it was. Yeah, that's what the other voice said, that Leif belonged to the Copper Clan, whatever that is. Besides, my real dad is dead." I looked down, feeling horrible. I had never met my real dad, and now I never would.

Mom tilted up my chin. "The Scottish people had clans." she said softly. "But I never heard of any clans here in the United States. Maybe they're Scottish transplants. I wonder what this Forrest guy is like. If it was you they were talking about, I think it's kind of scary to think that someone's been keeping an eye on us all your life. I'm sure Ben wouldn't like the idea of that. Maybe Ash and the other guy were not talking about us." But he was, and we both knew it.

Then Mom got her determined look I knew so well and said, "It doesn't seem as if this Ash Woodson guy and the guy he was talking to are trying to make your birth public knowledge. Try to stay away from Ash, and let's see what happens. Maybe if you ignore him and go on about your business, he'll leave you alone. I really don't want to move, but if things get worse, we may have to. I think I've wanted this house my whole life, but you mean more to me than this house."

Just thinking of making my mom give up her forever house, especially so soon after arriving here bothered me more than some stupid boy and his mean comments. I was stronger than that! I vowed to get past this. Just because Mom wasn't married when I was conceived did not mean I had no value. I had a mom and dad who loved me.

"I'm not going to be liked by everyone, I know that. I've made some good friends here. I don't like Ash, and I know he doesn't like me, but he keeps to himself. I think we can get through this," I said fervently.

She hugged me again and got up off of the couch. "I'm sorry you're going through this," she said, "But I'm not sorry that you're here, in my life. You mean everything to me." Yeah, I knew that. Mom never made me feel like I was a mistake.

Mom carried her work clothes upstairs. She was starting her new job tomorrow. She was going in to get her office set up. She wasn't actually taking patients until Monday. She came back down, and we had hamburgers for dinner that night. At 10:00 p.m. the phone rang, and Mom answered it. I could tell by her voice that it was Ben. She told him everything that I'd told her, leaving out the part about some guy named Forrest keeping an eye on us. At first I wondered why she didn't tell him, but then realized that it would probably freak Ben out, and there was nothing he could do about it from Iraq.

Saturday morning was bright and sunny. A chill was in the air. "Boy, it gets cold up here early," I said. "We'd still have the air conditioning on in D.C."

Mom smiled while we ate our breakfast. We had both gotten up early. She'd made us French toast.

"While I'm at the office this morning, do you want to come and see it from the inside?" Mom asked, taking a sip of her coffee. "Maybe I can call George, and we could head up to the reservation afterwards."

"Yeah, that'd be great!" I agreed. Mom went to call George. She told me he'd be expecting us after lunch.

Mom used her new key to open the clinic. There were no office hours on Saturday, unless a client had a crisis. Mental health didn't always keep normal work hours, and the clinic tried to be accommodating. But there were no cars in the parking lot when we arrived. The day was warming up, and it seemed like it was going to be a hot one after all. We propped the door open to get some fresh air in the office. The receptionist liked air fresheners, and the place reeked of some fake floral scent. Mom and I preferred the pine scent of the woods. Her office had a private waiting area. We opened all the doors from the front door to her office in the back. There was also a back door directly from her office to ensure privacy of her clients. This way, clients waiting to be seen did not have to see the clients that were leaving.

In no time at all, the artificial scent was washed away by the fresh, natural woodsy scent of the forest surrounding three sides of the building. I waited in the front room by the reception desk. There were magazines to look at, and some of them were actually current. The *People* magazine was less than a month old. I was amazed. I thought that all magazines at doctor's offices had to be at least two years old.

As I sat there leafing through the magazine, getting all of the dirt on famous people, I heard voices coming from my mom's office. I don't know why, but I didn't just walk in there to see who she was talking to. I guessed at first I figured she was on speaker phone.

"Hello!" I heard Mom say. "Can I help you?" Her voice wavered a little. She wasn't sounding confident. She didn't know this person. And she wasn't on the phone.

"My name is Forrest Oakton," he stated in his soft, so smooth voice. If European chocolate had a sound, it would be the sound like that. His voice was softer and smoother than the man in the library with Ash.

I couldn't help myself. I had to creep to Mom's office. She looked shocked and let out a little gasp at his name.

"You know who I am, don't you? How did you find out about me?" he asked softly. I had edged all the way to the doorway so that I could see Mom's face and get a glimpse of the guy in her office. He was tall, at least six-five, and thin. He had straight brown hair, about collar length and kind of slicked back behind his ears. His hair was almost exactly the same color as mine, although he had gray at the temples. He looked like a movie star, really good looking for an older man. His clothes were casual but obviously expensive—like designer clothes made just for him. He kind of looked like an older version of Ash Woodson.

"I think so. Please have a seat." Good old Mom, a nervous wreck, but still professional and polite. "If you're who I think you are, I hear you've been watching me and Laurel. Is this correct?" That seemed to throw him off guard. He didn't expect that.

"Well, yes. How did you know?" He seemed hesitant. Then he spoke more quickly. "You weren't supposed to know! Who told you about me?" This time it almost sounded like he was talking more to himself than to Mom.

Mom watched him for a minute, then said, "Laurel heard she was an abomination by someone at school, a boy by the name of Ash Woodson. Your name was mentioned in the context that you were keeping an eye on Laurel and me. So, this is true?" Mom had that determined look on her face now as she asked the question. Here was her chance to get some answers.

"Like I said . . . yes. it is true. I've been keeping an eye out for you and Laurel. She is most certainly *not* an abomination! She isn't a part of their clan, though. She's part of my clan." Forrest stated emphatically.

I couldn't take it anymore. I walked into the office. Forrest shifted so fast to look at me, I didn't even see his head move. One second he was looking at my mom, and a nanosecond later he had moved and was standing near me and looking down at me.

"Laurel," Forrest said, looking at me, his tone almost reverent. "I'm your Uncle Forrest. Forrest Oakton," he said, taking my hand. He smiled. "I always wanted to meet you face to face, but I didn't know how to do it, so I just kept an eye on you to make sure you were okay. I tried to make sure things were easy for you without getting in the way." He finished and glanced back toward my mother.

"You cleaned the yard and house before we got here, didn't you?" Mom said in a tone of voice I couldn't quite understand. "Why?" she asked.

Forrest sighed. "Yes. I knew you were coming, and I wanted to make it easier for you. Either of you could have been hurt trying to do everything. I know you don't have any known family in the area."

Known family, huh. What did that mean? Was he implying that we had family that we don't know about?

"There was a lot of debris in the driveway. Some heavy branches came down during the winter. I had them cleared away. I try to stay out of the way, I really do, but I just had to help you out. Please don't be upset," he pleaded with Mom. She stared at him. He seemed sincere enough. I liked the idea of not having had to do a lot of yard work. I also liked the idea of having family.

"What clan, and why now?" Mom finally asked. "After all of these years, why come forward now?" She paused then said, "How did you know we were coming? How did you know about this house?"

Forrest thought for a second, then said, "I'll tell you all about it, just not right now. Now is not the time." He looked off into space as if he were listening to something we couldn't hear. After a moment he said, "When you got pregnant, we knew immediately. The entire clan knew. We have a way of knowing about such things. Leif was killed less than a week after he met you. That's why he never came back to you. He loved you, and he was excited at the prospect of being a father. I should have come to you sooner and made myself known to you. Now I realize that." Forrest laughed in a sad kind of way. He started walking toward the door.

"I'll be back in touch. Now that we've met, I won't be a stranger. It's just not always easy to do what I want to do. I promise that I mean you no harm. Neither of you!" He looked at both of us from the doorway. "I am your friend, I truly am. If I had been able to come up with an acceptable way to meet you earlier, I would have. Please know that much. For now, I have to go. I'll be in touch. Tell Ben about me. He has a right to know. Oh, and try to avoid the area on Highway D from five miles out of town to the river. It is not a good area to be in, especially at night." With that parting remark, he slipped out of the door, not giving either of us a chance to respond. For a second we both just stared at the door.

I ran after him. But he was nowhere in sight. I ran around to the front of the building, thinking I could catch him getting in his car, but the only vehicle in the lot was Mom's Liberty. He had just disappeared. Where had he gone so quickly? Into the woods?

I walked back around the building and saw Mom leaning against the door jam watching me come back. "Wow!" she said. "I'm at a loss for words! I had no idea! First you overhear a conversation and now this! I wonder what other surprises are in store for us. I wonder when he'll come back?"

I agreed. Wow. I had a biological family! I had blood relatives other than just my mother. She was an only child. Her parents were deceased. She had no cousins that she knew of. It was just Ben, my mom, and me. Now, I had an uncle. It was exciting. Why didn't he tell us more about himself? Where did he live? Questions crowded my brain. I looked like him! It was obvious that I physically took after my dad's side of the family. Did I have cousins? I had family! He did not seem to think I was an abomination. He seemed happy to see me!

"I really don't know what to say other than it comforts me to know that Leif didn't abandon me," Mom said. "It's a relief to know your father felt the same way about me that I did about him. I went up to the cottage week after week for months. I wondered what had happened. I'm sorry he died. I wonder how he died. I wonder what our life would have been like if he'd have lived . . ." She paused. "I wonder what George will think about this," she finally said. "Let's close this place up and go see George." She walked back into the building to lock it up.

We got to George's house, and Mom and George sat at the kitchen table. George poured her a cup of coffee. George listened carefully as mom told him what happened. I then told George what I'd heard in the library.

"You're wonderful!" George said to me. "You deserve to live just like anyone else, maybe even more so . . ." he said thoughtfully. Then, after a long pause, he said, "The Woodsons and the Oaktons are not always nice people." He seemed to hesitate on the last word.

"You know the Woodsons and Oaktons?" I asked, curious. He had never mentioned them before.

"I know *of* them. I have met some of them, but I'm concerned about this Forrest guy." George said. "I've heard of the Copper Clan."

"You have?" Mom asked. "Really? What do you know about them? Other than Leif years ago, I never met any of them. I'd never even heard of them prior to meeting Leif, and as I told you, my memory of that weekend is sketchy at best. My dad and I went up there plenty of times. I wonder why I hadn't heard of them before?"

"You obviously met one of them." He said, looking pointedly at me. "Even though your dad owned a place up there by Presque Isle, you really weren't a local. The clans tend to be reclusive. Did you participate in any social activities in Presque Isle?"

"Not really," Mom replied. "Once when I was a kid we went to Muskie Days and a dance. That's all I remember doing in the town, other than grocery shopping or going to the Laundromat or bars and restaurants."

"Isn't it neat though, that we're finding out about my real dad's family?" I enthused. I couldn't wait to see Forrest again.

"Sure." George said, but he didn't sound all that happy. I wondered why he wasn't happy for me and my mom. Was he jealous that my mom might make other friends?

"Where's Adam?" I asked George.

"Probably at the clubhouse," George replied.

"I'm going to go there, okay?"

Adam, Jason, Jeremy, and Melody were there playing pool. Some other kids played pin ball and video games, too. "Hey, Laurel!" Adam called. "What's happening?"

"Hey!" I said to Adam and the group. "Mom and I met my dad's brother today."

"Really? I didn't know you had an uncle. Was he in Iraq with your dad?" Adam asked sinking the eight ball and winning the game.

"My step-dad is in Iraq. My biological dad was killed while my mom was pregnant with me. He has family in Presque Isle . . . the Copper Clan, whatever that is. Is there a Scottish group up there?" I asked.

"Scottish group . . . ?" Adam looked confused. "What Scottish group?"

"The Copper Clan, Adam!" I said. "A clan is usually Scottish, isn't it?"

"Uh, I don't think there's anything Scottish about *them*." He said. I saw Adam glance at his friends.

"What do you mean? How do you know? If they aren't Scottish, then what are they? Are they Native American, then?" I asked.

Looking like he'd said too much, Adam shrugged. "Sure, they must be Scottish. They aren't exactly Native Americans, that's for sure. What else could they be?"

I felt talked around. There was a secret here, and I wanted in on it. "If you don't think the Copper Clan is Scottish, then what do you think that they are?" I demanded.

"Maybe they're wood nymphs . . ." Jeremy said, looking at Adam. Jeremy turned away, busying himself with finding the correct cue stick for another game of pool.

"You guys know something! I thought we were friends. I'm going to leave if you don't let me in on this secret!" I threatened. "I've had a lousy couple of days, and I looked forward to being here. Not anymore!" I said, my own voice cracking a bit, as I fought to hold back the tears. I felt my face redden.

"Oh, Laurel!" Adam said, putting his arm around me. "There are always rumors about things we don't understand. We're not trying to keep secrets from you. There's just something different about the clan people. They avoid associating with other people. That's not a big secret. They're different. They've been here longer than our tribe. We're truly not making fun of you," he said softly.

Adam appeared very sincere. "Okay. Let's play pool," I said, linking my arm with his and headed for the cue sticks. "I get to break!" I grabbing a cue stick.

"Fine, we'll play partners against Jeremy and Melody," Adam replied picking up his own cue stick.

We played pool for a couple of hours. When I noticed the sun sitting low in the western sky, I told them all good-bye and headed back to George's house. Mom and George were on the street walking toward me. We walked back to George's house. Mom and I left shortly after that.

CHAPTER 7
REHEARSAL

Monday morning was chilly. It wouldn't be long before we saw frost on the ground. I was glad that we had a garage, or I would soon be scraping the ice off of my windshield each morning. I was almost to school before my car really warmed up.

Most of the day went by quietly. I ignored Ash Woodson, although only on the outside. Inside, I was aware of where he was when he was in the same classes, where he was in the halls. At lunch, my friends talked about the play. Everyone at the table had something to do with it. "It's too bad Ash is in the play." Mary said softly. "It would be a whole lot more fun if he wasn't."

Rodney said, "We can have fun whether he's there or not. He isn't anything to us."

Mary flipped her hair back and said, "We don't need downers around us."

I nodded in agreement, but when Ash walked by to turn his lunch tray back to the kitchen, I looked at him, and our eyes met. He didn't look away, but stared intensely at me as he walked by. At least he didn't look mad this time or say anything rude. Just then, the bell rang, and I had to return my own lunch tray.

In Drama, we were told that after school rehearsals were starting. Rehearsal would run from 3:00 p.m. to 5:00 p.m. Mondays, Wednesdays, and Fridays. On Tuesdays and Thursdays, rehearsal would run until 8:00 p.m., We were expected to bring something to eat on Tuesday and Thursday in case we got hungry.

After school, everyone with a part in the play met on stage with Miss Becker. The stage hands were back stage working with another teacher. Miss Becker handed out our scripts, and we just read our parts for the first half of the play.

Tuesday night, we read through the second half of the play. When it got to the part of the play where Mr. Darcy proposes to Elizabeth Bennett for the first time, Ash's face looked as if he was already in character. He looked uncomfortable with loving a girl not his equal. His acting skills were so good that Miss Becker had the whole class applaud his lines.

"Mr. Woodson, even though that was a first time reading of the lines, your facial expression and voice accentuation were perfect!" Miss Becker gushed. "You are a natural!"

Then it was my turn to read my lines, the part where Elizabeth Bennett turned down Mr. Darcy's proposal. I was thinking about Adam talking about how the clans felt that they were better than anyone else. I could actually see Ash Woodson believing he was too good for me. I was the illegitimate girl adopted by a step-dad who loved her, but that still didn't change the fact that I was born on the wrong side of the blanket, as the old expression went. If Ash Woodson's family didn't think regular people not of their clan were good enough for them, how could Ash ever find me desirable?

The truth was, I had been lying to myself. I was attracted to Ash Woodson. Every conscious thought not taken up by something else was filled by him. I imagined what life would be like if he actually smiled at me or showed me some kindness. I imagined him waiting for me when I got out of my car in the morning at school. But, this was never meant to be. I was a bastard in his eyes. I was thinking about this when the teacher called on me to read my lines rejecting the proposal.

As I read the lines, I could see clearly that Ash found me inferior. Projecting into the play, even if this Mr. Darcy ever did come to like me, let alone love me, how could I marry a man who felt he was above me? I would feel this way even if he did profess to love me against his better judgment. With these thoughts in my head, I was able to put myself in Elizabeth Bennett's shoes, to feel the revulsion she felt at being told that the man proposing to her found her and her family inferior, that he loved her against his will. I spoke with feeling.

"We have another person who gets the emotions of the scene and can express them perfectly! Bravo!" Miss Becker enthused. "With that, we're done for the night. I hope you all paid attention to those readings!" she said to the rest of the class. "If all of you can portray your parts with that much intensity, this will be a great play! Good night everyone, great job tonight!"

"Wow, good job, Laurel!" Rodney said as we walked to the parking lot. I glanced across the lot to the black Toyota. Ash met my eyes just before getting into his car. I drove home deep in thought about my new-found feelings toward Ash Woodson and wondering what I could do about them. Obviously this was going to be unrequited love. The guy couldn't stand me.

For the next couple of weeks, I did my best to focus on homework and getting a job. Two weeks after rehearsals for the play started, I got a weekend job at the local hardware store as a cashier. It paid better than minimum wage and the owner understood about my being a student and having school obligations. The owner suggested that I work weekends until the play was over and then I could work a couple nights during the week as well. I could pay my own gas and insurance! Between school and work, I had no free time to think about Ash Woodson. This was a good thing.

During the third week of rehearsal, Miss Becker brought in a dance instructor to teach us dancing in the Victorian style. We had to dance with the partners we would be dancing with in the play, so of course I had to dance with Ash. I noticed he didn't glare at me anymore. If anything, he was getting a puzzled look on his face when he looked at me. We seemed to have reached a point in our non-relationship where he was no longer angry just seeing me. If we were enemies, which I guessed we were, I'd say we had a truce going on. I'd have given anything to have been able to ask him about the look on his face. But I didn't want to spoil the truce by talking to him. I'd take intense scrutiny over glares any day. There were times I caught him staring at me.

I really wanted to know what he was thinking. Did he still believe me an abomination? Did it really matter about my heritage, that I was born illegitimate?

When we had to dance together the first few times, we just practiced the dance without speaking our lines. We would stand across from each other until it was time to get together during the dance, and he would move very gracefully and gently hold my hands while we danced the steps. His hands were warm and firm and, at the same time, soft. He had strong hands, but no calluses. It was like holding the soft skin of a baby over steel. He was a natural at dance. When I had to dance with one of the other boys, I felt clumsy and awkward, but when dancing with Ash, I floated.

"Miss Redmond, you shouldn't be looking happy!" Miss Becker called while we danced for what seemed like the millionth time. I thought, *Oh no! Is my face giving my true feelings away?* I focused on having a sarcastic thought and what the lines were during this part of the play.

"Sorry, Miss Becker, I was focusing on the dance steps, and I think that I like this dance!" I said as an excuse.

"That's fine, Miss Redmond. It's a wonderful dance. Just try to multi-task. Remember what your lines are during the dance. It'll keep your head straight and your facial features controlled." She corrected someone else's dance steps. After that, Miss Becker called the rehearsal a success and let us go home. It was almost 8:00 p.m.

When we got out to our cars, the parking lot lights were on, but it was a dark, overcast night. It had been threatening rain all day.

I was the last one to leave the parking lot. I had tried to call Mom before starting my car to ask if I should bring something home from town for dinner. I'd forgotten to bring a snack and was hungry. We had a Subway in town that was open late. But, my phone was dead. I'd forgotten to charge it. I didn't yet have a car charger for my phone. I was thinking I should buy one when I started the car to go home.

My Jeep made a funny sound. I wasn't a mechanic, but I knew the sounds my car made. If I hadn't been so busy thinking about Ash and the dance, I might have paid more attention to that sound. Maybe I was just hungry and mad because my phone didn't work. Either way, I decided just to head home.

I usually took Highway D home. I was a couple of miles out of town when my car started coughing. It sounded like it was having a respiratory attack, and then it died. Great. I was on an isolated part of the highway in the dark, with no cell phone. I tried to remember where the closest house was, and I couldn't. As far as I could tell, it was fifty-fifty which direction I should go to find help. The problem was, it was so dark, I couldn't see the road. I decided to wait for a car to drive by. Twenty minutes later, no car had come by. I remembered I had a flashlight in my glove box. I pulled it out. It wasn't a big flashlight, it had a nice bright beam when I flicked it on.

I grabbed my purse and keys and got out of the car. I started walking back towards town. I walked maybe a mile when I noticed that my flashlight was starting to grow dim. *Great, now what?* Was I coordinated enough to stay on the highway in the dark, or would I get lost in the woods? I figured if I lost the light completely, as long as I had pavement under my feet, I should be in good shape. As I continued, I heard a strange cry in the woods, an animal or night bird I didn't recognize. At first it was pretty distant, but it was getting louder, closer. Then I heard it really clearly, and it was a horrible sound, like a lunatic screaming. I was terrified. I started running, my footsteps echoing off of the pavement.

I could hear heavy, pounding steps in the woods right next to the road coming toward me. Branches crashed and broke as if something was charging through the woods. It was much faster than I was. I couldn't run anymore. Breathing heavily, I turned to face my fate from my unseen attacker. All of a sudden, strong arms wrapped around my rib cage and lifted me straight up into the air.

I was jerked up into a tree. The speed of which I was grabbed and lifted was so fast, I dropped the flashlight. Strong arms held me tight. I heard hooves or large claws clattering on the pavement under the tree as the monster searched for me. From the sound, I had to be at least fifty feet in the air. A hand was clamped over my mouth so I couldn't scream. My heart pounded. After a while, the creature below seemed to give up and wandered back into the woods. I could still hear it bellowing, its ungodly cry growing more distant. I realized I was shaking. I thought I was going to faint or knock both me and my savior out of the tree.

With one arm clamped around me, the hand was gently removed from my mouth. At the same time, a soft voice whispered softly in my ear, "Its okay. You're okay. You're safe now. I won't let anything happen to you. Please don't scream and bring it back." As he talked to me, he gently stroked my cheek with his free hand.

In the pitch dark, everything seemed unreal. I could hear the voice, though. It was real, as I could feel the arm around me. But it had to be a dream, because I recognized the voice—that of someone who hated me.

"Am I dead?" I asked.

"You're not dead," he said with a sigh. "You're about forty feet up in a tree. I have to get us down now, though. I have to jump. You won't get hurt. Can you promise not to scream or do I need to cover your mouth again?"

I was close on the height. "I won't scream."

He cradled me in his arms and stepped off of the branch. I felt the wind fly past for just a moment, and then we were on the ground again. He landed so lightly it felt as if he had stepped off of a curb into the street. I knew this wasn't so. I had felt the free-fall drop, felt my stomach lurch.

"Can you stand?" he asked setting me onto my feet.

"Of course!" I replied, and, when I tried to stand up, my legs promptly gave out. He caught me before I collapsed to the pavement.

"I don't know what the problem is." I said. "My legs used to work." After a moment, I was able to stand on my own, though not without support.

"You're in shock," he said, his arm still around me.

"W-why am I in shock?" I asked. *Okay, that sounded like a really stupid question.* I tested my legs. They were starting to function better. He kept his arm around me.

"You heard a Hodag. The sound's been known to drive people insane. Not only that, but the Hodag was after you. A couple more seconds, we wouldn't be having this discussion. It would've killed you. So, not only did you survive the scream of the Hodag, you survived a Hodag attack. That's rare."

"Hodag? The . . . the Hodag is real? Why are you being nice to me? I thought you hated me."

He reached down and found my flashlight, though I didn't know how he could in the dark. The switch must have been turned off when it hit the ground because when he flipped it now, it lit up. It wasn't bright, but compared to the blackness, it was a beacon. I took the flashlight from him and shined it on his face.

Ash Woodson. I knew that, knew his voice. Still I was startled. He jerked his head away from the light. "How did you know to find me?" I asked. "You left the school lot before I did. Will that thing come back?" I asked looked around.

Ash sighed. "I heard your Jeep when you started it. It didn't sound right. I waited up the road for you to drive past. When you didn't, I came looking for you. Oh, and, no, the Hodag shouldn't be back. They're territorial and aggressive, but they don't like to stay in one place too long. They go from one end of their territory to the other. They're not real bright. You were right in the middle of its hunting trail right when it was happening by. You couldn't have been in a worse place at the worse time." He gave me a wry smile.

"Isn't the Hodag a kind of a cross between a dinosaur and a cow? I heard something about how the screams of them would drive lumberjacks insane." I looked at him skeptically.

"Yeah, that's kind of what they look like. Lots of lumberjacks were killed by Hodags, though wolves and bears got most of the blame. And yes, many lumberjacks were driven insane by the cry of the Hodag." He took my hand and looked at my face closely, apparently making sure that I hadn't lost my mind during this adventure. We started walking towards my car. "We don't need to tempt fate anymore this evening. We need to get you home."

"I guess I'm glad that I couldn't see it. Why are we going this way?" I asked as I held his hand tightly. "My car isn't going to start."

"I parked less than a mile in front of you," he said. "I'll get you home safely."

I gripped his hand like a lifeline. Maybe he knew I needed this link to reality. He didn't try to remove his hand. As we walked, I felt exhaustion take over. Every step got harder. As we walked, we talked. Now that we were talking, I had some questions. "How were you able to hold me and jump so high into the air?" I asked, holding his hand tighter.

"You can't?" he replied, a totally unexpected response. I thought he was making fun of me, so I flashed the flashlight in his face, and I saw his surprised look.

"No, of course not." I stated emphatically. I had taken gym class and had tried the long jump. While I did pretty well, I wasn't Olympic material. I certainly couldn't jump straight up forty feet. Who could?

"I thought you might be able to, knowing who your father was and all." He replied thoughtfully.

"No, and I want to know how you could." I asked.

He looked back at me. "Genetics. It's all in the genetics. However, my family isn't like other families. I'd appreciate it if you didn't tell anyone about your misadventure this evening." He stated this while looking at me.

I gave a little laugh. "No one would believe me," I replied. Then I thought, "Why would you care whether I made it home or not? You hate me."

He sighed. "I don't . . . hate you. I may have hated the *thought* of you and what you are, but I never really *hated* you. I think you're the first of your kind."

"The first of my . . . what? What am I?" I was too tired to get mad. I just wanted to understand.

"I think you're beginning to know. You're a half breed of two species. You're half human and half wood nymph."

I stopped dead in my tracks. Though I had experienced plenty of shock this evening, this sent a new jolt through me. "Half . . . what? I don't know what you mean.

You hate me because I'm . . . part . . . wood nymph. *Wood nymph!* Okay, now I'm officially out to lunch . . . and so are you! I thought you hated me because I was illegitimate, that I wasn't good enough for you to associate with. But no. Your issue was that I wasn't all . . . human? Seriously?" I gave a humorless laugh. "This is rich. You think I'm not all human. Why did you even save my life? If I'm not human, I certainly am an abomination!" I whispered furiously, unbelievably hurt.

He stopped dead in his tracks. "No. Laurel, no. That's not it at all. Don't you get it? I'm a full wood nymph. I'm not a human. We look human and that is how we get along in the world, but I'm as far from being human as that birch tree is."

I, of course, really couldn't see the birch tree, or much elese in the wall of blackness that was the forest. It did connect with me, though, that he could.

"For a long time," he whispered, "wood nymphs didn't associate with humans at all, except to treat them as entertainment or pets." We started walking again.

He continued softly., "There are very few of us now. We're dying off as a species. Pollution is killing us off. We can't handle it. We used to have the lifespan of three humans. Now we have the life span of one. We never did have more than one or two children per conjoined couple, but now we're not having any children at all. I'm the last.

"I'd never heard of a wood nymph mixing with a human before. It just wasn't done. I mean, some of the women wood nymphs have had flirtations with humans, but none of them would allow themselves to get pregnant. I am the youngest of my clan. I don't even think your father's clan has any younger than I am. The married couples are trying to have babies, but they just are not conceiving. My mother is fifty-five, and I'm her only child. My father's sixty. The entire clan was ecstatic when they found she was pregnant. My closest cousin is thirty-five."

My mind seemed to be moving in slow motion. "So, you don't hate me?"

"If you expose me, you expose your uncle Forrest and the rest of them. I don't think you're the kind of person who would enjoy hurting anyone, even if you thought they hated you. And I don't. We've never really wronged a human. We just don't associate with them.

"I had never heard of you or about your mother until you moved here. While my parents knew about you, no one told me. No one told me specifically that wood nymphs could mate with humans. I always believed that it was just something that wasn't done. Calling you an abomination was a bit harsh, but I was taken by surprise." Then he asked, "How did you know I called you an abomination?"

I stopped and faced him, still clutching his hand like a security blanket. It seemed like the only real thing going on at that moment. I had almost died from an attack by a mythological beast, and just found out the guy I was in love with was not human.

"You said that in the parking lot I didn't belong here. And . . . and then I heard you talking to someone in the library. Who was that?" I asked.

He blinked at me. "You heard that? I didn't know you were listening. I should have been paying attention. That was one of my uncles. He's the school counselor. He always says—if you want to know what's going on in a community, get inside the kids' heads. Come on. We need to keep walking. It's really getting late. Your mother's going to be worried." He started walking again, pulling me along with him.

We were quiet for a few minutes. We weren't walking very fast. I was really tired and he didn't seem to be in any hurry either. I had time to think about all that he had told me. I believed him and what he told me frightened me, but, on a different level, it was okay. Hodags were real. Wood nymphs were real, and, according to Ash, I was half wood nymph. Okee dokie. What other myths and legends were true? Was this really happening to me? Should I believe this? I could be trapped in a weird dream.

"Does my mother know about this?" I asked finally. My Jeep was just ahead. The flashlight caught the glint of the bumper.

"I don't think so, but I think she will find out soon. Let her find out on her own, okay? The fact that she loves you may make it more difficult for her to accept the truth. Maybe not, though."

"Are other legends and myths true, too?" I asked with a yawn.

He smiled at me and said, "My car is just a little bit further down the road. If it was daylight, you'd be able to see it."

I picked up on the inference that he could see the car. "You can see it?" I asked.

"Yes. It appears that my eyesight is much better than yours. Wood nymphs can see at night almost as well as in the daylight. We also have better hearing. There's other stuff, but I think that's enough about me for tonight."

I was dead on my feet by the time we got to his car. He helped me in, and I fell asleep in the passenger seat of his car even as he started the engine. I woke up with the porch light on my house in my face. It didn't even occur to me at that moment that he knew exactly where we lived.

Mom came running out of the house. "Do you know what time it is? I've been worried sick about you! Where's your car?" Then she noticed Ash. I saw it in her eyes that she noticed his similarity to me. She stiffened. We really did look like brother and sister. "Who's this?" she finally asked.

"Hi, Mrs. Redmond. I'm Ash Woodson. Laurel's car broke down on the highway. She was trying to walk back to town to call you when I picked her up. We had to walk a couple of miles back to my car. With everything going on with school and the play, Laurel's exhausted." Ash helped me up the stairs and into the house.

Mom did see that I was exhausted and sat me in a kitchen chair. I guess she realized that this wasn't the night for twenty questions. "Are either of you hungry?" she asked.

"I'm more tired than hungry, but I could eat." I said. I looked at Ash.

"I have to go home, but thanks anyway. I'll take a raincheck," he said as he walked back to the front door. I forced myself to stand up to walk him to the door. He smiled and said, "I'll see you tomorrow."

My head filled with his words. "Raincheck." He intended to come back. He said raincheck. That implied a repeat chance at dinner.

CHAPTER 8
WHAT HAPPENS NOW?

I was still tired the next morning. I hadn't slept very well, but I didn't remember having any dreams. I got dressed, brushed my teeth and was down for breakfast earlier than usual. Mom was eating. If she didn't have clients first thing in the morning, she would leave for her office after I left for school so we could have breakfast together.

"I called the towing company and had your car taken to town last night. It is at the garage getting fixed. We should hear sometime today about the repairs," she said as she got me a bowl of cereal and herself another cup of coffee. "Isn't Ash the guy who hates you?" she asked gently. "He didn't seem to hate you last night. I thought he looked kind of protective."

"I *thought* he hated me. It surprised the crap out of me when he stopped to help me last night."

"You still look a little paler than normal. Did you sleep well?" Mom asked.

"Not really," I replied staring at my breakfast. I didn't seem to be hungry.

"That's quite a scare, having your car break down on a deserted and dark piece of highway." Mom continued.

"Sure." I said.

Mom was going to drive me to school on her way to work. As she was getting her purse and keys, she said she'd pick me up from school, too. As we walked to the front door, she said she hoped my car repairs would be completed today, and that when she picked me up, we could go and get the car.

As we walked outside to go to the garage, I saw a black vehicle coming up our driveway. We stood on the porch watching Ash Woodson's Toyota SUV approach.

He pulled up in back of the house, and Mom and I just stood at the top railing of the porch looking down at him as he got out of the car.

While both my mom and I were surprised by his appearance, my mom smiled and said good morning to him. Then I remembered my manners and said good morning, too.

He smiled as he stepped up onto the porch. "I knew you didn't have a car today, so I thought I'd pick you up. I hope you don't mind. I didn't have your phone number to call you first." He said leaning against the railing at the bottom of the stairs.

Mom looked at me, leaving this decision up to me.

"Sure, that'd be great," I said, walking down the porch stairs, book bag and purse in hand. I hadn't even noticed that Ash had grabbed my bag from my car last night until I saw it next to the front door this morning.

I waved good-bye to my mom as she went to the garage. I got into Ash's car.

As we pulled down the driveway, Ash glanced over at me and said, "I figure you have more questions. First, I want to make one thing clear. I don't hate you. I told you that last night, but you may not remember all of last night. You had quite a few frightening experiences for one night. The fact is, I . . . I like you. How much, I'm not sure, but I have decided that I definitely like you and would like to get to know you. Is that okay?"

I felt a warm glow spread throughout my body at his words. Did I think this was okay? No, this wasn't okay—this was great! "Yes, I'd like that. I'd like that a lot." I tried not to smile too broadly. Suddenly I was at a loss for words. I just basked in the warm glow.

"Do you have hobbies?" he asked me. "What do you like to do when you are not at school or at work?"

How did he know I had a job? Oh, yeah, this was Tomahawk. This was a small town. People who looked like him came into the hardware store, but I never thought that they noticed me. It'd make sense that these people would be his extended family.

"I like plants and fishing," I said. "I'm not very good at fishing, but a while back I caught enough fish for dinner for my mom and me." I laughed and said, "Yeah, I ordered the fish to bite my hook, and they did. It was the craziest thing."

"Really," he said softly, "That may be some ability you have. It may be that not just your appearance is wood nymph. We'll have to experiment with that, but you need to be careful. Water sprites don't take too kindly to our kind ordering their creatures about. There was a war once between us because of that kind of thing. Oh, it was centuries ago, but our kinds have long memories."

"Water sprites are real?" I asked, shocked, but then after thinking for a second said, "Sure, why not? Hodags are real, and so are wood nymphs." Then I thought of the face I had seen in the water, thinking it had been my imagination and said, "Do the water sprites have long, green hair?"

"Yes, some of them do. They don't associate with humans at all. They live strictly in the water. They really hate humans, as the pollution that humans introduce into the waterways is killing off their kind, too. I didn't think there were any left in this part of the river. I'm surprised one let you see it. They're usually very cautious around humans and avoid them. Perhaps your scent confused it, as you definitely smell both human and wood nymph," he said thoughtfully.

"You can identify scents?" I asked leaning back into the seat of his car.

"Oh, yes. Maybe with some instruction, you can, too," he replied and smiled.

Just at that point, I saw that we were on Highway D and wondered where the Hodag came after me, and stated such to Ash.

"I was parked right here," he said, pointing to the side of the road. "You were parked here, he said a minute later as we drove down the road. We drove a few minutes in silence and he pointed up into a tall maple tree that overhung the road, and said, "That's the tree we jumped into."

When I saw the tree, saw how high the branches were, it brought to the forefront of my reality what had happened last night. It was not a delusion or a hallucination. It really had happened. All of a sudden, I couldn't breathe. I was in the grip of what had to have been a panic attack. I started gasping for air.

"Are you okay?" Ash asked me in a concerned voice.

I couldn't respond. I just kept trying to force air into lungs that didn't seem to want any. It was almost like the feeling of having my breath knocked out of me. He was starting to pull over, really close to the tree, and I shook my head, no.

"I can't take you to school like this!" he said. "How about I take you to my house? We have a cousin next door who's a doctor. While we don't really get sick in the human sense, we can get injured. Plus, he's trying to find a way to fight off the pollution poisoning. With your mixed blood, I'd really rather not take you to a human emergency room in a hospital."

I nodded my consent, still gasping.

Away from the tree, I began breathing a bit more easily, but I was sweating and shaking. The sound of the beast kept echoing in my mind. The scream of the Hodag could drive people insane. Was I going insane?

Ash turned his SUV around and turned up the same road that our private driveway was on. A part of my brain registered that he didn't live very far from me. His driveway was only about a mile past mine. I had lost my breath as we drove past the tree, and I started gasping like a fish out of water again when I realized how close we lived. It was a good thing Mom took a different route to work, or we would have driven right past her. Knowing her, she would have turned around and followed us. That would have been more than I could deal with at that moment.

Ash's driveway wasn't gravel as ours was. It was concrete and about two miles long. It had a thick forest on both sides. When nearing the end of it, I saw that it branched out on each side into separate roads and also still continued on straight ahead. We kept on the forward branch of the road. We drove another half mile or so, and then came into a clearing and the biggest house I had ever seen. It had huge columns in the front and a wide circling porch that wrapped around the house in both directions. I had seen houses like this in the movies, but they were antebellum houses from the Deep South, a plantation style house. Lots of windows. It was gorgeous.

Ash parked right in front of the house and came around to my side of the door to help me out of the car. An older woman who looked just like Ash and I assumed was his mother came out the front door of the big house. She must have heard the car in the driveway. I found out later that the driveway had sensors that alerted the inhabitants of the house of vehicles coming up the drive.

"What's going on?" The woman asked, watching Ash help me from the car. I was drenched with sweat. It was obvious there was something wrong with me. She came and put her arm around me. I had Ash on one side and this woman on the other holding me up. For some reason my legs didn't seem to want to cooperate again.

"She heard a Hodag last night," Ash said. "I . . . I saved her from it. Just now, when we neared the place where it was, she went into shock." I caught a glance between the woman and Ash and realized he hadn't told anyone about our encounter last night.

"I couldn't take her to school like this! The only thing I could think of was to bring her here," he said. He sounded angry. Was our truce over? Was I too much of a bother? It wasn't like I wanted to have a meltdown. Was I really in shock? I'd never felt like this before. What was the matter with me?

I could breathe now, but I was still sweating. In the back of my mind I hoped my deodorant would hold.

"Put her on the couch," said the woman, her voice liquid and lovely. "I'll call Fraser. Oh, he already knows. Here he comes, now." The woman said looking toward the front door as she and Ash settled me on the couch, a plush, velvety pale mauve. An older man who looked similar to Ash and his mother came in the door.

The woman got up and went to him. "Hi, Fraser!" said the woman. "Apparently Ash and Laurel had an interaction with a Hodag yesterday. Of course Laurel wouldn't know about them or how dangerous they are. Damn humans and their lack of knowledge of the real forest," she complained to Fraser.

Ash sat next to me on the couch and put his arm around me. With his hand that wasn't around my shoulder, he held my hand. I held his hand in a death grip. With his hand in mine, I felt I was gaining control of whatever was going on with me. I didn't feel so much like I was drowning.

"That's my mother, Willow." Ash said.

"She knows who I am, doesn't she? I heard her say my name." I said softly.

"Yeah, she knew about you before I did. I told you that last night, don't you remember?" he responded as softly.

I didn't get a chance to answer. The man strode into the room and stood in front of me. "Hi, Laurel. I'm Dr. Fraser Woodson. I'm here to help. Tell me what happened." He took my pulse and looked into my eyes.

Before I had a chance to say anything, Dr. Woodson turned to Willow and said, "Expect a visit from Forrest. Olivia called me. If she know about Ash and Laurel being here, then Forrest will too. He's very protective of this one. He'll want to know everything that happened and what's going on." He smiled at me in a kind way and said again, "Please tell me what happened yesterday."

"If you don't mind, I'll tell you." Ash said. Dr. Woodson nodded and settled into a chair.

"After school yesterday, we had play rehearsal until 8:00 p.m. When we went out to our cars, I noticed that Laurel's car sounded off. It didn't sound to me like it would make it to her house. She let the engine run a few minutes and was the last to leave."

Did I really sit there for a few minutes before leaving? I could have. I was deep in thought about Ash.

"I started to go home, but then decided to go back and check on her. I was over halfway home when I got out of the car and listened. I focused my attention up the road and I heard her running steps about a mile away, running in the opposite direction. Then I heard the Hodag. I knew she was in Hodag hunting grounds, so I jetted to her. I grabbed her and jumped into a maple tree to get away from the Hodag. It was very close. She'd heard of wood nymphs as a myth, but didn't know we really existed. She didn't know she was a hybrid." After his explanation, he looked at me and gave me a tentative smile. He was really beautiful when he smiled.

"When the Hodag left, we dropped out of the tree. I told her she was half wood nymph. I don't know whether she'd inherited any wood nymph features besides her looks. Then, we walked back to my car. I took her home," Ash finished.

"What is jet?" I asked, starting to feel the panic coming on again.

"Jet is the word we use for a form of travel that we have," Dr. Fraser said in a most soothing voice. "There's no real human comparison. Think of . . ." he paused and then grinned. "Think of *Star Trek* and the way they transport people using 'beaming.' 'Beam me up, Scotty.' We just don't need a transporter. It's kind of like hyper speed, like . . . warp drive. We actually move so fast it's invisible to the naked eye. For some reason we don't set off sonic booms." He gave me a wry grin.

I didn't feel like smiling, though. I felt the panic coming back. I started gasping again, and Dr. Woodson said, "She's suffering from traumatic stress. She had to find out about things that aren't supposed to exist in her world. It is a lot to handle for a human. Then she was almost killed by what she'd consider a mythical beast. It's not surprising that her mind is rejecting this information."

"Is that what's going on?" Ash asked looking at me.

"Really, I can handle this!" I stated, gasping. "Just give me some time."

"How do you feel? Are you afraid?" Dr. Woodson asked me kindly. Doctors tended to cultivate soothing voices. His was pure comfort. He even had a touch of a European accent.

His question required thought. "No, I'm not afraid," I said truthfull. "I guess I'm a bit overwhelmed though. I'm embarrassed too. I would have loved to have met all of you under different circumstances."

Dr. Woodson smiled, and I smiled back. I was starting to feel kind of like my old self, and I was embarrassed. I was horribly embarrassed. As much as I wanted Ash to like me, I didn't want him to feel sorry for me. I wanted to get out of there. I think my embarrassment calmed me down more than anything else. My breathing went back to normal, and I finally stopped sweating.

"Good job, Laurel," Dr. Woodson said. "You're relaxing. I wouldn't have expected you to get control of yourself this quick. I think you know you're safe here. Your pulse is back to normal, too." He said while holding my wrist.

"Dr. Woodson, you have an accent different from Ash's or his mon," I said.

He smiled. "I went to medical school in the United States, but I did a few years of training in Europe in some specialized fields. There are some very old wood nymph clans in Europe. I wanted to see how they handled humans there. I guess I stayed there long enough to pick up an accent. At least I am not speaking in Old English. A lot of the clan members still speak that in Britain," Dr. Woodson answered.

"How many clans are there?" I asked, honestly curious.

"Lots. We live throughout most of the western world. Europe, North Africa, some parts of Asia. Our biggest ruling clan is in England. Some clans refuse to have any contact with humans at all," Dr. Woodson told me.

The older woman I thought was Ash's mom stood near us. She appeared to be hovering. When she noticed me looking at her, she said, "I'm sorry. I should have in-troduced myself to you earlier. I'm Willow Woodson, Ash's mother," she said to me as she reached out to shake my hand. "Can I get you something to drink? Water? Fresh squeezed juice?" she asked.

I realized that I was really thirsty. "A glass of water would be great, thanks," I said.

She went to go get the water. As she was bringing it to me, the front door bell chimed. It was such a beautiful, melodic sound. It had the deep tones of a huge wind chime blended with the higher tones of maybe brass bells and sounded like it came out of a Bose speaker. This place was amazing.

Dr. Woodson and Willow Woodson gave each other quick worried looks. It passed between them, then disappeared almost immediately. Who could make them nervous? I looked at Ash, but he didn't seem to have noticed.

"Forrest is here," Willow stated, going to the door. Everyone turned as the tall man entered the living room.

"I came as soon as I heard," I heard Forrest tell Willow.

He knelt down in front of me, his green eyes meeting mine. "Are you okay?" Forrest asked. He looked really worried. "Olivia said that she saw Laurel have some kind of attack or seizure. What happened?" Willow brought him a dining room chair, and he set it right in front of me and sat. This was a heavy, carved chair, and both handled it as if it was made of balsa wood.

Ash started to explain, but Forrest cut him off. "I want Laurel to tell me. Please, tell me all of it."

So I told my uncle the events of last evening leading up to our sitting in the Woodson's living room. I omitted the part about my thinking about Ash in the car, but I did state that I was the last to leave the parking lot. I found I was comfortable telling my new-found uncle about my car trouble. Even though I had only met him once before, he felt like family. I wasn't nearly as uncomfortable speaking to him as I had felt when I had been talking to Ash and his family, and I had known Ash longer.

I told Forrest how I had found the flashlight in my glove box and started walking back to town. I told him how, without the flashlight, I couldn't tell the difference between the road and the woods without feeling the pavement under my feet. I was completely blind in the dark without the flashlight. When I got to the part about hearing the Hodag, I started shaking again.

"That's enough!" Dr. Woodson growled while looking at Forrest, "We just got her calmed down."

"No, I want to do this," I said. "Maybe it'll be therapeutic to face my fears. Mom's a therapist," I added implying that she'd want me to do this, wondering all the while if she'd really think that this was a good treatment option for terror.

"When I heard the screaming of the thing in the woods, I got so scared I started running. I could hear my feet pounding on the pavement, and I didn't stop until I couldn't run anymore. Finally I had to stop. I was out of breath, and the fear was building so fast I felt paralyzed. I was completely blind to what was coming at me! And it was still coming. I heard the shaking of the trees and crashing of brush. It was almost upon me. I turned towards it, that thing coming to kill me. I was absolutely convinced

I was about to die. I have never been so afraid in my life. I was going to die." I shuddered as I recalled the events of last night.

"Go on . . ." Forrest said softly reaching for my hand not being held by Ash. He set my water glass on the table and took my hand gently in his. His hand was warm, baby soft, yet strong. Like Ash's.

I smiled at him and continued. "Just when I thought I was a goner, I was snatched straight up into the air." I looked at Ash. My shaking was getting under control I noticed. I continued after another deep breath. "Straight up into the air, and then my feet were on a branch. I was being held firmly in place, and there was a hand over my mouth."

I saw Forrest frown when I said that.

I said quickly, "He did it to keep me from screaming. I was already shaking. I was almost killed, and now I was being whisked up into a tree. I could see that my savior might think I would be screaming. He didn't want the Hodag to hear me. Ash didn't hurt me."

Forrest visibly relaxed at that and said, "Okay. What happened next?"

"I didn't know who had saved me until he started talking. I knew it was Ash when I heard his voice."

As I spoke I was looking into Forrest's eyes and felt a peace come over me. I forgot about everyone else in the room except for Forrest. I felt I could say exactly what I thought. As I stared into his beautiful, intensely green eyes, I said, "When I heard the voice, I recognized it as Ash's voice. But, I thought it couldn't be Ash. Every other time he had ever said anything to me, his voice had been hard and unfriendly. He hated me. He was the one I heard in the library call me an abomination."

Forrest's features tighten into a grimace, but he smoothed his face out quickly. I also felt a slight increase in pressure on my hand held by Ash. It felt like an apologetic gesture, that slight squeeze.

"Go on," Forrest urged, trying to keep my concentration on him.

It worked. My focus riveted on Forrest again. "Ash told me I was safe. He said he'd protect me and make sure nothing happened to me. I believed him. When he said he was going to remove his hand from my mouth and asked me not to scream, I was able to comply. Then he said he was going to drop us out of the tree. Now while I had no sense of vision, my hearing," as good as a human ears are I thought, "worked just fine. Before we jumped out of the tree I could hear the monster below us rustling in the leaves and bushes. I heard when it had left the area. I believed it was looking for me, as it was no longer running after me. It couldn't find me up in the tree. That was when I was convinced that it really had been after me. Otherwise, wouldn't it have kept on running?" I asked.

"Probably," Forrest admitted. "Go on." Forrest was so calm sitting there with me. I really did feel better having him with me.

"Okay. The day had gotten so weird, I was scared I was dead. The dark, the monster in the woods, going straight up into a tree . . . it was all pretty strange. And just that day I'd realized that even though Ash seemed to hate me, I didn't feel the same way about him. I was falling in love with him."

Again I saw Forrest's eyes tighten a bit, but he didn't want me to stop. "Then what happened?" he asked softly.

I was still in a kind of trance, my eyes locked in Forrest's gaze. "Ash hated me, I thought, so it couldn't have been his voice. This voice was soft and soothing. It was the most beautiful voice I'd ever heard in my life. I had to be dead. There was nothing that musical and beautiful in the real world." I gave myself a mental shake in order to continue. "Ash said he was going to drop us out of the tree. He picked me up like I weighed no more than a doll. The next thing I felt was dropping like a stone. It only lasted a moment. When we reached the ground, there was no jarring, no crash. It felt as if he had only stepped off a curb. He tried to stand me up, my legs wouldn't work at first. He found my flashlight. I thought it had broken when I dropped it, but the switch must have just shut off. When he tried the switch, it turned on. I aimed the light at my savior's face. I had to confirm who it really was. Ash Woodson. As I looked into that face, I felt as if I'd found my second half. With him I could be complete, like I'd never realized I was only half a person. Maybe it was that I had just realized that day that I loved him, and it just happened on the same day he saved me.

"Eventually I was able to stand on my own, and we walked to his car. He told me he didn't hate me, that he never hated me. He just didn't understand how I existed. He said I was the only human-wood nymph hybrid he'd heard of. I was exhausted by the time we got to the car, too tired to think about my mangled nerves. I felt like I had taken a ride on the biggest emotional roller coaster ever, and it'd left me in pieces. I guess . . . I guess I'm still a bit of a mess. Is that it?" I asked in a voice ragged with suppressed emotion.

"Apparently you've had a few too many experiences recently," Forrest said. "Come on. I'm taking you out of here." He got up from the chair and gave Ash a glance like loathing, but it was gone so fast from his face I wondered if I'd seen it at all. Surely he couldn't hate Ash, could he?

Then I realized we weren't alone. I had spoken my deepest thoughts out loud in front of everyone. I just told Ash and his mother and Doctor Fraser I was in love with Ash. Oh, my God!

What did Ash think of this? God, how stupid could I be? I didn't know what wood nymphs had for feelings, but the ones I had now were pure human, and they were smashed. The shattered pieces splintered into pieces. I was never going to be able to put the pieces that were Laurel Redmond back together again. Yeah, I thought of the fairy tale about all of the king's horses and all of the king's men. I was Humpty Dumpty. I was in pieces on the ground.

In the space of the time it took for me to stand up, I knew Ash didn't feel the same way about me as I did about him. He said he liked me and wanted to get to know me better, but was that sympathy? Had he gone from hating me to feeling sorry for me? Was that why he was holding my hand?

I snatched my hand out of his and gave Forrest a panicked look. I could feel my pieces splintering even more. I could feel myself losing my grip on sanity. The song "Crazy" by Gnarls Barkley came to my head. The song tells about how even your emotions have an echo when you're crazy. My emotions had an echo bouncing around the room. They bounced back and forth echoing off of the walls, screaming for a release or a form of security or peace. I felt like I was going crazy. Last night I found peace holding Ash's hands. How could I find a peace there now? He probably thought I was nuts. I was beginning to think I was too.

My emotions were running a gauntlet. I'd found the most wonderful true love, only to have it be a sad unrequited love. I had experienced the greatest fear in my life and discovered that I wasn't human. I was a freak.

"Look, I'm fine now. I want to go to school. Can you take me to school?" I asked Forrest. "I have a lot to absorb and I need familiarity. I need to get out of here. I need to get my books out of Ash's car. I need human things."

Ash looked shocked, "Hey, I can take you to school!" He said. He didn't get it. He had no real idea what I was going through. I'd had enough of his pity.

"Oh, no, you have done enough for me. Don't think I'm not grateful. I am. I thank you very much for saving my life. But, right now, I need some human experiences. I've had enough supernatural experiences in one day to last a lifetime."

I looked over at Willow and saw the sympathy in her eyes and that was just about enough to break my last handle on reality. But, I forced myself to be polite while I could feel my face turning red and tears wanting to spill. "Thank you for your hospitality. I'm sorry to be a burden and an imposition." I mumbled to both Willow and Dr. Woodson while heading towards the door. They didn't say anything.

I looked with quiet desperation at Forrest. He appeared to see my need to get out of there. He took my hand and told Ash pointedly, "I will get her books. Why don't you leave her alone for a while? She needs to adapt to her new situation."

"I could help her with that!" Ash suggested, looking at me with concern. I saw the look on his face and felt more splintering.

"You've done enough. It's not that I don't appreciate your saving her life, but look at her. Does she look like she can handle any more?" Forrest stated. My eyes were huge with unshed tears. I turned away from them.

I was no longer shaking. I was almost running to the door. Forrest got my book bag out of Ash's car, and we got into Forrest's car. We headed out down the driveway. My last view of the house was Ash, his mother, and Dr. Woodson standing on the porch staring at us as we left.

CHAPTER 9
A HISTORY LESSON

That did it. The sobs started and the tears began streaming down my face. Forrest handed me a tissue, and then a whole box of tissues. "Come on. We'll go for a drive before taking you to school. I'll take your mind off this and tell you about my family and a little more about wood nymphs in general. Would you like that?" He glanced at me while he turned onto the highway with concern written all over his face.

He let me bawl for a few minutes before he started. When I started to gain some composure, he started talking.

"Wood nymphs have been around longer than humans. We used to have really long life spans, two hundred years or more. Now, we are lucky if we live to one hundred years. We don't have many diseases or illnesses. In fact at one time, we had none at all. Our bones can be broken, but they heal in less than half of the time it takes a human bone to heal. In the beginning, when humans first came here, we avoided them completely. They didn't know we existed and we didn't want them to. Then more and more of them started moving into our areas. We found that, with a little effort, we could blend into their society without their knowing we were different from them. We looked human enough to be accepted into their communities without question. When the humans first started coming to Wisconsin, we were already here. By the time they realized we were here, they just thought we had settled here before they did. We realized we had to adapt to human culture. We started building homes like theirs. We used to live in elaborate branch-entwined natural homes in the trees. Some of us can talk to trees and plant life and get the plants to do what we wanted. We live in harmony with nature. Your pier is one that I made." He smiled smugly while glancing over at me.

"Oh, my gosh! I saw it when we first moved here. I love it! It is so beautiful! Can I see more things like that?" I asked excitedly. This was a part of being a wood nymph that was interesting and not scary.

"Yes, I'm sure you will see a lot of things like that in the time to come. I'll make sure that, now that you know of us, you are well informed on your cultural heritage from your father's side," he stated.

"Tell me about my father," I asked softly, looking at him. His face softened, and there was obvious pain there when he said, "He looked a lot like you, but then we all kind of look alike. At least clan members in this area tend to look alike. I loved your father. Everyone in our clan did. He was full of life and always had a smile and a helping hand. It was his altruistic nature that led him to your mother. It was also his altruistic nature that killed him. But I'll get to that."

"As a child, he was curious about everything—especially humans. He was instrumental in getting the rest of Copper Clan to associate with humans on more than a limited basis. It was his suggestion that we go to their schools and learn their culture. He believed that, if we understood them, we could relate better to them. He was genuinely fond of humans. He was amused by their limitations, but he didn't put them down for them. It's not a human's fault he can't communicate with plants or animals. It's not a human's fault he can't see in the dark or move as fast as we can or hear like we can. He got us to understand, even as a young wood nymph that being different was not always a bad thing. We learned multi-culturism because of your father. Because of this, I believe we've existed as long as we have. The isolation we preferred prior to your father's influence may have been what was killing us. With our interactions with the humans, we learned about pollution. We're still in the process of learning how to deal with the pollutants though. Many of us have gone on to human universities to study agriculture, botany, and chemistry to learn how to counter the affects of pollution. We have learned some, but not enough."

We didn't drive into town but north on Highway 51. He continued as we drove.

"We can eat only natural foods. Preservatives make us sick. We can't eat packaged or processed foods. We eat meat, vegetables, and fruits. But, they have to be natural. We can drink packaged food if it's all natural. But, we've found the hard way that sometimes packaged foods say they're natural, and we find out later, when someone gets sick, that there were some additives or preservatives. Those are the only things that make us sick. Artificial anything and pollution make us sick. We used to love fish, but with the toxins in the water, we can only eat limited amounts."

"Yeah, we have the same problem. We love Lake Michigan Salmon, but we can only eat so much due to the mercury and toxins in the lake water," I told him. I had no idea where we were going, as I had never been north of Minocqua. We drove through Minocqua, still heading north. I didn't care. I loved hearing his soothing voice. I needed soothing. *Ash's voice is soothing too*—the thought impaled my brain without my wanting it too. *Yeah, but this voice doesn't cause me discomfort,* I argued internally.

"Where are we going?" I asked to shut my mind up. I had to think of something else besides Ash or I'd start crying again.

"I thought you'd like to see where I lived before I took you to school. You'll miss at least half of a day, but I think you can handle the loss," he said and smiled at me.

"Won't I get in trouble?" I asked. "I don't skip school as a rule."

"Hmm, yeah, good point." He pulled out a cell phone. He called the school and told the attendance lady that I was with my uncle, and I'd be in this afternoon.

"Now they won't call your mom," he said.

We drove in silence for a few minutes. "How did my dad die?" I asked sadly.

"There was some new construction. A heavy-equipment operator had a heart attack while driving a grader. The machine went out of control. Workers were in the way. Leif realized they would be crushed by the grader. He jetted over and pushed them out of the way, but . . . there wasn't much time. People wouldn't have been able to run out of the way on their own otherwise. By saving the three men, he got crushed in the process. A normal human would have died instantly, but Leif's body tried to heal itself. Olivia, just barely older than a child then, had her ability to see things and screamed out about the accident. I had her explain her vision. She told me where the accident was. I jetted there, picked up Leif and jetted home, but his injuries were . . . massive. He died in a few days. But, while he was dying, Olivia saw your mother and you. As Leif lay suffering, Olivia told him all about you and your mother. He knew about you before he died. He knew about you before your mother did. That's when he begged me to keep an eye on the both of you, and I did it to the best of my ability. He loved . . . even the idea of you. He wasn't ashamed for getting a human woman pregnant. He knew part of him would carry on in you. He had only known her for a weekend, but my brother did love your mother."

I thought about my father. After a few minutes, I asked Forrest, "What does your family know about me? Will they like me?"

He smiled over at me. "Like I said, we, the clan, knew about you before your mother did. We were amazed, surprised and yes, I'll admit, at first we were shocked, but that wore off with the wonder of you."

"You really are the first of your kind. Some female wood nymphs have had trysts with human men, but not because they were in love. They'd do it because it was fun. They haven't done it in decades, not since we came out to the humans as humans. Every once in a while, one of our females would wear their color-shifting clothes and tease a man in the woods. But, they didn't hurt anyone. Sometimes they'd do it to steer a man away from a potentially dangerous situation, like walking into a Hodag's den. When a human man sees a wood nymph in all of her natural beauty, they tend to get mesmerized. They're compelled to follow her. Thus, they avoid danger. When the female got the human safely away from danger, she'd just disappear either by blending into the forest or jetting away.

"What do you mean by a female wood nymph's natural beauty or color-shifting clothes?" I asked. This sounded really interesting.

"Wood nymph-made fabric can change color to match our surroundings. Also, we can change our skin color to match the surroundings. Watch this." He said. He .

pointed to the dark gray upholstery of his seat and then his skin blended exactly to the texture and color of the fabric seat.

I gaped and started gasping again.

"That was a bit much too soon, wasn't it?" he said in his soothing voice. He quickly flashed back to what I thought of as his normal skin color. But was it?

"What's your natural skin color?" I asked.

"The one you normally see. Relax. It's no big deal. All of us can do it."

"Not me," I shuddered.

"Have you tried?" he asked.

"No! Of course not!" I was stunned that he would ask such a thing! I had never even heard of such a thing except in stories and tall tales. Oh, yeah, wood nymphs could change to match their surroundings. I'd heard that before. It got me thinking.

"How do you do it?" I finally asked. I could imagine the possibilities of being able to blend in anywhere at anytime.

"Focus on the thing you want to blend in with. Focus on the texture, smell, color —everything about it. Then concentrate on blending in with it."

"Okay," I said, trying to concentrate. Did I shimmer just a bit? Was there a gray cast to my skin for just a second? "I can't do it," I sighed.

Forrest said, "No, I thought I saw a bit of a change. With practice I bet you could learn to do it. Ah, here we are." He turned onto a side road. We had been off of Highway 51 for a while, but I hadn't paid a lot of attention to where we turned. I was lost. I felt a tingle of apprehension, but I was with my uncle, so I was safe, right?

As we drove down the road, I saw paved driveways leading off into the woods with elaborate name signs. All had a plant sound to the name. One sign said "Ageratum." That was a kind of sunflower. I also saw "White" and "Alder." I knew there was such a thing as a White Alder tree, so were they related?

We turned off onto a driveway with a sign post that said, "Oakton, Forrest," and I knew we were at his house.

"I see you only have your name on the wood post. Aren't you married?" I asked.

"No, I was never conjoined . . . married as humans call it. As clan leader I should have been, but I never found anyone I wanted to marry." He wistfully staring off, and then with an obvious effort brought himself back to the here and now. "Come on. I'll show you around," he said, taking my hand.

When we got out of the car, I stared at his house. It was very similar to mine! It was also a two story log cabin type of house! "Hey, this house looks like mine!" I said in a kind of awe. While there were similarities, there were also big differences between this house and mine. This one was made out of real wood, but it looked like the logs were from the same tree, and I knew that wasn't possible. They were exactly the same and of a type of wood I hadn't seen before. It looked like cedar, but I wasn't sure. It was more beautiful than my house, and I had thought my house looked good. But this one . . . this house was magnificent. It wasn't bigger than my house, but the skill and care in the construction of the house was evident everywhere. My house looked cookie cutter by comparison. My house looked made by a construction company. This house looked like it was made by artisans.

We walked up the front steps and across the porch and into the house. There was a small foyer as we entered, and on the left, there were French doors leading into a living room with a massive fireplace. On the right was a stairway that led to the second level. The stairway looked like vines that grew together to make the steps and railings. It reminded me of my pier.

"You did that, didn't you?" I asked him with more than a bit of awe in my voice.

"Yes, I built the whole house." He replied with a smile. He looked glad that I liked the house.

"I even put in a room for you. I had always hoped that some day we would get to know each other. Come and see it!" He said, leading me up the stairs.

"A room for me, why?" I asked. I wasn't exactly afraid, more in wonder about the whole situation.

"If anything were to ever happen to your mom, I planned to come forward as your nearest living relative. You'd need a place to stay. Not that I want anything to happen to your mom. In my own way, I love your mother," he said with a smile.

I looked at him squarely. I believed he loved my mom, as well as me. Wow, I hadn't expected that. I suppose after watching out for us, how could he not love Mom? She was easy to love. She was fun and loving and an overall great person. Maybe he felt a little familial obligation in there, too.

"Anyway," He continued, "I was hoping that some time you could come and visit me, but it never worked out that way."

"Why didn't you ever come forward? Why didn't you let us know you existed?" I asked, curious. I was openly gawking around at the house.

"I live under the rules of our clan. We have a democratic society, and it was agreed that I could watch over you and your mom, but I could never let you know that we existed. We aren't human, and there was always the possibility of a slip up about letting you know what we were. Plus, it was easier on me to watch you from a distance. A few times I almost broke the rules before Ben came into your lives. Then, when I saw how much your mom loved Ben, and how much he loved both your mother and you, well, it would have been painful to come forward. It was easier to keep an eye on you without you knowing of me. If Ben would have turned out to be a non-desirable entity, I would've eliminated him from your lives." He said this with a look that really did scare me.

"Olivia said you would move back to Wisconsin. She said she saw the house in Tomahawk before it was built. We just weren't sure when you'd be back here. This is your room." He said with a flourish, opening a door.

The room was beautiful. It was big and had huge windows on two walls. Everything matched in a light floral pattern that fit perfectly with the rest of the house. The bed was a full-sized canopy bed with a veil-like cover that matched the curtains, comforter, and bed skirt. The carpet was a short, very thick luxurious type that I didn't have a name for. It was the palest green that matched everything else perfectly.

"Oh, it's gorgeous," I said. "Everything looks brand new!" I sat on the bed and it had just the right amount of cushion to it.

"Every couple of years everything gets replaced. I wanted it perfect for you," he said sitting on the vanity chair that went with the Victorian style vanity in a corner.

"This is kind of creepy," I said. "No one does stuff like this without knowing someone."

"I know you," he said. And it was clear he did. He obviously had been paying attention to what I liked throughout the years. If I could have picked out my room exactly, this would have been it.

"I'm only here, this room is only here, if you need it. I'm not a threat to you. I love you and would like you in my life. But, I don't want to scare you. I want to be your loving uncle," he stated quietly.

"Why now?" I asked. I had heard what he had said about clan rules, but when did that change?

"I came to your mom's office because I couldn't stand it any longer. I had to let you know that I existed and took the risk of Olivia seeing and telling the rest of the clan that I did that. So, I jetted over to you, to your mom's work place to meet you without telling the rest of the clan. It was such a joy. I couldn't tell you much about me as you didn't know about wood nymphs. But, now that you know what you are, I can come and be a part of your life with your knowledge and the rest of the clan's knowledge. That's only if you want me to be?" He looked unsure about my response. "I think I can tell your mom now. We'll have a clan meeting this week and discuss it. We may have to go down to the Tomahawk clan and have a joint clan meeting."

I thought about everything he'd told me and all I had learned in the last day or so. "I want you in my life," I said emphatically. "I want to see you and be with you unless you're going to do something weird and scare me."

Scare me? A whole lot of things had scared me recently. I didn't want Forrest to be one of those things. And, weird. Everything was weird now. My life was weird. All these experiences were weird. The new abilities I was finding out about, understanding that I was a hybrid—it seemed everything about my life was full of weirdness.

"The Hodag scared me. The rest I think pretty much fascinates me," I said as I looked at him. "So, who is Olivia? I heard you mention her a couple of times," I asked as I sat on the side of the bed.

"I am Olivia," said a woman's voice from the stairway. A graceful woman who looked to be about thirty floated into the room. She didn't actually float, but she was so graceful it seemed like that. She wore a flowing caftan that seemed made of silk. It was a multi-pastel in color and brought out the green of her eyes. She was beautiful, easily the most beautiful woman I had ever seen. She had the same straight brown hair I had, but her hair flowed down to her waist.

On most people, really long hair tends to get thin and whispy at the ends. Her hair was just as thick at her waist as it was at her neck. It was the healthiest head of hair I'd ever seen. When I could take my eyes off of her hair and had a chance to look at her face, she had the most perfect skin and her features were gorgeous. She had the bright-green eyes I expected. I thought she was more beautiful than a model or a movie star. We were exactly the same height, but that was the only similarity besides hair color and green eyes I could see between us.

She laughed musically when she caught me staring open mouthed at her. Her laugh was like the tinkling of expensive champagne glasses connecting in a toast. The laugh was just as beautiful as she was. "I'm used to men staring at me, but not usually lovely young ladies!" She smiled at me. "Hi, Laurel. I'm your cousin Olivia. I'm very pleased to finally meet you."

"Uh, hello, Olivia. I . . . sorry for staring. I just can't get over how beautiful you are!" I blurted as I felt my face flush. She laughed her musical tinkling laugh, and, without meaning to, I joined in.

"Have you looked in the mirror lately? You're a beauty yourself," she said to me, taking me by the hand to stand with me in front of the mirror on the vanity table.

"You are lovely," Forrest agreed.

I stood side by side with this perfect creature and realized there really were a lot more similarities than I'd imagined. Her hair was longer, but her hair and mine had the same thickness. Side by side, even I could tell that I looked a lot like her.

My nose wasn't as perfect as hers. I had my mom's nose. For a human nose, it wasn't half bad, but hers looked like a sculptor's design. I thought the plastic surgeons in Hollywood would love to have a photo of her nose to use in their catalogs. My chin wasn't as perfectly defined, but we had the same cheek lines, the same clear skin, the same eye shape. Anyone could tell we were related.

I had never thought of myself as having the potential to be this kind of beauty, but there it was in front of my face. *My* face. Wow. I brought my hand to my face to touch my cheeks and my lips. My lips were exactly like hers, too—full and perfectly shaped—I had never noticed that before. I never wore makeup, just a touch of lip gloss. This was an unexpected wonder, and one I really liked. I stared at my reflection.

"I want to try an experiment. Here sit on this vanity chair. Get up Forrest and let her have the chair." Forrest did as she asked. "Sit here and put your face real close to this lighted vanity mirror and look at your eyes and tell me what you see." She put her face right next to mine in the mirror. We had the mirror tilted to the magnified side, so our eyes were huge. She turned on the lights that surrounded the mirror and our pupil's shrank down to small circles. Only, then, when I looked closely at her eyes, I saw that her pupils were just slightly elongated like a cat's eyes. It was hard to see, unless someone were really looking, but it was definitely there. I then looked at my eyes and saw the same elongation. I did not have perfect human eyes. I had wood nymph eyes. *I had the eyes of a wood nymph.* Too bad I didn't inherit the night vision. Wow. Forrest came next to us and his eyes also had the barely discernable elongation when the pupil shrank down. We stared at our eyes for a few minutes.

"Can you come back soon?" she asked, and only then did I realize how late it was. "If you're going to make your afternoon classes, you have to leave now, unless you jet." She giggled, emphasizing the word "jet."

"She'll have to meet the rest of the family later. We'll definitely take the BMW." Forrest said as he looked at his watch. So, wood nymphs didn't have perfect time pieces in their heads. They needed watches to stay on time, just like humans. I smiled at the thought. I liked finding similarities between the wood nymphs and the humans. I liked that they weren't completely perfect.

"It was great to meet you. I'm so glad you finally know the truth about us," Olivia said as she floated down the stairs beside me. "We'll see each other again. You need to meet my brother Douglas. He'll feel bad that he missed meeting you. He's at UWM studying chemistry. He should be back for Thanksgiving break," she said thinking ahead to the future and looking a bit distant for a moment. "Yes, he'll definitely be here for Thanksgiving dinner, and you and your mother will be here, too." She smiled a huge smile at me. *Oh, that's right,* I thought, *Olivia can see the future.*

Forrest and I got into his BMW and left for Tomahawk. I felt pretty good on my way to school. I had an extended family and I liked them! Even more important, they seemed to like me. We stopped at a grocery store and picked up some fruit for

Forrest's lunch. I had a hamburger from a drive-through fast-food restaurant. As we ate, Forrest said, "I don't know how you can eat that stuff. That'd make me sick." I laughed thinking this was one good thing about being a hybrid, I could eat fast food!

Forrest dropped me off in front of the school with about five minutes to make my first afternoon class. As I was getting out of the car, he handed me a card with his name, address, and phone numbers on it. He was an architect. I smiled. That figured. "Call me on my cell anytime you want me. I will be there."

Just as he dropped me off, my phone rang, and I answered it as I waved good-bye. It was my mom.

"Hi, honey. I just talked to the car repair shop. Your car is ready. It had to do with the injectors or something like that," she said. She was no mechanic. Neither was I. *Injectors*, I thought, *whatever*.

"Is it expensive?" I asked, wondering if I had enough to pay for repairs.

"Well, kind of." She hesitated. "I got it, though," she said. "What time do you get out of school today?"

It was Friday, so I got out at 5:00 p.m. I told her that.

"See you then!" she said and hung up. I had to check in at the office and then race to my next class.

When I got to Drama, Ash was waiting for me. "Where've you been?" he hissed. "I've been looking for you all day!"

"What . . . are you my keeper now?" I hissed back. "You save my life and then you own me?" I strode into the class without waiting for an answer. For the first time, I was glad people sat on each side of me in the front row and that Ash had to take his normal seat in the back row. My feelings were way too raw to deal with him. I'd had a pleasant morning with Forrest, though, and was able to put aside the acute feelings for Ash. I wanted them to stay there. I'd met other wood nymphs, family who liked me. I didn't need Ash or his family. I loved him but I didn't need him. *Okay, that's a weird kind of feeling.* He didn't love me. I certainly didn't consider it an improvement going from having him hate me to his feeling responsible for me.

I thought about how he'd said that morning that he liked me, just not how much. Yeah, sure he liked me. He felt responsible for me, like a wayward little sister or some-thing. Well, he could keep his responsibility thoughts to himself. I sure didn't need his obligation or whatever he felt. Then the thought that I wanted his love flashed in my head. I suppressed that thought quickly. Yeah, like that would ever happen.

I was agitated all through class and not looking forward to rehearsal. We prac-ticed facial emotions during Drama class and the sarcastic and angry emotions were easy for me.

At rehearsal, we continued practicing the dance. This time we were added our lines while doing the dance steps. I had the sarcasm down perfectly.

"Perfect, Miss Redmond!" Miss Becker crowed. "You have the intonation of Elizabeth Bennett's mood perfectly!"

"Mr. Woodson, you need to work on your facial emotions. We just went over them in class. You don't need to look so worried. It's okay to look a bit confused, but not that full-blown worry look. Save that for a later scene." Miss Becker said to Ash.

Ash sighed. Miss Becker saw it and gave him a reproving look. I saw it and smiled, and not a nice smile. "Keep your focus, Miss Redmond!" Miss Becker reminded me.

For the rest of rehearsal, I focused on my lines, dance steps, and facial expressions. I was so ready for the weekend. I really needed some down time. I gathered my stuff from the back of the stage and headed for the front door to meet Mom.

Ash ran to catch up to me. "Laurel! Really, where were you? I was worried!" Ash said.

"What do you care?" I stopped and faced him. "Mom's outside waiting for me," I said and started walking again.

He grabbed my arm. "I happen to care what happens to you!"

I jerked away from him. "Since when?" My voice had raised.

We were drawing a crowd, and I had enough humiliation earlier in the day. Rodney came up to us and, glaring at Ash, took my hand and pulled me away. Ash just stood there. I could almost feel his eyes peeling the skin off of my back.

Rodney walked me to Mom's car. "See you Monday!" he said.

I tossed my stuff into the back seat and got into the front.

"You don't look very happy," Mom observed. "Did you have a bad day?"

"Well, I guess it was good and bad. I want to talk about it, but not until we get home," I replied. We went to the repair shop. Mom went inside to pay, while I took my keys and got in my car.

Soon after, Mom came to my window and handed me my spare key, a magnetic one I had bought soon after getting the car and had attached under the frame. "Don't forget to put this back," she said. We drove our own vehicles home.

CHAPTER 10
MOM LEARNS THE TRUTH

My car drove better than ever. Whatever the problem was, it was fixed. Mom drove behind me all of the way home, just in case though. I felt my breath catch in my throat when I passed the tree, and I couldn't help but look carefully on both sides of the road as we drove home. But I didn't lose my breath or start sweating. Still it was good to be beyond that spot. Better to be home.

"So, what's on your mind?" Mom asked as she hung her jacket in the closet.

"After dinner, I'll tell you everything." I replied as I hung up my jacket. We both went into the kitchen.

Mom made us a tuna casserole, while I did my homework. I had to focus hard on my homework with so much new information cluttering my brain. And I had more than usual because I'd gotten what I missed from my morning classes. I had mumbled to my teachers about a family emergency that was now fine. My homework was completed by the time dinner was done.

After we finished dinner and the dishwasher was running, my mom said, "Okay, now spill it."

"You might want a glass of scotch first," I suggested.

"That bad, huh? Okay," she said as she poured herself a double with ice.

She wanted to look at me, so we sat across from each other at the dining room table. I could hear an owl hooting outside and wondered whether it was moral support.

I gave off a huge sigh and tried to start. "I've never lied to you, right? I mean, you know when I'm trying to hand you a line, right?" I watched her facial expression.

"Sure," she said, watching me closely. "Go on." .

I put my hands on the table as if to brace myself. "Don't interrupt, okay? Let me get through this, okay?"

"Okay," she said slowly, watching me really closely now, getting nervous.

I started with my personal revelation about my feelings about Ash Woodson in school yesterday. That was the easy part. It wouldn't have been easy a week ago, but that was the most normal thing I had to say.

I told her about starting my car and the noise it made, and she made appropriate nods and then I told her about my car breaking down, and she nodded at that, too. When I got to the part about the Hodag, her face froze, but I couldn't stop now. I told her everything. I told her about Ash and the tree. I told her about my meltdown this morning and his driving me back to his house. I told her about the wood nymphs. I told her about Forrest showing up and taking me to his place outside of Presque Isle. As I talked, her mouth slowly dropped. Her eyes got larger or smaller depending on what part of the story I was at. When I told her about the Hodag her eyes got wide. When I told her about the wood nymphs, her eyes got wide. When I told her about my meltdown, her eyes narrowed. When I told her about this afternoon and how I thought Ash only liked me because he felt sorry for me, her eyes narrowed.

"That's it. That's everything," I finished. I went into the kitchen to get a drink. I heard the ice in her glass clink. When I got back, her glass was empty, though she hadn't taken a sip the entire time I was speaking.

I came back to the table and sat down. She was still staring at me. "I believe you believe you're telling me the truth," she said, clearly picking her words carefully. "There was no guile or bullshit in what you said. But, if I buy what you're telling me, everything I know and understand is either a lie or some kind of half truth. You're telling me that I fell in love with someone who . . . wasn't human? That's not possible."

Was that the only thing that processed in her mind?

I sighed. "Yes, it is possible. Come with me." I took her upstairs to her bedroom. She also had a vanity table with a lighted mirror with a magnified side. "Sit at the table here. I want to show you something." She sat. I could see she was cautious, but also curious as to what I was up to more than anything else.

"Watch this. Watch my pupils really closely. Watch mine, then look at yours. Tell me if you notice anything." I said, turning on the light and putting my head down next to hers like Olivia had done with me just that morning.

Mom saw my pupils shrink. Then she looked at her eyes. She looked back at my eyes and then back hers. She jumped up from the table with a bellowed, "NO! I don't believe it!" I saw the telltale sweat and the gasping of panic. She was having a meltdown, now. Good thing I was experienced with such things.

I grabbed her bedside phone and pulled the card out of my pocket. I called Forrest's cell, and he answered on the first ring. "I expected your call," he said.

"Jet here, now, please!" I said and the phone was already dead.

My mother was still staring into the mirror gasping. She was mumbling something about a possible birth defect. I knew she was mentally trying to come to terms with what she had just seen, and she was trying to come up with some kind of a "plausible" explanation.

I walked downstairs believing that, by the time I got to the door, Forrest would be there. He was. He wasn't alone. He'd brought Olivia.

All three of us knew why they were there, why I had called Forrest. "Please come in. I'll bring her down. She'd feel funny having you guys in her bedroom. She has enough to process. I . . . told her everything." I waved them to the living room as I bolted back upstairs.

Mom was still sitting at her vanity, staring into the mirror, tears silently falling. I gently took her by the hand. She had this stricken look on her face as she faced me. "I have some help downstairs," I said softly. "Please come with me."

She got and followed me downstairs. When she saw Forrest and Olivia she stopped cold. She looked from one to the other, then to me and then to them again. I saw what she saw. I looked more like Olivia's daughter than hers. She started gasping again. Olivia and Forrest both got up at the same time and sat her in the middle of the couch. Tears flowed down her face.

"What is going on?" she finally asked, looking scared.

"This is a lot to deal with. Let me explain," Forrest said, as he and Olivia sat on each side of her and I sat in the recliner opposite.

Mom stared at Forrest exactly the way I imagined I had looked at him earlier that day at Ash's house. He spoke to her softly and gently. He told her that both she and I had been loved, even though we didn't know it. As he talked to her, Olivia gently rubbed my mom's hand. Mom didn't pull away.

Forrest told her the entire history that he had told me. He omitted the skin color changing part, which I appreciated. He told her about jetting and some other abilities, like jumping really high and Olivia's ability to see the future. She just stared at him until he told her the part about my biological father dying. He told her a bit about that the first time we'd met him. Tears flowed down her face as she listened.

I went to the dining room table and got her glass. I refilled it with scotch and ice. I knew she liked a good scotch especially for bad news. I set it on the coffee table in front of her. She didn't notice. She was caught in Forrest's gaze. Forrest glance at me, saw the glass and realized it was for her. "Here, drink this," he said, handing her the drink. She sipped and said, "'Crazy,' by Gnarls Barkley." It was a song both of us liked.

"'I remember the time I lost my mind,'" she quoted the song softly. "'I just knew too much. Does that make me crazy? Possibly.'" She said finishing the quote.

"Do they know about wood nymphs too? Was it your kind he was talking about in the song? Is finding out what I thought was fantasy and is actually something real making me lose my mind? What I have believed was myths is actually the truth?" she said trying, to make some sense of it all.

I started laughing. "You know, Mom. When I heard all of this, this morning, I thought of the same song, just a different quote. We do have similarities."

She started laughing too. I think it was a stress reaction. In her case it may have been the need to find the connection to me.

"I love you, Mom!" I said coming to hug her. "Just because I found I have other family does not displace you in my affections, you know."

"But I'm just human. Do you have abilities, too?" she asked me suddenly.

"The only thing I think I can do is call fish," I said sheepishly. "Ash seems to think that may be an ability, but I need to be careful about using it as the water sprites don't like wood nymphs ordering their water creatures around. I saw one when we first got here."

That made Forrest and Olivia stand up and look at each other and then at me. "You didn't tell me about that," Forrest accused. "Water sprites can be dangerous. Our relationship with them is tenuous at best. They have no relationship with humans." He frowned.

"We have to be careful about our relationships with all other species," Olivia stated in her musical voice. Mom turned to stare at Olivia. It was the first time that she had heard her voice, and she was just as struck by the beauty of this woman and her voice.

"Yeah, I thought her voice was beautiful, too," I said to Mom while looking at Olivia. Olivia smiled at me and Mom just stared at her.

"You have unbelievable beauty," Mom blurted to Olivia. "The people in Hollywood would love to get their hands on you. Between your looks and your voice, you could be a superstar."

"Thank you," Olivia said, "But I have no intention of going to Hollywood or being in the public eye. In fact, I rarely leave our small community. I really don't like the stares I get from humans, but I don't mind yours." She smiled. She took one of my mom's hands in both of hers. "You just found out we're family, and it does take a bit of getting used to. It was a shock on our side to find out about you, but we've had the last eighteen years to get used to having you two in our family. We very much like the idea that Leif left a part of himself in Laurel. Truly, I'm relieved that our differences have been aired. We can be friends, now. You do understand that you can tell no one that we aren't human, right?" she implored my mom.

Mom snorted. It was a very unladylike snort. "Who would believe me?" she asked, laughing. "I'd lose all credibility as a therapist. My career would be in ruins. However, when people come into my office telling me that they are seeing little green men, I may not be so quick to judge them!" She laughed, though it sounded off.

Mom was adapting, adjusting. That was a good thing. I was afraid that her logical mind would not be able to handle the new facts she had been handed.

"A good scientist has to be able to accept new evidence when presented with it," she stated. "The scientific world is constantly evolving and rearranging as new evidence is found. Columbus wasn't the first to discover America. Oh, well. We still keep Columbus Day even though we know different. I can and will adapt to this new reality."

"Bravo, Valerie!" Olivia trilled in her beautiful voice.

We got to know each other better for the next few hours. It was amazing how well Mom and I liked and got along with our new family members. Forrest and Olivia seemed just as happy to get to know us. We talked about my childhood, and Forrest interjected things that he remembered from the times he watched out for us.

"Maybe it's not a good idea to try to tell Ben about us while he's overseas." Olivia mused. "It may make him crazy, or make him think that you are."

"Yes, that's probably true. I hate keeping secrets, though." Mom complained.

It was late when Mom and I started trying to hide our yawns.

"You're tired. We should leave," Forrest said reluctantly. I could see he liked being with us. We were getting to know them, and we certainly liked them a lot. I truly believed that Mom, Ben, and I would all learn to love them. Ben just had to meet them first.

"Yes, you're right," Olivia agreed sadly, getting up from the couch beside my mom. Mom stood and discretely stretched. I knew she stretched, because I did the same thing, also trying to be discrete. Neither Olivia nor Forrest seemed to have any discomfort from sitting so long.

"You can stay here," Mom offered. "We have the space and extra beds."

"That's okay. We will be home in a minute or so. Remember we can jet!" Olivia said laughing.

Chapter 11
Dealing with Embarasment

Saturday morning came way too quickly. I had the late shift at the hardware store and didn't have to be there until eleven o'clock, but I woke up at ten and had to scramble with my shower and breakfast to get to work on time.

"Hey, Jane!" I said as I walked in the door of the hardware store and headed into the office to punch my time card. Jane Smith, an older woman who worked full time, was a nice single lady with a quick smile. She'd lived in Tomahawk her entire life. She was easy to work with and taught me the job when I first started there. There were only two cashier lines, and she worked at the register next to me.

"Good morning, Laurel!" she called to me as I went into the office.

I came back out with my cash drawer and logged myself into the cash register. "Has it been busy?" I asked while setting up.

"Not really. Ash Woodson was here earlier asking about you, though," she said watching for my reaction.

I gave a disgusted sigh. I didn't want to deal with him today. I had family now. I did not need anyone's pity. "Whatever!" I said, grumbling.

"Now, Laurel honey, it's not like you to be rude. What's the matter?" she asked.

I was saved from having to answer as a customer came up to my check-out station. By the time I rang up his purchases and bagged up his stuff, I had a line in my check out lane and so did Jane. We didn't talk to each other while waiting on customers. It was considered in bad taste by management, and we agreed with the rule. At six o'clock, Jane closed out her cash register and brought her cash drawer to the office and punched out. I waved good-bye as she left. She waved back. We closed at 7:00 p.m. Right at closing, as there were no customers in the store. I locked the doors. I closed out my register and brought my cash drawer to the office. "Good-bye, Mr. Reichert. It was a good day, I think," I said as I grabbed my jacket.

"Yes, it was a good day. Thank you, Laurel. See you next week," he said as I left.

Oh, yeah, I was off tomorrow. I'd forgotten. I hadn't had a day off between school and work in weeks! I wore a big smile as I walked to the parking lot. I didn't see the black SUV next to my Jeep until I got to my car. Ash Woodson leaned against it.

"Laurel, you have to talk to me," he implored.

"Duh, no I don't," I snapped back, opening the door to my Jeep and getting in. He stood behind my Jeep so I'd have to run him over to leave the parking lot. There was a car parked in front of me, so I couldn't move. I huffed and got out of my car and put my fists on my hips as I faced him. "Haven't I humiliated myself enough in front of you?" I almost shouted at him.

"Please don't, Laurel," he implored again with that soft, melt-my-heart-into-butter voice. "Please, can we talk somewhere? Can I buy you dinner?"

"A date? You want a *date*? I'm not allowed to date without a group," I said while still standing stiffly by my car.

"What if I call your mom? Would you allow me to do that? What if I asked her if you could go out to dinner with me? There'd be other people in a restaurant."

He looked so good standing there. I could feel my heart melting. "Yeah, sure, call her." I was convinced she'd say no. She never liked my old boyfriend, and I figured she wouldn't like any guy eho wanted to go out with me. I handed him my phone. "It's on the speed dial setting HOME." I said. I crossed my arms and leaned against my car as he figured out my phone and called my house.

"Mrs. Redmond? Hi, this is Ash Woodson. Yeah, no, Laurel is fine, she handed me her phone. I asked her to go to dinner with me, and she said she couldn't go unless I asked you first. I'm asking you for permission to take Laurel to Silver Bird for dinner. Is that okay? We're leaving for there, now. We'll leave her car in the lot here, and then come back for it after dinner, okay? Really? Great! Here's Laurel," he said and smiled as he handed me the phone.

"Hi, Mom," I said glaring at Ash. He'd said he wanted to take me to the Silver Bird. That was a nice restaurant! No fast-food kind of place. I had a decent shirt on, a clean pair of new blue jeans, and tennis shoes. Was I dressed appropriately for the Silver Bird?

"Do you want to go to dinner with Ash?" she asked bluntly. I don't know what happened to my brain or my mouth. I tried to say no, but my mouth said yes. The word just came out of me. It was like it had a mind of its own.

"All right, dear!" she said. "Have Chris at the restaurant call me if you are delayed too long at getting a table. I know how crowded that place can get on a Saturday night. I don't want to worry. Then, call me when you leave the restaurant, okay? I'm still not real keen on solo dating, but I guess it has to happen sometime."

I said, "Okay," and we hung up. Just like that, I was stuck with Ash. What made it worse was he gave me a big grin. I really didn't want to be one of his conquests, but I could feel my resolve slipping.

"Stop with the grinning. You won this round!" I acquiesced.

He didn't listen, he just kept grinning like an idiot. The next thing I knew, I was grinning, too. Why was I grinning?

I didn't know what to say. I guess neither did he, as we didn't talk during the few minutes it took to get to the restaurant.

"Why, it's Ash and Laurel, together!" Chris, the owner said to us as we walked in the door to the restaurant. I suspect Mom had called her. "Are you here for dinner?" she asked. Ash told her we were, and she led us to a nice quiet table in the back.

"They have good food here. Food I can eat," Ash said.

"Yeah, I don't think that they use preservatives here," I replied looking at the SPECIALS board on the wall.

"No, they don't," he said, and the look he gave me made me smile. He was wondering if he had told me that wood nymphs couldn't eat preserved foods.

In just a few minutes, our server arrived and asked what we wanted to drink. Ash ordered water, and I ordered a Coke.

"I'm really glad you came with me," he said. He placed his napkin on his lap, giving him the best manners of any teenage guy I'd ever met. Funny, this table manners thing was a human thing, and the wood nymph had it down better than most human guy that I knew. I laughed.

"What's so funny?" he asked. I told him about how most teenage guys I knew didn't have a clue about manners, but he apparently did. I think he understood the innuendo about his being a wood nymph and not human, and he smiled. "When in Rome, we do as the Romans do, right?"

Yeah, I understood all right. He was following a human culture since we were in a human establishment. Humans wouldn't be able to understand and accept his culture, and so he and his kind were adapting their lives to the human culture.

"I really like you," he stated bluntly. He pulled his chair a little closer to my chair.

"I think you feel sorry for me," I replied just as bluntly, leaning away from him. At that moment, our server brought our drinks. I sat back and waited for the server to leave. Then I said, "You know how I feel. I shouldn't have blurted that out at your house. I'm sure your family thinks I'm an idiot, and I'm pretty sure you think that makes me easy for you. My pride may have been shredded at your house, but I'm picking up the pieces."

He opened his mouth to say something, but I continued. "I'm not sure why you have this misguided notion that you have to save me from the world, but I'm not buying it. In fact, I don't want it. I remember what I said at your house, and my humiliation is complete. You can drop the liking nonsense. Maybe this is all an ego trip for you. Oh, the poor human girl!" I was whispering now, but viciously, "She hasn't the sense to take care of herself so let me take care of her. I have a news flash for you! I have a guardian angel. My Uncle Forrest watches out for me." I finished, glowering at him. I could see that he didn't like what I had to say.

"I don't feel sorry for you. I'm not sure exactly where you got that idea, but really, I don't. I find you fascinating and have almost from the second I saw you. I didn't like the idea that my family knew all about you. Everyone knew except me. I didn't like how they found the thought of you so interesting. We've never had mixed blood in my family. We didn't interbreed. We never went outside our species. You're different from us. Sure. It doesn't matter what you look like or who your father was. You were different, and I didn't like it." He took a drink of his water.

"But, that was very prejudicial. Almost immediately, I found myself attracted to you. I didn't like that. I tried to fight the attraction. Didn't work. I found very quickly that I dodn't want to fight my feelings. I only tried out for the school play because you did." He sighed as he finished.

"You're just saying that. I'm not falling all over you now that you've decided to pay attention to me, and, because of that, you find me a challenge. Trust me, I'm no challenge. I'm just me, a plain old human girl. I don't have any amazing abilities. Okay, I caught some fish, but that doesn't mean I have a special talent. Humans catch fish all of the time." I leaned toward him over the table and lowered my voice during this discussion so not to be overheard. He leaned toward me.

Our server came over. "I don't mean to interrupt, but are you ready to order?" she asked. We must have looked like a happy couple from her angle of approach with our heads together over the table. I thought, *If she only knew the truth!*

Ash hadn't looked at the menu yet and neither had I.

Ash smiled politely at her. "Can we just have a couple more minutes to decide?" That smile would disarm a harpy, I thought, rolling my eyes as the server stared at him with undisguised admiration. Wood nymphs did draw admirers.

"Of course. I'll be back in a minute," she said. She'd barely given me a glance. I rolled my eyes again.

Ash saw that. "Oh, now don't be that way, Laurel," he said as he handed me a menu.

I wanted the cheesiest, most fattening, preserved item on the menu. I looked and found a casserole on the SPECIAL board that had cheese, noodles, shrimp, and who knows what all else in it. The cheese alone had to be loaded with unhealthy preservatives. Mom wasn't there to censor what I ate, and I wanted to show Ash I was more human than wood nymph. I didn't belong in his world. I knew I was contradicting what I really wanted, but the ones I wanted were of the Copper Clan. I admitted to myself that, had he been human, I would still have wanted to avoid him.

"Do you know what you want?" Ash asked me.

"Yes, I'll take the cheese and shrimp casserole with noodles," I stated. Ash stared at me.

"Do you know what is in that stuff?" he asked, shocked.

"Yeah, it's got cheese, noodles, and shrimp. It has lots of cheese and fat," I said with a sarcastic grin.

"There may be preservatives in the cheese. Are you sure you can eat that?" he asked.

"Sure, I'm human!" I whispered. "And with the salad, I'd like blue cheese dressing." I never ate anything like this. Once in a while I'd have a cheeseburger, but my mom never cooked really fattening, heavy-cholesterol foods. This would be a treat.

When our server came back, I ordered the casserole and the salad with the blue cheese dressing, and Ash ordered a plain vegetable salad with lemon juice, a steak cooked rare with no seasoning, and a plain baked potato.

"That meal is going to make you sick," he said. "Why are you doing this?"

"I'm not doing anything," I said. "Humans eat this stuff all the time. It's just rich."

He just shook his head.

"Really, why did you want to take me out to dinner?" I said giving him a level look with no sarcasm.

"I really do want to get to know you. You were pretty impressive after your experience with the Hodag. Yeah, you had a bit of a melt down the next day, but you didn't go crazy. Most people would not have handled the situation as well as you did."

I snorted. "Yeah, right. Did you forget how bad the meltdown was? Or, how about how I embarrassed myself so completely in front of your mom? I don't think I handled anything well. As a matter of fact, I'm still not handling things all that well. I'm still putting the pieces back together."

He smiled softly. "You really don't see how remarkable you are, do you. I think the pieces you're referring to are emotional. Look at you. You can work, get mad at me and not freak out. I can say the word Hodag, and you don't hyperventilate. You've learned more about . . . us." He glanced around to make sure no one was listening. The tables near us were filling with people. He leaned in. "You found that the world around you wasn't what you always believed it was, and you're adapting."

I was thinking about what he said when our salads arrived. I usually have the salad dressing on the side. That way I could dip my fork in the dressing and get the flavor of it with each bite of salad without soaking the lettuce. I could stay healthier-avoid the extra calories that a thick gob of dressing eaten the normal way provided. My salad was coated with dressing. I couldn't taste the vegetables because of it. It was a very good blue cheese, however, and I ate it all. Shortly after we finished our salads, our meals arrived. My casserole was delicious. There was a lot of cheese and cream in the sauce, and the shrimp were cooked just right. I had to concentrate on eating slowly as I realized how hungry I was.

Ash cut his steak meticulously into small bites. I couldn't get over how perfect his manners were. He was very neat and tidy. When I ate a baked potato, I'd smash it down and add toppings. It'd be spread all over my plate by the time I finished mixing in the margarine and sour cream. His baked potato just kind of disintegrated as he ate it. He made no mess at all.

We finished eating at about the same time. I couldn't quite finish my meal as there had been a lot of food. I was really full. I had my leftovers boxed up and was wondering if my mom would notice how rich in sauce my meal was and say something about it. I really didn't eat heavy foods. I couldn't remember the last time, if ever, that I had such a rich, creamy sauce. It was delicious, but by the time Ash paid the check and we headed out the door, my stomach wasn't feeling very good.

Not good turned into feeling lousy about halfway to my car. I started sweating and I was nauseous. I had this metallic taste in my mouth.

"Pull over, now!" I shouted, opening the door and throwing up just as Ash pulled the car over onto a gravel side road that was deserted and had stopped the car. "Oh, Laurel!" Ash said softly as he reached over to hold my hair out of my face as I barfed my dinner onto the side of the road. Just as I had opened the door, Ash had unbuckled our seat belts. This gave me more room to lean out of the door. This also allowed him room to hold my hair as I balanced myself on the door frame.

After I completely emptied my stomach, I looked to see if I had thrown up on his car - and to my relief - I saw that I had not. Ash had pulled over far enough to the side of the road that everything that came out of me had gone over the shoulder of the road and into the grass.

"Are you ok now?" He asked me when I was finally able to sit up. He was still holding my hair out of my face. I pulled a tissue out of my purse to wipe my face and lips. I shuddered at the whole situation.

"I am not. Do I look like I am ok?" I stated. "I am an idiot and can't seem to stop embarrassing myself in front of you. Have you had enough of me now? Now will you leave me alone?" I cried out wishing I could just die right there.

Ash brought out an unopened bottle of water and handed it to me. "Here rinse out your mouth. You will feel better."

"I doubt it." I said, but I did take the bottle of water. I opened it, rinsed my mouth out and spit out the water over the grass. Hey, I thought to myself. He just watched me barf my guts out. A little spitting in the grass isn't likely to shock him.

"Thanks." I said, closing my eyes and leaning back against the seat with a sigh. I was pretty disgusted with myself. I had meant to show off and all I succeeded in doing is to make an idiot out of myself.

"Feel better?" He asked as he gently pushed my hair behind my ear so he could get a better look at my profile.

I turned in my seat to look at him. "My stomach feels better." I said. "I don't know why I ordered all of that rich food. I guess I just wanted to show how human I was. I really don't eat a lot of fattening foods. Almost never, I guess." I continued. "Mom believes in light and nutritious meals. She'll have a stroke when she sees what's in that leftover box." I sighed again, leaning back in the seat and closing my eyes again.

"We can take care of that." He said putting on his seat belt. "Buckle up. I think it is time to leave." I put my seat belt back on and he started the car. We drove back into town. He pulled over by the first dumpster he saw in a parking lot. He grabbed my leftover box and took it and threw it in the dumpster. "No evidence." He said, "Can I get you anything else to eat?" He asked after tossing the box.

"No, I don't think my stomach will take anything right now. I guess I should just go home. Can you take me to my car?" I asked softly.

"Sure." He said. The hardware store was only a block away from where we were at, so we were there in no time at all. He pulled his car up behind my Jeep. When I got out, I went to the drivers side window and said, "Thanks for dinner, sorry I tried to show off and threw it all up." I actually said this very calmly. I wasn't even embarrassed anymore. I had gone beyond that. What little dignity I had maintained prior to this evening was pretty much gone.

"Goodbye." I said and waved at him as I got into my car. After I started my car, Ash backed out of my way so I could pull out. He followed me home until I pulled into my driveway. Once I pulled down my driveway, he kept going on down the road.

When I walked in the door, Mom called from the living room, "Hi honey!" She called when she heard the front door open. "Did you have a good time?" She said this last part coming to greet me. She followed me to the coat closet as I hung up my jacket.

"Not particularly." I stated. I looked at her and rolled my eyes. "I am such an idiot! I tried to show off that I was human and could eat any human food! I ordered some very fattening cheesy casserole. After we finished eating, I got sick. Ash pulled over so I could barf it up outside of his car. I didn't particularly want to go to dinner with him anyway, as I was still embarrassed from the last time we were together. Now, I think I can safely say I will never hear from him again. I wouldn't even be surprised if he quits the school play because of me. I think he has had enough of my embarrassing behaviors. Maybe I have finally scared him away for good."

"Oh, honey, I'm so sorry!" Mom gave me a big hug. Then she looked at me, "Did he act appalled? What did he do when you threw up?" She asked me. Mom lifted my face with her hand since I was looking at the floor.

"He was nice to me. He even had the consideration to hold my hair so I didn't throw up on it!" I said sadly.

"That's actually a good sign, I think," Mom mused. "It sounds like you didn't gross him out. A lot of guys might have been grossed out. I mean, this was your first date, and what do you do? You puke." She was trying to be funny, and it worked. We both laughed. I tried to shrug it off. "Whatever," I said. "I don't really know what he thinks."

"Are you hungry?" She asked me.

"No. I'm going to go upstairs and play on the Internet and try to relax. This has been a rough couple of days for me," I said heading for the stairs. I turned half way up the stairs and said, "Guess what? I don't have to work tomorrow. I actually have a day off and I am sleeping in!"

"Good for you!" Mom said. "Don't worry honey. It will get better. I promise. See you when you get up. Good night!"

"'Night, mom!" I called from the top of the stairs.

I went into the bathroom and washed my face and brushed my teeth. I used mouth wash to ensure that I had removed any vomit particles that may still be floating around in my mouth. When I went into my bedroom to put on my pajamas, I looked out of the window into the dark and wondered what Ash was doing right then. He was home by now. I wondered if he was telling his mom about the human girl that tried to show off and barfed. I wondered if they were having a good laugh at my expense.

All I could wish for was that none of the Woodsons would ever go into the hardware store when I was working. I never wanted to see any of them again. It wasn't like Ash had a bunch of friends at school. There were plenty of girls that followed his every move. If he just smiled at any of them, all of those girls would be at his beck and call. So far, he had shown no interest. But then, why would he? They were only human. He was so much better than any human. He didn't just have to think it was so, I knew the truth. I believed it, too. I turned on my computer and looked up wood nymphs. I knew about some of the things that they could do. I knew they could move faster than sound and probably faster than light. I knew that they could change colors to match their surroundings. Wood nymphs were all beautiful, at least all of the ones that I had seen. They had musical voices. How could a human compete with that?

When my computer was ready, I logged onto the internet and looked up wood nymph. According to Wikipedia, the wood nymphs were very musical. Well, why not, I thought. They have everything else. I wondered what kind of music? I would have to ask Uncle Forrest about it. Then, I saw that Wikipedia said that they were beautiful, yeah, I already knew that one. Wikipedia also said that wood nymphs could move swiftly and invisibly. Yup, I knew that one. Ride through the air and slip through small holes? What does it mean to ride through the air? Hm, those were new ones for me. I would have to ask about those, too.

I had to look up the word nymphomaniac. That was a word associated with wood nymphs. I had forgotten all about that. According to Wikipedia, it was a person that would engage in sexual behavior at such an extreme as to have the behavior considered a problem. I hadn't seen any of those activities from any of the wood nymphs I had met. Truly though, why would I see anything like that? Who would get excited over me? No one I knew. I could see a human man going all crazy for Olivia. She was so very beautiful. Maybe this was a label thing from early male psychologists. They see a beautiful woman and get all hot and crazy for her and then blame their reaction on to her. It is like saying that just because a woman is attractive; her beauty is what causes men to become crazy. That's a pretty crazy way of thinking.

As I went to sleep, I was thinking of Olivia in her special color changing clothes flitting through the forest.

CHAPTER 12
SOME THINGS CHANGE AND SOME STAY THE SAME

I got up on Sunday morning with the sun in my face. I had slept well considering the events of the last couple of days. I decided I'd take life slow and easy. I needed to go nowhere, and no one I needed to see. I looked at the clock. Only 8:00 a.m. Still early. I had been so tired when I went to bed, I thought I'd sleep until noon. I had left my curtains open, and the morning sun was shining full on my face. I thought about rolling over and going back to sleep, but decided that I'd enjoy my one day off.

I went downstairs. Mom was sitting at the dining room table looking out at the river. She turned and smiled when I entered the room. "How did you sleep last night?" she asked as I went into the kitchen to get a bowl of cereal. I was really hungry.

I looked at her as I pulled my cereal bowl out of the cabinet and set it on the island in the middle of the kitchen. "I slept really well last night. Before I went to bed I had looked up wood nymphs on the Internet to see what I could find. I went to sleep thinking about Olivia running barefoot through the trees." I chuckled at the thought.

"Yeah, I can picture her doing that. She's so poised, so graceful, I can see her running barefoot through the trees. What did you find out about wood nymphs?" She sipped her coffee.

"I knew some things, like color changing. Forrest didn't show you, but they're like chameleons. They can change their skin color to match background colors and even take on the texture of whatever substance is next to them. It's really unnerving to watch." I poured the cereal.

"You've seen them do it? Who?" Mom asked.

I thought, *We're really taking this well.* We would never have believed that so many things we had considered stories and myths were actually true!

"When Forrest picked me up from Ash's house," I said as I poured milk, "tried to take my mind off the terror I'd felt at hearing a Hodag. I still can't remember the sound without shuddering. Will I ever get over that?" I asked my mom as I sat down.

"I hope so. Only time will tell, but who changed their skin color?"

"Forrest. He was sitting in the driver's seat, when his skin changed to match the color and texture of the upholstery of his seat. It kind of made me queasy. While it was fascinating in a way, it was also creepy." I heaved a sigh, then shook it off. I looked down at my cereal and took up my spoon.

"That must have been something to see," Mom said thoughtfully. "I think I would like to see something like that."

"There's more!" I said. "They have a special fabric that can also change to match their surroundings. Any of them could stand right next to us in the woods—or any-where—and we wouldn't even see them. That's kind of cool and spooky at the same time, don't you think?" I said, spooning up some more cereal.

"That's something all right. But, what else? What did you find on the Internet? What else have they told you?" She put her elbows on the table and steepled her fingers and then rested her chin on them while looking at me.

"Well, you know about the hyper speed. You know, what they call the jet thing. Wikipedia said wood nymphs were beautiful. We know that too. Wikipedia also said they could get through really small spaces, but I don't know anything about that. The website also said they were musical, and that makes sense, but I didn't see that beyond their voices. The site mentioned nymphomania. My theory on that is that humans see someone like Olivia and fall in love with her. Then, like the old stories, the guys think that, because they love her and she doesn't love them, she's bewitched them. Really, I think Olivia's beauty doesn't make her a sex-starved harlot. I just don't see it. She seems far too dignified for that." I said, eating some more cereal.

"I agree," Mom said getting up to get more coffee. "You have to admit that the wood nymphs are certainly interesting."

"I'm glad you think so, since I am half one!" I said grinned. This was pretty neat, I thought. I didn't feel any different, but why would I?

I said to Mom, "I've been who I am my whole life. It's not like I suddenly find out that I'm half something else, and suddenly I should feel different? I kind of think it's like finding out you're a different nationality from what you thought you were. What would it be like if you thought you were Italian, or German, or Irish, or African American, and then find out that you're that, but you are also something else? Would that change a person? It's still the same person. It might make someone curious about their history, I would guess, I don't think finding out that my background is different than what I'd believed all of my life can physically change me. I mean, I've already learned right from wrong, right? I know how to tie my shoes and drive. What my her-itage is shouldn't change anything. But now I have relatives." I smiled at Mom.

"Honey, this is all new to me, too. You're probably right in that you're still the same person you've always been. You're nice, kind, conscientious in what you do, and you're smart. Those things won't change. Who you are deep inside won't change. We just have to deal with things as they happen. We've both been through a lot this week. We're strong women. We can handle it. We won't let life change that. I agree with you.

And I also like the idea of relatives. They're not really my relatives, but they seem to accept me as if I was. I like Forrest and Olivia . . ." Mom left that kind of hanging.

I swallowed the last of the milk from my bowl, and my mom sipped her coffee. We both looked out at the river. "You know that Forrest cleaned up the place and made the pier, right?" I asked gently after a couple of minutes. "He's also an architect. He gave me one of his cards the other day."

"He did a great job with our pier. That was really nice. He's certainly talented. I wonder if their special talents help them make money. All the wood nymphs we've met seem to have plenty," Mom said with a thoughtful look.

"Olivia has a brother at UWM, studying chemistry," I said after another few minutes of silence. "I wonder if he's as handsome as Olivia is beautiful." We both laughed.

"I've got some case notes I want to put in the computer at work," Mom said, getting up. "What are you going to do?"

I leaned back from the table and stretched. "Looks like a beautiful day. I may go for a walk. Maybe I'll do some fishing. Maybe I won't do anything except lay on the futon in the screen room and watch the river roll by."

Mom said, "It's already getting warm, and it is only nine. I think we have an Indian summer kind of day going on. Nice for early October. Hope it's as nice tomorrow on my birthday. I'm too old to have birthdays," Mom said and laughed.

"Oh, you're only as old as you feel," I said and gave her a hug.

"Sometimes, I feel pretty old," she said and sighed.

"Do you want to go out to dinner tonight or tomorrow night?" I asked. We always went out to eat on our birthdays.

"Tomorrow. Definitely, tomorrow," she said going up the stairs to get dressed. "I'll meet you here after school tomorrow. It's not one of your late nights, is it?"

"No, I can be home by 5:30," I replied, following her up the stairs. We each had our own bathroom and got downstairs at the same time. We were both dressed in jeans and long sleeve shirts. She had on tennis shoes, and I had on hiking boots.

"Call my cell if you need me. I'm not answering the office phone. We have a messaging service on weekends, I'm not on call." She hit the garage door button.

I grabbed a Jane Austen book, *Emma*. I carried the book outside. It was warm enough that I didn't need a jacket. I walked out onto the pier and sat at one of the benches, the side that had more sun. I faced the deer path heading into the woods. After a while, I stretched out on my stomach with my head on my hands reading. I was so engrossed I didn't hear anyone until footsteps sounded on the pier.

I sat up quickly. It was Ash. That surprised me. I didn't expect to see him again ever, and here he was standing next to me on my pier. With the morning light on his face and hair he was so gorgeous. I looked at the river to compose myself and make sure my expression was neutral. "I didn't hear your car," I said as I got up.

"You wouldn't have," he responded as came closer. "I walked here."

"Oh, yeah," I said. "You can *jet!*" I gave a sarcastic emphasis to the word.

"I could have, but I didn't. I really just walked here," he said. "I wanted the fresh air and time to get my thoughts in order before I saw you. I had a feeling you might be a little difficult this morning, and I wanted to prepare for it." He sat and crossed his leg over his knee on the bench across from me.

"Difficult? You thought that I might be difficult? In what way? Why would you think I would be difficult?" I said glaring at him.

"Well, we haven't exactly had a stellar relationship so far, and I wasn't sure how receptive you'd be about my being here. You seem to have it in your head that you should be perpetually embarrassed around me. So I walked here. I came up the deer path between our houses." He said, pointing the way down the dead end deer trail.

"How did you get through the bushes? I've gone down that path and hit the biggest knot of thorns and shrubbery I've ever seen. No one could get through it." I stated. Now I was curious.

"I did," he said with a shrug. "You just have to know how to do it. Would you like to see?" he asked and stood up.

"Yeah, I would," I said. "Let me get a jacket and put my book in the house."

I was in and out in a minute with my jacket over my arm. I hated to be too warm, but I hated to be cold even more. "Show me."

I followed him up the path. Every now and then, I'd trip on a root, or almost twist my ankle stepping sideways on a stone and have to catch myself. Ash never looked at the ground. He walked like a panther in the jungle. He wasn't tripping over anything but was entirely graceful. I rolled my eyes at his back, tired of my human side being dominant in terms of my personal mobility. A little grace would've been nice.

"Would you like some help? Should I hold you up?" he teased after one especially difficult lurch.

That bad step had hurt. "No, I got it," I mumbled behind him. "I may not be as graceful as you, but I still can walk." I watched him walk and almost fell again.

He didn't say anything to that, but I could just imagine the stupid smug grin on his face. It seemed in no time at all, we were at the thorny hedge.

"Do you see this darker short, stubby branch, right here, the darker-colored thick one only about a foot long?" He pointed to a branch that looked different from the rest once it was pointed out to me. It was attached to the bush, but was a slightly different in color from the rest of the bush.

"Yes," I said standing next to him. He reached in and pushed the branch down. It was a lever. A five-foot section of the bush swung away like a gate. Once it was opened, I saw the continuation of the path on the other side. Ash closed the gate. I expected to hear a click, but there was no sound except leaves mashing together.

"Now you do it," he said and stepped away. I reached in and put my hand around the branch. It was smooth to the touch. I pushed it down the same way that I saw Ash do it. Immediately the gate opened again. "It's easy once you know the trick." He smiled at me as I stepped through the opening.

"Are we on your land now?" I asked. I started walking again, looking around to see if the land on this side looked different from the other side of the hedge fence.

"We've been on my family's land for a while now," he said.

"How far are we from your house?" I asked stopping.

"Not too far. Just around that bend in the river." He stopped next to me. "Why? Do you want to go there?" he asked.

"Absolutely not! That's one place in this world I don't want to go. Your mother probably thinks I'm an idiot. It's bad enough that you do. I didn't invite you over. You just showed up. I'd like to avoid more embarrassment. So, no, I don't want to go to your house." I turned back to the bush fence. Ash's mom had seemed pretty nice, but the day I met her wasn't one of my bright and shining moments. I didn't want to see either condemnation or humor in her eyes. I'd absolutely hate seeing pity, too. I just couldn't imagine a way for us meeting again without major embarrassment for me. No matter what she thought, I'd still feel stupid.

"She doesn't think you're an idiot—" he started to say.

I cut him off. "Whatever! I'm not going there," I said and faced him.

"Ever?" he asked, arching his eyebrow at me.

"Maybe. Probably," I replied. I don't think he liked that answer but apparently decided not to push it. "I want to go home," I said after an uncomfortable moment of us just standing near the hedge staring at each other.

Ash opened the hedge, and we walked in silence back to my pier.

"This is really beautiful wood nymph craftsmanship. Is this Forrest's work?" he asked, running his hand along the top of the railing. "I don't think I've ever seen a pier made this perfectly. Whoever did it can really sing to the trees."

"Yes, Uncle Forrest made it," I said proudly. "He's an architect." I ran my hand along the smooth wood of the top railing.

Ash looked at me, "Actually, I knew the architect part. Our clans do talk, you know. We used to be pretty close at one time. Not so much anymore. There was some kind of problem. But that's ancient history." He sighed. "I think Forrest really loves you." He said this last part simply. It wasn't a question, just a statement.

"Yes, he does. I love him and Olivia, too," I replied.

"Olivia. I know who she is. She's the beautiful one who can foresee the future. I think she's part of the reason for the rift in the family. Oh, yeah, I remember now. One of my cousins, Hawthorn Woodson, had a hard time after a breakup with Olivia. He lives on the other side of me, a couple of houses down. If I remember correctly, they'd gone out for a while, and he found that he loved her. Apparently she didn't love him back, and he got upset. He moved away for a few years to study agriculture with a European clan. He only recently came back. I guess it was easier to be away from here. He never did marry. Olivia didn't either, did she? We actually don't call it getting married. We called it being conjoined. There's no religious part to it. We have a cere-mony, and I suppose that 'married' would work, but it just isn't the term we use. Are you interested in this stuff?" he asked as he sat on the bench on the pier.

"Yeah. I'd like knowing the words you use for things. I want to know all I can about my family. No, as far as I know Olivia never married . . . conjoined. She's so awesome, though. I wonder why she never did." I sat beside Ash.

We spent the rest of the morning and early afternoon on the pier talking. I forgot I was uncomfortable around him. We were getting to know one another. At one point, we took a break and went into the house for fruit and a salad for lunch.

I learned his favorite color was the spectrum of color maple leaves make after the first frost in the fall. He didn't have one particular color he liked. I couldn't get him to pinpoint an orange or a red or a brown. He liked the whole look of the trees in fall color. Just one leaf he explained was not a complete picture of the change of season.

I told him my favorite color was a dark pink. Not quite a red and not really a purple. The closest colors I could imagine were magenta or fuchsia, I explained. While at first, I was a little hesitant about his showing up unannounced and the awkward way I usually felt around him, I thought this day felt good, and it was going well. I hadn't done anything horribly embarrassing, and I was getting comfortable around him. Was this a good thing? His favorite colors were all around us and in full bloom.

In the afternoon, a bald eagle came by and sat in the same tree where I had seen an eagle before when I had been fishing. This one flew onto a branch even closer to us after watching us for a while. He cocked his head as if to listen to our conversation.

"Is that a friend of yours?" Ash asked.

"I doubt it. To be honest, I'd like it to be my friend. Aren't bald eagles beautiful? He's such a magnificent bird," I said, looking at the bird. The bird let out a screeching call and opened his wingspan as if to show off how wonderful he was.

"He knows you," Ash said. "He's a shape shifter from a reservation. Do you have friends on any reservation?" This question took me by surprise.

"Yeah, I have friends on the Lac Du Flambeau reservation. Are you telling me that this bird, this magnificent bird is *not* just a bird? He's . . . a person?" I said as I got the feeling that more legends were about to come to life.

"Um, yes," Ash said with a touch of smugness. "Real bald eagles don't normally come this close to humans unless you're feeding them. Besides, I can feel the difference."

"You can *feel* the difference—" I started.

The bird let out a particularly raucous cry. It was close enough that, if it was human, it would have been able to hear every word. And apparently did. As we talked, it looked at me and then Ash and back again according to who was talking at the time. It really was listening. After this last exchange, the bird looked up and down the river as if to make sure the coast was clear and flew down to the railing on my pier.

I stopped mid-sentence to gawk.

The enormous bird was now about three feet away from me. It jumped as if to hop down onto the deck of the pier, and as it jumped, it shimmered. I then saw a flash that looked like someone had set a whole truckload of sparklers on fire at the same time. But, the sparklers were in the shape of the bird. At first, it was shaped like a bird. After a second, it changed into the shape of a man. Just as the sparkling human shape looked as if it was about to set my pier on fire, it flashed even brighter. Then the light went out, and Adam Whitestone stood in front of me in nothing more than a leather loincloth. But he didn't even look at me. He glared at Ash.

"Wood nymph!" he spat. "I didn't rat you out. Why would you rat us out? We didn't tell Laurel about you other than to tell her about legends. I told her about our legends, too! But they were just legends to her! They weren't real! I surely didn't tell her that shape shifters existed in her world!"

Trying to hide my shock, I was thinking *I shouldn't be shocked.* I took a couple of deep breaths while Adam and Ash squared off at each other. Just about then, I thought to myself, *If the little green leprechaun from the cereal box walks onto my pier and says, "How do you do?" I wouldn't be surprised. If a unicorn ate grass on my lawn, I'd tell it that it was welcome and ask if it, too, could talk.*

I took another deep breath. "Hi, Adam." I said in what I thought was a normal voice. "So, you turn into an eagle?"

Adam turned to me, and his face softened. "I'm sorry, Laurel. I couldn't tell you the truth. It's forbidden to tell White people the truth of our legends. Please don't be mad at me." He was looking between me and Ash. Apologetic at me, glaring at him.

"I'm not exactly 'White people,'" I said, with my hands on my hips.

"But you didn't know! You look like a wood nymph, but you don't smell exactly like one. When I met you, you didn't know what you were! I mean, you believed you were just human! I knew you weren't, but I'd never smelled that kind of scent before. I could tell by our conversation. I've met lots of regular humans before, and you acted just like one. I never met a wood nymph-human mix. I didn't know it was possible. When did you find out what you are?" he asked sitting on the bench across from me.

"Last week after I was almost killed by a Hodag," I replied. "Ash saved me by grabbing me and jumping forty feet up into a tree."

Ash hadn't said anything during this exchange, but he kept his eyes on Adam. I guess he might be concerned Adam would punch him, and he did look pretty mad.

"You couldn't sense I was more than an eagle?" Adam asked curiously.

On one hand, I wanted to continue this conversation. On the other, I didn't want to talk about what I couldn't do. "You don't have clothes?" I asked him glancing at his skimpy covering.

"Oh, yeah," he said sheepishly. "I'm lucky I've got this much. Normal clothes don't shape shift. Only specially made leather loin cloths will shift with us. Otherwise, I'd be naked right now. That might've been fun." He gave Ash a big grin.

"I wouldn't have liked that much," I said. Ash scowled at that thought, too.

"Hey, okay, at least I'm covered!" he said.

"Not by much," I muttered. "Can you talk to me as a bird?"

"Yeah, but I'm really hard to understand," Adam replied. He seemed really relaxed in less than his underwear sitting on my pier. I was glad I didn't have neighbors who could see him.

"I'll chance it. If you want to visit me without driving down, bring some clothes in your claws, or stay a bird," I stated firmly. I was so proud of myself for not freaking out about finding out that my friend from the reservation was a shape shifter. I was about to ask him if the other kids I'd met there were shape shifters, too.

"What a prude you are!" he said, scoffing. "Okay, yeah, whatever. Hey, I hear your mom's car coming up the driveway. I better go. She shouldn't see me like this. She doesn't know about shape shifters. I'll leave it up to you whether you tell her or not. Keep in mind that she's been friends with George a long time and that this might upset her!" As he finished speaking he took one quick look at my house and then launched himself into the air from the edge of my pier. Again, he looked like a million lit sparklers shaped in a human form and molding to the form of the eagle with wide spread wings. Just before he hit the water, he was the eagle and flying away down the river.

Ash and I watched him go until he was out of sight around the bend in the river. "I'm not going to keep this a secret from my mom. If she finds out later that George was a shape shifter and that I knew about it, she'd be upset with me. Come into the house with me," I said to Ash as I walked toward the house.

Ash and I came in through the screened in porch room. Mom was coming in the back door.

"Hi! I didn't know you had company. Ash, it's nice to see you. I didn't see a car in the driveway," Mom said as she hung up her jacket. "I really didn't need the jacket. I shouldn't have been inside. It's been a great day! Too bad I had paperwork. Did you guys have a nice day?"

"Oh, this morning. I walked over along the river. Our property is right next to yours. It is just a couple of miles from here to there. On a nice day, it's a nice walk." Ash explained.

"We spent the day on the pier," I said. "We were outside except we came in for lunch. We ate most of the fruit. Sorry." I looked at my mom's face to see if she would be mad about my having a boy in the house or about our eating the fruit.

"That's okay. I only work a half day tomorrow. I'll just do some quick grocery shopping before we meet for my birthday dinner." Mom walked into the kitchen with a note pad and paper in her hand to make a grocery list.

"Your birthday is tomorrow, Mrs. Redmond?" Ash asked.

"Yes, I can't keep it from coming. So, instead of being miserable about being a year older, I prefer to celebrate it!" She laughed as she looked in the refrigerator and wrote something down on her pad.

"We're going to have baked chicken for dinner tonight. Would you like to stay?" Mom asked Ash as she set the package of chicken on the counter.

"Oh, thanks, no. I'd better get home," Ash replied. Then he looked at me, "Can I pick you up for school tomorrow?"

"Okay," I said. "That'd be great! See you tomorrow." I walked him to the door. He paused there, and I wondered if I was supposed to say something.

"Bye, Laurel," he said. He looked at me intently for a minute and then left. One second he was standing on the porch at the top of the stairs, and, then the next, even though I was looking right at him, he was just gone. In a blink he had vanished. It was going to take me a while to get used to that jetting thing.

Mom was just putting the chicken into the oven. "Mom, there's some more news for you. You need to sit down." I could tell by Mom's face that she was preparing herself for some new kind of supernatural phenomenon.

"Oh, my. Let me get a glass of scotch. I'll meet you by the dining room table." She reached for a high ball glass and opening the freezer for some ice. After she had poured herself a double, she sat across from me at the table.

I told her about Adam being a shape shifter. I told her about how I'd seen the eagle when I'd been fishing, and how Ash and I had been talking on the pier when the eagle landed in the tree. I explained how the bird seemed to be listening to us talk and how Ash had known it wasn't a normal bald eagle. Mom's eyes got really wide when I talked about how the bird glowed like a bunch of sparklers as it changed into Adam. I finished by telling her that all of the Indians on the reservation could shape shift.

"What does George turn into?" Mom asked.

"I don't know. Just as we were getting to that part, Adam heard your car in the driveway, and he didn't want you to see him in his loin cloth. He knew you didn't know about shape shifting, and he didn't want to be the one to tell you. He left it up to me. Adam jumped off of the pier, flashed like a million lit sparklers and changed into the bird again. He was gliding away down the river when you pulled up." I said.

"Oh, my!" Mom said softly. "I can see how this would be difficult to tell me." Then she said, "I've got to call George and let him know I know! I don't completely understand all this, I can at least let him know I know it happens, and he can explain it to me."

She got up from the table and called George. She didn't appear to be upset at all. I wondered if it was her training in psychology that made this easier for her to deal with, or if, on the inside, she thought the whole world had gone crazy.

After a half hour or so, Mom got off of the phone. She finished making dinner while I set the table in the kitchen for the two of us. After dinner, I went upstairs to get ready for school. While many things had changed in my life, some things stayed the same.

CHAPTER 13
FRIENDS OR MORE?

Monday morning dawned cold. My room felt cool when I got up. Mom was already at the table. She said she'd watched the news, and the weatherman had said there was the possibility of flurries today. Just yesterday, I didn't need a jacket outside.

In D.C. the temperature would still be in the seventies and eighties this time of year. We'd still have our air conditioning on! The housing people would just now be talking about the switch to heating. Talking. After breakfast, I put on a winter jacket. I wanted to be ready when Ash arrived to take me to school. I wondered if there might be a chance he'd change his mind and not want to pick me up. I didn't know him yet, not really. We'd just started talking. Were we becoming friends? I thought we were at least approaching friendship. I thought about my feelings. I liked being friends a lot better than being enemies, but was that enough for me?

When I had blurted out how much in love I was with Ash last week, I had the feelings of a normal human girl and thought Ash was just a normal human guy. I wasn't sure how I felt anymore. Did knowing I was a hybrid and Ash was a wood nymph make a difference? I understood now that Ash didn't call me an abomination because I was illegitimate but because I was a mixture of two species.

I wouldn't have thought different species could mate. I'd seen the offspring of a donkey and horse in the zoo. Was that similar? I wasn't sure I liked the idea of having a wood nymph for a boyfriend. While there were neat things about being a wood nymph, I wasn't altogether sure I was comfortable with the whole interspecies thing. That was kind of a hypocritical thought, but I wondered if I'd be here if Mom had known my biological father wasn't human. Did wood nymphs have the same emotions as humans? What about their thought processes? Obviously they had adapted to the human world, but what was their world really like? Their culture? Was it similar to human culture? There were a lot of human cultures. Asian culture was different from African culture. European was different from American. Different countries also had vastly varying cultures. Were wood nymphs similar?

I was standing by the front door considering these things when I saw Ash's SUV come up the driveway. I went outside. The wind had a biting edge to it. I was glad I'd worn my winter jacket. I quickly hopped into the passenger seat.

"It's really cold outside!" I complained as I shut the door.

"It's going to get a lot colder," Ash replied with a smile. "How are you doing today? You look like you have something on your mind."

"I do. I want to know some things. First, you've been around humans your whole life. How are a wood nymph's emotions? Are they different or the same as a human's?" I looked at him as he turned around and backed out of the driveway.

"I believe wood nymph emotions are more intense than a human's. We mate for life. I suppose calling it being married would work, although I think I told you that we don't have the religious aspect of it many humans have. We don't get divorced. At least, I've never heard of that. As a rule, we treat our males and females equally. We don't believe in a male or female dominated society. We don't fall in love easily, but, when we do, it's forever. Humans are always getting divorced or trying to control each other. We don't do that. We aren't forced into marriage for either convenience or power. We form a bond strictly for love. When one dies, the other does not usually take another mate. Most of the time, the surviving spouse follows the spouse into death."

"Okay. I see the point about humans getting divorced, but could it be that different human cultures cause that? Mine might be a male-dominated society and women sometimes still struggle with being treated like equals but not as much as it used to be. It's getting better.

"Some men are kind and wonderful to women until they get married, then the woman becomes his property. That's not fair, but not all men are like that. And, yes, sometimes men and women marry for money or power.

"Mom's told me of people getting divorced because one or the other was too controlling. She wants me to marry for love and not some perceived need. I think humans are working toward more perfect equality," I said. I liked wood nymph equality.

I asked, "I don't think because you don't get divorced makes you have more powerful emotions. Do your emotions ever get out of control?"

He shrugged. "I've heard of that, but it's not a common problem. Take my cousin Hawthorn and your cousin Olivia. That caused a rift in our families for years."

"My cousin Olivia," I said softly. "It feels strange to think I have blood relatives beyond my mom. It's a new experience for me. Olivia's very beautiful and nice, too. Because of the attention she gets from men, she keeps herself isolated. Did you know that?"

"No, I didn't, but I guess I can understand it." Ash added, "I wouldn't want to constantly be the center of attention."

I couldn't believe he said that. Didn't he pay attention at school? "Oh, yeah? Don't you notice the way girls at school follow you with their eyes. Are you blind? You're the center of lots of girls' attentions."

"Yeah, but they're just humans," he said with a shrug. "I don't pay any attention to them." I guessed he hadn't thought about what he just said, or to whom he was talking. I was offended for myself and for each girl in school. Just because we were humans didn't mean we didn't have feelings. None of the girls knew he was a wood nymph. They just thought he was a good-looking guy. He pulled into the school lot.

"Just human, huh?. So am I. At least half human." I got out of the car. I wanted to get away from him. When I saw Rodney heading into the school, I saw my escape. "Hey, Rodney! Wait up for me."

"What are you doing?" Ash whispered furiously as he got out. He slipped his hand around my elbow. "I don't want anything to do with him."

I jerked my arm away from him. "Yeah? Well I do! He's my friend. I know he's just human, too, so you don't want anything to do with him. Too bad no one around here is good enough for you. It must be awfully lonely on your perfection island with no friends." I turned away and jogged over to Rodney who was waiting for me.

Rodney and I started walking into the school together. Ash strode past us, looking like a thunderstorm. He didn't look at either of us. Rodney asked, "Did you just ride in with Ash Woodson?"

"Yes, I did," I answered, suddenly wondering how I was going to get home. I could take the bus, I supposed. Maybe I would ask Rodney. He lived on the other side of town, so it'd be completely out of his way, but maybe he wouldn't mind, just this once.

As I was thinking about this and walking with Rodney, Ash turned around in front of us and said, "See you later. Don't forget you're riding home with me."

"Wow. That sounds kind of controlling, doesn't it, Rodney?" I said. We had both stopped in the hallway to stare at Ash.

Rodney looked from him to me and back. "Yeah," he said tentatively, probably knowing he'd stepped into the middle of something. "Yeah, that was kinda controlling."

We had two minutes to get to first hour before the bell. We were doing experiments in chemistry. I liked that. I liked seeing chemical reactions take place. I hurried to class and focused on the lab experiments. I didn't even think about Ash until I saw him by the door to Physics. I had calmed down and needed to deal with the issue. "What's up with you?" I asked. "What you said in the car . . . well, it was very uncool."

I couldn't go into specifics with so many people able to overhear us. "Also, telling me I was riding home with you also sounded kind of bossy. And your family doesn't believe in controlling another person?" I tried to keep my voice down but made no effort to hide my anger. I walked past him and took my normal seat in the front row. Ash sat next to me. We didn't have seat assignments, but people usually kept the same seat all semester.

When Mary Clarkson, the girl that normally sat in that seat came and stood next to Ash with a confused look on her face, Ash gave her a big smile. He said, "You don't mind if I sit here today, do you?" He was intentionally charming her.

With his full attention on Mary for the first time, and that beautiful voice and disarming smile turned to max, Mary didn't have a chance. "Uh, sure. I'll just . . . ah, I'll just take your seat in back then. Would that be okay?" Mary looked completely mesmerized, staring at Ash with undisguised awe and fascination.

"That'd be great, thanks!" he said smiling as she walked away. Poor Mary backed down the aisle, bumping into legs on her way to Ash's regular seat, almost falling over a couple of times. It was unnerving to see her lose herself like that.

"Stop that!" I hissed at him. "What do you think you're doing? She doesn't understand! You don't have the right to do that to someone."

He tried to give me an innocent look. "What did I do? I just asked if I could sit here. What's wrong with that? It's not like I ordered her to sit back there."

I narrowed my eyes at him. "Yeah, like she stood the slightest chance against your charm. I can see they didn't come up with the word 'nymphomaniac' for nothing!" I whispered furiously.

Mary was the brainiest of the senior class. As far as I could tell, her entire focus was to graduate at the top of the class. I had never seen her look at any boy. I thought she even might be a lesbian. If Ash could make her stammer and stagger, I wondered what he could do to the girls who did notice him. It made me shudder. Maybe it was a good thing he didn't pay attention to the human girls. They wouldn't stand a chance against him.

I hadn't gone to my locker since arriving at school, so I still had my winter jacket and book bag with me. When I shuddered, Ash noticed and asked, "Are you cold?" He grabbed my jacket and tried to drape it over my shoulders.

I slapped his hands away. "Stop it. I'm not cold. You're freaking me out!"

He sat back stiffly and gave me a hurt look. Did he really not realize how he treated girls? Was there the slightest chance he was innocent of the effect he had on them? Didn't he realize the girl now sitting in his back-row seat was probably fantasizing about him? Or that he had treated her in a very controlling way. If this was the case, we needed to talk. In any case, we needed to talk about this.

"Meet me in the cafeteria at lunch," I hissed just as the bell rang and the teacher started the class. He gave me a short nod. I had a hard time focusing on physics. I was glad we didn't have a pop quiz. We got a lot of pop quizzes in Physics to make sure we were keeping up with the concepts.

When I got to the cafeteria, Ash was already there, leaning against the entrance door. He rarely ate in the cafeteria. I knew why now. He didn't seem to notice that the majority of girls going past him ogled him on their way to the lunch line. To him, they seemed almost invisible. He was watching for me. When he saw me coming up the hallway, he came and met me and gave me a tentative smile. We went through the lunch line together without speaking. At the cashier, he told her to put both our lunches on one bill. I started to argue but decided not to make a scene in the lunch room, but issues were compounding in my head. I decided to pick my battle, though and deal with a more important point. He could win this one. I let him buy me lunch. We took a table at the end of the cafeteria by ourselves.

Rodney came over and asked me, "Hey, what's up? Aren't you going to sit with us for lunch today?"

"Not today," I replied with a smile. I gave Ash a meaningful look that Rodney could see. "Ash and I need to talk. Later, okay?" I smiled again at Rodney.

Rodney blinked a couple of times. I thought I saw confusion on his face, which I took as his trying to understand. He finally said, "Yeah, right. See you at rehearsal, then."

Rodney returned to his table. Everyone at the table looked at me. They didn't look happy. Rodney started talking, probably telling them what I'd said. I waved at them to show that things were just fine. I really hoped they didn't think I was abandoning them. Mary smiled tentatively and waved back. Then the rest kind of waved in a hesitant way. I could tell they didn't understand what was going on. I had sat with them since the beginning of the year. I felt like a traitor. That made me angrier.

I started in on Ash. "You shouldn't charm people the way you did Mary in Physics. She didn't have a chance, and you know it. She'll be lucky if she can get her head back into her studies after the smile you turned on her."

Ash snorted. "And how's that different from what you just did to Rodney?" he asked in his beautiful voice, seemingly enjoying this conversation.

"What? Rodney's my friend!" I stated. "He understands I needed to talk to you. It is not like he's my boyfriend or anything."

"Oh . . . so you didn't notice his face?" Ash glanced down at his hands, polishing an apple with his paper napkin. I could tell he was still smiling, acting very smug.

"Okay, so he might have been confused about why I wanted to talk to you." I replied, taking a bite of my sandwich. After I swallowed, I added, "But I didn't mesmerize him the way you did Mary."

"Are you sure? Are you really sure he wasn't drawn in by your smile? Maybe you have the attraction of a wood nymph and just don't know it." Ash took a bite of his apple. He was looking me in the eye now. He thought this whole thing was funny.

"Look, I have known and hung out with Rodney all semester. He's just confused by my having lunch with you. That's all! I don't have the charm you do."

"Are you sure?" Ash asked looking at me and then at Rodney.

I looked at Rodney. He looked devastated, like a baby who had lost his lollipop and was trying hard not to cry. Okay, not that bad, but pain was all over his face.

"Oh, crap," I breathed. "I didn't think he cared that much." I rolled my eyes. This was getting out of hand. I didn't want this. I liked Rodney. He'd been my first and best friend since I'd started school here. Obviously he had some strong feelings for me. It was written all over his face.

"I think he wants more than friendship from you," Ash stated truthfully.

I hadn't wanted this. I liked Rodney but not, apparently, as much as he liked me. The poor guy. "No, no, no," I said softly. I put my elbow on the table and leaned my head into my hand. Ash was quiet, too.

Then I remembered what I'd wanted to talk to him about. "Why did you say I had to ride home with you after school?" I asked suddenly.

"Did I say you *had* to ride home with me?"

"It sounded like that. You said, 'Don't forget you're riding home with me today.' Yup, I think those were your exact words," I said and then whispered fiercely, "If your kind didn't control other people, how could you say that?"

He blinked. "Oh, I guess I can see where you'd get the idea I was pressuring you. Sorry. I was just reminding you that you didn't have your car here. I didn't want to have to search for you after rehearsal."

Yeah, right, like that could happen, I thought. Ash could just jet the entire school in a second, search everywhere in the time it'd take me to take one step.

"Well, this's been fun. Gotta get to my next class, though. Thanks for lunch. See you in Drama, right?" I picking up my lunch tray and headed to kitchen counter.

"I'll be there!" he called. He followed me out of the cafeteria, then headed in another direction for his next class.

I went to Art and finished my project. I wanted to have Mom's gift ready so I could wrap it for her before we went to dinner tonight.

What am I going to do about Rodney? He was a good guy, but I only wanted to be friends. The next class dragged, and then I had Drama with Ash. He sat next to me in the front, again in another person's spot. When the guy showed up, he didn't say a word. He just looked at Ash with a strange look and went to sit in the row behind us.

In class, we discussed unrequited love. I sighed. *Yeah, that's my life nine ways to Sunday.* I loved Ash, but he didn't love me back. Rodney loved me, but I didn't love him back. Sometimes life sucked.

We practiced looking hurt. Not a stretch today. We were each given a sheet of paper with lines from various plays. Since Ash and I were lead characters in the play,

Miss Becker asked us to practice together. When Ash tried to fill his face with love lost, he looked so incongruous, I had to laugh. I just couldn't imagine Ash being in love and not having it returned. Granted, there apparently weren't many wood nymph girls to choose from in this neck of the woods, but there were other wood nymphs enclaves in the world. For all I knew, Uncle Forrest's clan had girls his age. Ash should be able to find someone. I was sure of that. In my dreams, I hoped that person could be me. But that was ridiculous. I should feel lucky he only wanted to be my friend. It was highly unlikely that he'd settle for someone like me as a permanent partner. But could I handle being just his friend?

At rehearsal after school, we practiced the end of the play. Mr. Darcy was going to kiss Miss Elizabeth Bennett. I wasn't sure how I felt about that. As it happened, we got hung up on some script changes and didn't get to the kiss.

After rehearsal, Ash took me home. He was nice in a polite kind of way. Almost too polite. His was treating me like an important guest. It made me nervous. I'd have felt more comfortable if he was a little less formal. I found myself wanting to see his crooked grin.

When we got to my house, he dropped me off and told me he'd see me tomorrow. I said okay and went into the house. Mom was sitting at the dining room table with two huge bouquets of flowers. I had never seen such lovely flowers. The colors were magnificent.

"The first bouquet was on the dining room table when I got home!" she said pointing to the larger arrangement. "It's from Forrest and Olivia. I wonder which one wrote out the birthday card? I can't imagine these flowers came from a florist. They must have their own greenhouse. I don't even know what most of these flowers are. And look at the handwriting on the card. Have you ever seen such a beautiful script? It's almost Victorian. The card's hand made, too." She handed me the card.

"This second bouquet was on the porch when I got here. It's from Ash and his parents. Aren't they just breathtaking? You must have smelled them when you came in the door. Such a lovely scent!" Mom handed me the second card.

It had similar lovely handwriting and also looked hand made. "Have you ever seen such lovely paper?" Mom asked. "This is no Hallmark card. Is there nothing they can't do better than us normal people?" She put her face in the bouquet and drew in a deep sniff. I breathed in the other arrangement.

The only identifiable flowers in the first bouquet were the roses. There were red, pink, and white roses. And blue. A true, amazing blue. That wasn't supposed to be possible in roses. The rest of the flowers, which I didn't recognize, were different colors and were a perfect accent to the roses in the arrangement.

Mom looked at me and smiled. "It's nice to be remembered on my birthday. I got a package from Ben today, too. My favorite perfume. He must have ordered it weeks ago. I wish he were here. I really miss him. He'll be so surprised when he gets home," Mom said showing me the box with the perfume.

After making the appropriate responses, I excused myself to run upstairs to wrap my gift. I changed clothes. I was downstairs in fifteen minutes.

We went to dinner at the Silver Bird, both ordering broiled walleye. It was seasoned and cooked perfectly. We also had their homemade onion soup, steamed asparagus, and a rice pilaf. It was all delicious. I should have ordered this the last time I was here.

The same server that waited on Ash and me, waited on us. "Nice to see you back so soon!" she said to me.

I was surprised she recognized me since she'd given Ash all of her attention. I smiled and told her it was my mom's birthday. After dinner, the server gave Mom a piece of chocolate cake with a birthday candle in it. I gave her the copper ring I'd made in my seventh-hour art class while she was eating her dessert.

She opened my gift. "Laurel, this is lovely! You made this? Really? It's wonderful!" She tried on the ring. It fit.

For a beginning art student, I thought it wasn't a half bad piece. It had a wide band and swirls carved into it. It was smooth and shiny and quite unique. I had coated it with a lacquer to keep her finger from turning green when she wore it. She put it on her ring finger of her right hand and admired it a long time.

We had a great time at the restaurant. Mom fairly glowed on the way home. I was glad she'd had a nice birthday. When we got home, she retired to her room, and I did my homework before going to bed.

FOR THE NEXT WEEK, Ash and I fell into a pattern. He picked me up for school, and we met for lunch. We sat next to each other in our joint classes. Rodney wouldn't talk to me. I tried to talk to him, but he just ignored me. He'd give me some lame excuse about being in a hurry for a class or to get home. Every time I tried to talk to him, he gave me the same cold shoulder.

I saw Mary from my lunch table one day in the hallway. "Hi, Mary!" I said. I was happy to see her.

"Hey, Laurel, nice to see you!" she replied. "We miss you at our table, you know," she said, "but we girls totally understand. I'd sit with Ash Woodson if he gave me the time of day, too!" She sighed and blushed at the same time. "See you later!"

I thought, *Sweet little Mary's affected too?* Was there a girl that didn't want to be with Ash? If there was, I hadn't met her. This was getting ridiculous.

Rehearsal that day was going to include the kiss scene, and I was scared. I'd never had more than a couple of kisses with my first boyfriend, and that had felt like he was trying to suck my face off. Either that or he slobbered over me with his tongue. I didn't like that at all. I wondered if it would be the same with Ash. Would I like it? Would it be like getting licked by a friendly dog? Worse, would it be like getting kissed by Mom or Ben? I'd hate that. When they kissed me, it was a quick peck, usually on the cheek. They loved me, and they didn't mean anything bad by kissing me, so I tolerated the kisses. But, theirs weren't kisses I particularly liked. I guess I was waiting for more.

I didn't aspire to being some famous actress, but I did want to do a good job in my role in the play. I resolved to ask Miss Becker what to do. She'd coach me how people were supposed to kiss in the play.

At rehearsal, there were a couple of assistant teachers working with other kids in other parts of the play. This was a mass rehearsal night. Everyone had to do their own scenes. Next week we were going to have our first real run through of the play. We were getting close to dress rehearsal night.

When Miss Becker saw me and Ash, she called us over. She wanted to do the kiss scene where Elizabeth agrees to marry Mr. Darcy and the final kissing scene at the end of the play. Miss Becker said to me, "Remember now, Miss Redmond, as Elizabeth, you're in love with Mr. Darcy. You finally realize he isn't the bad guy you thought he was. When he proposes this time, you happily accept." Miss Becker turned to Ash and said, "As Mr. Darcy, you realize that Elizabeth really does love you. When she accepts your marriage proposal, you smile broadly and then kiss her. Do you need instruction on how to do the kiss?" she asked looking at each of us.

"Nope. I got it." he said with a confident grin. This was the first time that I saw that particular grin.

I didn't get it. What was he so happy about? I knew I was going to ruin the whole scene. Well, that was okay. We were just high school kids, right? Wasn't that what the teacher was for? To teach us stuff? Whatever.

"Do you want me to start now?" Ash asked. He and I were on the stage in our correct positions for the scene in the garden. The stage hands had already completed the garden set and props and had set the scene up.

"Yes, start where Mr. Darcy has just taken Elizabeth to the garden to propose," Miss Becker said.

I felt totally self-conscious, like half the school was watching us. I don't know how Ash managed to look so calm. We didn't need a script to remember our lines. We'd practiced them a lot and with the facial expressions required for each scene. We almost had the whole play memorized. He began, and I responded with my lines, trying to look and act appropriately for the scene. Next thing I knew, it was time for the kiss. Ash, as Mr. Darcy, got the appropriate loving look on his face and bent to kiss me.

For days now, I had been practicing the appropriate behaviors for the scene. I hoped I had the right look on my face. I hoped I adequately portrayed love and trust.

Ash put his hands on my arms while he slowly bent forward and tilted his head just a bit. He looked me in the eyes. As his lips touched mine, he slowly closed his eyes. He started with gentle pressure against my lips. As his lips found the right position, he applied more pressure and eased open his mouth just a bit. He slowly put his arms around me, pulling me deeper into his embrace and the kiss.

My mind spun with the intensity of it. This was supposed to be a rehearsal, not the real deal. My mind was screaming that this wasn't acting. The whole world dissolved. All that was, was this kiss. My knees started to buckle, but he held me firmly in his arms. I lost myself in the moment, feeling heat shoot through my body in a flash.

"Wow!" said Miss Becker. "Okay, Mr. Woodson, that was a bit intense for this scene, but it certainly looked real enough. Miss Redmond, I loved the weak in the knees aspect you gave it. You two are naturals. Do we need to do it again in case the first time might have been a fluke? Maybe we should run through the scene again just to make sure. Please start from the beginning of that scene."

I was brought back to earth by her voice. Could she tell how affected I was by the kiss? Did she believe it was all acting? How she failed to see my body screaming in response to that kiss was a mystery to me! I was surprised that the whole rehearsal room wasn't staring at me. I needed to clear my head. "Miss Becker, can I run to the restroom first?" I asked, looking anxious.

Miss Becker saw my distress, and took it to mean that I needed the bathroom. Yeah, I sure did, but it wasn't what she thought. I hurried to the restroom back stage and went into a stall. There was a makeup room just inside the door with chairs and big mirrors for makeup application and touch up. Inside this room was the bathroom. I wanted privacy. I put my face in my hands. I had to get myself together. After a few minutes, I came out and went to the sinks. I washed my face. It felt so hot.

Back at rehearsal, Ash was leaning casually against one of the stage props talking to Miss Becker. He smiled when he saw me and winked. What did the wink mean? I didn't get it. Usually someone would wink if there was some kind of joke or something funny, but I didn't get the joke or feel very funny. Actually I did feel very funny, but not in a humorous kind of way.

"Ready?" Miss Becker asked, "Places! Get into your places and start from the same spot."

"Yes," Ash said. *No*, I thought. We had to do the lines prior to the kiss a few times since my brain had stopped working. Maybe it was my subconscious trying to fend off the severity of the kiss coming. I knew it'd be just as intense as the first one. That kiss had ripped me up, torn me apart and put me back together. I was shattered, but not in the same way as my meltdown after my experience with the Hodag. This one was pure feeling! I felt as if I was going to explode with the depth of the feeling. I tingled in places that I didn't even know existed. I felt hot and cold and sensations I couldn't begin to describe. A dorment part of me had been awakened, and I didn't know how to handle it. I focused hard on the lines, and we got to the kiss.

The second kiss was just as exciting as the first. It made my blood sing. Afterwards I looked into Ash's eyes. They were glowing. I mean, they were *really* glowing. In the stage light, it looked as if little light bulbs behind his eyes made the green of his eyes brighter. I had the feeling that in the dark, his eyes would be little green flashlights.

"That's a wrap. Good job, you guys! You can go home a little early today. See you tomorrow!" Miss Becker faced the stage, taking her eyes off of us once the kiss was finished. She missed the part where Ash and I stared at each other as if we were the only two people in the whole universe. When we heard her voice, we came back to reality, separated and went for our books and coats. I knew when Ash got back to earth because his eyes stopped glowing. We didn't talk until we were in the car.

"That was a good rehearsal, wasn't it?" Ash said looking at me as he buckled up.

"Yeah, I guess," I said. I stared out the windshield. I wasn't thinking about rehearsal, just the kiss. Only the kiss. It felt authentic. It was the most real thing I had ever experienced. We were supposed to be rehearsing parts in a play. It was supposed to look real without actually being real. I would have thought Ash had felt the intensity the way I had, but apparently not. He thought we had a *good rehearsal*. That's what he said. A good rehearsal! Maybe his body wasn't doing the crazy things on the inside mine was. I was an idiot. Again.

I didn't talk on the way home. I just stared out of the windshield. I didn't know what to say. When he dropped me off, he said he'd see me in the morning, and I mechanically said okay. He asked if anything was wrong. I said no. I grabbed my book bag and ran to the house. I was an hour earlier than usual. I hung my coat up and stepped into the living room. Olivia sat on the armchair talking to Mom.

"Hey, Olivia!" I yelled and went to give her a hug. Gosh, it was nice to see her! Once in a while, either Olivia or Forrest would pop in to see us. I loved that. She sure was a sight for sore eyes to me tonight.

As I stepped away from Olivia, I knew I was surrounded by love. Mom loved me. Olivia loved me. Ben and Forrest loved me, too. I thought of how much I was loved and, for some reason, started crying. Immediately, Mom and Olivia came running up to me, "Honey, what's wrong?" Mom asked softly, hugging me while Olivia rubbed my arm.

"Ash kissed me tonight!" I wailed. I felt like an idiot saying that, but there it was. It was out in the open for all to see my pain and anguish.

Mom stepped back. So did Olivia. "What?" she said. "What happened? Come sit down and tell us all about it."

"At rehearsal tonight." My voice broke, hard to get the words out. I felt like so stupid. "We had the big kiss scene at the end of the play. When Ash kissed me, I don't know how he did it, but . . . he rocked my world!" More softly, I said, "He doesn't even know. To him it was just rehearsal. An act. Pretend." I reached for a tissue.

"Oh, honey! You've just never experienced a kiss before," Mom said. "Some kisses are better than others."

Olivia nodded in agreement. "It's true! It depends upon who you're kissing!"

"Remember my boyfriend from D.C? He kissed me a couple of times. I hated it. It felt like kissing a Saint Bernard puppy!"

"I didn't see this coming," said Olivia, "and I should have."

"We can't be everywhere at once, now can we?" Mom said. "And you see more than anyone I know. Don't be too hard on yourself." Mom then looked back at me.

"How do you feel now?" she asked me.

"I feel stupid and young. I feel I've just touched the edge of life and it's scary and wonderful at the same time. I don't know what I want to do," I finished slowly.

"Yeah, that makes sense," Mom said. Then she asked Olivia, "Are wood nymph emotions much different from humans? I know you once told me that they are monogamous. Do you think Laurel has wood nymph emotions?"

She shrugged. "I don't think our emotions are a lot different from humans'. I think they're more mature in some ways and are not usually violent. As a rule, we're a peaceful species." Olivia smiled. "We do feel certain emotions quite intensely, though. A kiss can be quite overwhelming, even for us. For someone not used to this kind of intensity, it could easily have been hard to deal with."

Then Olivia said to me, "Feel the experience. Don't be embarrassed by it. I think you're going through a normal phase of life." Then she got up and said, "I've got to go, but I'll be back soon. I love you both!"

We walked her to the door. I saw her walk down the front porch stairs. Then just like that, she was gone. I really wished that I could do that jetting thing!

CHAPTER 14
THE PLAY

The play was about to start. We'd been going through dress rehearsals for the last couple of days. Tonight was the night. On one hand, I was excited. On the other hand, I was sad it would be over. I had enjoyed this closeness with Ash. Once the play was over, there would be no reason for him to hang around with me anymore. Rodney seemed to be thawing out. He was at least talking to me again. The comfort zone that he and I had together before I started hanging out with Ash seemed to be gone though. I felt bad about that.

Ash was still so polite to me when we were alone. He never looked at me the way Mr. Darcy looked at Elizabeth in the final scenes of the play. Not when he was out of character. During the play—especially the love scenes—he looked so tenderly at me, I could pretend he really did love me. I wanted him to. I wanted that kind of intensity. I realized now my feelings for him were very strong. It didn't matter to me that I was a hybrid (I liked that word better than "half breed") and he was a wood nymph. I loved him. I feared that Ash considered me a half breed, and that sounded so negative. He never said it, but that's what I thought. I knew I wasn't his equal, nor could I ever be. I didn't have the looks, talents, or anything else of a wood nymph. He'd never be able to accept me for myself. I just wasn't good enough.

He was polite, and that was it. I lived for the kissing scenes, but no one knew that! I kept my emotions locked up tight. I did what Olivia said. On the inside, I reveled in the kiss and the feelings they brought me. No one knew that the "acting" was the real me. The nonchalant person outside the play was the one acting. In the last month, the only time I saw Ash was when he picked me up for school, at school, and when he drove me home. He didn't come over unexpectedly anymore.

On many days when I didn't have to work or go to school, Mom and I went to the reservation or up to Forrest's home. Mom liked how welcoming Forrest's family was. He was always happy to see us. Olivia knew when we were coming and had a nice meal ready for us. She was a great cook.

I couldn't concentrate on my new family today. I had to focus on the play. In drama class, all we did was talk about exiting, entering, and facing the audience. We concentrated on last minute advice from Miss Becker. My mother had told all the people at her work about my being in the school play, and they were coming to see the it.

The play would run today, tomorrow, and Sunday. On Saturday and Sunday, we were doing an afternoon and an evening show. We'd be exhausted by the time this was over.

We spent a couple of hours in makeup getting dressed and ready. I had dyed my hair a dark brown with a washout hair dye. Because Ash and I looked so much alike, we would've looked like a brother and sister standing on the stage. We had to do something to look different. I came up with the hair dye idea. Miss Becker agreed. One stage hand's mother was a professional hairdresser. The girl asked her mother to do the girl's hair styles. She was generous enough to do up our hair. Stage hands took care of last minute issues, and we were at the point back stage when we could hear the people getting settled into the audience. Everyone was getting nervous. "Places everyone!" Miss Becker said. *Way too soon*, I thought. It was show time!

We'd rehearsed and rehearsed. There were no slip ups. No one made any obvious blunders. When it came to the kissing scene, for once I didn't lose myself in the kiss. The last thing I needed was to have the whole world see me lose myself in Ash's arms. This would be one time I couldn't bring myself back to reality. At the end of the play, we received a standing ovation. The applause was deafening. It had been a full house. It was hard to tell with the stage lights in my eyes, but I thought I saw Mom in the front row with Forrest and Olivia. The relief I felt was wonderful.

After the play was a reception in the gym. In full costume, all the actors joined family and friends who had come to see the play. A refreshment table held cookies and drinks and was staffed by students without a part of the play. Rodney, Noreen, Ash, and I all made our entrances. Rodney and Noreen walked in holding hands, and Ash and I walked in holding hands. Again, we received a round of applause. Mom, Forrest, and Olivia came up and hugged me.

"Oh, honey!" Mom exclaimed and handed me a bunch of roses. "You were fabulous!" I received flowers from Forrest and Olivia, too.

Ash's mom and a man who looked like an older version of Ash greeted him. Dr. Woodson and other family members also congratulated Ash. One guy stood out. He was obviously a wood nymph, so I figured he was a relative. In fact, there were a lot of wood nymphs clustered around us. There were very few humans in our immediate circle. People who worked with Mom were the only humans in the crowd.

While we were being congratulated, Ash held my hand. Even though I was getting hugged by more than one person at a time and cradled flowers in my other hand, so it would have been easier to hug people with one hand free, I didn't let go.

I saw Olivia stiffen and wondered what the problem was. At first, I thought it was being in public that made her nervous until I looked where she was looking. The male wood nymph I had noticed earlier from Ash's family was staring at Olivia. I saw him stiffen too. He broke away from Ash's group and approached Olivia. "Hello, Olivia," he said softly. He was staring at Olivia as a man dying of thirst would look at a glass ice water. I thought, *This is the guy who was in love with Olivia.*

"Hello, Hawthorn," Olivia replied just as softly. There was a special look in her eyes. Not hate. I saw some pain perhaps, and what appeared to be love, and I was well versed in facial expressions after this drama class and having been in the play.

Forrest also noticed the exchange between Olivia and Hawthorn. I thought I saw him flash angry and wondered if he'd make a scene. I couldn't imagine Forrest being angry, but his look was thunderous. I sure wouldn't want that look directed at me. Olivia put a restraining hand on his arm and whispered something to him. Forrest calmed.

Willow Woodson said, "Forrest, Olivia, and Valerie, we're having a party at our house tonight after the reception. Will you please join us?" I wasn't sure whether I hoped they'd refuse or accept. I couldn't do anything too embarrassing tonight, could I? Could I be with Ash and his family without feeling like an idiot?

Willow then looked at me, "You were wonderful tonight, Laurel. Both you and Ash played your parts perfectly. We're very proud of you. It'd be nice to have both the stars of the play at the party tonight."

I wasn't sure what to say. I finally realized that, at the very least, I should be gracious and said, "Thank you. The play was a group effort and wouldn't have worked without the hard work of a lot of people, but thank you for the compliment." Mom smiled.

To my surprise, Olivia said, "Yes, we'd like to come to your house." She looked at Forrest, and, while his eyes tightened just a bit, he nodded. Mom had complete trust in Forrest and Olivia's judgment, and I'm sure she was curious about Ash's parents. She'd heard the story about the day after the Hodag attack, after all. Besides, Ash's parents had sent her flowers on her birthday.

Mom raised an eyebrow at me as if to question what I thought about going to their party. "I'll go with the family's decision. Sure," I said. I really did like the idea of family. I smiled. Mom smiled, too.

We stayed at the reception at the school for another half hour or so, receiving congratulations from students, faculty, and other parents. Being the center of attention wasn't a bad thing. Soon though, I wanted to get out of my costume. I excused myself. Ash did the same. We walked back to the dressing rooms behind the stage.

"You really did a great job tonight, although the kissing scene could have been better," he said, squeezing my hand as we walked down the hallway. At that moment, we were alone. "Let's try the kiss again. I think you need more practice." He leaned his head down to kiss me, and I looked up at him. At first I was going to argue about the need for more practice. But his lips reached mine before I could speak. He started with the gentle pressure he had on our very first kiss. When I didn't pull away, he leaned in. I felt that heat shoot through me. He put his arms around me and I put my arms around him. I don't know if I was holding onto him to keep from sagging, or if he was holding me up, but this kiss was better than any one I had received from him. I had no idea how long we stood in the hallway locked in that embrace completely oblivious to the world around us.

Noreen suddenly was tapping me on the shoulder. "Get a room!" she said and busted out laughing. Ash and I broke apart, and I know I went beet red in the face. Noreen continued to the dressing room, laughing.

"I love you," Ash whispered and took my hand. He steered me toward the girl's dressing room. I was so busy staring at his beautiful face, I paid no attention to where I was going. When I found myself in the dressing room, I wondered if I'd walked in or floated. I didn't remember my feet touching the ground. I didn't even remember opening the door.

"He said he loved me!" I said in quiet wonder to Noreen who was taking her makeup off at the big mirror.

"Duh! I've known that for ages. Are you saying you didn't? You two've been an item for like the last month." She looked up with half her makeup off of her face.

I sat next to her and grabbed the pot of makeup remover and some tissues to clean my own face. "I didn't know. I've loved him almost since I met him, and I had no idea he felt the same," I said, wiping my face.

Noreen giggled. "You couldn't tell? *Everyone* else saw it." She rolled her eyes and went into the bathroom to change clothes. "Well, you know now!" she called out. "The question is, what are you going to do about it?"

"I don't know. I guess I'll just have to play it by ear." I replied.

Noreen came out in her jeans and sweatshirt and hung her costume in the wardrobe closet. "See you tomorrow! I can't wait to hear how the rest of your evening goes!" She sang as she left. I finished my makeup removal and quickly changed clothes. I hung my costume up and ran out of the door.

Ash was in the hallway waiting for me. "I heard what Noreen said," he said. "She's right, but . . . I didn't notice either. I've loved you for a while now. I don't care. I'm not going to fight my feelings for you anymore. I mean what I said. I don't care what anyone thinks." He grabbed my hand and kissed it.

"I love you too," I said, still in awe at this turn of events.

"That makes me glad!" he said happily. We almost skipped to meet our families. I don't think either of us felt the floor beneath our feet.

Mom and Olivia looked at each other when they saw us. Mom gave me a slightly puzzled look. *Hey*, I thought, *we'd just had our first performance as leads in the school play. We have a right to be happy and proud, right? Okay?* Maybe we were a little too happy and certainly walking closer together than usual. And we both had huge smiles on our faces. But our big grins could have been because the play went great, which it had. But I think my mom saw that our elevated mood was much more than just the pride of doing a great job in the play. I heard Forrest sigh as we walked to the cars. Did he realize that something had changed between us too? If I had to guess, I'd say that the sigh represented knowledge that he had to accept something he really didn't want to.

When we left the school, we drove in a convoy to Ash's house. I rode in Ash's car. At Ash's house, every light was lit. Yard lights I noticed for the first time gave us a clear path. While it was a cold night, the house looked warm and inviting.

Ash never left my side the entire evening. I'd never seen him so happy. I can't remember me being so happy. His mother would look at him and shake her head. I wondered if she realized something had changed for us. Ash's father didn't look quite as happy. Dr. Woodson gave me a big hug. "It's so nice to see you again, especially looking so happy." He was looking at Ash. I wasn't sure if he was speaking to him or me or both.

Forrest busied himself introducing my mother to Ash's family members. They obviously all knew one another. After a while, I looked for Olivia and didn't see her. I said to Ash, "Have you seen Olivia?" I looked around again. "What about Hawthorn?"

We both looked. There were a lot of wood nymphs in the house. I didn't know there were so many between the two clans. Ash had said that all of his clan was there, as well as the majority of mine. I hoped, in time, to get to know all these people. Right then I couldn't remember many of their names. I hoped to know all my clan's members in time.

Ash and I slowly worked our way through the crowd, smiling and accepting congratulations, and looking for Olivia and Hawthorn. I had the feeling if we found one we'd find the other. We searched the huge living room, family room, dining room, and den. No Olivia or Hawthorn. Ash tried listening for their voices, but with so many people talking, he couldn't pinpoint her voice. We finally made our way to the kitchen. There was Olivia, sitting on a counter, with Hawthorn standing in front of her with his hands on the edge of the counter on each side of her. He was really close to her, their faces only inches apart.

"I have been a fool. I'm so glad you're here. I've truly missed you," Olivia was saying softly to Hawthorn as we entered the kitchen. They didn't hear us enter. Their world consisted only of the two of them. I knew the feeling. A wood nymph could have heard us a mile away if paying attention. They weren't. Ash cleared his throat. They both turned to look at us, but Hawthorn didn't move his hands from where they were on the counter. The doorway was along the same wall as the counter, so they only had to turn their heads to look at us.

Olivia said, "This is my cousin, Laurel. You saw her in the play, but I don't think you've been introduced." She added, "She's my deceased cousin Leif's daughter."

"Hello," I said as Ash and I joined them. I felt kind of shy meeting Hawthorn, as if Ash and I had just intruded on a very personal moment, and we had.

"It's nice to finally meet you," Hawthorn said. "I've heard a lot about you." Then he turned to give Olivia the intense look I'd seen at the school.

"It is nice to meet you, too," I said, and then turned to Ash. "We should get back to the party."

Ash looked at Olivia and Hawthorn and smiled. "Yes, let's do that." I don't think that Olivia and Hawthorn saw when we left.

In our search for Olivia, we'd noticed the den was empty. We went back there. "I want to kiss you again," Ash said simply.

"And I want you to kiss me, too," I said

He bent his face down and kissed me. It was wonderful. I could feel my blood sing. I could feel my heart pound like it was trying to come out of my chest. I'd never felt so alive in my life. I was in love, and all the world was wonderful. With effort, we forced ourselves to rejoin the party given in our honor. We should be there. I felt like a star had lit my heart. I felt like I glowed like a star.

We had to be at school at noon the next day. Just after midnight, Mom said it was time to go. Ash kissed me on the forehead when we left. I assumed he didn't want to embarrass me by kissing me full on the lips in front of everyone. I appreciated the gesture. I thought it was too early for public displays of affection.

I smiled at him and waved good-bye. Mom and I drove home with Forrest in his BMW. Olivia had come with us, too, but she and Hawthorn weren't finished talking. They had left together earlier. I assumed they went to Hawthorn's place. I guessed they had a lot to catch up on. They hadn't spoken in years. Besides, Olivia could just jet home when she was ready.

"What did you think of the party?" Mom asked Forrest once we were in the car.

"The party itself was well prepared," Forrest said hesitantly. He seemed to be hedging away from what he really wanted to say. I didn't know what Mom was looking for, so I paid attention to the conversation.

"And?" she pushed. Clearly she wanted to hear Forrest's take on the day's events. Apparently she heard the hesitation in his voice, too.

"Well, the clan was very gracious. I had worries about how they would respond to you and Laurel. But, the truth is, they handled themselves well. I think you're the first humans they've ever invited to their house."

Mom settled back in her seat, so maybe that was the answer she was looking for. To be honest, I had worries, too, especially after the last time I had been there.

"It appears that you and Ash are getting pretty tight," Forrest said looking at me through the rear view mirror as I sat in the backseat.

I couldn't help the smile. "He said he loved me tonight." I probably should have filtered that statement.

"What?!" Mom said turning around to look at me. "Are you kidding me?"

Yup, should have filtered. "Nope," I said. She let out a big sigh.

I saw a lot of different emotions cross my mom's face. She looked at me a moment longer, then turned back. She said, "I'm not sure what I think about that. You're a little young for love."

"I don't know. I don't think so," I said.

Mom spun back around to face me. "How do you feel about him?" At that moment we were pulling up to our house.

As I got out of the car, I said simply, "I love him."

Forrest walked us to the porch. He waited while my mom unlocked the door and then hugged me good-bye. "Be careful with Ash," he whispered. "Are you sure he's the right one for you? Anyway, you really were great tonight. I may have to come and see every performance." He smiled and kissed me on my forehead before returning to his car.

Mom and I went inside. "Seriously, aren't you a little young to be in love?" she asked as she shut the door and we hung up our coats.

"I'll be eighteen in April. In some cultures, girls my age are already married with babies." It was a lame argument.

She pursed her lips. "I sure don't want to think that far ahead, and you shouldn't be, either. You're way too young for babies. What colleges have Ash applied to?" We sat in the dining room, our place for serious discussions. "You just got accepted at UWM. Please don't do anything to ruin your chances at college." Mom said, worried.

Why did parents always go there? Take everything so far? I stood. "Mom, I have to be at the school in just a few hours. I need to go to bed." At the stairs, I paused and said, "You raised me with decent values, Mom. I know I need to go to college. I know it is all well and good to love and be married, but I also need to be able to take care of myself. Does that pretty much cover it?" I asked.

That seemed to calm her down. She smiled. "Yes, honey. You know I only want you to have a good life. You're both so young. I don't want you to lose sight of your future because you're blinded by love. Good night. I'll see you in the morning. Oh, I'm assuming Ash is picking you up?" She got up and turned off the downstairs lights. She was trying to be funny, so I didn't have to answer.

I knew she was was really talking about sex. Why did parents always have to worry about sex? It wasn't like I was going to go jump in the sack with Ask now that we were officially dating. Okay, I only thought we were officially dating. Didn't telling someone you loved them lead to a more intensive relationship? And while I was eager for intensity, I wasn't ready for sex. I did love the idea that Ash was my official boyfriend though. At least official to me. I was still stunned by the idea that Ash had said he loved me. I knew I wasn't good enough for him. I didn't have any special talents. I couldn't even jet with him like Olivia and Forrest did together. I could see Hawthorn and Olivia jetting back and forth. Ash loved me now, but would he get tired of me because I was a plodding human without wood nymph capabilities?

As I got ready for bed, I put my hair in a scarf to keep from having the hair dye stain my pillow. I had to keep this goop in my hair for two more days. As I went to sleep, I imagined Ash's glowing green eyes and smiled as I drifted off to sleep.

WHEN ASH AND I GOT TO SCHOOL IN THE MORNING, Noreen started in on us about our budding relationship. Rodney at first looked surly when he found out that Ash and I had been kissing. But after a while, he seemed to accept the idea. Noreen was right. Everyone did think we were already boyfriend and girlfriend. The entire cast already thought we were a couple, so they yawned at the fact that Ash and I believed we were in a very new relationship.

After each performance, the school had a reception for the people who came to watch the play, the actors, and the stage hands. In the same way, we walked hand in hand into the reception. Noreen kept laughing at me. It wasn't a mean laugh. She just had great fun telling everyone that she had caught Ash and me kissing in the hallway. It seemed we just finished with the reception when it was time to get ready for the next performance. By the time we finished the second performance, we were all exhausted. Forrest was at both performances, and Mom came to the second performance of the day. I didn't see Forrest's car in the lot as we walked out after the second reception. Mom had parked close to the woods on the far side of the parking lot. One second Forrest was talking to me and her, and the next second he was gone. I guess he figured it was safe to jet if people thought he was riding with us. I rode home with my mom after agreeing that Ash should pick me up tomorrow to take me to school.

One more day of the play—two more performances—and it was all over. I had mixed feelings about it while I cleaned up for bed. I'd enjoyed the play and thought I would do something like this again. It was a good thing there was only one big play a year though. I didn't think I could handle more than one school play in one school year. That night I think I was asleep before my head hit the pillow.

Sunday was almost an exact repeat of Saturday. Forrest came to both shows, and Mom and Olivia to the second show. The big difference was that Hawthorn came to the play with Olivia. Other than Ash, none of the wood nymphs came in a car. They would walk to our cars with us, and then, when they knew no one was looking, they would quietly disappear. There was a pizza place in town where the cast party was to be held after the last performance. Ash and I walked my mom to her car. Ash told her we wouldn't be too late as there was school tomorrow.

The cast party was fun, but, I ate little of the pizza. Ash ate only the salad. The play had been a success and everyone knew it. Miss Becker basked in joy. There had been no last minute problems. None of the sets fell. No one forgot their lines. She stood up and said with tears in her eyes, "This has been the best play put on by this high school ever. You're all stars today!"

We all agreed that it'd been great fun and were glad we'd taken part in it. Ash and I didn't stay at the cast party very long. Neither did anyone else. Everyone needed to get some sleep.

Ash drove me home, When I walked in, Mom said Ben had called. He hadn't been near a phone and had been unable to text or call us for a week. Mom said he was sorry he hadn't been able to talk to me, but she'd been instructed to tell me how proud Ben was of me for being the lead in the school play. The coolest thing was that Ben told Mom he was going to be able to take some leave and was coming home for Christmas. Boy, would he be surprised about all of the changes when he got here.

I told Mom how excited I was about Ben's coming home. That really was great news. What an exceptional couple of days. I had been in my first play. I was in love for the first time. I only wished Ben could have seen the play. He would have liked it.

I was in bed by midnight, knowing I had to get up for school even though I was going to be exhausted. My last thought before sleep was the good-night kiss Ash had given me at the front door. Even though it had been cold outside, he'd made me quite warm on the inside.

CHAPTER 15

I found out from Forrest a couple of weeks or so after the play that he was concerned about Ash's feelings for me. While a wood nymph didn't take feelings between wood nymphs lightly, Forrest was wondering if Ash was considering me a wood nymph. Did he consider me an equal or something or someone he could cast aside later without thought? Uncle Forrest did not want to see me get hurt.

I loved having family to care about me. This was new and sweet. I'd always had Mom and Ben, but now it had been months since I found out that we were not just the three of us anymore. My family no longer consisted of just Mom, Ben, and me. I was still getting used to the idea of extended family.

It was a Saturday, and I had just gotten off work. I'd worked the early shift that finished at 5:00 p.m. Forrest and Mom were in the living room drinking coffee. "Hi, honey!" Mom had called as I walked in the door. "Forrest has a couple of issues he'd like to discuss. Do you have a couple minutes?" she asked. I noticed she didn't look really comfortable. Forrest had always had my best interest at heart, so I believed it couldn't be anything bad.

"Sure. What's up?" I asked and sat down next to Forrest. "What's on your mind?" I loved seeing Forrest. He was fun to be around. He treated me as if I had value, that I mattered. He took my thoughts and feelings about things seriously, too. He never treated me like a child.

Forrest smiled as I sat down. "How are things going with you and Ash?" he asked.

This was an easy question. "Great! He's the most sensitive and loving guy I've ever met. He's a million times better than my other boyfriend." I smiled.

"How do you get along with his parents?" Forrest asked, watching me closely.

I quickly said I did. Ash and I had gone to his house a number of times in the last couple of weeks. Sometimes I ate dinner there. We wanted to be together all the time. There weren't enough hours in the day for us. Mom was patient with us, talking about "new love." She didn't know if our love was the real thing or an infatuation, but she treated me with respect about it. I figured she thought I was smart enough not to blow it out of porportion. I think once she realized we weren't doing anything stupid, she relaxed.

Kids at school seldom hid the fact they were in intimate relationships. Some had break ups after sexual relationships, and it was awkward to be around them. The girls seemed to feel self-conscious and quite frankly, they said they felt used. Their hearts were broken, and they had a hard time dealing with it. Occasionally, it would be a guy who had the broken heart. All in all, it was really sad to see this happen.

Ash and I had only been going out for a couple of weeks. We talked about what we liked and what we didn't like. We talked about our goals. There were certainly sexual feelings between us, and I felt as time went by that I was getting closer to the idea of a physical relationship, but I just wasn't quite ready for one yet.

Forrest didn't know what an intimate relationship would be like between a wood nymph and a human. I told him that it must work the same as with two humans because I existed. Regarding sex, I guess I felt that one didn't miss what one never had. At least, that was what I told myself. Neither Ash nor I had experience with sex. Right then there were too many negatives. We'd settled on kissing and holding hands.

We did study together. It wasn't unusual for Mom to come home from a long day at work to find books all over the dining room table while we did our homework.

I'd been accepted at UWM as an undergraduate in Chemistry. The school also had a great grad school program in Chemistry, which was what I wanted my Ph.D. in. The school also had a great Physics program, the area Ash wanted to major in. We could go to school and stay together. Ash had received his acceptance letter from UWM that week. We'd both excelled in our classes. Difficulty in academics wasn't an issue for either of us as long as we kept our head in the game. We felt we could love each other as long as we also stayed focused on the long-term goals.

We studied at Ash's house, too. We tried to divide our time evenly between the two homes. I was over my discomfort about being around Ash's mom. She was always nice. Sometimes when she was cooking, she'd allow me to help her. It wasn't unusual to have some of Ash's cousins come to have dinner with us. Ash's dining room table could seat twelve comfortably. They had a huge kitchen, and Willow made cooking for that many people look easy. After watching her work in her kitchen, I felt she could easily have been a caterer. She had never gone on to college. I don't even know if she went to a human school. She'd met Ash's dad, Elm, as a teenager, and she had bonded with him. They'd been together ever since. Ash had told me this.

Elm Woodson traveled a lot. Even though he could jet, he had projects that drew him away from home for days. He was a geoscientist and did surveys and studies throughout the world. Ash explained to me one time that geoscientists studied the earth, what it was made of, and analyzed all aspects of the land, rocks, and water. They looked for natural resources like metals, water, and fuel. His dad was particularly interested in finding minerals and metals. His wood nymph gift was being able to locate metal ores or fossil fuels in the ground. He pretended to use human equipment to work with humans.

He enjoyed working with human equipment and admired many of his fellow human scientists. Ash told me he had no patience with people not of his intellectual level, however. Elm ignored me when I was there. Did that mean he thought that I was intellectually his inferior? But I wasn't at his house to be his pal, right? He'd ask Ash questions about his studies and showed appreciation when Ash told him at dinner one night that he'd been accepted at UWM for Physics. Ash's dad never talked to me. As I thought about it, I couldn't remember his congratulating me after the school play. At the time, I didn't think anything of it. But now, with Forrest's questions, I wondered if there was something to be concerned about.

"I know Willow likes me." I told Forest. "Ash's dad's never speaks to me. I've seen him around, of course. But we've never had a conversation or anything."

"Don't you think that's peculiar? Doesn't that bother you?" Mom asked.

"Should it?" I asked. Even though Forrest's questions were making me doubt my relationship with Ash, I didn't want him or Mom to know that. "It's not like we have anything in common." I gave Mom and Forrest a level look.

"I'm not sure if it should matter or not," she said thoughtfully. "I would've expected at least a hello or good-bye or something. I find it odd he doesn't talk to you at all."

"Well, Ash brings me home with him, so it is not like Elm has had to answer the door and greet me. I think he just has other things on his mind."

"I'm not trying to hurt you," Forrest said, "but I think you should be aware of something. I don't think Elm thinks you're right for his only son. I think he only tolerates you for Ash's sake. I absolutely believe Elm thinks Ash'll get over you. I've heard that he's been in contact with some European wood nymph clans with teenage daughters. He plans for them to come to the Wisconsin north woods for a visit."

Forrest scowled. "If we had a wood nymph in our clan who you liked, I'd certainly feel you were good enough for him! This is part of why we had our last falling out between the clans. That whole clan tends to be narrow minded and prejudiced. "

"Are you telling me that Elm's trying to match Ash with a foreign wood nymph? Ash'd never tolerate that! He loves me!" I laughed, but it sounded forced.

"We love you, honey. No matter what happens." Mom said. Then in what appeared to be an afterthought she said, "You're right. Of course, Ash wouldn't hurt you. He does love you," but her expression didn't match her words.

"You feel threatened for me, don't you? You think Ash's dad really could influence Ash. You think there's the possibility that some new wood nymph girl from Europe will take Ash away from me." I was astounded. "Not a chance in hell." I stated emphatically. I wasn't one to swear, but this whole idea had me upset. The idea was appalling. But were they right? Was I being set up for a broken heart?

I could almost feel my old fears coming to the surface. I had felt the same way, thought I wasn't good enough for Ash. I was also the closest thing to a female teenaged wood nymph in the north woods. Was that the only reason Ash fell in love with me? Because I had no competition? A partial wood nymph was better than no wood nymph?

"I hope for your sake you're right," Forrest said. "I don't want you to get hurt."

I didn't want to get hurt either. Was that what was happening? "Is that it?" I asked, ready to end that conversation. Ash was due over in twenty minutes, and we were going over to Hawthorn's house to have dinner with him and Olivia. Whatever had caused Olivia and Hawthorn to separate all of those years ago appeared to have been resolved. I wouldn't ask questions, but I would be there to listen if Olivia ever wanted to tell me about it. In the meantime, I didn't want to think about Ash not loving me. I wanted him to love me forever.

"Yes, I'm sorry to upset you. That wasn't my intention. I just want you to know what's going on," Forrest said softly, standing up to give me a hug. "I think you're perfect," he said.

I knew he didn't care about my mixed blood, but did it really matter to Ash's family?

"Don't worry about it," I said, trying to ease his mind and my own while I was at it. "I'm not going to worry about it." I went upstairs to change out of my work clothes. The problem was, I was going to worry about it. This idea was going to worry me and fester like a gangrenous sore. I didn't want it to, but there it was. Could a beautiful wood nymph take Ash away from me? The same insecurity that had kept me from believing that Ash really loved me in the first place flooded back with a vengeance. It was like the vengeance gods had decided that I was too happy.

I put on my best pair of jeans and a nice top with a nice sweater. I even applied a bit of makeup. I wanted to look good tonight. I needed to believe that I looked as pretty as Olivia. Right now, I felt like the dumpy frumpy girl in school. I knew I was not dumpy and frumpy, but I also knew that only applied in the human world. In the human world, I was quite attractive. But in the wood nymph world, I was the frumpiest. one of all. I was a half breed, tainted. Ash would meet someone better and dump me.

I was sitting on my vanity seat pondering about this when I heard Ash's car pull up in the driveway. I blinked back the tears that had gathered.

"No later than midnight!" Mom called as I ran down the stairs.

"Okay," I said as I got my coat. "See you tonight."

"I love you!" Mom and Forrest said at exactly the same time.

I yelled back, "Yeah, I love you both, too!" No matter what happens, I was loved, I told myself as I went to the car.

But would that be enough? If Ash dumped me for another wood nymph, would I be able to get over it? I walked to his car and looked through the windshield at the guy who owned my heart. Would being loved by others be enough? Would I be able to handle Ash leaving me for someone so much better than I was? Did Ash's dad really believe any wood nymph was better than I was? Was it true that he was actually importing female teenaged wood nymphs? While not all of them had lots of abilities, each wood nymph had at least some kind of ability, as far as I knew. I had no special abilities. At least no abilities that mattered.

"What's the matter?" Ash asked as I got into the car. "You look like something's bothering you."

"Yeah, I guess there is something bothering me," I said, not sure how to start this, but deciding to come right out with it. "According to Forrest, Olivia saw your dad bring some European clan members to your place for a visit." There, that was harmless. There was no accusation in that statement.

"Funny you should say that. My dad did mention something about that today. Some European clan guy wants to come and see the Wisconsin woods. They're supposed to be here in a few days and stay for Thanksgiving, maybe longer. Apparently this geoscientist is bringing his whole family on the visit."

"Interesting. Did he tell you what his family consists of? Is the family a wife with sons?" I asked.

"No, no sons that I know of. He is bringing his wife and three daughters." Ash said and smiled at me. "It's a good thing we have a big house."

I didn't respond. I just looked out of the windshield.

"Is that a problem?" Ash asked, slipping his arm around me.

I leaned into his arm, but I didn't reply. I usually had a comment for everything, but not this time. I didn't know what to say. Should I tell him that Olivia saw his dad trying to set him up with another wood nymph in order to get rid of me? We drove in silence for a while and then we were going down the private road to Hawthorn's house. I hadn't been to Hawthorn's house before.

When we pulled up to the front of the house, the yard and driveway lights were on. It was getting darker earlier every day. We were a week away from Thanksgiving. That was a human holiday. The winter solstice was on December 21st, the shortest day of the year, and was a big wood nymph holiday. Most wood nymphs celebrated both the winter and summer solstices.

Hawthorn and Olivia came to the door to greet us together. They were holding hands. "Hi, come on in!" Olivia said smiling and coming to give me a hug. The house was just as beautiful as I had expected it to be. Hawthorn liked modern human styles of furniture. Nothing on the inside of his house reflected that he was a wood nymph in any way. His house and furniture matched beautifully, as if he'd an expensive interior designer come in and set it up.

Hawthorn hung up our coats as Olivia brought us into the living room. She was smiling, looking very comfortable here. She would look perfect as the mistress of the house. She had a pitcher of ice water with lemon slices on the coffee table. Olivia poured us each a glass of water and handed them to us after we were seated. I ran my hand along the fabric of the couch. It looked like the set for an expensive magazine.

"How's school?" she asked looking at both of us as she sat in the loveseat set perpendicular to the couch.

"We both got straight A's this semester," I said proudly looking at Ash. He smiled back. He raised his glass in a mock toast.

"How does it feel not to have to rehearse for the play anymore?" asked Hawthorn as he sat down next to Olivia.

"I don't miss the memorization of the lines, but I did like the kissing scene!" Ash said laughing and raising my hand to his mouth to kiss the back of my fingers. I smiled. Sometimes he was so old fashioned. I couldn't imagine a modern-day teenage guy kissing the back of anyone's hand.

"Me, too," I said. Then I remembered what Forrest had said, and asked Olivia, "Olivia," I started, "Forrest told me you saw some wood nymphs coming from Europe. What did you see, exactly?" I leaned toward Olivia, and Ash looked from me to her.

Olivia kind of stared off into space and I wondered if she was trying to clarify her vision. Maybe she was trying to put it into words. After a moment, she looked at us and said, "In a couple of days, a family will come. There is a father, mother and three daughters. The three daughters will be sixteen, seventeen and nineteen years of age. They will be staying for a few weeks. They will be here over Thanksgiving and possibly stay and celebrate the winter solstice with Ash and his family. The last part gets a bit fuzzy." This last part she said looking at Ash.

Olivia continued to look at Ash and said, "Your dad would prefer for you to find someone more suitable to you. He wants you to lose your infatuation with the mixed-blood human. That is what he's told the visiting family's father."

Olivia then turned to me and said, "I didn't want to tell you both this, but you asked. I guess it's better to hear it now and not to have this dropped on you out of the blue later. Oh, honey." She said reaching to take my hands. "I'm sorry. I love you as if you were my own daughter."

"There's no way my dad would do that to me," Ash said looking at Olivia and me. "He knows I love Laurel. What could he be thinking? I'll always love Laurel."

"He's thinking that I'm not good enough for you," I said softly, looking down. I missed the sad look that passed between Olivia and Hawthorn.

"You're perfect for me!" Ash almost yelled. He stood up and started pacing the living room.

"Oh, Ash, I knew this was too good to last. I really don't know all of your cultural rules, as you people . . ." I saw Olivia flinch at the "you people" part. I took a deep breath and continued. "Wood nymphs conform to human rules to blend in with human society. If your father really wanted you to break up with me, would you have to do it?" I was almost in tears. Ash hadn't broken up with me yet, but I knew it was going to happen. It was just a matter of time.

As we sat there in silence for a while, the timer in the kitchen went off. Dinner was ready to be served. Olivia and Hawthorn went into the kitchen. The dining room table had already been set. Ash and I sat down where Olivia pointed us to sit.

I kind of picked at my food. I had no appetite even though everything looked and smelled delicious. In fact, as I looked around, I saw that no one had much of an appetite. After dinner, we returned to the living room

"What can we do?" Olivia asked Hawthorn. "You know Elm best. What can we do to help Laurel and Ash?"

"Nothing. Once Elm sets his mind on something, it's almost impossible to change it. He tried to break us up, remember? It worked for all of those years. He thought you were too beautiful and would never be able to settle down with me. I listened to him, and I blamed you." Hawthorn said with a big sigh.

"I could have fought harder for us at the time, though," Olivia said.

"What are you saying?" Ash asked, getting defensive. "Dad's not a bad guy."

Ash had no idea that his father was apparently a manipulator. "He is just bringing some friends to the house for a visit. It's not a big deal. Let's not overreact."

He looked at me. "Laurel, you know I love you. That won't change. Will you please give me some credit, here?"

Hawthorn and Olivia tried to change the subject, but everyone was uncomfortable. I tried to shake off the feeling of impending doom, but I just couldn't. I tried to smile and enjoy myself, but it was a weak effort. After an hour or so, I said I had a headache and wanted to go home. I think everyone knew I didn't really have a headache but didn't know what to say to make me feel better. I was working myself into quite a state of panic by the time we left the house. Both Ash and I were quiet as we left Hawthorn's house.

"I don't have to take you home," Ash said as we got into his car. "We could be alone somewhere for a while. Why don't we have some alone time?"

"I'd like that," I said. He drove toward my house. Since my driveway was a private road a mile long and we were the only house on the road, Ash stopped about halfway down the driveway and he turned off the car. It was highly unlikely anyone would just happen to come across us.

We took off our seat belts and I scooted over next to him. We hugged. We stayed that way for about an hour, just hugging and enjoying the quiet solitude of being alone. Finally, my body was starting to cramp. "I hate to say this," I said, "but my back hurts. I'm getting uncomfortable. Maybe I should go home, now." I said getting back into my seat and putting my seat belt back on.

Ash started the car and drove to my house. "I really do love you," he said. "No one can change that." Outside my front door we hugged again.

"I know you do," I said. And I did know it at this moment. But would it last? I kissed Ash good-bye and waved as I went into the house.

"You're home early," Mom said as I walked in. I walked into the living room. Mom was stretched out on the couch reading.

"Yeah, I just wasn't real good company tonight. I talked to Olivia about the European family coming to stay at Ash's. She said they'll be there in few days. I just can't stand it. I can't stand that Ash's dad hates me. It drives me crazy to have his dad think I'm not good enough for his son. I don't like to be told I'm not good enough! It's bad enough when I believe I'm not good enough for Ash! No one ate much at dinner and then I told them I had a headache," I said with a big sigh.

"Do you want to talk about it?" Mom asked as she stood up. "We can sit here in the living room."

I really didn't feel like talking. I'd said all that I wanted to say. I didn't want a bunch of sympathy or words of encouragement. I wanted to be alone with my misery and horrible thoughts. "I'm pretty tired. I think I'll go to bed," I said softly.

Mom didn't press. She gave me a hug and said, "I'm here if you need me."

"I know. Right now I just want to be alone," I replied. I felt as if my world was crashing, and I didn't know what to do about it. I had to figure out how to cope with the feelings of despair crowding into my mind.

"If you and Ash love each other as much as you think you do, you'll get through this!" Mom called to me as I headed up the stairs.

I hoped she was right. I kind of wished I'd tried harder to have a close human girlfriend. Mary would be a good friend, I thought. After Ash and I had made our relationship public, we started eating our lunches with my old lunch table crowd. Even Rodney accepted my relationship with Ash. While we would probably never be as close as we had been, it was nice that Rodney was accepting that I loved Ash.

If I had a human girlfriend, what would I tell her? That my boyfriend's dad didn't think I was good enough for his son? I'd guess that would be safe. I sure couldn't tell her the whole truth.

I sat on my bed. What could I do? Ash didn't think his dad was doing anything wrong. That probably meant that his dad never told Ash that he thought I wasn't good enough. I wondered if Ash didn't fully understand Olivia's talent or if he didn't believe it. Either way, a family of wood nymphs was coming and at least one of the daughters was expected to take Ash away from me. Could she do it? Of course, she could. They could jet together. Who knew what else they could do together! It'd be likely they would have more in common. Ash and the European girl would both be pure wood nymphs. I sat on the edge of my bed in the dark and stressed myself out until I heard my mom go to bed. I sighed, cleaned up, changed into my pajamas and went to bed. It was a long time before I fell asleep.

CHAPTER 16
THANKSGIVING

Ash came over on Sunday morning and we talked about the visitors coming to his house. I tried to be open minded and think of them in the way Ash did. They were a clan family coming for a visit. This didn't mean anything. The fact that they had three teenage daughters didn't mean anything. I did my best to put it out of my mind. We watched TV and played video games and the day flew by.

The rest of the week had school and work. We spent time doing homework or hanging out at my house. We didn't go to his house anymore. I had to work on Wednesday evening, so I drove to school that day. It was easier to just drive from school to work without wasting the time to drive home to get my car. I didn't see Ash that night.

The next day was Thanksgiving. I had hoped to take Ash with me to Olivia's house for Thanksgiving, but Ash's dad had plans for his family on Thanksgiving Day and prevented him from going with us. We were originally going to have Thanksgiving dinner at Olivia's house, but most of the clan wanted to celebrate the American tradition of Thanksgiving by being with their new human family members. They didn't care I was half wood nymph or even that my mom was fully human. They wanted to get to know us. Mom was the first full human that they wanted to get to know personally. I think my being the first human and wood nymph hybrid made them curious about me.

They had a place used as a celebration house between their homes in a kind of park put together for social gatherings when one house just wasn't big enough.

Mom and I drove up to the celebration house in her Jeep. I was looking forward to this dinner and wished that Ash could have come with us. I wished he could see how other wood nymphs accepted me.

The food was always good when Mom and I visited Olivia. I believed she and the rest of the clan would make this event something particularly special.

I loved how welcoming the clan was. Celebration house looked like a huge log cabin from the outside and like a banquet hall on the inside. It had a combination of wood nymph and human decorations, including the silly little fold-up turkey table decorations on each table.

There were four chandeliers down the center of the ceiling that could be electric or candle lit, depending on what kind of ambience whoever was throwing the party wanted at the time. Today I saw that they used electricity. I thought they might have had this because electric lights gave off more light for human eyes. There was a kitchen off one end of the banquet hall area, and I could smell turkey cooking. I could also smell other wonderful cooking smells, but I couldn't identify all of them. The whole room smelled amazing.

Just inside the door, Hawthorn, with Olivia, waited for us. While he smiled at me and said hello, I noticed that his smile didn't quite reach his eyes. I think I made him uncomfortable. He loved Olivia and would put up with anything to be with her, but I don't think he fully accepted the whole human-wood nymph togetherness thing. I saw the surprise in his eyes when Forrest and a lot of other wood nymphs came over to hug me and Mom and tell us how welcome we were as we entered the hall. I think Hawthorn was impressed by their sincerity.

A young male wood nymph stood next to Olivia. He looked a lot like her— gorgeous. Getting to know the different wood nymphs and separating them was kind of like learning to tell identical twins apart. All wood nymphs looked a lot alike, but there were differences between them. While all were beautiful; some were more beautiful than others. This guy was breathtaking in his perfection.

"This is my brother, Douglas!" Olivia said bringing him over to us while holding his arm. "This is Laurel and her mom, Valerie."

I could tell by his expression that he'd heard of us. I shouldn't have been surprised. Everyone in this clan had known about me years before I knew anything about them. He looked interested. I wondered if he was just curious about me, or if he was genuinely interested in me. He didn't look appalled or disgusted at all. He gave me a measuring look, and it appeared what he saw pleased him. I wasn't sure in what way, but I didn't really care. I just liked the idea of being accepted.

"Hello. It's very nice to meet you, Douglas!" Mom said, holding out her hand to shake his. He looked at her hand for a second and then reached out to shake it. For a second, he looked confused. This was a human cultural thing. I'm sure he knew about the practice from study of the human world, but shaking hands didn't seem to be a natural reaction for him. That made me think—what was normal for wood nymphs when meeting someone new?

"Me, too!" I said, holding out my hand as well. After he shook Mom's hand gently, he took my hand, but instead of shaking it, he brought the back of my hand to his lips and kiss it. Ah, I'd seen that before. Ash did it all of the time. It was so Victorian. I thought it was Ash showing affection. Maybe not. Just a greeting?

Mom raised an eyebrow at that. I'd explain it to her later. We were in their village, and in their comfort zone. We would see more of their normal behaviors here than anywhere else, I thought. And, when in Rome . . .

I was almost mesmerized by Douglas's beauty and manners. I couldn't help but stare. I had to force myself to act normally.

"Valerie, I'd like you to meet some of the village elders," Forrest said, taking her hand. "You've met some of them, but there are more."

As Mom allowed Forrest to sweep her away, she looked back at me. Olivia tucked her hand around my elbow and led me to a table near a raised band stand. "Laurel, come and talk with us for a bit. Okay?"

I saw Mom and Forrest at a table with a group of elderly wood nymphs. As humans aged, their facial skin often looked like creased leather or papery, dry and thin. Older wood nymphs' skin took on the look of wood bark, wrinkled and folded like the bark of an ancient oak tree. The look was similar but not identical. I smiled at my mom, thinking I'd have more fun with Olivia and her brother than chatting with a bunch of old people. Mom smiled back at me between introductions. I knew she'd be fine.

Olivia and Douglas led me to a table that looked as if it was made of cedar. It didn't look so much "made" as a tree that had been "grown" into a table. Like my dock. It had a "natural" flat side on top. The base curved up to the table top in one flowing piece, spreading out and flattening to form the top. All the tables looked like this.

I couldn't help but notice Douglas as he walked in front of me. He was dressed casually in earth tones. The clothes looked human made, but they were tailored to fit his body. He had a Henley-style shirt that wasn't too tight, but showed how perfect his body was. I could almost see his muscles ripple in his back under his shirt. His pants fit perfectly, allowing that, perfect flowing walk characteristic of all the wood nymphs I'd met. He had a catlike grace. His body reminded me a lot of Ash's. Douglas's body was just a bit more mature. That was probably what Ash's body would look like when he was a fully mature adult wood nymph. While I'd thought his body was great, in comparison to Douglas's, Ash's face and figure were only a good rough draft of the ultimate final product.

After we sat down, Olivia asked how my last few days had gone since she'd seen me, and I said that I was still worried about the visitors.

"What visitors?" Douglas asked.

Someone came out of the kitchen and looked around. Olivia said, "Oh, I've got to help in the kitchen. Laurel will answer the question. Please excuse me as I tend to the turkey." She excused herself to go help in the kitchen.

"Can I help with anything?" I offered starting to stand up.

"No, no. I've got it. You're a guest here! Enjoy yourself! I always wanted you to get to know my brother! I'll be back soon." She hurried into the kitchen.

Left with Douglas, I was instantly self-conscious. I sighed and then asked the obvious question, "How much do you know about me?"

"Um, I know that your dad's from our clan and your mom's human," he said simply. His voice was soft and soothing, the perfect tone to carry to my ears without his having to raise it over all of the voices in the room.

"Does it bother you that I'm a half breed?" I asked.

He sucked in a quick breath. "I like to think of you as a hybrid. Half breed doesn't sound very complimentary. I think you're unique and interesting. I'm glad to meet you. I've heard of you, of course. But, other than what Forrest's observed and told us about you, I don't know much." He shrugged and smiled. I almost fainted at the beauty of his smile. His teeth were perfectly white, and he had a dimple on one side of his face when he smiled. He looked like he smiled a lot.

"I've only known of you for a couple of months," I told him. "I've only known I'm part wood nymph for just a bit longer. This is still very new to me."

"We have the rest of our lives to get to know each other better. I think I like having you as part of my family!" He reached over to hold my hand. "Now what were you going to tell me about visitors?" He released my hand and sat back.

"Oh, right." I said, folding my hands in front of me on the table. "I have a boyfriend, Ash, who's a wood nymph. His father doesn't approve of my hybrid status. He feels I'm inferior. He's bringing a family of European wood nymphs to visit. They have three teenaged daughters. I think that they arrived yesterday."

"Ash? Ash Woodson's your boyfriend? Okay. Wow. That's interesting. You move to Wisconsin, and you get a wood nymph boyfriend instead of a human one." He smiled. "So? Is that a problem?" he asked, his head tilted to one side.

"Well, Ash's father's trying to set him up with a full wood nymph girl. That's why he's having this particular family visit. Olivia said she had a vision where Ash's father actually said he wanted Ash to be with a pure wood nymph girl. Elm doesn't think I'm good enough for his son. I wanted to bring Ash with me today, but his father told him he couldn't come."

"What nonsense! I think you're fabulous!" He leaned over the table toward me again. "Do you know our whole clan thinks of you as our future? The birth rate of wood nymphs has slowed down. Fewer and fewer children are being born throughout the world. Some clans are doing better than others, but all of them are getting smaller."

"Yeah, but I don't have abilities. I can't even jet!" I said, sitting up straighter. "Why would anyone want to blend with a human and lose abilities?"

"Isn't it better to lose some abilities, than to lose a whole people?" he asked softly. "Our minds and values are very similar to a human's. We have pretty much the same feelings and emotion. I spend most of my time interacting with humans, so sometimes I think I'm more human than wood nymph.

He shrugged and looked away. "I'm the youngest in the clan, next to you. A lot of older clan members think our species is dying off. If things don't change, they believe we may become extinct in the not too distant future! Your existence breathes new life into our world! Just think of it! If wood nymphs can have children with humans, and the hybrid offspring have babies with wood nymph fathers, it could save our species from extinction. While we may not be pure wood nymphs anymore, wouldn't it be better to have hybrid wood nymphs than none at all?"

I stared at him. Was I the future? If I ended up with Ash—and we had children —would more wood nymphs look to humans as potential mates?

"Um, I hear what you're saying. But, uh, just hypothetically speaking, what if who I want to marry ends up not being a wood nymph?" I asked. I was beginning to feel like a science experiment.

His eyes grew large. "Oh, no! I didn't mean to make you feel uncomfortable. I'm not necessarily talking about you alone! All I'm saying is, you're the first of your kind! Wood nymphs, as far as I know, never wanted to have a human spouse before. Sexual activity maybe, but there's never been a child before. Now, maybe with having you in the clan, other wood nymphs can see that a relationship with a human isn't a bad thing. Leif really loved your mother. I believe that, in the short time your mother knew Leif, they really did bond! No one knew a wood nymph could bond with a human. It hadn't been done before! Your birth opens up a whole set of new possibilities! A mixed couple can bond and produce offspring. That's huge!" Douglas said excitedly.

"What do you mean by the word 'bond'?" I asked.

"Wood nymphs mate for life. Once one wood nymph conjoins with another, that bond is for life. Neither could ever be happy with anyone else. Sadly, when one spouse dies, the other usually dies shortly thereafter," Douglas explained to me.

"How old are they when they bond?" I asked, getting a strange feeling about this conversation.

"That's not set. They could be as young as teenagers," he said thoughtfully. "Although, I've heard of instances where two wood nymphs didn't bond until they were in their forties or later. But, that was when wood nymphs had much longer lives."

"Is it possible that Ash and I have bonded?" I asked feeling a bit lightheaded. What if we had?

Douglas looked closely at me. "Yes, I suppose. There is no time table, or in your case, not even a precedence. But humans don't always bond for life. A great many couple get divorced. Some humans even remarry if their spouse dies. Look at your mom. After she thought Leif had abandoned her, she was able to find a human mate and find happiness.

"If Ash bonded with you and you didn't bond with him, it could be really bad for him. I guess the question is, did the wood nymph characteristic of bonding get passed on to you?" Douglas sat back in his chair and waited for my response.

I sighed and said softly. "It might have. I can't imagine life without Ash in it."

"If you and Ash have bonded, then Ash's father's a fool to try to keep you two apart." Douglas said.

I was relaxed around Douglas. He made me feel as if I had value. Was I the only possible future for the wood nymphs? Douglas made me feel as if I was the start of something new and good. I didn't feel inferior around him. We talked until it was time to eat. Olivia and others flitted about bringing dishes to the tables.

They wouldn't let me or my mom help with anything. A group of male wood nymphs gathered in a corner on what appeared to be a bandstand near the table where I sat with Douglas. They opened some cases and took out what appeared to be musical instruments. Some looked like wood-wind instruments I knew. Others looked kind of like violins mixed with something else. There were percussion instruments, too.

I had a lot on my mind when Forrest sat at the end of the first table as the head of the clan. Douglas, my mom, Olivia, Hawthorn, and me, as well as a lot of the elders sat at the head table with him. I was glad no one seemed to think this strange. I wondered if most of the wood nymphs at this gathering saw me as someone to bring new life to this clan and to wood nymphs in general.

The day would've been perfect if Ben and Ash had been here. I couldn't wait for Ben to see all of this and meet these people. I smiled. He'd have a hard time believing all of it. I thought he'd like the idea of extended family, though. I wondered what he'd think of my being the future hope for the wood nymphs.

For dinner, we had the traditional stuffed turkey, but the stuffing was unlike anything I'd tasted before. I tasted water chestnuts in it, but it had a lot of other flavors in it, I couldn't identify. I knew that whatever was in it and the other foods was healthy. Healthy never tasted better. And everyone was having a great time. Maybe other human traditions could be brought into the clan culture. I liked that thought.

I only received a short text message from Ash on Thanksgiving afternoon. He had said he was thinking of me and missing me. He also said he'd met the visitors. I wasn't psychic, but I figured that was why Ash hadn't come with me today.

The pleasant music the band played before dinner, seemed just a warm up to the amazing, beautiful music that they played after dinner. After everyone had finished eating, the tables were cleared. It took little more than a minute for the women wood nymphs to clear the tables. They jetted to the tables in a blur, and when they blurred away, dirty dishes were gone. After the tables were cleared, the band started playing.

There was an open area between the band and the tables. After dinner, some of the women changed into traditional flowing color-changing dresses.

"This is the traditional wood nymph celebration dance!" Douglas whispered.

I thought this might have been the dance my grandfather probably saw in the woods when he told my mother about seeing the wood nymphs. The dance reminded me of exotic belly dancing. The dresses looked like they had layers of a variety of earth tones and greens that shimmered and complimented their bodies while showing off the women's curves.

The movement that the dresses made reminded me of leaves reflecting sunlight and shadows that flitted through the woods in a gentle wind. The dance was seductive, sensual, yet innocent, all at the same time.

More dances followed, a couple with men and women dancing together. The men wore the same colors as the women, but their clothes were more substantial and less ethereal. They reminded me of Peter Pan clothes, the pants similar to tights, without the foot portion and the tops tunics that flowed like the women's dresses. They all danced with bare feet.

Some of the dances looked like a cross between a gymnastic routine and ball room dancing. The grace and strength was obvious in the intricate steps and agility. Professional ballet dancers would be envious of the skill and grace of these people. I felt honored to see this facet of this very old and interesting culture.

When we finally left for home, we were still full from the magnificent dinner. I think my mom had made some new friends among the elders in the village. I had definitely made a new friend with Douglas.

"I'm only in the north woods for a couple of days," Douglas had said as we got our coats and walked at the door. "Will I see you again before I have to leave?"

"Sure. Here is my number. Give me a call," I'd said, handing him a piece of paper with my phone number as I waved good-bye to everyone. Just before I went out the door, Forrest hugged me. "I like your human tradition," he said.

Mom and I got into her car still waving and drove slowly out of their village. We agreed that was one of the best Thanksgivings ever. Next year, Ben would be with us. I hoped Ash would be, too. I liked Douglas, but I liked him as a cousin. I was sure he felt the same way.

The next day, I drove to work. I had the day shift. We didn't have school as it was the Friday after Thanksgiving. I noticed it was snowing as I walked to the garage. We'd flurries, but no heavy snows yet. We had a skiff of snow on the ground, and I wore my hiking boots to work. They were waterproof but didn't look as clunky as regular snow boots.

After work, I found Ash standing by my Jeep. "Our guests arrived Wednesday," Ash said. "They seem like a nice enough family." I looked at his face. He didn't look any different. But then again, what did I expect? Did I think he would lose interest in me already? What if we hadn't bonded? What if only I bonded? Would my human part be able to live with it if he bonded with one of the European girls?

"Are the girls really pretty?" I asked. I expected them to look like Olivia only younger and maybe a little like me only prettier.

"They look okay. They are all blond with blue eyes," he replied blandly. He didn't seem to care what they looked like.

"Blond? I thought all wood nymphs had light-brown hair and green eyes," I said.

"Apparently, different clans from different parts of the world have different looks," he replied.

"Will I get to see them?" I asked. I leaned against my car next to him. I liked being near him. I'd missed him. He gathered me into his arms, and I put my face in his neck and breathed in the scent of him.

He leaned away from me so he could see my face. "Uh, my mom and dad want just us around with no other company while the visitors are here," he said slowly. "Dad's also keeping me close to the house. I'm only here now because I had an excuse to run to the store. Do you want to meet them?"

"No other company as in human company, too, right?" I stated. "The rest of your family or even Olivia would be able to come over, right?" I seethed.

"He didn't say that." He said pulling me into his arms.

"But that's what he meant, isn't it?" I pushed away from him. He looked surprised. I was mad.

Ash didn't answer. I was livid. His family was so embarrassed about me that Ash had to keep me away from the house. I didn't need a picture drawn. I could figure this out for myself. Why was Ash so dense? How could he not see the truth? His father hated the very concept of me.

I sighed. With effort, I controlled my anger. "Mom's waiting for me. I have to go home." I walked around him and unlocked the driver-side door.

Ash turned around, pulled me to him and held me close for a minute. "I love you, you know."

"I love you, too." I said, sounding muffled since my face was pressed to his chest.

When he let me go, I felt colder on the inside than I did on the outside. What would I do if Ash bonded with one of the blondies?

Saturday morning I had the late shift at work. A half hour to closing time Ash came into the store with a fashion-model-gorgeous blond girl at his side. She had a narrow face with the most exquisite features and very pale blond hair. Her eyes were the lightest, palest blue. She was beautiful. The worst part, she hung onto his arm.

"Hi, Laurel!" Ash called. The only other person in the store was the owner in the office. It had been snowing all day, and even though it wasn't deep, the wind was blowing pretty hard. People had been coming in all day for shovels, salt, or winter supplies.

"Hi, Ash. Who's your friend?" I asked.

"This is Stella Quince. I thought you'd like to meet one of our visitors. Yesterday I got the impression that you wanted to see what the Europeans looked like. Mom sent us into town for groceries, so I thought I would stop in and say hi."

I wondered why Ash really brought her in to where I worked. It was really hard on me. Was he so ignorant as to think I wouldn't hate seeing him with another girl?

I wasn't about to let Ash get me upset in front of this girl, though. She was beautiful and held his arm possessively. In his defense, I did see him try to extract her hand from his arm, but she'd have none of it. She held on tightly. She even gave me a smirk.

Ash looked at the girl. "This is my girlfriend, Laurel," he said to her. I was surprised he said that. I was glad, but I still couldn't figure out what he was doing there.

"This's the half breed I heard about?" she said in her musical voice that sounded like small wind chimes made of steel.

"Who called her that?" Ash asked, sounding both surprised and a little sharp. He looked furious and puzzled at the same time.

Duh! I thought. Obviously someone in his household was talking about me. While he was questioning her, and I was beginning to think he'd forgotten I was there. I sighed, closed out my register drawer and brought the cash drawer into the office.

"Mr. Reichert," I told my boss, "we haven't had a customer in an hour, and it's almost closing time. Do you mind if I close up?" I asked, holding the drawer out to him.

He laughed. "Sure, Laurel." Then Mr. Reichert looked out into the store. "Say, isn't that your boyfriend with another girl? And such a pretty one. He's got a lot of nerve bringing her in here. If he does it again, I'll have to talk to him. I don't care for it. Are you two, broken up?" He scowled. It appeared that Mr. Reichert assumed Ash was either an idiot or showing off his new friend. It was just what I thought other people would think when I saw Ash with that girl.

"It's just a family friend," I said. "Not a new girlfriend. He's still my boyfriend." I grabbed my coat and headed out of the office.

"If you say so!" Mr. Reichert responded.

I forced a smile and waved as I left the office. When I got back to Ash, I said, "I've got to lock up." They went outside. I got my keys out and I locked the front doors. Mr. Reichert would finish the lock-up later.

"Laurel, I didn't mean for this to happen. This wasn't what I expected to happen when I came here to see you. The truth is, I just wanted to see you! Plus, I thought you wanted to meet one of them." He explained to me as we walked into the parking lot. We were walking side by side, me and blondie on either side of Ash.

"Will you please let go of me!" he hissed at Stella, yanking his arm out of her grasp. Forced to let go of his arm, Stella was pouting when I faced him by my car.

"Laurel, I only wanted to introduce you to Stella. I didn't know she was going to be a parasite! She hadn't acted like this before! And if I'd known she was going to say something mean, I wouldn't have brought her at all." He glared at her when he said the last part. She just smiled smugly at him. I rolled my eyes at his back.

"I haven't seen you in a couple of days, and this was the only way I could think of to see you." He still glared at Stella. He was talking to me, but he was giving her his attention. She smiled over his shoulder at me.

I sighed. I wasn't about to get into an argument. I wanted to tell Stella just what I thought of her and her lack of manners. I wanted to scream at her to get her hands off of my boyfriend. Maybe she was one of those spoiled girls who knew she was beautiful and could get anything she wanted. I wanted to tell her just what I thought of her high handed way of acting with *my* boyfriend, but then she'd be able to go back to Ash's house and laugh about how she upset the half breed.

So, I refused to show my extreme jealousy. I was fairly new to this whole dating and being in love thing, but I really believed that if you loved someone and they loved you back, there was no need for jealousy. Jealousy was a wasted emotion. If you had a real reason to be jealous, then you didn't have a relationship worth being jealous about. I mean, if the guy loved you, he wouldn't do anything to make you jealous, right?

As calmly as I could manage, I said, "Ash, come and see me when you get some time to yourself, okay? I don't think I want to meet any more of your visitors, though. This one was more than enough."

I hoped that my tone implied just how rude I thought Stella was. Wood nymph and beautiful she may be, but she was a a twit, an example of how beauty was sometimes only on the outside. Ugly however, can go right down to a person's core.

I thought Ash was too embarrassed to do anything except get her out of there. I knew I would have been embarrassed. "I'll see you later, okay?" he said to me as I finished scraping the snow and ice off of my windshield and climbed into my Jeep.

I wanted to say, "Yeah, whatever," but that wasn't what I really meant. I had to think about what to say. "When you can. I love you."

"Oh, yuck!" said Stella with a grimace. "How can you love a *human*? You don't really love her, do you?"

That was the last I heard as Ash and Stella got into Ash's SUV.

I put my head on my steering wheel. I thought, *Do you love me enough, Ash?* I took a deep breath, straightened and started my Jeep. Ash hadn't even waited around to see if my Jeep started okay.

I got home and made myself a sandwich. It had finally stopped snowing. I got a text from Ash stating that he was going to be tied up the entire weekend. No surprise there! He said his father had him doing different projects with him, and he couldn't get away. Yeah, right.

Yeah, I knew what the projects were. The main one was getting to know the rude wood nymph girls. I didn't know if they were all rude, but I just assumed they were.

Saturday night, I got a call from Douglas. He asked if it was a good time to come over. I said it was. A couple of minutes later, I heard a knock at the door. It was Olivia and Douglas. "I was just on my way to Hawthorn's house and thought I'd show Douglas the way," Olivia said brightly. She gave me a quick peck on the cheek and was gone.

I brought Douglas into the house, and we sat at the dining room table. We talked about UWM and his classes. He was a junior, majoring in Chemistry. I had told him that I'd been accepted into the Chemistry program, and he told me what to expect in my freshman and sophomore classes. We were both excited to know we'd be at the same school in the fall.

Douglas didn't stay long. He said he had to go back to Olivia's house and pack. He was driving back to UWM in the morning, and we talked about Christmas vacation. I had told him all about the scene at my work. While Douglas seemed interested enough, I wondered if he expected Ash to dump me for one of the European wood nymphs. When he left, I was sad to say good-bye to my new and beautiful friend. The thought went through my head, *Why couldn't I have bonded with Douglas!*

Monday morning, I had just opened the garage door to drive myself to school when Ash pulled up. I shut the garage door and grabbed my book bag and went to his car. I opened the door and sat down to shake the snow off of my boots before getting in.

"I'm sorry I haven't called as often as I should have. I miss you!" he said. He looked rough, like he hadn't been sleeping. "The only reason I'm here now, is because I have school! The girls are home schooled. They do not attend a human school."

He said bitterly, "To think I used to be like them!"

I knew what he meant. He was talking about the bigoted way he used to feel about humans, that they had no feelings about anything other than themselves. While this was true for some humans, it was far from a species characteristic.

I actually felt sorry for him. "You're not that way, now. You've even made some human friends." He had. The lunch table crew.

He looked at me and reached over the seat and gave me a long kiss. "I hate being away from you! My parents are parading the two older girls around me like they're slaves at auction! I think Stella actually likes it! The older one, not so much. They wear some kind of transparent gauzy fabric that flows when they walk! It's disgusting! It's like Stella's trying to look like or be the stereotypical nymphomaniac. I swear, it seems as if I were to throw her down on the floor and go at it with her, both sets of parents would applaud. It's disgusting." He complained bitterly.

He looked at me and said, "I only think of you! It's you I want to throw down on the floor. Ok, not exactly like that, but the only girl I want to touch intimately is you! I only want it to be you! I could go through a hall of naked beauties and if it were you at the end, I wouldn't see a one of them while I walked to you."

Wow. I thought of the dances I'd watched at the Copper Clan. While some of them could be considered seductive, those dances also had a sort of innocence about them. I'm glad that my wood nymph culture wasn't like Ash's. No wonder Ash's family didn't have humans over to their house. I wondered what other things they did behind closed doors.

During the whole week following Thanksgiving, the only time Ash and I saw each other was school. There were no after school study periods or dinners. On the days that I had to work, we couldn't even ride to and from school together. Our time was way too short, and I felt as if I was losing my mind.

CHAPTER 17
BLIZZARD

I t was Saturday morning, and I didn't have to work today. Ash called and said his dad had some stuff for him to do that morning, but he'd try to escape and come to see me in the afternoon. No surprise about his father keeping him busy! This waiting and wondering if I'd get to see Ash each day was getting old. I was restless, and the last thing I wanted to do on my day off was sit around and wait to see if Ash really could get away to come see me.

I couldn't stand sitting around wondering what was going on over in Ash's house. Was the teenage nympho getting through to Ash? Was there a day coming when Ash would call or text me to say our relationship was over? Every day I expected some kind of "Dear Jane" text. I wondered if he'd have the nerve to tell me in person that he no longer wanted to see me. My heart was already breaking. I could wait all day and Ash still might not be able to come over. I wanted to hate Ash's dad for what he was putting me through. But, if I had only one son, and I saw him doing something I thought wrong, wouldn't I try to change his mind? Was I the best thing for Ash? I was a half breed with no talents. I wondered what the European girls could do. What were their talents? They were beautiful. There was no doubt about that. I wondered how many super models were wood nymphs. After seeing Stella, I was convinced that at least some actresses and models I'd seen on television and in movies were. I was going to drive myself crazy thinking about Ash and Stella. I had to get out of here. I decided to drive up to the reservation. I thought maybe Mom might want to go, too.

When I went downstairs, Mom was already eating breakfast. "Good morning! How'd you sleep?" Mom asked me as I got my cereal.

"Not great. It took me a long while to get to sleep." I said. "Being away from Ash is killing me! I hate it. I need to do something other than sit around the house feeling sorry for myself. Do you want to go to the reservation today?" I asked her.

"Oh, honey, I'd love to! But I have to go to the office. I have clients this morning. You go. It may do you some good to see Adam and the rest of the gang over there." She replied. Then after a moment, she said softly, "No Ash again today, huh?"

"He thinks he might be able to get away this afternoon," I replied getting out the milk. *Yeah, right,* I thought. Ash's dad was coming up with more and more stuff for him to do to keep him away from me.

"It's supposed to snow today, so drive carefully," Mom said as she put her dishes in the dishwasher. "It's supposed to be the first bad storm of the season. Are you going to be home for dinner?"

"Yup. I'll be home this afternoon just in case Ash can come over. I hope we get to set an extra place for dinner."

Mom smiled. I almost couldn't stand the sad edge to it. Pity.

"Well, I better hurry up. It's an hour's drive to the reservation. But if I leave soon, I'll be able to stay for a couple of hours before heading back," I replied.

Mom grabbed her coat and purse and put on her boots before hitting the garage door opener next to the door. "Bye! We'll have broiled chicken for dinner just in case Ash can join us."

"Bye!" I called back to her, still hoping that he would.

I called Adam. He said he'd meet me at the clubhouse. It was snowing hard by the time was dressed and ready to leave the house. The sky visibly darkened during the drive north. It was almost as if the day was moving into twilight instead of reaching to late morning. Usually, it was only an hour's drive to the reservation. Driving more slowly with the snow, I knew it would take me longer. I immediately engaged the four wheel drive as I drove onto the highway. Even with four wheel drive, I soon was having trouble staying on the road. It was really windy and my Jeep was light.

Quickly I found it was difficult to see where the highway ended and the shoulder began. I began to see cars in the ditch on either side of the highway as I drove along. The wind was howling, and the snow was blowing horizontally. The snow in my headlights was almost hypnotic in the way it seemed to reach with fingerlike tentacles across the road. I could actually watch the snow accumulate on the ground at the ends of the fingers. After a few minutes of creeping along, I was beginning to think I should turn around and go back home. But, the thought of just sitting at home and watching the snow fall wondering if Ash would be able to come over was too depressing. At least difficult driving was giving me something to do.

Even if it took me two hours to get to the reservation and I only stayed with Adam for an hour, I'd still have time to make it home. After another few minutes of creeping along, it was dawning on me that this might just be the worst blizzard of my life. If I continued, it'd take me more than two hours to get to the reservation—maybe a lot more—if I arrived at all. I'd be better off home and bored than getting stuck and freezing to death. When I hadn't seen another car on the highway for at least a couple of miles, I decided this was nuts and I should head back home at the next exit.

I saw the sign, indicating the exit in a mile. I didn't want to miss the exit ramp and started to slow down. I was concentrating on what was in front of me and didn't look in the rear view mirror. I didn't see the semi behind me. As it passed me, I lost control of the Jeep. I wasn't sure if I spun out in the blast of wind coming off of the truck combined with the wind of the storm or if the truck actually hit my Jeep. All I remembered was losing control. The Jeep spun—maybe a couple of times or more—until I hit the shoulder. It was steep right there. My Jeep rolled down the embankment. I remember seeing a glimpse of the semi truck, and a hurge cloud of snow as it continued down the highway.

My Jeep had roll bars and a fiberglass removable hard top. The hard top was destroyed almost instantly as the Jeep hit the embankment and toppled. Because of the snow, the crushing sound was muffled or I was too scared to remember it. It seemed to roll, over and over, for a very long time. When, finally, the Jeep came to a stop, I felt the wind as it blew through the shattered side windows and windshield. I had no protection. At least the roll bars seemed to have done their job. The main cabin was intact. As I assessed myself for pain and damage, all I felt was an ache where I'd hit my head on the steering wheel. My seat belt and the roll bars had kept me firmly in place. Maybe my Jeep was destroyed, but I seemed to be only slightly wounded.

But I was hanging upside down. While holding onto the steering wheel to keep from falling on my face, I worked my seatbelt off. It didn't want to release due to the pressure of my body against it. I was glad that I wore gloves, a hat, and long pants, as the glass from the windows would surely have cut me struggled as I inside the smashed car. I crawled out of the seatbelt and looked out the side window opening. The snow littered with glass all down the embankment and the roof of my Jeep looked like a taco.

I reached for my purse to get my cell phone, but it had spilled during the roll down the embankment. After a frantic search inside the Jeep, I looked along the scraped slope. I spotted my cell phone. It had smashed against an exposed rock during the roll and lay in pieces.

I had to take my jacket off to wriggle through the windshield opening to get out of my vehicle. I pulled my jacket out behind me. Once free of the car, I sat on the hood and rubbed snow on my bleeding forehead. I felt the beginning of a headache, and I felt a little faint when I stood up. The snow at the bottom of the embankment was more than knee deep. I looked up at the road, but, because of the blizzard, I could hardly see the top of the embankment. I put my jacket back on and zipped it up while reviewing my situation and looking around. Should I stay down here with the Jeep and wait for help? Would I have better luck of a rescue up on the highway? Did the sheriff's department look for stranded or stuck vehicles along the highway? I had never been in an experience quite like this one. I wasn't sure what to do. I had never realized how much I depended on my cell phone until that moment when I had no way to call for help. I started to get scared, but I knew that would get me nowhere.

I wondered if I should I try to get to the exit. I could barely see ten feet in front of me because of the blowing snow. Without windshield and side windows, the Jeep was no protection from the cold wind or snow. Also, I could smell gas. I didn't think that was a good sign. I had over a half of a tank when I left the house. I feared my car could catch fire. Then again, if it did, maybe that would draw some attention. At the bottom of the embankment, it was highly unlikely that anyone would see my Jeep. Even though my Jeep was black, in a few moments it would be covered with snow.

I needed to flag down some help. For that, I needed to be up by the highway. It took me a few minutes to crawl through the blowing snow up the side of the embankment to the road. In the snow, the highway pretty much looked like a field. As I looked up and down the highway, I saw nothing moving. I wondered if I could get lost in the blowing snow trying to get anywhere. Was it in my best interest to try to walk to the exit, or taking the chance of staying put and freezing to death?

I had on a well-insulated ski jacket and heavy jeans. I'd chosen my Icelandic snow boots, Mom had bought for me and had on a pair of ski gloves. My mother always believed in being prepared for the worst. Right then, I was glad she tended to be overprotective. I was glad I'd learned it was better to be overprotected than under protected. I wondered how long I could last in the storm, how long before I found help or someone noticed my absence and came to look for me. I decided I needed to find shelter. I was getting colder quick. I was near an off ramp, so maybe there were houses in the vicinity.

I headed in the direction of the off ramp. I couldn't see anything. I walked for a while. Was I still on the highway? I should have noticed the off ramp by now, I thought. It wasn't that far up the road, or was it? The sign had said that it was one mile to the off ramp. How far past the sign had I gone before I went off of the road? Could I have missed the off ramp in the blinding snow? My face was cold and my feet were getting cold in the boots. My fingers, even curled inside my gloves were starting to feel the cold. I knew if I didn't find help soon, I could be in trouble.

I walked for a couple of hours against the wind. Didn't it just figure that the direction of the off ramp was against the blowing snow? I was getting tired. Walking was difficult in the accumulating snow. I had to lift each leg to clear the snow and it was getting deeper by the minute. It was worse than walking through sand. I had not seen one car since I'd been walking. It was so dark with the storm, I had no idea what time it was. I didn't wear a watch. I usually relied on my cell phone for the time, but it was broken. I felt as if I had been walking the entire day. I was tired, hungry, cold and getting scared. I was getting really scared. I sure wouldn't make it through the night in this weather. As far as I knew, wood nymphs didn't have special powers to protect them from the elements. I didn't think they had super human abilities regarding snow that I'd inherited as I was freezing as I walked. If I had super-human abilities, would I feel so cold? I believed that in the worst situations, wood nymphs could freeze to death the same way a human could. I wondered if they could jet in this kind of weather. I'd think the snow would certainly slow them down.

Finally, I couldn't walk any more. I needed to sit down to rest for a bit. My head hurt. I looked around, but all I saw was snow and more snow. Some snow was higher than other levels of snow. Was this where plows had pushed aside some earlier snow or humps in the ground? There were no tree branches or downed trees that I could sit on. I saw no covered area under trees that would protect me from the elements. I seemed to be in a clearing. Was I still on the road? Had I wondered away from the highway? I knew if I sat in the snow, my jeans would melt it and the wet would be really uncomfortable and maybe even dangerous. Wet jeans would sap my body heat that much quicker. As it was, my legs were wet and icy from the knees down.

I couldn't take it anymore. I sat in the snow. The snow was at least two feet deep where it hadn't drifted. The drifted areas had filled in the landscape. I sat on the far side of a drift and was a little bit out of the wind. At least it didn't seem to blow as hard where I sat. I was really scared. I didn't want to die in the snow.

I crossed my arms in front of me to try to hold in whatever body heat I had left. I was getting really cold. "Help me!" I cried out, knowing no one could hear me, but wishing for a miracle. "I'm freezing to death!" I screamed. I hollowed out a small space for myself in the back of the drift. No one was going to find me. I had to do what I could to survive. Maybe the snow could work as insulation, but for how long? Wasn't that how an igloo worked? Wasn't an igloo basically a frozen snow house?

I was tired. I was cold. I feared I was going to die in the snow. I curled up in the hollow I had scooped out. I felt sleepy. I had walked so far. I drifted off to sleep wishing I could tell Mom, Ben, and Ash that I loved them. I was going to die right there in a snow drift. Would they find my body before spring?

The next thing I noticed was that I was moving. I wasn't walking. I was being carried. Was I dead? It was still snowing and blowing. I could hear the howl of the wind and felt the ice particles hitting my face. I looked to see who my rescuer was and I saw I was being carried by a large black bear. I must be dead. Either that or I was this bear's dinner. Did bears eat people? I thought bears hibernated in the winter. I could feel the heat of its body where my body was cradled next to thick fur. That felt kind of good. It was holding me very gently. It looked down at me. It had a huge head and huge brown eyes. It looked me right in the eyes. "Laurel, can you hear me?"

I must have been hallucinating. I'd learned a lot of things that I'd taken as stories and legends really were true. But, talking bears? Bears didn't talk. Was this one of the things that a person goes through before dying from the cold? Not only did the bear talk, it knew my name. How likely was that? The voice was unlike any I had heard before. It was difficult to realize that it was English. I had to listen closely to understand the words. While the voice was deep and gravelly, I could understand it.

"Yes, I hear you. You talk good for a hallucination." I told the bear. The bear then opened its mouth and, while the teeth were frightening, it looked like it was smiling. It gave a kind of grunt that just had to be a laugh. Yeah, I was dead. To think a bear was talking was just plain nuts. For me to believe it was laughing, well, I must be crazy. Just at that moment, I saw a bald eagle circling about ten feet over us calling out its piercing shriek. It sounded like it was trying to say English words too, but I couldn't understand.

"Yes, she's conscious," the bear mumbled in its deep voice.

I noticed that we were definitely off the highway and heading into the forest. The wind was not nearly so bad here, and other than the crunching of the bear's big paws in the crust of snow, and the occasional eagle cry, the forest was silent and still. The tree tops created a natural barrier to the worst of the storm, and the snow on the ground wasn't as deep or drifted as out in the open. We walked for a while—I'm not sure how long—and the storm twilight darkened to night.

Some time after dark, I realized we were no longer in the woods. I heard the sound of gravel being moved by heavy paws. It was very quiet. Then I saw the millions of lit sparklers flash of the eagle turning into Adam, I knew I was safe and not a talking bear's dinner. With all of the supernatural things I had seen since moving to Wisconsin, a talking bear hadn't seemed all that unrealistic. While the sparkling phenomenon of Adam changing from the eagle to a human was going on, the light from the change lit up the space around us. We were in a cave. A couple of minutes later, I saw Adam in his loin cloth on the floor setting a match to a pile of wood. After he had the fire lit, he walked deeper into the cave. In a couple of minutes Adam returned—dressed in jeans, a sweatshirt, and boots—and sat down cross legged in front of the fire. The fire caught quickly and burned brightly.

I looked around for my rescue bear and saw George pulling a shirt over his head in a corner of our cave.

"Were you the bear?" I asked George.

"Yes," George replied. He sat next to Adam at the fire. I was still standing, a little confused. "It'll get quite warm in here in a little bit. You can take your jacket off and let it dry. Here is a blanket for you to sit on." He handed me a thick Indian blanket. I set it on the ground near the fire and planted my bottom on it.

"How did you find me?" I asked. I was still light-headed from being so cold. I was shaking pretty hard, too, shivering so that my teeth chattered.

"When I saw how bad it was snowing and that you hadn't shown up yet," Adam said, "I called your house phone and cell. I got no answer, so I called George. He called your mom. She said you'd left. With the weather worsening, we came looking for you. I heard your call for help and that pinpointed your position. You do have a wood nymph gift Laurel. It's a wood nymph trait to be able to call for help the way you did, but it's not a common gift. Only a few have the ability to call for help. I have no idea how far the command for assistance travels, but it is almost a compulsion to have to try to help if you happen to be someone who hears it. As far as I know, I wouldn't be surprised if all of the wood nymphs in the north woods heard that call."

"A few of us Native Americans can also hear that kind of call. The call came through like a beacon through the fog. Once you called for help, it's as if it was projected in all directions, like an invisible line that anyone who heard it could follow directly to you. We were only a couple of miles up the road when we heard it. We were about to be stuck in the snow, so we changed into our spirit guide forms to get us to you quicker," Adam said. "We knew you were in trouble, as the call doesn't work unless the caller actually is in serious trouble. We were hoping we wouldn't be too late. Are you okay?"

Adam did not appear to be the least bit cold. He was sitting there on the floor as if it was a camp fire in the middle of the summer.

I was still shaking when I realized I was starting to thaw out. My fingers and toes were tingling in a painful way that let me know that blood circulation was getting back into them. I took my jacket off and hung it on an outcropping of rock that jutted out from the wall.

"Are you hungry?" George asked pulling a large round metal container out from under a shelf of rock that I hadn't noticed before.

"I think so," I admitted, curious about what was in the container. I thought I felt hungry, but I was also feeling really weak. I thought that now that I was rescued, I should be feeling better, but I was starting to feel worse. Maybe some food would improve things.

"We have caves throughout the north woods. We keep a bit of non-perishable food items and water in them in case of an emergency." George said pulling the lid off of the container.

Inside the container were breakfast bars, juice boxes and other assorted drinks and snacks. I noticed that all had packaging that could easily be burned in a fire with no leftover waste. I reached for a breakfast bar and opened it up. It tasted okay, but I found that I wasn't as hungry as I had thought I should be.

"Let me check your head," George said, seeing the dried blood on my forehead. He reached for a package of antibacterial skin wipes also in the metal container. He pulled out the package and removed a wipe and gently pulled my hair from the dried blood on my skin. He then proceeded to clean around my gash. It stung a bit, but I held as still as I could while he cleaned my foreheard up. After he finished with the wipe he threw it in the fire. My head had stopped bleeding.

"It looks like you hit your head pretty hard. We saw where your car had rolled off of the road. I saw it while I was flying as the eagle. The snow was covering it quickly, but eagle eyes are very sharp," Adam stated as he came over to rummage in the metal container for something to eat. "Did you hit a patch of ice?" he asked sitting back on his blanket by the fire and munching on a breakfast bar.

"A semi truck and trailer drove past me. I think it made the Jeep spin. Then I went into the ditch. I don't know if he hit me or pushed me or if it was just the wind that blew me off of the road. Ouch!" I said as George hit a particularly painful spot as he cleaned my wound with another antibacterial wipe.

"Do you feel dizzy or anything? You don't look good," George said, watching me closely, still tending to the wound.

"I feel kind of faint. I'd have thought I should be starving, but I'm really not all that hungry. I was pretty sure I was a goner when I went to sleep in the snow," I said while pulling off little bits of the breakfast bar.

"Is your mind clear? Your head feels pretty warm," George said looking at me closely and resting his hand against my forehead.

"What is this ability you seem to think I have?" I asked George. Did I really have an ability or some kind of gift? Were there other things that I could do?

"You have the call. Wood nymphs and Native Americans have been mostly allies throughout the centuries. We keep to our cultures, but, our stories tell us there have been many instances of wood nymph-Ojibwa collaborations. For some reason, I don't know why, we never intermarried. However, we could always count on each other in emergencies," George said thoughtfully.

"It's likely wood nymphs heard your call. I'm surprised we haven't seen any yet. I'd imagine we'll have company before long." George looked towards the opening in the cave.

"That would be correct," I heard a voice say. I couldn't see anyone at first, but when the speaker had finished the sentence, I saw that Forrest had come into the cave.

Forrest had on clothes like nothing I'd ever seen. They were fitted and looked like a cross between a ninja outfit and something Middle Eastern. It made me dizzy to look at him as the fabric changed colors to match anything he stood next to. The clothes flowed like silk. When he moved and the colors changed, be became almost invisible. At the moment, the clothes had melded with the dark of the rock wall of the cave. Forrest had told me about such clothes, but I had never seen them in action.

"Are you okay?" Forrest crouched next to me to look me over. "I heard the call, but I almost lost the scent in the snow when George picked you up and moved you. That's an awesome call that you have! It appears you do have at least one wood nymph skill."

I smiled.

He said, "It took me awhile to get here because of the snow. We can't jet through snow. We're still faster than humans, but not as fast as we can move on a hard, level ground. I drove as far as I could and then hiked from there. I was hoping I wouldn't be too late. Once I smelled the bear, I realized help had arrived. I just followed the bear's, well, George's scent, through the snow. Here put these clothes on."

Forrest handed me a small bundle of fabric. "No one will look. They'll warm you up. They're designed for cold weather. You look kind of flushed. Have you been standing too close to the fire? How's your head?"

I was getting warm because of the fire, and I was still wet. The idea of dry clothes was welcomed, even if they hurt my eyes. I was feeling kind of nauseous. I went into a deeper corner of the cave and changed quickly into the clothes. They were light, like silk, but warm against my skin. I could feel warmth wrapping me like a blanket. I walked back to everyone by the fire, but my head was starting to spin.

"Your mom's worried about you," Forrest stated while looking at me closely.

George and Adam nodded. "Yes, she was worried before we set out to find you and that was hours ago." Adam said.

"Mom! Oh, my gosh! I have to get home! Can you get me home? What time is it?" I cried. Now that I knew I was safe, I worried about Mom. She must be out of her mind. She probably thought I was lying in a ditch . . . which I had been.

"It's dark out, almost night. I'd call her, but I have no cell service out here because of the weather. She knows we're looking for you. Come on, I'll carry you home. Those clothes will keep you warm and dry. George, Adam, thank you for getting to her before I could. However, I'm faster than a bear. I'll take her home." Forrest said, smiling at George.

"Right. And though Adam can't carry her as an eagle, he can let Valarie know Laurel's safe before you arrive," George said, cleaning up around the fire and burning the trash.

Adam said, "That's a good plan. I'll become my spirit guide and go to Valerie. She'll be home when? In an hour or so?"

Forrest nodded. Adam went into the corner where I had changed to take off his clothes so that he could change into the eagle. I knew he had changed into the eagle when I saw the sparkler effect reflect off of the rocks of the wall of the cave.

"See you in a little bit, Laurel!" Adam cried in his high pitched eagle bird voice as he flew out of the opening of the cave. This time I could understand what he said, but it was like listening for words through a scream.

I was near Forrest when I coughed. I covered my mouth with my hand. It was no big deal, but it caught Forrest's attention. "Laurel, your color is all wrong. You look more than just wind burned." He put his hand to my forehead. "You're burning up," he said.

George came over and looked closer at me. "She really doesn't look good, Forrest. I think you need to get her home, fast. She might need medical care."

Forrest agreed and picked me up. As we left the cave, he tried to protect me as much as he could from the cold but I was shivering again in no time even in the warm wood nymph clothes. I felt as if I had breathed in too much cold and my lungs were raw. The coughing worsened the whole way home, which took about half an hour. I kept my eyes closed. I could feel Forrest's strong body flex and a breeze blew around me, but I wouldn't have guessed we were moving it was so smooth. We must have been moving pretty quickly to get there in a half hour in this weather.

Adam had beaten us to the house and my mom had the outside porch lights on and was waiting at the door when we got there. Forrest carried me into the house and up to my room. Mom and Adam followed him up the stairs. Adam had clothes on, so he must have carried his clothes in his claws.

But I was tuning out. I know Mom and Forrest got me into my room, but I don't remember making any effort on my own. I was like a five-year-old, helpless and depending on the adults around to take care of me.

CHAPTER 18
ILLNESS

S he's burning up with fever," I heard Forrest tell my mom as I sank down on the edge of my bed. "I need to get a doctor. Wood nymphs as a rule don't get sick easily. This looks like pneumonia to me." At that, Forrest left the house.

Mom helped me out of my color shifting clothes and get my pajamas on while Adam waited outside of my bedroom. Once I was tucked into bed with my comforter snugged under my chin, Mom allowed Adam in my room.

Mom brushed my hair out of my face with her hand. I could see her concern. She said to Adam, "Thank you for finding her. I don't know what I would've done if anything happened to her. Laurel and Ben are my life."

She then said to me, "Honey, your head is really warm. I'll be right back. I want to get a cold compress."

I heard Mom go into the bathroom. The water ran. A minute later, she returned with a cold, wet wash cloth to lay on my forehead. I gave my mother a wry smile, "Yeah, just what I need, something cold and wet after being so cold and wet."

"Oh, honey," Mom sighed, "just leave it there for a minute. I'm going to get a thermometer." Just as my mom left again, I heard the door bell ring. Adam got up and said he would answer the door.

I heard George's voice as he came up the stairs with Adam. Mom had just come from the bathroom and was turning on the battery-operated thermometer when George and Adam got to my room. "How's she doing?" George said outside my door.

Mom leaned over me and put the thermometer into my mouth and said to me. "You know the drill. Under your tongue."

She then looked up at George and said. "I'm not sure how she's doing. Forrest went to get a doctor, I think. Thank you so much for finding her! You're the best friend anyone ever had." She gave George a big smile.

"Of course we had to find her. Me heap big Indian. Good tracker!" George said looking pleased.

"Yeah, George, laugh it up. Seriously, even though she's sick, it could have been much worse if you hadn't have found her when you did," Mom said seriously.

The thermometer beeped, and I had a coughing fit as Mom pulled the thermometer out of my mouth. She looked at me and said, "That's a nasty cough."

She looked at the thermometer, and I could see the shock fill her face. She whispered, "Your fever is 104. You should go to a hospital." She started looking around my room as if to find something in my room to dress me in to take me to a hospital. She looked a little panicky. I felt dizzy. One minute I felt hot and then I was cold. I coughed.

I heard the doorbell ring again and Adam went to answer it. I heard footsteps on the stairs.

"I brought Dr. Woodson," said Forrest coming into my room with the man I remembered from Ash's house.

"Dr. Woodson, I'm so glad that you are here! Please help my daughter! Her temperature is 104!" Moom said, wringing her hands.

The whole room was getting surreal. I was getting really dizzy, and I felt like I was starting to black out or something. People and things started getting fuzzy and losing their shape. I felt someone poke a tongue depressor into my throat and assumed it was Dr. Woodson. I had my eyes closed. Everything was getting to be too much trouble to pay attention to. I felt as if I were a million miles away from my body, like I was drifting away. The last thing I remember for a long while was a prick in my arm.

When I woke up, the sun was shining brightly in my room. Mom was in the my bedroom chair. Ash, Olivia, and Forrest sat on chairs they had brought in. Everyone looked so sad. I felt like I was the dead guy in an old funeral movie.

I read in a history class that over 100 years ago, dead people would be laid out on the dining room table before they were buried so people could pay their last respects to the deceased person. What a creepy thought.

Everyone looked worn out. Mom was the first to realize I was awake and looking around, and she jumped to her feet and ran over to me. "Laurel, honey, I'm so glad to see you awake. Can you hear me? How do you feel?"

Ash, Olivia, and Forrest crowded around my bed and looked down at me. I felt so tired. "Um, I feel really tired and thirsty, but I think I am okay. I'm going to live, right?" I asked. My throat felt scratchy and I was really thirsty!

Just as I said that, Dr. Woodson walked in with his medical bag. He looked like a stereotypical doctor. He had on a black suit and carried a black medical bag. He didn't wear them, but a little pair of spectacles sitting on the end of his nose would not have looked out of place on his face.

As he walked in the door, he saw that I was awake and said, "You gave us quite a scare, my dear. You've been unconscious for four days. How do you feel?"

"I'm really thirsty and tired," I said as I tried to sit up and fell back down. "I feel pretty weak, too," I said with a sigh.

"We thought we were going to lose you a couple of times. It appears that your hybrid status made the pneumonia harder for your system to handle rather than easier. As wood nymphs usually don't get such diseases, they have no natural immunity to it. The human part of you had to fight off the illness alone." He sat next to me on the side of my bed. He checked my eyes and my tongue and looked into my ears.

He put his hand on my forehead and with a smile, he said. "I think you are out of danger. I no longer feel the fever."

When he said that, everyone in the room cheered. I was embarrassed. "Can I get a drink of water, please?" I said. The doctor nodded.

Ash came forward with a glass of water with a straw in it. He gently held the straw to my lips. "I was so worried about you. I felt like a part of me was dying. I never want to go through that again," he said softly that only I could hear.

At that moment, two more people entered my bedroom. The first was Douglas. He came over, looking at me from the foot of the bed. "I heard you were really sick so I had to come. I jetted from school."

When Dr. Woodson stepped away from me, Douglas came over and kissed me on my forehead. He was so handsome in his polo shirt and jeans. I felt a warmth wash over me that he would take time out of his scholastic schedule to come and be with me. Ash stepped aside to allow Douglas and the second person who had entered the room with Douglas to come to the side of the bed.

The other person was obviously one of the European clan wood nymphs. "I'm Rebecca Quince," she said, smiling at me. She had a beautiful voice, soft and gentle. "I hope you don't mind, but I helped Dr. Woodson treat you while you were unconscious. When I heard you were ill, I volunteered my services to Dr. Woodson. I'm very interested in humans and human culture, and I plan to attend a human college to be a nurse. I sincerely want to be able to help humankind. I like humans. I really like the relationship that the Copper Clan from northern Wisconsin has with you and your mom. I think it could be the start of something wonderful throughout the world."

I started to be appalled at the thought of one of the horrid European wood nymphs being anywhere near me while I was unconscious. But, as I looked at her, she seemed really sincere. "I find the thought of you being a hybrid of wood nymph and human fascinating. To the best of my knowledge, you are the first one!" she said reaching down to touch my hand.

"I was grateful for the opportunity to assist Dr. Woodson in helping you." Her beauty was staggering and with her incredible smile, especially so sweet and sincere, it was really hard to dislike her. Could wood nymphs be false and look like this? I didn't think so. What a contrast in sisters I thought. I thought of my first experience with the European family. While Stella was beautiful, she couldn't hold a candle to the beauty of this sister. Plus, Stella wasn't beautiful all of the way through her soul like her sister was.

"You're the oldest sister?" I guessed. I gave a little cough, and Ash came back to sit beside me on the bed. He held the straw in the water glass to my lips. I took a drink. The water felt good on my throat.

"Yes," Rebecca replied in a soft, flowing voice. I was imagining the soft sigh of leaves in a gentle breeze while I listened to her voice. She wore a flowing caftan-style gown similar to what I'd seen Olivia wear. As I was thinking of the caftan, I looked at Olivia. Still sitting in the chair she had been in when I woke up, she smiled at me.

Olivia was wearing jeans and a sweatshirt today. I looked at her, and then I looked at Rebecca. It was breathtaking to see Olivia with her perfect features. She had such soft-looking light-brown hair and green eyes. It was interesting to see the contrast between Olivia and Rebecca in the same room. Rebecca also had perfect features, but had blue eyes and blond hair. I have never seen a super model as beautiful as either of these women. I thought maybe some super models were wood nymphs masquerading as humans.

"I'm so glad to see you awake," Douglas said, squatting down to be on my level. Rebecca glanced down at Douglas, and he lifted his eyes, and their eyes met. For a moment, they couldn't seem to look away from each other. There was definitely some attraction. I wondered if there could be some bonding going on in my room.

"Douglas, how long have you been here?" I asked breaking the connection between the two of them. Douglas looked back at me. I wasn't jealous of the attraction that they had between each other. I found it interesting.

"Three days," he said. "You've had a crowded room for the last few days. Everyone has been so worried about you. I met Rebecca while she was taking care of you with Dr. Woodson."

He smiled at me and then looked back at Rebecca. This definitely looked like a budding romance. It was nice to see that my illness brought someone happiness. "I really have to get back to school now that I know you'll be okay. I'll be back at Christmas. See you then!" Douglas said as he glanced at me and then returned his attention to Rebecca.

"I should go now, too," Rebecca said. "I truly hope I can get to know you better." Rebecca smiled at me, and then looking at Douglas. "Maybe I can talk my parents into allowing me to study nursing here in Wisconsin." She said the last part directly to Douglas. They waved at me as they left. As Douglas and Rebecca walked down the stairs, I heard Douglas say something about UWM having a nursing program.

"I'm so sorry you got sick," Ash said. "If I had been with you, this never would have happened. I won't let my father keep us apart again. You were right. My father was keeping us apart." Ash held the straw to my mouth again.

I was looking at the straw and Ash as Olivia came over.

I looked up from the straw and I saw that Olivia was next to me. "Please don't put me through something like this again!" Olivia pleaded with a sad smile. "We were really frightened about you." Ash backed away as Olivia reached down to give me a hug. She not only looked good, but she smelled really good, too.

Dr. Woodson came over and put his hand on Olivia's shoulder to look at me and she smiled at him. "Thank you for saving our Laurel." Olivia looked up at Dr. Woodson with her breathtaking smile. Of course with Dr. Woodson being a wood nymph, he probably didn't even notice how beautiful her smile was. Dr. Woodson saw the look on Olivia's face and smiled back at her in a professional manner.

I wondered if he knew about Olivia and Hawthorn. He had to have known. He must know that Olivia and Hawthorn had made up their differences and were figuring out how to build a life together. We all anticipated formal vows in the near future. It was obvious that they had bonded.

Dr. Woodson said to Olivia. "Well, it looks like the little lady will be just fine. I was glad that I was here to help." He nodded his head as if to add to the conviction of his statement. "If you need me, just call me. Good-bye for now. Try to avoid germs that make humans sick!" He said with a smile. We all said good-bye to him. As I watched him leave, I thought to myself how lucky we were that we had a wood nymph doctor as a neighbor. I wondered what would have happened to me in a human hospital.

My mother had gone to get me something to eat. I heard her outside my door talking to Dr. Woodson. He said, "Only light foods for the next couple of days. Let's see how well she tolerates them. Light broths, maybe some cottage cheese and Jell-O."

"I have some chicken soup here. It's mostly broth. Is that okay?" Mom asked.

"That should be fine. Start with small amounts and increase slowly if she can handle it. Oh, and get her up and walking as soon as possible. We don't want the pneumonia to settle in the lungs again. If you have any need of me, send Ash, and he'll find me. Good-bye." I heard Dr. Woodson say. I heard heavier steps going down the stairs and lighter ones coming into my room.

"Can you try to sit up?" Mom asked me.

"I think I should go now, too," Olivia said. "I'm so happy to see you awake. I'll come and see you tomorrow." She leaned over Ash to kiss me on the forehead.

Ash helped me sit up. It was harder than I thought it should be. I had almost no strength. Without Ash's support, I think I'd just have fallen back into my pillows. Mom sat down to feed me lunch.

Ash kind of sat behind me while my mom sat on the edge of my bed in front of me. Mom spooned some soup into my mouth. It was wonderful! I was starving!

After a couple of spoonfuls I took the spoon to do it myself. My hand shook, but I was able to get a half of a spoonful into my mouth without spilling. I finished the bowl and leaned back. Ash helped me lie back down. I felt better but very weak. Mom set the tray on my dresser and sat down on the edge of the bed again.

I looked at her. "What happened to me?" I asked.

Mom asked me, "What do you remember?"

I lay there feeling Ash's warm body next to me and remembered being cold. "I remember coming home with Uncle Forrest carrying me. I remember coming into my room and you helping me change into pajamas. I sort of remember Dr. Woodson coming, but then nothing at all," I replied.

Mom folded her hands in her lap and took a deep breath. "You were burning up with fever. Dr. Woodson gave you an antibiotic shot. He wasn't sure if it was viral or bacterial pneumonia, but your lungs were filling with fluid, and you had taken a nasty chill. You almost froze to death in the snow! At one point I wanted to take you to a hospital, but Dr. Woodson talked me out of it. He felt that your blood work would send up some red flags as to your genetic background. He had a full array of hospital equipment, even a portable x-ray machine to determine how bad the pneumonia really was. At one point he suctioned mucous from your lungs! I have to tell you, that scared me." My mother stated, wiping a tear from the corner of her eye.

"You had an IV for a couple of days, but then last night you ripped it out of your arm and cried out in your sleep that it hurt. Dr. Woodson said that if you didn't regain consciousness today that he was going to give you another IV. He was here almost twenty-four hours a day monitoring your condition. After the first day, he asked if he could bring Rebecca to help him. I said yes. While I have training in mental health, I have no nursing training. Rebecca was very gentle with you. She bathed you and cleaned your hair. She changed your sheets and pajamas. You certainly couldn't have had better nursing care." Mom smiled at me.

"What happened then? When did Douglas get here? How did he find out?"

"Well, honey, it appears that you have something they describe as the 'call'. Douglas heard your call and knew it was you. Olivia heard the call too, and saw in a vision that George and Adam would find you and that Forrest would bring you here. Olivia saw that you were going to be extremely ill. Douglas was here the next day."

"When did Ash get here?" I asked, not looking at him, but focusing on my mother. I felt him move next to me.

"Ash was here the same night you were brought home. Dr. Woodson was at Ash's house when Forrest found him. According to Forrest, while Dr. Woodson was gathering up his medical supplies, Ash's father banned him from coming over here." Mom said this last part while looking at Ash. I couldn't see Ash's face as he was sitting just to the rear of my vision on my left side.

I turned my head to look at Ash. "You disobeyed your father?" I asked in awe. "I thought wood nymphs didn't defy their parents."

"As a rule, we don't. But, what my father was doing was wrong. He had no right to keep us apart. Wood nymphs have always been respected in making their life mate choices. He doesn't believe that I could bond with a human. He had no right to parade other female wood nymphs in front of me trying to change my mind about you. As long as he was so in the wrong, I felt justified in defying him to come here. He hasn't spoken to me in four days, and, just now, I really don't care." Ash told me kissing my hand. "I never want to be away from you again."

Mom smiled at Ash and then looked at me. "You have had so many visitors checking on you. George and Adam have stopped by here a couple of times. The first time George showed up, he showed up as a bear carrying a bundle of clothes. That really rattled me. I knew George was a shape shifter, and I knew he was a bear, but I'd never seen him actually transform before. He didn't know I was watching from your bedroom window when I first saw a bear in our yard and then saw the flash of light that changed the bear into George. I told him I saw him change his shape in front of the house. George knows I saw him in his loin cloth. I guess having the little leather thong is better than nothing, but not by much," Mom said with a half-embarrassed chuckle.

"The truth is, it was really touch and go with you for a while. You'll have to continue with bed rest for another few days. But, according to Dr. Woodson, we need to get you up and walking, soon. So how about now?" Mom asked.

"Can you stand?" Ash asked me. "I'll help you." He stood and reached to help me get out of the bed.

I felt so weak. It took me a minute to get my legs over the side of the bed. They felt like lead weights. Ash took my left arm and Mom took the right and also reached around my waist. When I first tried to stand, I felt dizzy and had a hard time. My legs tried to give out. It took a bit to get my legs to hold me, but ultimately I was able to stand, although I was extremely wobbly.

With the help of the two of them, I was able to walk around my room. I made one lap and was exhausted. "Please, I can't do anymore!" I wailed. "I need to lie down!" I was so tired. I just wanted to sleep. Mom and Ash helped me back to my bed and tucked me in.

I was falling asleep fast. "Don't leave me," I mumbled.

I heard both of them say, "I won't."

CHAPTER 19
WINTER SOLSTICE

The day after I gained consciousness I was able to go downstairs with help and lie on the couch. For the first couple of days I slept most of the day, and Ash came to see me in the evenings. We spent many quiet evenings at my house that week. Ash brought me my homework from school each day. Most nights he had dinner with us. Ash didn't mention his father. Ash's father continued to try to ban Ash from seeing me, but Ash ignored him. Ash told his father he didn't like what he was doing. His father remained unhappy with our relationship.

The European wood nymphs were still at Ash's house. Rebecca visited. I really liked her. On Saturday, Ash brought her, and on Sunday, he brought Rebecca and her younger sister, Pom, short for Pomegranate. She was a younger version of Rebecca and just as sweet, though very shy. She had not associated with humans at all in Europe and was afraid of them.

She had been told humans were the cause of most of the pollution in the world and thought all humans were evil monsters. She had been told by her parents that humans lied to each other, killed each other and did all kinds of terrible things besides polluting the world. I explained that while there were evil humans in the world, there were also a great number of very good ones who did wonderful things for the world. I found her ignorance about humans interesting. We spent many hours discussing human habits and traits as well as wood nymph habits and traits. We both communicated verbally. We had different languages, but could learn new languages to get along. Wood nymphs and humans used utensils to eat and cooked much of their food. Wood nymphs and humans wore clothes and lived in homes.

I explained about apartments and condominiums. There were no such things as a building with various homes in the same building as in an apartment complex for wood nymphs. Rebecca told of an instance of a huge oak tree in Europe in an isolated area of a forest. She had visited the community with her parents when she was a small child. She said that the wood nymphs had several homes built on the branches of the huge oak tree. We all agreed that this must be similar to a human apartment complex.

By the end of the day, Pom was very comfortable around Mom and me. Forrest and Olivia had come to visit on Sunday. Pom was surprised to see how close my mom and I were with them. After Forrest and Olivia showed up, she really started to relax.

164

We were all very curious about each other and had a good time making comparisons. Stella, the seventeen-year-old wood nymph didn't come over at all. Fine by me.

On Saturday night after everyone else had left and just Mom, Ash, and I remained, I asked Ash what Stella was up to. He sighed and said that Stella wanted nothing to do with any human. He hadn't realized this when the European family had first arrived. They did not associate with humans except on a professional level as in the father's work as a geoscientist. Now, because of his father and Stella, Ash found the whole anti-human attitude bigoted and avoided Stella whenever possible.

By the following Monday, I was still a little weak, but, after a week, I felt I'd missed enough school. If I missed any more school, I took the risk of not being able to graduate. At least, not on time. That wasn't an option for me. I had to graduate. On time! I wasn't going to redo senior year or drag out graduation. Even though I had kept up with most of the homework, there were a few areas that I was having trouble understanding. Ash helped me where he could, but I needed to get back to school.

Both he and Mom were concerned I wasn't ready. "You can't handle a full day of school!" he said. We were sitting on the couch in my living room.

"I have to go. If it gets too bad, I'll go home. I promise." I replied as I leaned against him.

"If you get tired during the day at school, have someone find me, and I'll take you home. Immediately. Promise me." He kissed the side of my head, and I nodded.

When Ash came to get me Monday morning, I was ready to go. I still didn't feel perfect, but I felt I was good enough for school. We drove to school with the heater running full blast. Ash wanted to make sure that I didn't get chilled. I appreciated his concern, but I almost felt baked alive by the time we got into the school parking lot.

The first day in school went by fairly quickly. Everyone I knew seemed to have known that I was sick. I got a lot of "Welcome back!" and "How are you feeling now?" comments. All the people at our lunch table seemed genuinely happy to see. When we had gone through the lunch line and sat at the table, I hadn't realized that Ash had made a point of sitting with my human friends while I wasn't there. Mary told me he had sat with them all that week I was gone. It made me feel good that he was making an effort to maintain human friends. I had to smile as I discretely watched Mary and the other girls at the table interact with Ash. I could tell that they were all a little in awe of him. Most girls in school had a crush on him. I knew the feeling. He couldn't help it that he was so good looking.

The guys at the table were talking about their various sports. Ash said that he might try out for the track team, and I choked on my sandwich. As I was coughing, he patted me on the back and looked at me in all innocence and said, "Everyone seems to be involved in some kind of sport. I should too. I think I might be good at track, especially cross country."

That made me choke harder. Ash patted me harder on the back. While I got some funny looks during my coughing fit, no one wondered why I was choking. Bob Hansen said to Ash, "I've been on track since I've been here. I'll help you with what you need to know." Bob Hansen was a blond, tall, skinny guy built for running.

"Thanks, Bob. That'd be great," Ash said. "I think it'd be neat to earn an athletic letter." Ash grinned at me. I tried to give him a meaningful look, but he just winked. He had to know what I was thinking.

Could Ash actually pull it off? Could he run without jetting? When we were alone together on the ride home, I was going to ask him about it. I couldn't wait to get out of school and ask him what his reason was for feeling the need to letter at the Tomahawk High School.

I was tired by the end of the school day, but I quickly walked with Ash to his car. He had to walk briskly to keep up with me. There was no way I could say what I wanted to say with a bunch of people around. I wanted to be alone with him. Once we were in his car and the doors were closed, I turned to face him while fastening my seat belt. "What are you thinking? Whyever would you want to try out for track? How does that work for you? Can you just run without jetting?"

"Of course I can, silly girl!" he laughed as he started the car. "You want me to blend in with humans, and I will. I'll letter in track. Don't worry, I know how to act around humans. It'll be fun." He laughed again.

"I don't think it's funny," I said darkly. "Is there any way that you could accidently jet while running?"

Ash looked over at me and had the gall to laugh harder. "Of course not. Do you accidently run while you're walking? It's the same principle. You consciously run or you consciously walk. As a wood nymph, I can consciously jet or not."

The next day, Ash talked to the track coach. At lunch, he met me at the cafeteria entrance and said that he wouldn't be meeting me for lunch today. He was going to run around the gym at lunch so the coach could see his style. Since Ash hadn't been in the school before this year, the coach had no idea if he had potential or not.

"Mind yourself. Don't run too fast and surprise the coach too much," I admonished him. He kissed me on the cheek and gave me a big grin, and then he loped toward the gym locker room to change into gym shorts and a T-shirt. I shook my head as I watched him go. Was he going to be the first wood nymph track star? The fact that he would be a track star was a no-brainer to me. I fully believed he could outrun every guy on the track team. I just hoped that he didn't get too carried away with his attempt at acting like a human. It wasn't enough that he was the most handsome boy in the school. It seemed he wanted to be the most handsome boy with a letterman's jacket. I shook my head and went through the lunch line before joining my friends at our table.

"Where's Ash?" Mary asked, trying not to sound too inquisitive.

"He's in the gym showing the track coach what he's got," I said nibbling on a carrot stick. "He wants to be a track star."

"Hey, how cool is that?" Bob said while eating a hamburger. "He looks like he's in good shape. I bet he will do well."

"He should have tried out for football, but the season's almost over," said Sam Anderson, the biggest guy at our table. He was a full back or tight end or something on the football team. He was a nice guy who lived and breathed sports. No one messed with Sam. He didn't take any grief from anyone.

I didn't see Ash again until we were in Drama together. During the class when the teacher had her back to us and was writing on the board, I whispered to him. "How did you do? What happened? What did the coach say?"

He smiled at me and squeezed my hand under the desk. He leaned over and whispered, "I'll tell you later."

That last class seemed to drag. Since we'd finished with the play, Drama wasn't as much fun. The good thing was that it was only a semester in length. I had an ecology class the spring semester in this time slot. Ash made sure he had the same class.

Talking about being on the track team would sound like a normal human conversation. As soon as we got out of our drama class I turned to face Ash. "Well, how did it go?" I said walking backwards down the hall.

"I think I'm on the team!" he gloated. "He liked my style." Ash laughed.

I wasn't sure whether to be proud of him or worry about him. What if he let down his guard and ran too fast? Would Ash realize how fast was too fast?

"Don't worry! For the first couple of races I'll either let someone win, or just beat the guy by a small margin. I'll be sure to look adequately exhausted at the end of the race." He put his arm around my shoulder and turned me so I walked by his side. He still had a big grin on his face. I rolled my eyes at him. When he had that cat-in-the-cream grin, I couldn't help but smile with him.

"Track practice starts right after the Christmas break. Will you miss me while I am on the track team at practice?" he said giving me a quick kiss. He seemed really pleased with himself.

The next two weeks went by pretty quickly. We had to study for semester finals. On December 20th, Ash came over to my house like he usually did in the morning and said, "I have to leave for home right after school tomorrow. We have our winter solstice celebration, and I can't miss it. It's as close as we get to a religious holiday in our clan."

I had remembered hearing that the winter solstice was important to the wood nymphs but didn't know much more. "I really wish I could go with you. I'd love to see that part of your culture," I sighed wistfully. We both knew it wouldn't happen. Ash's dad wouldn't allow a human to their celebration.

"I wouldn't go if it wasn't so important to my whole family. I wish you could go, too," he sighed. We drove the rest of the way to school in silence. We got through that day, and he came over for dinner. Afterwards we studied for our exams.

After school the next day, while he drove me home, he said, "I'll think of you during the ceremony!"

I watched him drive away. I slowly entered the house to find Mom and Forrest waiting. "Forrest came to take you to the winter solstice celebration with the Copper Clan." Mom said. "The only way to get you there in time is to carry you and jet. He has a surprise for you, too. Are you up for that?" I knew that my mom would have loved to have been invited to the celebration. But, it started at dusk and there was no way Forrest could carry both of us.

"Here put on these clothes, and we will go." Forrest said handing me a bundle of something that changed colors in his hands. I recognized the color-changing fabric and felt the nausea in my throat. I wondered if I'd ever get used to it.

I had a hard time figuring out what was the front of the shirt as it kept trying to blend in with whatever was next to it. I had the same trouble with the pants. This time there were shoes in the package. They color shifted too. They looked like a cross between moccasins and ballet slippers. Then I figured something out. It took a couple of seconds for the fabric to match the background. I'd move them from one background color like my carpeting to my bed spread. It would take the shoes a couple of seconds to change colors so I could look quickly at them to tell which shoe went on which foot. I wore my normal socks. I figured if the pants were opaque, they'd cover my socks. After I got dressed, I looked into the mirror above my dresser. I looked like I had a head and hands and no body as the clothes had already blended into the background of my room.

"This is so cool but weird," I said aloud as I left my room to go downstairs. Forrest had a solid-colored long coat on over his color shifting clothes. I think he did this for my mother as she wasn't used to seeing them. She had seen me in them when I got home from the blizzard, but I don't think she paid a lot of attention to what I was wearing.

When I came downstairs, my clothes would color shift to match the steps and wall behind me. "Wow, that's hard on the eyes," Mom said. "I'll concentrate on your face. My trying to focus on your whole body is making me a little nauseous."

"Yeah, I feel the same way," I said laughing and watching my mother's face.

"Maybe I don't want to see the celebration after all. If everyone's wearing those color-shifting clothes, I might get sick," Mom said shaking her head.

I turned to face Forrest when I got to the bottom of the stairs. "Are you sure you can jet while carrying me?"

"No problem. Come on. We've got to go or we'll be late." Forrest held the front door open for me.

"Take care of her. She's precious!" Mom called out to us. I knew she was trying not to be worried. She walked with us to the top of the porch and watched as we walked down the steps. Forrest picked me up and I started to say, "Bye," but I don't think Mom heard anymore than maybe the "B" as we jetted.

Immediately after Forrest picked me up, I lost sight of the world. It didn't even feel like I was moving. I felt and saw a shimmer of various colors around me for a few moments, but I didn't feel the wind like I thought I should have. Were we going so fast I lost the sensation of speed? Astronauts traveled at extremely high speeds, but that didn't show when they walked in space. In an airplane, I didn't feel the forward propulsion or rapid deceleration. Was jetting something like that? My eyes couldn't handle the speed of the surrounding countryside. All I saw was a shimmer.

In the time it took me to realize that we were jetting, we were stopping. I think for my sake, Forrest slowed down slowly. One second I felt and saw the shimmer of speed, and the next second we were trotting up to the same building we'd had Thanksgiving dinner in. Forrest's car was in front of the building. He put his overcoat in his car. Next to his car, I saw a brand new Jeep Wrangler. While mine had been black, this one was a light blue. It was the same style and model as mine had been, but it was shiny and looked like it had just driven off of the showroom floor. I felt a pang of regret at no longer having my car.

I forgot all about the Jeep as we walked around the back of the building. I had never been back there last time. We'd arrived just at dusk. I saw a clearing behind the building. A million little lights fluttered about the clearing. I noticed that the lights were moving like fireflies, but there were no fireflies in the winter.

"What are those little glowing things?" I whispered to Forrest.

"Those are fairies," he said as we walked to where at least 100 wood nymphs were gathering in the clearing.

"What's a fairy?" I asked. I had heard the word before. I kept thinking of Peter Pan, but that was a fairytale. But, wasn't my life becoming a bunch of living fairy tales?

"Do you remember the story of Peter Pan?" Forrest asked as we walked toward the gathering.

"Of course," I replied thinking *Here it comes*. This is the part where another mythical creature comes to life and sure enough, I was right.

"Well, Tinkerbelle in the Peter Pan story is real. At least, fairies are real. They are wonderful entities. They've been around longer than wood nymphs. Would you like to meet one?" he asked.

"Sure!" I said. *Wow, fairies.* I was wondering what other mysterious creature I didn't know about. I didn't meet many interesting creatures as a human.

Forrest made a humming sound. He wasn't exactly humming a tune, more like one or two notes. One of the bright spots bouncing around near the other wood nymphs flitted over to us. It flew in a kind of erratic pattern, like a moth.

"Hold out your hand," Forrest said, and I did, holding it flat, palm up. A tiny, bright, glowing spot landed on my hand. The spot was about half an inch tall. I didn't feel it, but I could see it. After it landed, the light dulled a bit. It still glowed but now I could see what it was. It wasn't just a glowing sphere above my hand.

It looked just like a little Tinkerbelle from Peter Pan, only this one appeared to be a male. It had on the same little green outfit Tinkerbelle wore. I had to look close to see him, he was so small. He looked just like a tiny human with transparent gossamer wings. He looked up at me, his little body glowing, and bowed. I smiled at him. "This is Frederick Brightspot," Forrest said to me.

"Frederick, this is my niece, Laurel Redmond," Forrest said to the fairy.

Frederick bowed again. He then looked over his shoulder toward the rest of the wood nymphs and popped into a bright glowing circle again and took off toward the other glowing spots near where all of the rest of the wood nymphs were gathered.

"The ceremony's about to start. Come on!" Forrest said and took me by the hand. I noticed when we got over by the rest of the wood nymphs that there were various benches of different heights surrounding a circle with an opening in two places across from each other, kind of like parentheses. Most of the wood nymphs took seats on the benches. A few stood behind them. Forrest and I sat on a bench in the front facing the clearing in the center. I didn't see musical instruments, but I could hear them—a lot more instruments than what I had heard in the building at Thanksgiving.

The music flowed right through me and seemed to come from various directions. I felt as if I was listening to some kind of surround-sound system. I heard string instruments, wind instruments, something that sounded like a harpsichord and a harp. Deep tones came from some kind of bass horn. I heard notes from every spectrum of the known scale and thought some might be beyond my hearing capabilities. At times the chords in the music seemed to be from various octaves, like four-part harmony, but in many more parts. Nothing sounded flat or wrong. It was beautiful, hypnotic.

Just when I was beginning to think that the ceremony was a concert, I saw a flash of movement on the far side of the clearing. The fairies flew to the opening and lighted the movement at the end of the field. I saw dancers. The fairies were giving light to the wood nymph dancers.

They wore flowing caftans like I saw Olivia and Rebecca wear. The clothes seemed to flow as if through water. There were eight dancers, and four came around one direction of the clearing in front of the benches and the other four came around the other side. Each group had two women and two men. The movements were rhythmic and perfectly synchronized. The music seemed to follow the dancers.

When the dancers were right in front of me, the music was coming from right behind them. It seemed almost as if the music was coming from them. They slowly danced from one opening into the clearing to the other opening on the other side. After they had departed, the dancers immediately returned as an escort to a really old wood nymph. As the old wood nymph came out into the clearing, the music stopped. If he had been a two-hundred-year-old oak tree, his skin couldn't be more wrinkled.

He walked with a measured pace to the center of the clearing carrying a glowing bowl. When he got to the center, the old man let go of the bowl. It stayed suspended all by itself. The dancers dispersed in all directions and disappeared.

I had seen the clearing, but I had not seen any kind of table or pedestal at that spot where the old guy hung the bowl in the air. The old man raised his hands to the sky and started chanting. I couldn't understand the words. After a few minutes of listening to the chanting, which seemed to grow louder and stronger, the wood nymphs started humming. They started soft but that started building in intensity. They hummed in various chords, kind of like the instruments.

When the humming reached its crescendo, the old man clapped his hands together. Instantly, lightning seemed to flash out of the bowl. It came out in really quick flashes, one immediately followed by another but happening so fast that it looked like a strobe of light coming out of the bowl. As I watched, I saw that each wood nymph was getting hit by a lightning bolt. So much light streaked out of the bowl, I couldn't see the faces of individual wood nymphs around the clearing. As the lightning would touch each one, the wood nymph would raise his or her face to the sky and close his or her eyes in what appeared to be some kind of rapture. They didn't look like they were in pain. This was happening in a matter of seconds as I took all of this in. The lightning worked from near the openings to the centers of each side of the benches. Forrest and I were in the middle on one side. And then the lightning hit me.

I felt energy pulse through me. It felt kind of like a cleansing. I only felt the lightning for a moment and it was gone, but I felt a peace and tranquility that I had never felt before. It felt as if any contaminant in my body was now gone. It felt as if the lightning burned it out without hurting me. I felt refreshed and awakened. I felt really alive, wonderful. I too leaned my head back and closed my eyes and gave myself over to the feeling of rapture that had invaded my body. I had no idea what had just happened, and I didn't care. Anything that felt this good could not be bad.

After a few moments, minutes—I'm not sure how long—I brought myself back to the here and now. The lightning stopped flashing. The bowl and old man were gone. I looked over at Forrest to find him staring at me. "How do you feel?" he asked.

"I feel great!" I cried. "That was the greatest experience of my life! Absolutely incredible." I knew I was grinning like an idiot, but I couldn't stop myself. I didn't know such a feeling was possible. I wondered if I could experience it again.

When he heard that, Forrest got a big grin on his face. "Yeah, it is something, isn't it? It is one of the benefits of being a wood nymph."

"What was that?" I asked. "I've never experienced anything like that before."

"That was the Essence Bowl ceremony. We do it twice a year. If someone were to take all of the goodness of the world and bottle it, that would be the essence. The fairies gather it from different places throughout the world and bring it back to share with us. Every good deed or an altruistic act emits something like smoke into the air from the person performing it. It's a form of energy. The fairies gather this energy and save it for our ceremony. Doing a good deed makes a person feel good. In a way, this is the essence affecting them. It's nature trying to push cognitive species to do good things. The best essence comes when someone or something does a good deed without expecting anything in return. Most of the time, fairies are invisible unless on their hallowed ground. This is hallowed ground. Once in a while someone might catch a glimpse of one outside the fairy special areas, but rarely. Sometimes if you're looking into a forest or across a body of water and see a sparkle of light, you just might be seeing a fairy. They're intelligent but rather fragile creatures. We try to keep their habitat healthy and they bring us the Essence of Good Will," Forrest explained to me.

I tried to understand what he was saying, but I didn't get all of it. I figured I would think about it more at a later date. Right now, I just wanted to concentrate on this wonderful feeling.

"If you have abilities or natural gifts, sometimes the essence will magnify them," Forrest told me as we got up.

That would be something, I thought. I'd love to have another ability.

"Come on, we're going to a party!" Forrest took me by the hand and led me toward the celebration building. Wood nymphs were laughing and dancing all around us and heading in that general direction.

"Laurel!" I heard Olivia call. I didn't see her through the throngs of wood nymphs, but I'd recognize that voice anywhere. Then there was a break in the crowd in front of us, and Olivia rushed up to me. "I'm so glad you could participate in this! Wasn't it wonderful? It's nice to know that there's a lot of good left in the world!" She said, smiling widely.

"Do all wood nymphs receive essence?" I asked.

"Yes, but we have the largest grouping of fairies so we have a more concentrated essence during the ceremonies. In other words, the feeling of rapture you felt would not have been felt as intensely at another wood nymph gathering," Olivia explained.

Then Olivia looked at Forrest and said, "Has she seen it yet?" Olivia had a conspiratorial grin on her face as she said it.

"Well, yes, she's *seen* it, but doesn't know anything about it," Forrest responded with a wink.

I figured they were talking about fairies or something related to that. I was trying to understand everything, but some of it was a bit overwhelming. I didn't say anything as there was so much going on around me in the celebration hall. There was so much to see! There was dancing and music. Our Thanksgiving dinner didn't have this many wood nymphs in attendance. The ones here were dressed in a variety of colors and styles. But none of the clothes looked human. Not all wore color-changing clothes.

For the rest of the evening, we laughed and ate chunks of fresh fruits and drank the coldest, sweetest ice water I'd ever tasted and had a wonderful time. Some of the wood nymphs were drinking wine out of rams' horns. Forrest said I could try some when I got older.

I learned some of the easier dances. I loved this place! I loved learning about my father's culture. When Forrest said it was time for me to go, I wasn't ready. I was wide awake and having the time of my life. He reminded me that I had school tomorrow, and I sighed. I knew he was right and agreed to leave.

We walked out of the building and instead of going to the BMW, Forrest stopped by the blue Jeep. He handed me some keys. "This is for you," he said. "All these years I've wanted to do stuff for you on behalf of your father, and your father's people, but I haven't been able to. Now, I can. And before you ask—yes, your mother knows about it. Are you okay to drive home?"

Was I okay? I was great! I had just had the most intense feeling of my life with the essence and now I was given a new car!

"Is it new?" I asked tentatively. I ran my hand over the beautiful blue paint job. It sparkled with the lights from the celebration house.

"Yes. The odometer has about twenty miles on it. Do you like it?" he asked.

"I absolutely love it! Thank you! This is the coolest gift I have ever received!" I threw myself into his arms. I couldn't help myself. I wondered if I should feel funny about taking this expensive gift from my uncle. But he did say that he was giving it to me on behalf of my father. My father would have given me gifts, right? I looked at the keys. On the fob was Tinkerbelle from Peter Pan. I showed the key fob to Uncle Forrest and said, "How appropriate!" It would remind me of this night forever. I hugged Uncle Forrest tighter. I was delighted with my new family, my new culture, and my new car.

I got in my new car and immediately noticed the new car smell. I was checking out where all of the controls were when I rolled down the window. Olivia came up to the car. She hugged me through the window. "Do you like it?" She asked, smiling.

"I love it and I love you!" I said with a big grin. I couldn't remember this kind of happiness before. I was sure some of it was from the essence, but the feeling of being loved was so huge it made my heart want to just explode in my chest.

Forrest and Olivia stood and waved to me as I turned the Jeep around to drive away from the ceremonial house. I took it slow and easy going home. I knew I would be tired tomorrow. But, I was enjoying myself and my feelings and my new car. I wanted to prolong the moment as long as I could.

CHAPTER 20
BEN ARRIVES

Mom was waiting in the doorway when I pulled up to the garage. Forrest even had a garage opener put in the Jeep for me. He must have gotten that from my mom. I could see her through the glass in the door.

She opened the door as I crossed the porch. "Did you have a good time?" she asked. She was already in her pajamas and robe. She looked at my radiant face. "You look like you had a good time." She finished with, "How do you like your new Jeep?"

"I love it! Thanks for letting him give it to me," I said giving her a big hug as I walked into the house.

"Well, Forrest is your father's brother. He wanted you to have a nice car. I don't think it was a financial strain for him to buy it. Plus, he paid the insurance for a year. How could I deny you something from your father's family?" she said simply and then asked, "How was the ceremony?"

"Mom, it was great! I'll tell you about it." We walked into the living room and sat on the couch. I proceeded to tell her all about the evening, including the Essence Bowl ceremony.

"It's like lightning flashing out of this big old bowl. As I understand it, each bolt of lightning was a piece of energy. Each flash touched a wood nymph. It was wonderful, the feeling that the Essence gave me. Like it washed away any contaminant in my body. It gave me a feeling of peace, but in an energetic kind of way. I feel like I want to do nicer things with my life and for other people. I feel great!"

"What's this essence stuff? It must be safe, or Forrest wouldn't have allowed you to have anything to do with it, but . . ." Mom asked.

"Forrest tried to explain it all to me, but I understood only part of what he was trying to tell me. Ask Forrest about it. I'm sure he'll tell you everything you want to know. The only bad thing I can think of regarding the whole night is that the essence won't go to humans," I said softly.

"I'm sorry, Mom. I think that's why Forrest didn't bring you along. They weren't even sure if it would come to me, since I'm only half wood nymph. It seems no one has control over the essence. The fairies gather it up, and, when it's released, it goes where it wants to. It's not harmful. It's a good thing." I finished with, "It appears to be a wood nymph thing."

Mom thought about that for a minute and said, "Fairies, huh? More mythical creatures that are real. Huh. Well, it sounds like that's a good thing, and you're right. I'd love to experience such a thing. I'm glad you could. Is there a way I can watch the ceremony even if this lightning essence stuff passed me by? I mean, it isn't harmful to humans, is it?" Mom asked me.

"I don't know. I can't see a problem with you attending the ceremony and watching, but it's really not up to me," I said looking at my mom.

"Yeah, I guess I can understand that. So many of the wood nymphs have invited me into their hearts and homes. I hope they'll eventually allow me to come. If they don't I'll respect their decision," she replied.

This whole concept of wood nymphs accepting humans into their private domains was new to everyone concerned. Wood nymphs had adapted to human culture to be accepted in the human communities. But, inside their own clan villages, they could be themselves. The wood nymph elders of my father's clan liked my mom. But, would they allow her into their private lives? The solstice ceremonies were a wood nymph cultural thing. Would they want to share that with my mom? They had shared other things with her that they had never shared with another human being.

"Thanks for letting me go and thanks for letting Forrest buy me a car," I said hugging my mom. I got up and headed for the stairs to study for my last final.

"I'm glad that you had a good time. But, it is midnight. You have tests tomorrow." Mom said as she shut off the downstairs lights.

"Yeah, but it's only half a day tomorrow! " I scampered upstairs to clean up for bed.

I saw that my mom had already left by the time I went downstairs to have breakfast. She must have had early clients, I thought. Ash picked me up at the usual time. I saw him drive up and ran out. He saw my radiant smile as I got into his car and smiled back. "You seem in a good mood," he said.

"I am. How was your solstice celebration?" I asked. I couldn't wait to tell him about mine!

"Uh, it was okay. I really am sorry that you couldn't go," he said sincerely.

I blurted out. "When I got in the house after you dropped me off yesterday, Forrest was here. He jetted me to the Copper Clan. I attended their ceremonies. I was able to participate in the essence ceremony. Then Forrest gave me a new Jeep." I smiled smugly.

"You went to an Essence Bowl ceremony?" He stared at me, incredulous.

"Yup. Uncle Forrest had me there in time for the ceremony. I saw fairies and met a fairy by the name of Frederick Brightspot. They're really tiny. I had to look close to really see him," I said smiling. I liked the incredulous look on Ash's face. Maybe his family didn't see me as a wood nymph, but my father's clan did. Not only did they accept me as one of their own, they took me to their ceremonies.

"I was touched by the light energy thing, too," I said smugly.

Ash whispered, "My dad said there was no way you could attend such a thing. It'd make no sense to you, and when everyone around you was touched by the light and you weren't, you'd feel left out."

"Ah, but the light *did* touch me. What a magnificent feeling it gave me, too. Hey, you better start the car or we will be late for our tests," I said to Ash.

"I knew your wood nymph side would prevail," he said. "I knew that the energy would touch you. I told my dad that. He was convinced it wouldn't. I can't wait to tell him how wrong he was." Now Ash was smiling, too. He started the car.

The half day of school flew by. The tests were completed in no time, and we were out of school for Christmas break. The garage door was open when Ash and I pulled up in front of the house, and I saw Mom's car in the garage next to my new Jeep.

"Is that your new car?" Ash asked. "It really looks nice."

"It is nice. It handles great and has that wonderful new car smell. I wonder why Mom's home," I replied.

Then, I looked up at the front door and I saw a familiar face in the open doorway of the house. "Dad!" I screamed, threw open the door of Ash's SUV and flew up the stairs and into his arms. Ben was home! I couldn't believe it! I remember hearing that he would be home for Christmas, but I didn't know when. That must have been where my mom was when I got up for school. She was at the airport picking him up.

Ben hugged me so tight I thought for a moment that he was going to disconnect my spine. "It's so good to see you!" he said as he held me close. Just then, he noticed Ash. The way he looked from Ash and back to me, I knew he saw the similarity.

"You must be Ash," Ben said. With an arm around my waist, he extended the other hand to Ash.

"Yes, sir." Ash said walking up to us and shaking Ben's hand.

Ben had military bearing. Everything about him screamed organization and efficiency. He was precise in everything he said and did. Ash looked nervous until Ben smiled. Then Ash smiled, and I knew everything was going to be all right.

"Oh, Dad, it's so good to see you!" I said. "How long are you home for?"

"About three weeks," Ben replied, letting me go once we were inside the house.

Mom came out of the kitchen wiping her hands on a towel. "I was just making lunch. Are you hungry?" she asked me and Ash. "It's broiled chicken breast and a salad." She turned to Ben. "Ash has a special diet. His people can't eat anything artificial. They can't even eat fast food," Mom said smiling.

Ben caught the "his people" comment and raised an eyebrow. Mom saw it.

"I'll tell you everything," Mom said. "There are some things that need to be shown as well as told, and I had to wait for the kids to come home to tell you."

The four of us sat down to eat the salad and chicken. I really liked having the four of us eating together.

"Valerie told me that you found out that you have family here," Ben said to me. "How do you feel about that?"

"Oh, Dad, it's great! We're not the three of us anymore. The whole Copper Clan has been great to both me and Mom, and they're looking forward to meeting you, too." I gushed at Ben.

"Copper Clan? What's that? Are they Scottish?" Ben asked.

"Ah, no, Dad. They're not Scottish." I kind of stammered at him.

Ben put his fork down and looked at Mom and then at me and said, "Okay, spill it. Someone's hiding something. What are you trying to tell me?"

We'd never held anything back from him, and he was confused. He was right, we had been less than completely honest about the wood nymphs, but how do you tell someone about wood nymphs over the phone? How do you tell your step-dad that you are not completely human?

"Ben, you are absolutely right," Mom said earnestly. "We're trying to tell you something, but it's hard. It is not a bad thing, but you have to have an open mind about it. I'm going to tell you a few things that are going to make me sound like I've lost my mind. I haven't. A few of these facts were a bit hard to accept for me, but after seeing the evidence, I had no choice but to accept them as truth. But I couldn't tell you over the phone. Some things need to be shown as well as told." .

Ben said tentatively, "Okay. I'm ready for the facts."

"I'm glad Ash is here," Mom said looking at Ash and smiling. "He can help with the facts." Ash didn't smile. I think he remembered my melt down and didn't want to deal with a grown up man having a melt down.

Mom took a deep calming breath and started with, "You know I've never lied to you, right? I'd never tell you something in all seriousness and then tell you later it was a joke, right? What I'm about to tell you isn't a joke. It's real and we can prove it."

Ben looked at each of us in turn. "I'm listening," he said softly.

Mom sighed again. "This was really hard for me. I didn't take this information easily. I had a kind of melt down when I realized the truth, and I knew I had to accept the information as fact."

Ben nodded and Mom continued. "Do you remember hearing about wood nymphs?" she asked.

Ben narrowed his eyes. "I guess so," he replied slowly. "Mythical creatures that live in the woods or something like that, right?"

"Well, they live in the woods, but they're not so much mythical. They're real. They look human and act human to fit in with human society. They're a different species, but their DNA is similar enough to human that, when conditions are perfect, a human can mate with a wood nymph and create a child."

Mom looked intently at Ben. She sighed again and pushed on. "Do you remember when I told you about the weekend with the man in Presque Isle? The weekend I got pregnant with Laurel?"

Ben nodded.

"I found out that Laurel's biological father is dead. I also found out that he's a wood nymph. Laurel's half wood nymph." We all looked at Ben for his reaction.

Ben looked at each of us as if waiting for the joke part, but we all had very serious faces. "You really believe that," Ben said astounded.

"Oh, I don't just believe it, I know it," Mom said. "Ash and Laurel can prove it. We'll start with the first piece of proof. Come upstairs. Ash, you and Laurel come, too." Mom took Ben's hand and led him toward the stairs.

Ash sighed as we went up the stairs, following behind my mom and Ben. I squeezed his hand and whispered, "This is going to be fine. Ben's smart. He'll get it."

Mom had Ash and me stand in front of her vanity table. Instead of having us all lean down to the table, she picked up the mirror and turned on the light so that the magnified side was facing us. "Ben, Laurel and Ash are almost as tall as you. Hold this vanity mirror to Laurel's and Ash's faces. Then look at their eyes. After looking at their eyes, hold the lighted mirror to your own eyes and tell me what you see." Mom sat on the vanity chair and watched.

Ben stood between Ash and me while we looked into the mirror at a close range. Our pupils shrunk down. At a certain point, instead of turning into a round dot for a pupil like Ben's eyes, there was the slight elongation like a cat's eye. Ben then held the mirror equally close to his own eyes and then handed the mirror to me and said, "Hold it in front of your face again."

He had seen the difference, but didn't believe it. "There's a difference in the pupils. I see that, but that just could be a natural birth defect that runs in the family. You're not related to her are you?" Ben asked Ash. "You sure look like her."

Ash looked at Ben and said, "No sir, we are not related. Not that I know of. We're from different clans."

"So it could be some kind of defect of the eye. That doesn't prove anything," Ben stated as he turned off the mirror and put it back on the vanity table.

"Ash can jet, Dad. He can run faster than the human eye can see. Do you remember *Star Trek* and warp speed? It is kind of like that." I said holding Ash's hand.

I could see the incredulous look on Ben's face. He was beginning to think we were crazy. He looked from Ash to me and then to my mom, shaking his head. "Really?" he said with a laugh.

"Really, Dad, it is true. Ash, will you show him, please?" I asked.

Ash sighed again and nodded. We all went downstairs. "Do you want a jacket?" I asked as it was cold outside.

"I won't get cold in this short a period of time." Ash replied in a resigned way. I could tell he hated this show-off stuff. It was one of the reasons why wood nymphs didn't show their true selves to humans.

Ben, Mom, and I put on jackets and stood on the porch. Ash walked down to the driveway.

"Watch Ash closely, Ben. Don't blink," Mom said.

I believe to humor us, Ben did indeed concentrate on Ash. I think he believed Ash was pulling some kind of trick. Ben watched as Ash turned to look at me and said, "I'll be back in a moment." Ash turned down the driveway and was gone. Just like that. There was no rush of wind, no sonic boom, nothing. First Ash was there, and then he was gone.

"Where are the mirrors?" Ben said, smiling. "That's a pretty good trick."

Mom was getting upset. "We're not playing tricks. Ash can go from here to Presque Isle in about two minutes. Forrest and Olivia come down here all of the time by jetting. It's much quicker. Watch the driveway."

Ben turned to face the driveway, and I think for effect, Ash concentrated on slowing down coming toward us on the driveway. At first he was a blur and then came into focus. He wasn't even breathing hard.

"That's either a really good trick, or you're telling the truth." Ben said soberly.

"Ash can jump really high, too. Ash, see that huge pine just there? Can you show Ben?" Ash sighed and nodded. I kind of wanted to see him jump, too, as I had never actually seen him do that. I had just felt it when he jumped with me in his arms.

"He grabbed me and jumped into a tree when the Hodag attacked me," I said as Ash got into position in front of the tree. Ben turned to look at me with shock and Ash waited until Ben turned to look at him. As soon as Ash knew that Ben was looking, he bent his knees just a bit and shot straight up about thirty feet into the tree. He stood on a limb for about thirty seconds so that he knew that Ben had seen him jump, and stepped off of the branch and came down to the ground. He landed so softly, the snow wasn't disturbed except where his feet landed.

Ben's jaw hung open. He stared at Ash. Mom looked at Ben and used her index finger on his chin to close his mouth. When Mom touched his chin, Ben jumped. I had never seen Ben startled before. He was usually so calm and collected. This was unnerving.

Ash walked over to us slowly. He didn't want Ben to freak out.

"Wow. That was incredible. What else can you do?" Ben said, staring at Ash as if he was a freak. Ash looked down at the ground. He was getting really uncomfortable.

We needed reinforcements. I took out my new cell phone and called Forrest. "Uncle Forrest? Hi, yeah, it's me. Um, my dad's here from Iraq. We are trying to explain about you and Ash. Even though Dad saw Ash jet and jump up into a tree, he is having a hard time. Can you help? This human education thing is making Ash uncomfortable. Thanks." I hung up the phone and looked at Ben.

"We'll have help with this whole explanation thing, soon." Ash looked at me relieved. Ben was making him feel like a freak, and he didn't like it.

I pulled Ash to the side to talk to him where Mom and Ben couldn't hear. Ben was talking to Mom. "I'm sorry he is making you feel like a freak," I said softly.

"How do you know what I'm feeling?" he asked just as softly. He narrowed his eyes as he looked at me.

"I can tell. Maybe I can see it in your face. You're uncomfortable, aren't you?"

"Yeah, I really am. I'm not a freak," he said fervently.

I smiled at him. "No, you're not. Neither am I." I kissed him softly on his lips.

Ben had just turned back to me and was walking over to us when Forrest showed up right in front of him. Forrest stood between Ben and me. "Hello, Ben." Forrest said, holding out his right hand.

"How did you get here? Have we met?" Ben said backing away from Forrest.

"This is Forrest. I told you about him," Mom said, holding Ben's arm and guiding him to Forrest.

"I know you, Ben. We haven't actually met, but I'm Laurel's Uncle Forrest. I just jetted here. Olivia will be here soon. Ah, here she is," Forrest said, spotting Olivia.

Olivia had stopped farther up the driveway and was walking so gracefully she seemed to float up to us. She was wearing her color-shifting caftan that hurt human eyes. She was in full wood nymph form. Ben stared at her as if he was seeing a vision or a ghost. He put his arm around Valerie as if to protect her.

Mom shook off Ben's arm and went to hug Olivia. "Oh, Olivia, Forrest, thank you for coming. We're having a hard time with the wood nymph explanations."

Ben just stood where he was. I knew he could see the similarity between Olivia and me. I really did look more like Olivia than Mom. If he looked a bit closer, I knew he could see the similarity between Forrest, Ash, and me. We all were tall, thin, with light-brown stick-straight hair, and green eyes, although Ash had styled his hair with gel.

"You're the one who gave Laurel the new Jeep," Ben stated as he turned back to face Forrest.

"Yes. I asked Valerie if it was all right, and she said yes. As her uncle, I want to do things for Laurel. I love her. I've been watching over her for a long time," Forrest responded extending his right hand to Ben again.

Ben stared at Forrest, and then at his hand and said, "For a long time? What do you mean?"

Smiling to try to put Ben at ease, Forrest dropped his hand and said, "I've known that Laurel was my niece since before she was born. As her uncle, it was my responsibility to make sure that nothing bad happened to her. When you came into Laurel and Valerie's lives, I watched you to make sure you were a good guy. Because you have been so loving and caring and accepted Laurel as your daughter I didn't need to interfere. As you can see by Olivia's clothes, we can go places without being seen. If you had been a bad character, I would have had to eliminate you from their lives."

Ben didn't like the sound of that and scowled. He thought for a minute and said, "How did you know about Laurel? As much as I don't like the sound of the threat, in a way, I'm glad you've been looking out for Valerie and Laurel." Ben sighed. "They mean everything to me. In a weird kind of way, I'm glad they've had a protector other than me. I try to do the best I can for them and I certainly love them. But if you know anything about the military, it can take me away from them. I hate being away from them." Ben finished speaking and looked from Forrest to Olivia.

"Come into the living room," Mom said, holding Olivia with one arm and grabbing Ben with the other. Ben came along meekly, staring at Olivia. I knew how he felt. I'd never met anyone as beautiful as Olivia when I had first met her, too. If Ben saw Olivia with the European wood nymphs, I think Ben's heart would stop. I knew he loved my mother, but wood nymphs had an attraction about them. No doubt about that.

Mom sat on the couch between Ben and Olivia. Ash and I sat on the loveseat and Forrest took the recliner.

"We showed Ben the pupils of our eyes. He saw Ash jet and jump about thirty feet or so into a tree," Mom said. "He's having a hard time believing his eyes."

Ben just shook his head and didn't say anything. He was staring at Olivia and watched her caftan disappear into the couch as it matched the colors and fabric.

"This is a special fabric made by wood nymphs and used by wood nymphs only." Olivia said. Ben stared at Olivia trying to see her body but only seeing the couch like the rest of us. He then looked at her face with what appeared to be awe or shock.

"I can see how you could blend into the background," Ben stated as he tried to look only at Olivia's face.

"We can change to match our surroundings. I wore this outfit since it changes color to match whatever I'm up against. I wanted to show you something strictly of the wood nymph culture," Olivia said as Ben continued to stare at her.

"The Army sure could use fabric like that," Ben murmured. Olivia smiled and then seemed to have disappeared. She had changed her face and hands to match the fabric and texture of the couch.

"Where did she go?" Ben asked suddenly as Olivia seemed to have disappeared.

"Dad, Olivia didn't disappear. She's just changed her skin to match the texture and color of the fabric of the couch. Look at her from an angle, and you'll see that the couch does not conform to its usual lines. There's a bulge where there shouldn't be, and the bulge is Olivia." I said, smiling.

Ben turned to look at where Olivia was sitting from different angles. With effort, he could see where the couch did not have its natural shape. There was the shape of something bulging from the front of the cushions on the couch. When Olivia put her hand out in front of her, Ben could see the texture and color of the fabric of the couch for just a moment before Olivia's hand changed into the color and texture of the wall behind her hand.

"Incredible." Ben stated in absolute awe. "You should be in the Army. Many special operations could be completed with a skill like that."

Olivia changed her face and hands back into their normal color and texture. She smiled at Ben and said, "No. That'll never happen. Most humans can never know of us. You do understand that you must keep our secret. We blend in with humans, but humans do not need to know that we're different from them and that we have talents and skills that they don't have."

"Why the secrecy?" Ben asked. He was starting to relax. He leaned back into the cushions of the couch.

"Most humans would try to use us in ways that we would not want to be used. We would be exploited. We blend in by working in human jobs and we do human things. There's no need for humans to know about wood nymphs. We look enough like humans to blend in to their communities." Forrest stated intently, looking straight at Ben.

"Can't you see how some government would try to control the wood nymphs? They'd have no peace or freedom. They've given up much to live in human society. Let's not take their culture away from them or exploit it." Mom implored softly.

Forrest sighed. He knew it was important to get Ben to understand and to like wood nymphs or me and my mom's life would become difficult.

"Ben, I've been watching out for Laurel her whole life," Forrest started and then told Ben about how my mom and Leif had met, and how Leif had died.

Olivia told Ben about her limited ability to see the future. She didn't see everything, but the things she did see all came true.

Olivia sat quietly for a second and then started naming the people in Ben's platoon. These were things Mom and I didn't know. She told Ben about a secret mission he could never have told us about due to security.

Ben's eyes were almost bulging from their sockets. I could tell he was starting to really believe. I remembered how hard it was for me and Mom to believe the truth. I kind of felt sorry for Ben at this moment. It was disorienting to find out that myth was actually truth.

"There's no way you could know that," he stated flatly. "No one outside of my chain of command knew about that mission. Is it that you're able to see things like a psychic or something?"

"It's something like that. I can't see everything I want to, but sometimes if I don't concentrate too hard, I can see what I need to." Olivia said softly.

"We've grown to love Laurel and Valerie," Olivia said softly. "Our social interaction with humans was almost nonexistent, but we embraced Laurel and Valerie and invited them into our homes. Please be the kind of person we can embrace. Laurel has opened a new dimension between humans and wood nymphs. She has added a new life to an old species."

"My family dislikes humans," Ash said. "I'm trying to change that. I used to hate humans because I thought they were selfish, rude and tried to impose their rules on others. Then, I met Laurel and her mom and got to know them. I realized that not all humans were selfish."

For a few minutes, Ben contemplated all of the information that he had just received. After a moment he sighed and said, "Bottom line is, I love Valerie and Laurel, and I think they're special. I guess I can understand how someone else could think that they're special, too. I'm having a bit of difficulty understanding the whole different species thing. But, it's obvious that you're family. You look just like her. As long as no one tries to take Laurel's affections from me, I won't complain about having an extended family for Laurel."

We spent the rest of the afternoon and evening discussing the similarities between wood nymphs and humans and explaining the differences. During the conversation, Mom cleaned up the lunch plates and made dinner. No one had finished lunch.

"Wood nymphs can't eat anything artificial," Olivia explained as we all sat at the dining room table for dinner. Mom made a broiled fish with mashed potatoes and a salad.

Ben watched Forrest and Olivia as they ate. I think he was surprised they ate with a knife and fork just like he did.

After dinner, Forrest went to our fireplace and added some logs. There had been plenty of times I had come home to find Forrest or Olivia with Mom, and there generally was a fire in the fireplace. But, this was the first time I watched Forrest start a fire. He put some logs in the grate without any kindling or paper. He hummed softly with his hand outstretched to the wood. In a second, the wood caught fire as if someone had saturated the wood in gasoline and tossed a match on it. A nice roaring fire that would normally take quite some time to develop was accomplished in seconds.

"Holy cow!" Ben muttered as he watched Forrest light the fire.

"I've never seen Forrest light a fire before. Have you, mom?" I asked as she rinsed the leftover food off of a plate into the garbage disposal.

"Of course. Many times," she answered looking at me curiously.

"I didn't know they could do that!" I almost hissed at her.

"Me, either," mumbled Ben, still staring at the fire and at Forrest.

"Oh, I thought you knew," Mom responded.

I turned to look at Olivia. "Can you do it too?" I asked.

"Yes. So should you with some training," she stated, smiling.

I turned to Ash. "Can you start a fire like Forrest just did?" I had never seen anyone light a fire at the huge fireplace at Ash's house, but there always seemed to be a roaring blaze in their fireplace when I had been in the house.

"Yes." Ash looked at me quizzically. "How do you light a fire?"

I gave a disgusted sigh. "I have to use a match or a lighter, and a starter log or paper and kindling. If I use paper and kindling, the fire starts slow, and most of the time I have to light it two or three times before it stays lit."

"Me, too," Ben said, still staring at Forrest and the fireplace.

I touched Ben's hand to get his attention and rolled my eyes. "Dad, as you can see, we're still learning about each other."

We all looked at Ben. He thought for a moment and then said with a sigh. "Today has been an incredible experience. I'd never in my life believe that such things were possible. The truth is, no one would believe me if I did tell them," he said with a chuckle. We all smiled.

"Yeah, wait until you meet the shape-shifting Indians!" I laughed.

"What?" Ben said looking startled. I was beginning to think that he was getting his brain fried.

I gave him a brief overview about George and Adam. "Oh, Dad, this is just the beginning of your education. There really are Hodags. I haven't seen one, but I was attacked and Ash saved me. I know what they sound like," I said with a shudder. "There are fairies, too."

"Really?" Ben asked looking at my mom.

"Yes. George takes the form of his spirit guide which is a black bear," Mom said sipping an after-dinner coffee.

"My friend Adam from the reservation turns into a bald eagle," I stated. "George and Adam helped find me when I almost died in the snow. I have at least one wood nymph talent. I have the call."

"The call is a special talent that some wood nymphs have," Forrest explained. "When a wood nymph is in danger, he or she can project a call to all wood nymphs and certain Native Americans in range. Humans may not actually hear the call but may find themselves compelled to go somewhere. The sound carries great distances and hooks up a kind of link between the caller and the receiver. The receiver hearing the call is instinctually driven in the right direction."

I could tell that Ben was shocked but was really starting to believe what he was hearing. He understood that wood nymphs were real and that Mom, Ash, Forrest, Olivia, and me were not lying to him. I felt it when the acceptance took place. He kept glancing at Olivia like she was not quite real in her color shifting clothes and un-believable beauty. But the fact was, he accepted that wood nymphs were real.

"Dad, being different isn't bad. It's just different," I said giving him a hug.

"Oh, Laurel, this is some heavy-duty stuff you and your mother have dumped on me. But, these people seem to really care about you and your mom and that makes them all right in my book," he whispered in my ear while he hugged me.

"Wait until you meet Adam and see George shift," I said going to sit next to Ash.

Ben laughed and shook his head. "Not today. I've had enough for one day."

"Tomorrow, though, you have got to see the pier. Uncle Forrest made it. Uncle Forrest is an architect," I said smiling proudly at him.

"I knew there'd be changes when we moved to the north woods, but I never ex-pected anything like this. If Valerie can adapt and thinks the things you do are good, I can accept them. I trust Valerie's judgment." Ben reached over and kissed Mom. She looked back at Ben and smiled.

"I better get home," Ash said at that moment. He was having a little trouble dealing with the whole human acceptance of wood nymph culture. Even though Ben was trying hard to be understanding and accepting, Ash kept thinking of Ben as a stu-pid human. I felt what Ash was feeling. I could feel his emotion.

"I'll walk you to the porch," I said. Once we were out on the porch I said to Ash, "Please be patient with Ben. This is hard for him. He's not just a stupid human.

You didn't like the idea of me when you first met me because something like me had never existed in your world before. There are times when we find that the truths and beliefs we have had all of our lives turn out to be lies. Do you know about Santa Claus? What about the Easter Bunny? When I was little, I believed in Santa Claus as the great old guy who loved kids and delivered presents to them on Christmas Eve. I found out later that it was a lie. Ben was pretending to be Santa Claus, and I saw through the disguise. It broke my heart when I found out that Santa Claus was a lie. Sometimes i's a shock to learn something new. That's what Ben's going through now, but he's accepting you, me, and the whole wood nymph concept." I wrapped my arms around Ash.

Ash whispered, "Okay. I'm trying. But, how do you know? How are you so confident that he won't tell the wrong people and destroy our world?" He held me close.

I pushed myself back far enough to look Ash in the face. "I know. First, because I know Ben and I know he's honorable. Second, I felt it when he accepted the truth."

"You felt it?" Ash said narrowing his eyes.

"Yeah, you didn't?" I asked. "I thought everyone could feel it."

"No, I didn't feel it. Very few wood nymphs are Emotion Readers. I've heard of only one in my life, and that was a distant cousin. Have you always been able to do this? I don't remember you telling me things like this before." He stared into my eyes.

I could feel confusion and an undefined emotion coming off of Ash in waves. "I feel your confusion and something else," I said, looking at him. "I don't remember knowing anyone else's emotions before today. I mean, other than what I could tell from their facial expressions."

"The essence has affected your abilities. I wonder what other ability you have that's been lying dormant," Ash said holding me and kissing my face.

I realized what the emotion was that I hadn't identified earlier. It was respect and appreciation. He liked me having wood nymph abilities.

"You like it that I have abilities," I stated as a fact. It gave me a warm and fuzzy feeling to have some kind of wood nymph abilities. It made me feel closer to Ash.

"Of course I do. It'll help my family accept you more easily. I can't wait to tell my dad that you experienced essence and that you have other abilities. I wonder if you have more," Ash said as he kissed the side of my face.

"You're shivering. You better get in the house. You don't need to get chilled. I'll see you tomorrow." He kissed me one last time on the lips and ran to his car. I went into the house and watched through the glass as he drove away.

I wondered what other abilities, if any, I would manifest. I went back into the living room and stood in the doorway watching Ben and Forrest talk about their careers. I looked over at Olivia and Mom. They were discussing recipes. If someone came into the house, and if Olivia was wearing normal clothes, no one would think Olivia and Forrest were different from any other human. It appeared that Ben had decided to accept that not only did I have an extended family, I had an extended family that wasn't human. Good old Ben could handle anything, I thought. I was so proud of him, Forrest, Olivia, and my mom. This was my family, and I loved them.

Ben looked up at that moment and saw me looking at him with a special smile that I had always reserved just for him. Since I was a little girl, I'd look at him in this way. He blew me a kiss and I caught it, just like we used to do when I was a little girl. I ran up to him. He stood up, and I threw my arms around him. "I'm really glad you're here. I'm really glad you met my biological father's family, and it means everything to me to have you all get along," I said holding Ben tight around the waist with my face in his chest.

"Honey, these seem to be good people. I think you couldn't have asked for a better extended family even if they aren't human. Just because they're different, I can't judge them negatively. I'll just have to have an open mind. I've always believed that people should be judged on their merits and not their appearances." Ben looked at Forrest and smiled. Forrest smiled back and got up from his chair and walked to Ben.

"Thanks Ben. I knew for years that you were an honorable man," Forrest said extending his hand to Ben. Ben shook his hand and it almost appeared as if an unspoken agreement had been initiated between them. Whatever their thoughts and feelings, they did not appear to be bad. I sensed caution, acceptance and the beginnings of trust emanating between them.

Olivia and Mom got up, too. It was late and we were all tired. The fire had burned down to ashes. Mom, Ben, and I were tired. I could feel exhaustion coming off of Ben in waves. I had yet to see Forrest or Olivia even yawn. Didn't wood nymphs get tired?

"How much sleep do you get a night?" I asked Forrest covering my yawn with my hand.

Forrest laughed at me and said, "It varies. Sometimes I can go days without sleep or I sleep four or five hours every night. It depends on the need, I guess."

"I usually sleep five or six hours every night. I need my beauty sleep." Olivia said and we all laughed. It was funny because there was no one more beautiful than Olivia.

Ben, Mom, and I walked Olivia and Ben to the door and said our good-byes. As Forrest and Olivia were putting on their jackets, Forrest asked Ben, "How long will you be here before you have to go back?"

Ben had his arm around mom and said, "Just about three weeks."

"Great! That gives us time to get to know each other better. Oh, if you don't mind, we'll come back tomorrow and discuss Christmas," Forrest said as Olivia and

Forrest walked out of the door. They got to the bottom of the stairs, took two steps into the driveway and disappeared. In unison.

"Do you ever get used to seeing that?" Ben asked shaking his head.

"Not yet, I haven't," Mom replied chuckling.

"I wish I could do it," I muttered, and we all laughed as we walked back into the house.

I thought about how nice it was to have my family together as I went up the stairs to my room to go to bed.

CHAPTER 21
THE NEIGHBORS

I woke up feeling great. It was December 23rd. There were only two more days until Christmas. As I stretched and got out of bed, I caught myself smiling about my life. Ben was home for Christmas. He'd be here for just about three weeks. He knew about me, and he knew about wood nymphs, and he'd accepted the truth of it! I'd have to call Adam to come over. I couldn't wait to see Ben's face when he saw Adam and George change into animals. I couldn't stop grinning about that.

Mom and Ben were already sitting at the dining room table. "Good morning! What time is it?" I asked. "Did I sleep late? I didn't even look at the clock when I woke up."

Ben answered, "No, honey, it is only eight o'clock."

"What are your plans today?" Mom asked taking a sip of her coffee. "We plan to decorate for Christmas and hoped you'll join us."

"Yeah, that'll be fun!" I said happily. I loved decorating for Christmas. I loved the lights, the garlands, the music and the whole festive atmosphere. Maybe part of what I was feeling was a residual from the essence stuff, but whatever the reason, I felt great. My family was together! We were going to be doing human stuff. As much as I liked the idea of being a wood nymph, I didn't want to lose my human side.

I wondered if Ash would like to help us. I wonder if he'd ever had anything to do with human traditions and holidays at his house.

"Can Ash help?" I asked. I knew Ben was still adjusting to me having a boyfriend. However, I thought, compared to the other stuff Ben had dealt with yesterday, my having a boyfriend was not even a blip on his radar.

"Sure," Ben said pouring some more coffee into Mom's and his coffee cups. "I'd like to get to know your boyfriend better." The last part he said with a wink.

Cool. I think he likes Ash.

It did really seem that Ben was trying to take all of his new knowledge in stride. Just for the fun of it, I tried to reach out intentionally to feel Ben's emotions. I could feel that he was very happy to be home. He was having a hard time adjusting to his new reality, but he was coping with it.

I went into the kitchen and called Ash on his cell phone. Since I knew his dad didn't really care for me, I felt uncomfortable calling his house phone. He picked up on the second ring. "Good morning, Laurel!" he said with a smile in his voice as he answered the phone.

"Hi, Ash. We're going to decorate for Christmas today. Would you like to join us? We usually have pizza while we decorate the tree. Mom bought special natural ingredients for the pizza, and I don't think there are any preservatives in it. She always makes it from scratch."

"Do you think that is a good idea?" Ash asked tentatively. "Not the pizza, I'm sure that'll be fine. But what about Ben? How's he doing today? I really don't want to come over and feel like a freak. How's he coping?"

"Well, I think he's doing fine. I really think Ben's handling the information well. Maybe his Army training helped him adapt to situations, but I'm just guessing. While I believe he's a bit nervous about everything, he's trying to come to terms with it all. I'm sure he never expected to find his step-daughter is half human and half wood nymph. He was fine at breakfast this morning and even winked at me when I asked if you could come over. I can only guess why.

"Decorating for Christmas is a tradition for us. It'd be great to have you join in on a human tradition. There'll be times when I need human activities and traditions. This is one of them. I'll never give up Christmas," I stated emphatically as I got out my cereal bowl and poured my cereal into it.

"Okay. I'll learn about your customs. In the future, you'll learn more wood nymph things. I guess it won't be too bad to learn human traditions," Ash replied.

"Great! Come over whenever you can. I'm eating my breakfast now. I think we'll start digging out Christmas boxes when I finish." We said our good-byes, and I ate my breakfast at the dining room table with Ben and Mom.

After breakfast, Mom said that she had to go into the office for a couple of hours and would return just after lunch. After she left, I put my dishes in the dishwasher, and Ben and I went into the attic to dig out the Christmas boxes. We were looking for were huge plastic containers with lids clearly marked, "CHRISTMAS."

When we got in the attic, Ben sat on a box. "Sit down a minute. I want to talk to you before we get started." Ben motioned for me to sit on an adjacent box.

I sat on the box and waited for him to say what he wanted to say.

"You know that you and your mom really rocked my world yesterday. I had no idea that wood nymphs were anything but fiction. I'm really trying to come to grips with everything that you told me. I want you to know that it wouldn't bother me if I found out you were part alien. I know you and I love you. I may not have had a part in your birth, but in every way that matters, you're my daughter. You know I feel that way, don't you?" Ben said earnestly as he sat on the edge of the box facing me.

191

"Of course, I know that. I love you, too. I was a little worried about how you would respond to all this. Mom said that being a true scientist was being able to accept changes as the evidence warrants. Sometimes I think we just need to keep our sense of humor while we experience new things. I keep expecting the little leprechaun from the cereal box to walk into the yard." I laughed, and Ben laughed with me.

"After what I learned yesterday, I guess that wouldn't surprise me either," Ben said as he got up off his box. "However, I'd really appreciate it if there were no more secrets. I understand why you didn't tell me about wood nymphs and shape shifters before. But, please don't hold things from me anymore. However, don't tell me that there are little green men right now, or I'll start looking for them. Agreed?" Ben finished and picked up a Christmas box.

"Agreed," I said to Ben as we were lugging our first load of boxes down the stairs.

We made a couple of trips to bring down all of the boxes. On our last trip, I asked Ben. "Where do you want to start?"

"Since it's a nice day. Let's start with the outside decorations. It's cold, but the sun's shining. We can always trim the tree in the house after dark," Ben suggested.

"Sounds like a plan," I said as I sat on the floor and opened the box of outside Christmas lights. I untangled the wires of the icicle lights while Ben went out to the garage to get a ladder. As I sat there, I wondered how learning about the wood nymph part of my life would change me. Would I always be able to be both human and wood nymph? I wondered if Forrest and Olivia would have accepted me if I wasn't related to them. If I had been born with Ash's family's blood, would Elm have been more accepting of me? Or, would he still have hated me for being of mixed blood?

I watched Ben through the window as he set the ladder against the side of the house. He appeared either to be ignoring what had happened yesterday or had fully accepted it. He seemed very calm. Was it only less than a day since he had come home?

I thought about Ben as I laid out the untangled strands of lights. He wasn't related to me at all. He had adopted me, when I was a small child after he married my mother. His actions yesterday and today showed me much more than words that he accepted me without reservation. I really believe that he doesn't care what my blood is. He knows who I am and loves me for just being me. I always did believe that he loved me unconditionally. But, I really wondered if he would still love me when he found out that I wasn't completely human. Not for the first time, I thought about how lucky I was.

I tested the strands of icicle lights in the house before taking them outside to hang. Ben was on the ladder and I was handing him the strands of icicle lights when Ash drove his car into the driveway. "Decided to take the slow way here, today?" Ben asked over his shoulder from the ladder as Ash got out of his car.

"Yeah, we might have to go in town for something and it's easier to have the car handy. I don't always jet to get around, and Laurel can't jet. And, it is not a good idea to jet where humans can see. You know, I can't just jet into town," Ash replied.

Ben looked down at Ash and said, "Yeah. That's probably a good idea."

Ash came over and kissed me on the cheek. Ash watched me handing up the lights to Ben. When he realized that Ben would have to move the ladder to place any more icicle lights along the gutter, he said "I can help with this." Ash hopped straight up onto the roof of the house next to the ladder. Ours was a two story house. Ben didn't expect Ash to jump up beside him and gave a gasp when Ash squatted down next to the top part of the ladder.

"It's going to take me a bit to get used to things like that. Do try not to give me a heart attack, okay?" Ben said as he took a deep breath and continued with, "Okay, fine. You hang the lights. Take this bag of clips. Clip one onto the gutter about every foot or so, and hang the wire onto the hook."

Ben tossed the bag of clips to Ash and came down off of the ladder. Ash crouched down by the edge of the roof by the gutter and picked up the strand of icicle lights and reaching over, attached the clip and secured the wire. I handed up the strands so that Ash could continue hanging the lights. Ben made sure Ash had enough hooks. The job was finished in a fraction of the time that it usually took when it was just Ben and me. Ash didn't have to move a ladder.

"Well. That certainly saved time," Ben stated looking at the icicle lights hanging from the house. "Let's see how they look."

Ben took the end of the extension cord that he'd attached to the corner of the house and plugged it into an exterior outlet. Ash jumped off of the roof and came to stand beside me. The three of us looked up at the lights. While the lights were not as bright as they would be at night, we could see that each one was lit up.

"Do you want a real tree this year? I think I read somewhere that wood nymphs have some kind of affinity with trees. Is there a problem with cutting down a tree for Christmas? We haven't had a real tree in years, so it's not like it'd be hardship not to have one. But, it would be fun to have a real tree this year, and they do make the house smell nice," Ben said as he retracted the ladder to put it back into the garage.

Ash looked at Ben for a second before responding. "Thanks, Mr. Redmond, for thinking of my culture and asking me about the trees. Yes, we are kind of connected to the trees and the plants. If too many trees die off or are killed in an area where we live in, it does tend to affect our health. But, if we plant a tree to replace the one we cut down, we won't cause any harm. Humans cut down acres of trees every year for Christmas, and we are still here. Although there aren't as many of us as there have been in the past. Anyway, we'll have to plant in the spring as the ground is too hard to plant a tree now." Ash replied.

"Fair enough. Maybe we can plant a few trees in the spring," Ben replied thoughtfully. "Right here, we're surrounded by woods, but where to find the perfect tree for our purpose? When we do find the tree, do you have a special way to cut down trees or should I get the chainsaw?" Ben finished.

"Yeah, a chain saw would be good. We don't have a special way of cutting a tree. At least, I don't." Ash replied looking around. "There, over by the river. There appears to be a nice one for the Christmas tree. The tree also happens to block some of the view of the river from the house. When we plant in the spring, we'll plant away from the river."

The three of us went to look at the tree—a nice seven foot Balsam fir. We walked around it and couldn't discern any blemishes in its symmetry. It looked perfect. Ben walked back into the garage and came back with the chainsaw. It took a minute or so to get it started as it hadn't been started in a while. But then it took only another minute or so to cut the tree down. Even though we had never used it in my life, we did have a live tree stand in our Christmas stuff. I went to dig it out while Ben and Ash dragged the tree to the house.

By the time Ben and Ash had knocked the snow off the tree and were bringing it in through the screen porch, I had a spot set up for it between the living room and dining room. We set the tree up in the stand and decorated the rest of the house, giving the tree a chance to dry off in the house before putting electric lights on it.

When Mom got home around 1:00 p.m., we had garlands with lights set up around doorways and the windows in the living room and the screen room. We had Christmas figurines on tables, and the smell of pine permeated the air from our fresh-cut tree. The only thing left to do was to decorate the tree. Mom made the pizza, and we ate it while decorating the tree. We were just about finished when we heard a huge explosion come from the direction of the river.

"What the hell was that?" Ben asked looking at Ash. The sound scared me. When I looked at Mom, she looked kind of scared, too. We ran to the screen room to look toward the river. We saw the water falling in a mist back to the river over a huge hole in the ice in the direction of Ash's house.

"I don't know." Ash said slowly. "I have never heard anything like that."

We put our boots on and went to the river to look around. From the pier, looking down the river towards Ash's house, we saw just how big a hole it was in the ice on the river. It had to have been thirty feet across.

"Water sprites," Ash said. "What are they doing?" This last part was said really softly. If I hadn't been standing right next to him, I wouldn't have heard what he said.

"I don't mean to be dumb, but how do you know?" Ben asked Ash. I guess Ben had heard Ash, too.

"Water sprites are the only things I can think of who would do such a thing. Occasionally a snowmobile will come this way. However, at this time of year, the ice is too thick for someone to have fallen through there. Anyway, they would have crashed through the ice without causing an explosion. The only humans living on this part of the river is your family. You're not bothering the sprites. For them to blow a hole like that, I'd think that they must be really angry about something. Also, there's a deep spot in the river right there where their community is."

We stood there for a moment trying to figure out what to do. About then, Olivia and Forrest came toward us from the direction of the house.

Olivia and Forrest were standing by the house looking around, and then when they saw us, they jetted over to us. "The water sprites have taken Pomegranate Quince," Olivia stated. "I saw the explosion, and then I saw a small contingent of them when they went into your yard and took her," Olivia finished, looking at Ash.

"I have got to go home! Why would they do such a thing?" Ash stated turning away from me. Pom was such a nice girl. I was really worried about her, too.

"I don't know, but we'll find out. We'll go with you," Olivia said to Ash holding his arm to keep him from jetting.

"Ben, Valerie, and Laurel, please wait here. Stay in the house away from the river until we figure out what's going on. Water sprites can be unpredictable. Something big must have upset them to take a wood nymph child. We'll be back as soon as we have news," Olivia said. A second later, Olivia, Forrest, and Ash were gone. They had jetted away.

Ben wrapped an arm around both me and Mom. "We were told to get away from the river. I don't know anything about water sprites, but, until we know more, I think we should do as we're told. I'm getting out my shotgun just in case. Let's hope they're done with their mischief. I don't want any trouble with any of our neighbors."

Something was going on. Water sprites kidnapping a wood nymph? What was going on? Was it any wood nymphs they were after or was it just this particular wood nymph? Why did they take Pom? I really hoped she was okay. I thought about how cold the river was. I wondered if she was freezing to death.

As we hurried to the house, I thought about all of the things I'd heard about water sprites. According to the wood nymphs, the sprites hated humans, believing they were the cause of all of the pollution in the world. They believed humans were noisy and destructive. Yeah, I guess a lot of that was true enough. I thought of all of the dams and water craft humans used on the waterways. I felt the sprites might have had some justification in being afraid of and angry with humans.

Mom started a fire in the fireplace while Ben loaded his shotgun and placed it on the mantle above the fireplace.

"What do you know about water sprites?" Ben asked sitting on the couch. He kept glancing out of the window to the river.

"I know absolutely nothing," Mom said sitting next to Ben.

"I know very little," I said. "I believe they don't like humans. At least that is what Ash told me. Wood nymphs don't like water sprites, either. There was a wood nymph and water sprite war a few centuries ago around here. I think that the peace has been tentative at best. I saw one once, when we first moved here. It had long green hair. I think it was a female, but I'm not sure. I was sitting on the pier getting ready to fish and saw this green face with long flowing green hair in the water. I thought I was imagining it. It didn't look too friendly, but I don't think they're evil," I said thoughtfully. As I thought about it, I was more and more convinced that I was right.

We waited in the living room. I hadn't noticed it being cold earlier, but with this strange, scary news, I shivered. Mom must have felt this too, and added wood to the fire.

"Why was Olivia at Ash's house?" Ben asked to no one in particular. He was still staring out of the window.

"She probably wasn't at his house. She probably had a vision," Mom replied. "She doesn't see everything in her visions, but she sees a lot. Once in a while, she'll see something just before it happens, but mostly, she sees something as it's happening."

"I hate not knowing what's going on," I said softly. "I really hope Pom is okay."

"Who's Pom?" Ben asked as he turned to look at me.

"Pom is the youngest member of a European wood nymph family that have been visiting Ash's family." I told Ben. I turned to stare at the flames.

We sat in silence for a while. It was tough waiting for some kind of news about Pom. While I sat there, I noticed that I felt an emotion but couldn't tell where it was coming from. This one had fear, anger, and confusion all mixed up in it. It was unlike any emotions I had felt from anyone else. Where was it coming from? I looked around me. Mom had gotten up from the couch and was in the kitchen. Ben was staring at the fire.

I went to the three-season screen room and felt the emotion more intensely. It wasn't that whoever was feeling the emotion was feeling it more intensely, it was like I was getting a stronger signal. It was coming from outside! Was it a water sprite? Didn't I read somewhere that sprites had great hearing? I wondered if it could hear me.

I closed the sliding door to the main house so no one would hear me and said, "Can you hear me? I feel you. I want to help, but I don't know what's wrong." I felt the shock as the entity heard my words and comprehended what I said. Whatever it was, it had cognitive abilities. I felt hope coming from this creature.

"Can you come to talk to me? You seem to understand what I'm saying as your emotions are reflecting your thoughts. Are you a sprite?" I said out loud into the afternoon gloaming. I felt excitement and fear coming from whatever I had connected with. The emotion disappeared.

I ran into the main part of the house. "I heard something! Well, okay, not exactly heard it, but I got the emotions of it! I think I felt a water sprite!"

"What are you talking about?" Ben said coming over to me.

"Ever since I went to the Essence Ceremony, I've been able to read emotions. It's more like I feel them. I don't have to look at you to feel them, they come off the people around me in waves. The closer you are, the more intense the feeling is. It's kind of like the signal on a cell phone. When you're next to me, I have full receptive capabilities. The farther away you get, the harder it is to get the reception. If I concentrate on a specific person, I can get a good reading. I felt something outside! It was unlike any emotion I'd gotten from a human or a wood nymph. I felt fear and curiosity. I called out to it, as Ash told me that water sprites had great hearing, and I felt shock and then hope! It wanted to believe we can help! Then it disappeared," I said and sat on the couch.

"Laurel! That could be dangerous," Ben warned.

"What's dangerous? I'd be able to tell by the emotions whether it was dangerous or not. It's the emotion that I feel! They can't lie with emotions! They don't even know I know what their emotions are! It just knows that I sensed it by the emotions I felt."

I said, "They need help! Of course it didn't tell me that, but something is really wrong, and I believe that they took Pom out of some kind of desperation."

"You may be right, but you aren't going out of the house. It'd be nice if we could get some more information," Ben said thoughtfully.

After what seemed an eternity but was probably just an hour, our doorbell rang. I ran to answer it. It was Forrest.

"Forrest! We've been waiting and worrying! Where's Olivia?" I asked as I stepped back to allow Forrest to enter. Mom and Ben had followed me to the door.

"She's at the Woodson house trying to "see" something. The sad thing is, the harder she tries, the least likely she'll be successful." Olivia couldn't just focus in with her gift. She had to be relaxed and wait for a clear vision. This was not a situation that was helping her to relax.

As we went into the living room, I asked Forrest, "So, what's going on?"

"It definitely was the water sprites who took Pomegranate. There were witnesses. It was like she was singled out from the three sisters. Stella was closest to the water when the water sprites attacked. Pom was the one closest to the house. The girls were in the yard by the river. They heard the huge explosion. When they looked at the river, they saw a huge fountain of water falling back to the river. At first they saw the three water sprites on the shore and then the sprites were right next to the girls. Neither the girls or the water sprites said anything. They just grabbed Pom and darted back into the water through the hole in the ice," Forrest replied as he sat on the recliner.

"She'll freeze to death in the water!" I cried. I couldn't sit down. I was too upset. Mom and Ben sat on the couch.

"Maybe not," said Forrest. "The water sprites have an ability to put someone into a suspended animation or a coma. Once in that state, the sprites can place a barrier around the body that keeps the person from feeling hot, cold, or wetness. The person has no consciousness of what's going on around them."

"Why did they take her?" I asked again, pacing back and forth in the living room.

"I don't know. There must be a reason. Come sit down?" Forrest said softly.

"I don't want to sit down! What else do you know about water sprites?" I asked.

"Well, they can hear really well, even better than we do. They can hear us in here if they want to. They can move quickly on the ground, but not as fast as wood nymphs. They can move in the water almost as fast as sound travels in the water. They hate humans and are afraid of them. Sprites think if humans find out about them they'll want to find a way to destroy them. They aren't fond of wood nymphs either, but the sprites aren't afraid of them. There's a kind of understanding between our species since the wood nymph and water sprite war hundreds of years ago. Many on both sides died during the war. I don't think either wants to go through another war. So, we leave their domain alone. They leave us alone. This is a good reason not to call fish to bite your hook when you're fishing. The sprites don't like it when other species compel their water creatures. Truth is, that's what you were doing when you called a fish to your hook. The sprites don't mind having humans or wood nymphs fish in their waters if the fish have a choice in biting the hook or not."

Ben looked at me and said, "You can call fish?"

"Yeah, I guess I can," I said. "It sucks to have a skill I'm not allowed to use. I used it once, and Ash told me emphatically never to do it again. And, it might have been a coincidence. It's just that every time I said out loud for a fish to bite my hook, one did."

"Wow," Ben said. He was looking at me like I'd grown a third eye or something.

"Let's call Adam. Maybe he can see something from the sky!" I said jumping up to grab the phone in the kitchen. "Hi, Adam, it's me, Laurel. Can you fly over here? One of the European wood nymphs has been taken by the water sprites, and I want to know if you can see anything from the sky. Okay! Thanks." I turned to my family and Forrest. "Adam will be here in a few minutes," I said to Ben.

"What does Adam change into?" Ben asked.

"A bald eagle. It's his spirit guide. Adam is George's nephew from the reservation." I replied.

"Tell me again what George changes into?" Ben asked, looking from me to Mom.

"George is a black bear when he changes," Mom said simply.

"A black bear sounds like it could be an asset in a dispute," Ben said to her.

"Yeah, but in the winter, when George changes into a bear, he says he gets kind of sleepy and has to stay focused to keep from finding a place to hibernate," she replied.

I heard the scream of an eagle outside our screen room between our house and the river. I went out the door, and the eagle dropped a bundle into my hands. I could barely understand the screeching voice, but he was saying something about his clothes.

"I'll leave them in the screen room!" I yelled to Adam as he flew toward the river.

"I'll be right back," he screamed in his high-pitched eagle voice. Ben was standing next to me as I was holding the bundle of clothes.

"Adam, right?" he asked as he watched the eagle follow the river.

"Yes," I replied. I listened for that other emotion but felt nothing.

Ben stared at the bird. He shook his head as we walked into the house, and I smiled. It was strange to think of something funny at a time like this. But, I couldn't help but smile when I thought of how much Ben's reality had warped since he had been home. I put the bundle in the screen room. Ben and I went into the house.

A short while later, I heard the screen door open from the outside. A couple of minutes after that, Adam knocked on the glass of the sliding door leading into the house. He had his clothes on.

"I could see a light under the ice. A human eye would not have been able to discern it, but I certainly could see it with my eagle eyes," Adam said as he came into the living room with me. He sat next to me on the love seat.

"How far down the river?" Ben asked as he put some more wood on the fire.

"Between here and the Woodson's pier. I'd guess parallel to the bush fence. I would say about 100 yards beyond the hole in the water," Adam replied.

Mom came into the living room with a tray of hot chocolate. "I wasn't sure if you got cold while you were flying as an eagle, so I made some hot chocolate." She handed us each a mug.

"Thanks, Mrs. Redmond. It's not too bad. I get colder as a human," said Adam taking a mug from the tray.

"How deep is the ice?" Ben asked as he sipped on his chocolate.

"A foot deep in most places, but where the river has running water underneath, it'll be less thick. In places over a natural spring, ice might not form," Adam said.

"Where the water sprites exploded the ice it would just have a thin layer of ice at this time," Ben said thoughtfully. "How afraid are they of humans?"

"Oh, very afraid. According to water sprites, humans are the cause of all of the evils in the world. Wood nymphs are bad, but humans are the epitome of evil," Forrest stated, sipping his hot chocolate.

"Water sprites won't bother human boaters or water skiers, at least not where humans would see them. A propeller prop could hit a rock that shouldn't be there, or get snarled in weeds that that hadn't been in that spot before. A water skier could hit a submerged log. These could be the actions of water sprites. They would never intentionally show themselves to a human, though."

"What if a human entered their domain? What would happen?" Ben asked in a casual tone as he sipped his chocolate.

"It's never happened as far as I know. Humans have been scuba diving a lot of the lakes in the north woods, and I have never heard of anything bad happening. I think the news crews would pick up on a water sprite sighting. I think we would've heard something," Adam replied. Forrest nodded his head in agreement.

"Do water sprites talk? Can they speak English?" Ben asked.

"Yes. They speak all of the common languages in the areas where they live. This way they can stay aware of what's going on. They're extremely intelligent," Forrest replied. I could tell by the look on his face that he was wondering where Ben was going with these questions. Actually, I was, too.

"Are they reasonable creatures? How are their thought processes?" Ben asked after a moment of thought.

"Like I said, they're very intelligent beings. But, because they keep to the water, they have a lot of ignorance regarding the world outside of their domain," Forrest replied cautiously.

I said, "I know they understand English. I heard the emotions of one an hour or so ago outside our house. At least, I believe it was a water sprite. The emotions have a different flavor than human or wood nymph emotions. When I first felt it, I felt fear and anger. After I talked to it, I felt shock and hope! I said I'd try to help if I could, but I needed to know what the problem was. Then I lost the connection."

"Did you bring my scuba gear? I used to have a wet suit, a dry suit, a knife, and a spear gun," Ben asked my mom.

"Of course. I'd never dispose of anything of yours without your knowledge. It's in the closet in the spare room. Why?" Mom gave Ben and questioning look.

"At this point, I'm just curious," Ben said leaning back into his couch with a very thoughtful expression.

Mom, Forrest, and I were staring at Ben. Forrest didn't know Ben, but my mom and I did. He didn't like to sit and do nothing if there was something that needed doing, even if it was something dangerous. Maybe *especially* if it was dangerous.

"What've you got on your mind?" Mom asked Ben cautiously as she set her mug on the table in front of her.

"Will the sprites give a ransom demand?" Ben asked Forrest.

"They might. It depends on why they took Pom," Forrest replied.

"Can we find out?" Ben asked leaning forward towards Forrest.

"Maybe," Forrest replied. He gave Ben an odd look. Did Forrest think that Ben was up to something? Was Ben up to something?

"Water sprites don't have high-tech devices, do they? How's their technology?" Ben continued.

"They're not technical at all. They think technology is a human's way of polluting the world. Boats, power plants, and all other human technology is polluting their waterways. They want none of it." Forrest narrowed his eyes at Ben.

"Can you call Olivia and get us an update?" Ben asked. His emotions were wound up. He was in full military mode, and I wasn't sure what exactly that entailed. Mom looked scared out of her skull, but she didn't say anything.

Forrest took out his cell phone and called Olivia. "Hi, Olivia, what's going on? Uh huh, okay, really? Okay. Call me back."

Forrest turned to us. "Olivia says the sprites are angry about the European family's father wanting to drill for oil in the river. Apparently one of his gifts is to locate large quantities of natural resources such as oil, and he found a large deposit of oil on your land just this side of the two properties. That just happens to be where the largest community of water sprites live in the Wisconsin River. Chester Quince, Pom's dad, doesn't believe that water sprites have the right to say where he and his company can or cannot drill." Forrest sounded angry.

Ben nodded. He asked, "I'd think if the oil is on our land, I'd have some say about drilling, don't you think?"

"I don't think he would've told you. If anything, he would've drilled from the Woodson side of the property line underneath into your property to get at the oil." Forrest shook his head about the whole situation.

"Well, then I do have something to say about it," Ben said, getting up. "I'm going over there."

"Wait, Dad. Now that we know what the problem is, maybe we can talk to the sprites. We can show them we're not evil and mean. At least in this case, we are certainly on their side of the matter. Let me try to reach out to them," I implored.

"No. It's too dangerous. Water sprites are too unpredictable," Forrest said firmly.

I shouted, "They are only unpredictable to their enemies! I'm not an enemy! The creature I felt outside heard me, and I felt hope! They need us! I don't know how big their community is, but I can count the different emotions and get a sense of their size. I want to try to talk to them. I felt hope!" I stressed again.

I don't know why Ben agreed to it, but after a moment, he said to me, "Okay. I'll go with you onto the porch, and you can try to talk to them. Tell them we want to discuss the situation and try to help if we can."

"I'll be there, too," Forrest said furiously.

"We'll all stand with you for support," Mom said. Adam nodded his agreement.

We walked onto the porch, and I said gently, "Please hear me. Me and my family mean you no harm. We understand why you took the wood nymph girl and want to help you with the problem. You see, the problem affects us, too. We will prevent the drilling. We don't want any changes in our part of the river. You're our neighbors and are to be treated with respect and consideration. Please allow us to show you our sincerity."

I reached out with my new sense. At first I felt nothing. About the time I thought I was wasting my time and there would be no response, I felt three different emotions. One was complete anger and barely controlled. One was full of hope, and the last one was a combination of anger and hope. I could feel the emotion signal strength intensifying.

"Three are coming," I said confidently looking at Ben, then Forrest.

Forrest looked impressed. "Valerie, put a cover or something on whatever furniture you want them to sit on and towels on the floor, or everything will smell like fish," he told Mom. I wondered if he was speaking from experience.

Mom ran to see to it. I could feel the emotions from outside the house get stronger. At the periphery of the yard light, we saw the three water sprites walking to the house.

They were all dressed in green. They had on long green tunics trimmed in the same shade of brown as a dead leaf. They wore skin-tight leggings that came to their ankles. Their skin was green as was their hair, but it was a darker shade than their skin. Their fingers and toes were webbed. You wouldn't be able to see them in any seaweed or water foliage. But, against the stark white of the snow in the yard, they stood out quite clearly as they walked barefoot in the snow.

They came up the stairs and I opened the door and motioned for them to come inside. The main emotions I felt now were fear and tension. At least one of them felt that they were wasting their time coming here and that we may be a trap.

"Please come in and sit down," I said gently.

"We are sincere in wanting to help you with this issue, and we want to be comfortable together as neighbors," Ben added.

The sprites looked at the open door for a minute and then entered. They stopped when they saw Forrest. I felt the anger and hostility flare up in their emotions.

"Forrest is an ally in this situation. He's not the enemy. He's my uncle," I said holding out my hand to the first one entering. He was a large male.

He looked at my hand and then looked deeply into my eyes for a moment. Slowly he took my hand. His skin was wet and cool, but not cold. It felt like what I thought an eel would feel like. I led him into the house. Mom had put towels on the floor from the door to the living room and spread waterproof plastic table cloths on the furniture. All three of the water sprites were staring about themselves as they entered the house. It was obvious that they had never entered a human house before. I felt awe, confusion, anger, fear, and determination. The most powerful emotion I felt was the hope I had felt earlier. I guided the male that held my hand to the couch and sat down. He sat next to me, and the one female with them sat next to him on the other side. Mom held her hand out to the recliner for the other male, and he sat down. Ben and Forrest sat on the love seat and Mom and Adam brought chairs from the dining room table to sit on.

"Can you tell us what happened, please?" I asked the male I was sitting next to. He'd been looking about the room. When I spoke, his face snapped back to look at me. It seemed water sprites could move almost as fast as wood nymphs.

When he spoke, his voice was understandable, but there was a liquid quality to it, like trying to hear someone speaking from a swimming pool! It must have been his gills that affected the way the sound was projected. He had a set behind each ear.

"My name is Tyne. I'm the leader. This is Amadahy, the wise man of our community, and Geneva, his mate. Let me start by telling you that you are the first humans we have ever communicated with. We know your language because we want to know what's going on in the world. We just don't want any part of it. We have enough trouble trying to keep our stretch of the river free from human contaminants.

"We hear that evil wood nymphs want to drill nearby and the drilling will destroy our home. We tried to communicate with them, but we were ignored. We won't swim by and idly watch our homes and community ruined by human and wood nymph drilling."

Then Tyne said softly to me. "We have never experienced one like you before. You have a different scent and aura than other land-based two-legged beings. We, too, can feel a certain amount of emotion coming from different creatures. Mostly we get pride and superiority from humans when they think about the forest around them. We've never found a human that we thought worth meeting. But we wanted to meet you. You aren't even a human, at least not completely. We can sense that you're part wood nymph along with being human, aren't you?"

"Yes, I am," I replied, smiling at him. I wasn't getting any negative emotion from him. He was extremely curious about me, and I could work with that.

"Because we are new to each other and different, that doesn't make us automatically enemies. We have different cultures and lifestyles, but if we respect each other and each other's lives, communities, and environments, we can try to get along, right?"

Tyne stared at me for a moment, and then replied. "Yes. If you're telling the truth, there is the possibility that we can live in harmony with humans for neighbors. But, we still need to prevent the wood nymphs from drilling and ruining our habitat."

"I think I can help with that," Ben said, bringing everyone's eyes to him.

"What do you mean?" Tyne asked. Caution and hope was coming off of him in waves. I was wondering how I couldn't see it shimmering.

"I'm going over there and let them know I won't tolerate any drilling anywhere near our land. I'll threaten exposure of the wood nymphs if necessary," Ben stated.

We stared at Ben in disbelief. I couldn't believe he'd do this. A confrontation between him and Ash's dad! Ben was only going to be home for three weeks, and he was going to have it out with the neighbors.

But, as I thought about it, Ben had every right to be indignant. This European guy and Ash's dad was threatening the lives of our water sprite neighbors. Plus, they planned to drill on our land.

"I'll take you, Dad," I said, standing up to get my coat.

"We'll *all* go," Forrest stated.

"Me, too?" Adam asked excitedly. He came over to stand by me.

Ben grinned. "Sure. If there's a problem, we may need the help from the reservation."

"At least let me call them and let them know we are coming," Mom said wringing her hands. "It is eight o'clock. Civilized people just don't barge into other people's houses this late at night no matter what the provocation."

"Okay. Make it quick," Ben said as he got his coat out of the closet.

"We'll wait in the water until you return. The child will not be harmed. When you call us, we will hear you and come," Tyne led the other water sprites out.

Mom went into the kitchen. I followed her. I noticed that her hand was shaking as she grabbed the phone. She went through the speed dial list and saw where I had entered Ash's home number and called the house. She took a deep breath as the phone rang on the other end.

"Hello, Willow," Mom said. "This is Valerie. Yeah, Laurel's mother. My husband has something he wants to discuss with your husband, and it won't wait. We are on our way over. No, this is important. We'll see you in a couple of minutes."

"She didn't sound happy about it. She tried to talk me out of coming," Mom told me as we got our coats.

We all got into Ben's pickup truck and drove over. Like every other time I had gone over there when it was dark out, every outside light was on. As we got out of the truck, we saw Ash, his dad, his mom, and the European family standing outside watching us from the wide veranda.

At first they just stared at us. "Please, let's go in out of the cold," Mom suggested to Willow. Willow gave a curt nod. We all went into the Woodson's living room. I ended up sitting in the same place that I had the first time I had ever entered the house. Ash sat next to me, but I could see he was confused as to why we were there. I smiled at him in encouragement. I was not surprised when Willow did not offer us a beverage.

"Why are you here? You haven't been invited. This is an outrage!" Ash's dad, Elm, almost yelled at Ben and Forrest. He didn't acknowledge my existence.

"My name's Ben Redmond," Ben said firmly. "I'm Valerie's husband and Laurel's dad. I just got home and I find all hell breaking loose and that you're the cause. You have no right to drill on my land. This will be resolved tonight."

"How dare you come into my house and insult me!" Elm said, stepping closer to Ben. Ben didn't move. They were about the same height and faced each other eye to eye.

Ben said, "I may not have a lot of experience with wood nymphs, but I thought they were honorable. I'm not seeing that here. Let me explain before we all get hostile. A short while ago, Laurel had contact with a water sprite. She talked to it. She told it she wanted to help with whatever their problem was. Three of them came to our house." When Ben said the last part, there were shocked hisses and intakes of breath.

Elm said emphatically, "That would never happen. Water sprites do *not* have contact with humans. Not under *any* circumstance."

I said, "Oh, it did happen. I shook Tyne's webbed hand and welcomed him into our house. We met Tyne, the leader, Amadahy and Geneva."

"You told them the names!" Elm hissed at Forrest.

"I most certainly did not. However, I was there when they came to the Redmond house. Laurel speaks the truth," Forrest replied calmly.

"What did they say?" Elm asked cautiously taking a step back from Ben.

"They were a bit hard to understand, like listening to someone talking while gargling. But, the gist of it is that they had heard your plans to drill for oil by the property line. The most interesting thing they said was that the majority of the oil is on my land. Were the sprites correct? Tyne, the leader, said that Chester Quince and Elm Woodson intended to drill for oil on my land without my permission. Is that about right?" Ben asked quietly. When Ben got mad, he tended to speak very softly.

"Who are you to say such things about me?" Chester Quince bellowed, jumping up from his chair.

"I'm a human who lives in these United States. I'm a taxpayer with property rights that you appear to think are yours for the taking. I won't allow any drilling. If you don't back off, I'll go to the authorities. If I have to be, I can be the human who blows the whistle on your wood nymph world if you don't listen to me," Ben answered even more softly.

"You can't do that!" Elm cried.

"Can't? Oh, I can, and I will. The authorities may not believe me at first, but with Laurel's help, I'll show that there's more going on in this community than they know. Even if they don't believe you're wood nymphs, they will understand trespassing. It's illegal to drill on someone's land without their permission."

"I could kill you," Elm threatened. Ash and I looked at each other with horror.

"You can try. I don't plan to allow you to do that. However, if you do succeed, there are witnesses. Do you want to be known as a murderer? Are you willing to go to a human prison? Would you do this to your family? At the very least, you'd probably have to move away from here and live in some kind of wood nymph isolation the rest of your life away from all humans. Forrest's clan won't take you in. Is that what you want?" Ben stated quietly.

Ben didn't seem in the least bit afraid. He couldn't move as fast as a wood nymph, but I was pretty sure he had a few weapons on his person at that moment. Ben was always prepared. He was also well trained as a warrior by the Army.

Elm looked a bit surprised. Ben said, "I don't want to threaten anyone. I think you have every right to live in your self-imposed obscurity if that's your wish. I'd like to live in harmony with you as your neighbor. If that's not possible, at least you have to respect my rights of ownership. In other words, if you're not my friend, I want you to stay off of my land. I'm asking you to respect my rights and that of my other neighbors, the water sprites. It appears they've hated humans for a long time. I'd like to change that." Ben finished. That was quite a speech for him.

For a moment, no one said anything. Then, a woman that looked a lot like an older version of Rebecca Quince stood up and walked over to Ben.

"I am Monukka Quince. I am Pomegranate's mother. What about my daughter? Is she alive?" asked Mrs. Quince hesitantly.

As I watched her speak, she was glancing over at her husband.

I said, "As the water sprites left our house, they said she was fine. I didn't sense anything else, and I think I would have felt that in their emotions."

Mom said, "What Laurel's saying is we all have an opportunity here. Our initial contact with the water sprites gives us hope to establish some kind of rapport before making any kinds of demands. We found out why the sprites took Pom. How you respond now will determinine how to get her back." Mom stood next to Ben.

"My youngest daughter means a lot to me," Mrs. Quince said looking at me. "If you can get her back, I'll promise that my family will have nothing to do with drilling for oil or anything else on your property. In fact, I think it's time for us to go back to Europe. You get her back and we'll leave."

Mrs. Quince stared hard at her husband. She looked really angry. Her husband's shoulders slumped. He nodded.

"Please get my sister back," Rebecca Quince said to me softly. "I think the sprites will listen to you. There's something special about you. I feel it. Ash feels it, and it seems that the water sprites feel it, too."

I liked the emotions coming from Rebecca. While there was certainly worry, I felt the hope and confidence more strongly.

Ben confronted Elm again. "Do you promise not to do anything to upset the sprites? My family will leave nature as it was meant to be between our properties. Will you agree to do the same?"

Elm gave a disgusted sigh. He was still angry, and it came from him in waves. Was there any hope that Ash's family and mine could become friends? Probably not now, but who knows what might happen in the future?

Elm sighed. "Fine. I'll ensure that there'll be no drilling. At least not anywhere near here. It's embarrassing to have a human establish a friendship with a water sprite. I, too, will make sure that the land is not disturbed and keep peace with the water sprites. Please stay on your property side from now on. I agree to do as you demand, but I don't have to like it, and I don't have to like you." Elm stood and headed for the front door.

"Fair enough," Ben said. "However, while I'll stay away from you, I won't keep Laurel from seeing Ash if she wants to. She has to make her own mind up about her relationship with him." Ben followed Elm to the door with the rest trailing behind.

"Whatever. Ash will see her if he wants, to. I don't have to have her in my house," Elm said. He shut the door hard behind us and we piled into the truck.

"Do you really think that the water sprites will listen to Laurel?" Mom asked Ben as he drove to our house.

"Actually, I'd be kind of surprised if they hadn't listened in on that whole conversation and are not waiting on the porch by the river when you get home," Forrest said.

When I got out of the truck at home, I ran around to the river side of the house. I was almost there, when Ash appeared next to me. He'd jetted over. He took my hand and we walked hand in hand to the porch by the river. Ben, Mom, Forrest, and Adam followed behind. Sure enough, Tyne, Amadahy, and Geneva were waiting for us. Their emotions indicated shock when they saw Ash and realized who he was.

I said, "Thank you for being here. All parties have agreed that there'll be no drilling on any land on this part of the river. We even agreed that there would be no other disturbance of the land or water between the properties."

Tyne bowed to me and I felt relief coming from all three of them.

"We will bring the girl here. She won't remember anything. She won't even be wet. She's been kept in a containment bubble in hibernation. When she sees you she may be confused. This is normal," Tyne said and bowed to me. He backed away for a couple of steps and then turned and walked to the river with Amadahy and Geneva.

They had been gone for just a couple of minutes when I saw Pom coming out of the bushes by the river. Ash and I ran over to her. She looked around, and her emotions reeked of fear. She said. "What happened? The last thing I saw was these horrible wet green water sprites dragging me with them." She looked around at herself as if she was amazed to find that she was dry.

"You were abducted by the water sprites, but they didn't hurt you. Come on, I'll explain it all to you." I took her hand in mine, and we walked into my house.

I didn't feel too bad about keeping her a few minutes longer from her family. I felt she had a right to an honest explanation of what had happened to her. I told her that the water sprites had tried to talk to Elm and Chester about what would happen if they drilled, and that they wouldn't listen. I explained how drilling would destroy some water sprite habitat and that in desperation they'd kidnapped her. I told her that the issue was resolved, and so they had set her free. While she was horrified at the concept of being abducted, when she learned that her own father would have been instrumental in ruining another creature's home, she understood why the sprites took her.

"I guess we all do some pretty crazy things when we are desperate," she sighed after I finished telling her the story. At that moment the doorbell rang. It was Olivia.

She looked around quickly for Pom, then sighed in relief. "I told them she was safe, but they sent me to make sure my vision was accurate. I may not see everything, but what I do see is usually right on the mark."

"I have my car here. I can take you back to my house. We don't have to jet." Ash said to Pom. He gave me a big hug. "You really are incredible," he said to me. "Some day my dad will realize what a treasure you are and he'll come around." He kissed me good-bye. As he kissed me, I heard Ben clear his throat and Adam laugh. *Oh, so they saw that. Oh, well.* I watched as Ash and Pom got in the car and drove away.

"It sure is entertaining being around you, Laurel," Adam said, laughing. "You're some piece of work. Who would have thought the little human girl I met a few months ago would end up a mediator among species and the first human friend to the water sprites. I can't wait to tell the rest of the tribe!"

With that, he took off his clothes right in front of us, while still laughing and put them in a small leather bag. He set the bag on the railing on the front porch. Then he jumped off of the porch and flashed in his million-sparkler display as he changed into a bald eagle. He swooped once around the front yard. With his great talons, he grabbed his bag off of the railing and, crying raucously, almost like a laugh, flew away.

Ben took a deep sigh and shook his head and said as we turned and to go into the house. "Well, now ain't that just something to see? It seems like there are a whole lot of things we saw today that an average human would never see in a lifetime."

"You got that right," I said. Mom, Forrest, and Olivia nodded in agreement.

Forrest rested a hand on his shoulder. "I'm not sure if threatening was a good tact when dealing with Elm, but it seemed to work. I don't think you made a friend of him, but I do believe that you and Laurel have made great strides in establishing a relationship with the water sprites."

At that moment, I yawned. I tried to cover it up, but I wasn't very successful. Olivia smiled at me. "Oh, honey, you need to get to bed. It's late. We'll go home now. Is it okay if we come back tomorrow to discuss Christmas? Oh, and by the way, you all did a great job with the decorating. The tree looks wonderful. So do all the lights."

"Is noon convenient for us to return tomorrow?" Forrest asked as he got his coat.

"Sure. See you then," Ben said. I gave both Forrest and Olivia a hug before they walked out the door. They walked down the outside stairs together, took two steps into the driveway and disappeared as they jetted home.

"Gee, I sure wish I could do that," Ben said rolling his eyes and giving off a sigh. He put one arm around me and one arm around my mom.

I laughed at him and said, "Yeah, I wish that all of the time, too." We closed the front door and went to bed.

CHAPTER 22
CHRISTMAS

I woke up and realized it was Christmas Eve day. I hopped out of bed thinking this would be the best Christmas ever. I had been buying Christmas presents for the last couple of months when I worked on the weekends. It was easy to find gifts at the store I worked at. It was a hardware store, but they sold a lot more than that. I bought stuff for my mom and Ben and now this year, I had Forrest, Olivia and Ash to buy for. I even bought Douglas a little present. Buying more gifts meant spending more money, but I enjoyed trying to find things they'd like. In the case of Olivia, I had originally bought a joint gift for her and Hawthorn, but later, I bought a special little present just for her.

In art, near the end of the semester, we had pottery, and I had made a pot for Forrest. I was no Michelangelo, but for a first attempt at clay, I thought I did a fairly good job. It was green and brown and all of the colors swirled as the pot fired. It was tall and thin with a wide base. I thought it would go well with any room in Forrest's house.

Before I went downstairs for breakfast, I wrapped my gifts. I left them on my bed. When I got downstairs, mom and Ben were at the dining room table drinking coffee. "Would you like eggs and bacon for breakfast? Special treat," Mom said when I came into the room.

"Eggs and toast would be great, but I'll pass on the bacon," I replied sitting down next to Ben. Mom got up and went into the kitchen to get my breakfast. I got back up and asked, "Do you want some help?"

"No, honey, I got it," Mom said putting the egg pan on the stove. Mom and Ben were very relaxed. I could tell from their moods.

"So, what crisis are we going to fix today?" I quipped smiling. I really didn't expect any kind of crisis, but a lot had happened since Ben had gotten home.

"I hope nothing. I just want to relax today. I think there's a football game on that I'd like to watch. I haven't relaxed since I got here." Ben stretched at the table. "I still have boxes to unpack in the garage, but I don't feel like dealing with them just yet."

"Don't forget that Forrest and maybe Olivia are coming around noon," I reminded him.

"Yeah, okay, then Forrest can watch football with me," Ben said smiling. "Do wood nymphs watch football?"

"I don't know. Do you think that they'll want to do Christmas in the community center where they held Thanksgiving?" Mom asked from the kitchen.

"Is that a problem if they do?" I asked looking at Ben.

"Anything is okay with me. I've had you two to myself all of these years. Now we find that we have extended family. As long as I'm with you, I don't care where we have Christmas," Ben said leaning over to kiss my cheek.

"I love you, Dad," I said impulsively.

"Me too, kiddo," he replied with a smile.

Mom brought my eggs and toast, and I ate it all. I was hungry. After the crisis with Pom had been resolved, I had slept well. I had gone to sleep wondering how the water sprites would react to us now that we knew they existed.

After breakfast Mom curled up on the loveseat with a book. Ben turned on the television and started "channel chasing," which was my term for using the remote and scanning all of the channels, with a tendency to do it over and over again, like that would change what was on. By mid-morning, I didn't know what to do with myself. I'd already wrapped my presents. School was out for the holidays so there was no homework. After the scene at Ash's house, I didn't even want to call his cell phone if he was near his dad.

"I'm going outside for awhile," I announced as I went to get my coat.

"You should be here to discuss the Christmas plans. Be home by noon, okay?" Mom said without moving from her spot on the loveseat.

"Be careful. Oh, and don't find any more new creatures that can talk," Ben called from the living room. I could hear him chuckling. He had a weird sense of humor.

"Okay!" I said as I walked outside into blinding sunshine. There wasn't a cloud in the sky. It was around thirty degrees, so not bitter cold. The sun reflected off the snow and hurt my eyes. I had to squint. I had a couple of hours to waste, so I went for a walk. I had my new cell phone, but the signal strength was erratic. Right by our house we had great signal, but as I walked into the woods, the signal fell off quickly. My phone wasn't a fancy model, but it could take pictures.

I decided to walk along the river. It had been frozen over for some time, but I grabbed a walking stick so I could test the ice in front of me to check how solid it was. I knew those water sprites came out of the water somewhere, and I didn't want to fall through their hole in the ice. I'd had enough excitement in the last day to last a lifetime.

At times I could see the ice beneath the snow covering. I thought I saw green below the ice, and I waved. I felt a little foolish about waving to the river, but, hey, there might be a water sprite watching me, and I didn't want to be rude.

The wind that constantly blew along the river kept the large areas of the ice clear of snow. The ice looked like perfect for ice skating. It looked thick and clear of snow right down the middle of the river. Today there was little wind. Just the sunshine and the fresh cold pine scented air around me. As I walked along, I looked at the pine trees with their heavy layers of snow. I thought about how city people would pay extra money for an artificially flocked tree for Christmas. I was surrounded by trees that were beautiful in their Christmas snow raiment. I loved living in the north woods.

I was about to head back home when I heard what sounded like a puppy yipping. Where would a dog be around here? There were no houses for at least a couple of miles. I went into the direction of the sound, and I started to feel the emotion. There was terror and frustration coming from the little creature. While I could feel the emotion, I could not tell what kind of creature it came from.

As I rounded a bend in the river, I saw a bundle of fur by the side of the river. Something moved near it. I walked closer. Soon I could see the pile of fur was a large dog, but it was clearly dead. Next to it a puppy yapped at, what I assumed, was its dead mother in the trap. How sad. I didn't know what kind of animals were trapped along a river—mink or muskrat maybe—but the poor dog had gotten her paw caught and died as a result. I went over to the trap and carefully removed the dead dog from the steel teeth in the trap. The whole time I did this, the puppy watched me. I wasn't on our land anymore and this could be a legal trap. I was so angry that I wanted to destroy the horrible thing. I figured how to detach it from the tree and dragged it onto the ice. I wanted to drop it to the bottom of the river where it would never hurt anything again, but I didn't want to pollute the water sprites' domain. I saw a spot of thick foliage across the river. The trapper would never find it there. All the while, the puppy was nuzzling and curling up next to its dead mother and watching me.

"I need to get rid of this torture device, but how? If I put it in the bushes, and the trapper comes back today, he'll find it. I need some help." I muttered out loud. I saw a spot about three feet across and about ten feet in front of me, melt into water. The ice had to be a foot thick, but it melted like butter under a hot knife. A green head popped up through the ice. It appeared to be a young female water sprite.

"I'll help you," she said as she hopped onto the ice. I had to strain to understand her gargling words. "I'll take it where it'll never be found," she said smiling at me. At least I think it was a smile. If it wasn't for the fact that I could read her friendly emotions, I would've been scared to death. As she took the horrible thing from me, she said, "This device is one of the reasons we don't like humans. But, you want to destroy this thing. You are different from other humans. You are good."

She walked back to the hole in the ice and dropped into the ice cold water. I stared after her quite awhile. As I watched, ice crystals formed as the hole started freezing over. I also noticed that the sun wasn't shining as brightly, and it appeared to be getting colder. The puppy whimpered again. I turned to look at it. It would die if I left it by its dead mother. As I walked back to the pup, I looked at the mother. I wasn't great with dog breeds, but it looked like it might have been a collie crossed with maybe a German shepherd. The mother had a sable coat, a white ruff, and a brown head, but I thought collies had longer hair. I didn't remember German shepherds having that much white. The puppy was solid brown with darker shadings. It wasn't very big. I figured it couldn't be more than a couple of months old. It wouldn't live by itself in the forest. As I got closer, I noticed that it was shivering.

The puppy watched me and started yipping and whimpering. I squatted down and held out my hand to it. I said gently, "Come here, baby. Good, baby. Come here. I'll take care of you."

After a couple of minutes of listening to my voice, the puppy walked over to me and sniffed my hand. It licked my fingers. I reached down and picked it up. It whimpered but didn't struggle. I walked quickly as I carried the puppy home.

It was about noon when I got back to my house with my little brown charge.

"Hi!" I called into the house. "I'm home!"

"Hi, honey. Great! You are on time. No one's here yet. Did you have a nice walk? What have you got?" Mom froze when she saw the moving bundle under my jacket.

"Its mother was dead in a trap a couple of miles up river. I know it wasn't on our land, but I disposed of the trap. I wish I could have buried the mother." I said sadly still standing with the pup in my arms.

My mother sighed and said. "Okay, give me the pup and throw your mittens in the wash. We will see what we can do."

When I came back, Mom handed me back the pup and said, "What do you plan to do with this little guy? If you even think about wanting to keep it, keep in mind that dogs are a lot of work. There is feeding and the house training, obedience training and on and on. Are you up for all of that?"

I looked at the pup sleeping in my arms and felt I had no choice. Ben had been upstairs and when he came down, he saw us standing in the dining room.

"What's going on?" Ben asked as he came into the room.

"Laurel found a puppy," Mom answered as she and Ben followed me into the living room. She gave him the short version of the dead mother dog and the trap. I gently laid the puppy on the fireplace hearth rug.

"Damn traps!" Ben replied looking down at the sleeping pup. "What did you do with it?" Ben asked.

"I got it loose from the tree it was attached to and gave it to a water sprite to dispose of it," I said while looking at the pup.

"A water sprite?" Mom and Ben said at the same time.

"Yeah, I was looking for a place to get rid of it and I happened to mutter out loud that I needed help. A water sprite melted a hole in the ice and told me she'd dispose of the trap for me. She was young. A little scary looking. If I hadn't of been able to read her emotions, I would've been afraid of her." I looked up at Mom and Ben and they were looking at me in a strange way.

"I'm fine!" I said. I could feel their worry and tension.

"Sometimes I wish for the days of ignorance before all this," Ben said as he sat on the couch. The doorbell rang and Mom answered it. It was Forrest and Olivia.

When they had hung up their coats and came into the living room, I was sitting on the floor and petting the sleeping puppy.

"What have we here?" asked Olivia as she and Forrest walked into the room.

Mom told her about me finding the dead dog in the trap and the water sprite disposing of the trap.

"You do find interesting situations, don't you?" Olivia mused to me. I smiled at her. "You'll need a kennel for him," she said and turned to Forrest. "Can you run into town and pick up a kennel? Make it a big one. He looks like he's going to grow quite large. He'll need it during house training."

"Oh, hey, we didn't say we were going to keep it," Mom said looking startled.

"You said I could if I wanted to," I said. "You said if I took care of it and fed it and cleaned it and trained it, I could keep it." I looked at Olivia. "You said *he* will need it." I lifted its tail and sure enough, it was a boy dog.

"Will he get really big?" I asked. All I knew was his mother was big.

"He'll get big enough. Those are big feet. You may need a little extra protection. A canine guardian may be good for you." Forrest reached over to look at the pup's teeth and feeling along his ribs. "He's hungry. I think he is only sleeping because he's warm and exhausted. When he wakes up, you'll need to feed him. And you'll need to take him outside to take care of business."

"So, a puppy needs a kennel and food. You might was as well pick up bowls, too. Don't forget some teething toys," Olivia said to Forrest with a smile. "I'll work on Christmas details with Valerie."

With a sigh, Forrest agreed, and Ben said he would drive into town.

I'd always wanted a dog, but with us living on military bases, Mom thought it unfair to keep a dog locked up while I was in school and she at work. I watched the feet on the little puppy twitch in his sleep.

"One member of our clan is a veterinarian. James Basswood. I could call him if you like. We could have him checked out. What do you think about me setting up an appointment?" Olivia volunteered.

"Yeah, that would be great," I said. I was worried about the little guy.

Olivia used the kitchen phone to make the call. A couple of minutes later she came back into the living room. "We're in luck. He's making a farm call not too far from here. He'll stop by when he is finished. That'll save us a trip." Olivia sat at the dining room table with Mom.

The doorbell rang and it woke up the puppy. I brought him with me to the front door. It was Ash. I walked past him and down the porch stairs. No car. Ash had jetted over. I remembered what Forrest had said about what would happen when the puppy woke up. I didn't want him to make a mess in the house.

"An early Christmas present?" Ash asked me while I set the puppy on the ground. The little guy sniffed around and squatted. Forrest was right.

"Not exactly," I said." I found him by the river. His mom was killed in a trap." I watched the puppy sniff around the parking area. "I didn't call because I was worried I might get you when you were with your dad."

"Don't ever be afraid to call me. I want you to call me. I would've been here earlier, but the Quinces are leaving today for Europe, and I helped carry their luggage to their rental van. Mrs. Quince refused to spend one more night here. She's really pissed at her husband. I sure wouldn't want to be in that household for a while. But, on a happier note, Rebecca did get permission to attend UWM in the fall if she can get accepted. Mrs. Quince said it'd be fine, and Mr. Quince agreed." Ash smiled and gave me a big hug.

He looked at the puppy and asked again. "So . . . where did you get the dog?"

"Like I said, I went for a walk along the river away from your house. I didn't want to go anywhere near your property line." I looked from the puppy to Ash. He gave me a sad smile and nodded for me to continue.

"I walked for an hour . . . probably a couple of miles. As I got to a bend in the river, I heard yipping. I went to investigate and found an adult dog dead in a trap. I was so mad! There was this little puppy trying to get its mom to move. It was so sad. I removed the trap and was going to throw it in some bushes across the river, but then realized that if the trapper came back today, he'd see my tracks and gotten his trap back. I guess I said out loud I neede help to get rid of the trap, when, a few feet in front of me, the ice just melted, and a young green water sprite poked her head out of the water. She said she'd get rid of the trap for me. She was kinda scary looking. She had really sharp teeth." I shuddered.

"Some water sprites look beautiful to humans. Some don't. That doesn't mean anything. As I understand it, the toothier they are, the more attractive they are in their world. So, the girl you saw is probably considered quite lovely in her community."

"I'm glad wood nymphs aren't that way. Anyway, I wish I could have buried the mother dog, but I would never have gotten through the frost. The only thing I could do was rescue the puppy. So here he is," I said, picking up the puppy. It started chewing on my fingers with his little needle-sharp baby teeth.

"He's hungry," I said. "I hope Ben and Forrest get back soon. They're getting food and supplies for this little guy." Just then, Ben's pickup come up the driveway.

Ben hopped out and started unloading bags of food and bowls. "You're lucky this isn't Christmas Day. Everything would have been closed. We were lucky. Your hardware store carried everything we needed, and they were nice enough to let us use your discount."

Forrest and Ben pulled a huge metal crate out of the bed of the truck and brought it into the house. I handed the puppy to Ash and carried in the food and dishes. Ash followed with the puppy.

Ben and Forrest put the crate in the corner of the basement. Mom had some old blankets for it. Ben attached some brackets so the dishes could be mounted inside the kennel so that the puppy couldn't spill his food and water all over. After the kennel was ready for him, I put him in it. He sniffed the dishes and put his nose in the beefy puppy kibble bits Ben had purchased. He tentatively tried one, and then started to munch it down. Forrest said we needed to start him at half a cup of food because we didn't know how well his stomach would tolerate it. If he kept it down and didn't get diarrhea, we could give him some more after an hour or so. After he finished his food, he came out of his kennel and sat in front of me. I picked him up to take upstairs.

Mom and Olivia were sitting at the dining room table. "How's he doing with his new crate?" Mom asked.

"Well, we haven't left him in it yet, but he ate the food," I replied. I put the puppy on the floor and gave him one of the rawhide chew toys Ben had brought back from the store. He immediately started gnawing happily while we discussed Christmas.

The doorbell rang. It was the veterinarian, Dr. Basswood. He looked the pup over and gave him a shot of something. "He's thin, malnurished. What did you get him to eat?" he asked.

Ben told him the name of the puppy food, and Dr. Basswood said that brand had enough meat in it and was acceptable.

"Nutrition is going to be an issue," Dr. Basswood said packing away his stethoscope. "He's going to be a big dog when he's grown."

"We'll take care of him," I said reaching down to pet the puppy.

"Thank you for coming, James," Olivia said and slipped him some money. Dr. Basswood nodded, took the money and left.

"You didn't have to do that," Mom said to Olivia. "I should have paid him."

"It was my idea to have the pup seen by him. Let's finish discussing Christmas."

Mom could hardly stay concerned with Olivia flashing her gorgeous smile. Olivia led Mom back to the dining room. We all sat down to finish our Christmas discussion.

Olivia said that she hadn't discussed Christmas with the other Copper Clan members. Mom suggested that we have Christmas at our house, and we all agreed. Olivia would call Hawthorn to see if he wanted to come. She was pretty sure he would. We spent the rest of the afternoon discussing details, and then Forrest and Olivia left. Mom said she was going to the grocery store for last minute items.

Ben went outside to work on emptying more boxes in his workshop in the garage. We had a four-car garage with a heated workshop in it. Because Ben hadn't been around during the move to Wisconsin, we just had the movers put his tools and stuff in the workshop for Ben to put where he pleased on his return.

Ash and I were alone with the puppy. We sat on the floor playing with him. "I wonder if any of Adam's tribe shape shift into a wolf," I said out loud to Ash.

"Why don't you call and ask?" Ash said.

I got up to call Adam. Ash stayed with the puppy while I went into the kitchen. When I came back into the living room, I told Ash that the tribe did have a member that shape shifted into a wolf, John Mingan. Adam said he would try to bring him over in a couple of days.

"This is your birthday, isn't it?" I said. I had almost forgotten with the excitement of the last few days.

"Yeah, I turn eighteen today," Ash said smiling at me.

"Does your family do anything special for birthdays?" I asked him.

"Not really. It's no big deal," he replied, kissing my ear.

"I've got to run upstairs a minute. I'll be right back," I said and bounced up. "Watch the puppy." The little guy had gone to sleep. There wouldn't be much to watch. I ran upstairs to my mom's room to use her phone.

I called her cell phone. "Mom! Today's Ash's birthday. He turns eighteen! Can you pick up a cake?" She said she would.

I went into my room to get the present I had bought for him. Two necklaces. Each had a half of a heart. The pieces fit together to make one whole heart. I put my necklace on under my shirt. The other had been wrapped for Ash for his birthday.

I went back downstairs and sat next to him. I handed him the little wrapped box. "Happy birthday!" I said.

He stared at the box for a long moment. "I never got a birthday gift before," he said slowly as he took the box from me. He kissed me on the lips and then slowly unwrapped the box. When he pulled out the necklace, he saw it was only half of a heart. "Where's the other half?"

I pulled the necklace out from under my shirt. "Here. We're each only half of a whole heart. When we're together, we make a whole heart," I said. I hoped he wouldn't think I was stupid for giving such a mushy gift.

"Oh, Laurel! I feel that way exactly! I'll never take it off." Ash said as he put his necklace around his neck and tucked it in his shirt. "I'll wear it close to my real heart."

I thought my heart was going to burst out of my chest. I felt so good! He liked my present!

Mom came home and made a shrimp salad for dinner. We had cake afterwards. "The bakery made it in town. They promised me there were no preservatives in it," Mom told Ash after we had sung happy birthday to him. Mom and Ben gave Ash a sweater as a present. He really seemed to like it.

We spent the rest of the evening watching old Christmas movies and sitting on the floor with the puppy. The Christmas tree was lit, and I think everyone was in a festive mood. We didn't stay up really late. Everyone was expected around noon tomorrow, and there was lots to do before they arrived.

Mom and Ben had already gone upstairs to bed when Ash got ready to leave. "I really love my present. Thank you," he said. "I like celebrating birthdays. I think I like some of your human traditions."

I smiled. "I'm really glad you like it. I like birthdays, too," I said as I got our coats and we walked outside with the puppy.

There was a half moon in the night sky, shining brightly on the snow. "The moon reminds me of our necklaces," I said. "There's only a half moon tonight."

"I'll always remember this night," Ash said, pulling me into his arms. He put his hands on each side of my face and kissed me. Even though it was cold outside, I was warm in his embrace.

When he pulled away, I said. "Me, too. I love you!"

"I love you too. I will see you tomorrow!" I could barely understand the last word as he had started to jet before he finished his sentence.

I put the puppy in his kennel with some food and a couple of toys. He ate the food, lapped some water, and then curled up and went to sleep. I went to bed myself.

I woke up early. It was finally Christmas Day! I put my robe and slippers on and ran down the basement to get the puppy out for his morning business. He was awake when I got down there, but he had not made a mess in his kennel. I brought him outside, and the cold helped him get right down to business. By the time we came back inside, Mom was up making food.

"Who all's going to be here?" I asked her as I set the puppy on the floor by one of his toys. He attacked it, but was distracted when I put out a dish of food for him.

"Well, let's see," said Mom. "Forrest, Olivia, and Hawthorn will be here. I believe Douglas might be here, and you, me, Ash, and Ben. I think that's it."

The pup and I ate our breakfasts. Afterwards, I asked Mom. "How can I help?"

She looked at me gratefully and said, "Yes! You can help with the appetizers!"

After breakfast, I put on an apron. Mom and I worked side by side making appetizers and setting up fruit and vegetable trays. Every so often, the puppy would stop playing with his toys and sniff around. I'd take him outside. One time after I brought him in, Mom asked me, "What are you going to name him?"

I didn't know. I told her I'd been thinking, but no name was coming to me.

By the time people started coming, Mom and I had the food ready and all the presents under the tree. We had to make a barrier of TV trays on their sides to keep the puppy away from the presents. He wanted to tear them up.

Forrest and Douglas were first to arrive. I hadn't seen Douglas since I'd been sick. I was happy to see him. Then Ash came, followed by Olivia and Hawthorn.

Mom had food laid out all over the kitchen counters and dining room table. People could eat when they wanted.

At first, Hawthorn was very quiet. But, after a while, he relaxed. Everyone was sorry about the pup's mother, and no one said I shouldn't have disposed of the trap. Douglas was surprised to hear about my adventures with the water sprites, but we didn't go into a lot of detail with Hawthorn there. There was enough strain between my family and Ash's. We didn't want to make the matter worse by explaining how rotten Ash's father and Chester Quince had been. We glossed over the reason for the abduction, but I think Douglas knew that Forrest would fill him later. I saw Forrest give a discrete nod to Douglas when he raised an eyebrow toward Forrest.

Once everyone was caught up on the details of the puppy and the water sprites and Hawthorn knew we were not going to criticize the Woodsons or Quinces, he visibly relaxed. We just wanted to have a good time.

For the first couple of hours, we sat around and ate. Ash and I drank lemonade. Forrest had brought a type of ale that the adult men drank. Ben said he loved it! Olivia brought a bottle of wood nymph-made wine that she drank with Mom.

Just before it was time to open the presents, I let the puppy outside one more time and then put him in his kennel. He had been quite active making new friends, so when I put him in his kennel he curled up and went to sleep.

We had put the furniture in a half circle by the tree so everyone could see what was going on. I had bought a wall hanging for Olivia and Hawthorn and had both of their names put on it for when they had a house together. Olivia and Hawthorn both seemed to like it. For Olivia alone, I had a rose pin.

I gave my mom a beaded necklace I found at the novelty store in town. It looked like miniature ice cubes connected. She seemed to really like it. I gave Ben a pillow with WORLD'S GREATEST DAD embossed on it.

For Forrest I had the vase I made for him. He said it showed great craftsmanship. I wasn't sure if he was sincere or not, but it made me feel good. I gave Douglas a hand-stitched Periodic Table wall hanging that I bought at a craft shop in town. He laughed.

I gave Ash a bracelet of intertwined copper and brass that I'd made in my art class. It had a sealant on it so that it wouldn't turn his wrist green. It was kind of like a Celtic design, but simpler. He gave me a big hug and kiss in front of everyone.

I got a beautiful tunic from Olivia and Hawthorn. I wasn't sure if it was wood nymph fabric or not, but it was made in the flowing wood nymph style. Mom gave me real gold earrings, and Ben gave me a figurine from Iraq. Forrest gave me a shelving unit for my room that would take up half a wall. It was a good thing I had a large room. The shelving unit was made of the vine-like wood that reminded me of his stairway and our pier. Douglas gave me a Chemistry book he said would be helpful for my classes next fall.

Ash gave me a ring handmade out of silver. It had designs on it I didn't recognize, but apparently Hawthorn, Olivia, and Forrest did, as they all gave sharp intakes of breath when they saw it. It appeared to have some significance in the wood nymph community. I just thought it was beautiful. I kissed him for it and put it on. "This is to show you how much I love you," he whispered in my ear.

"Thank you. I love you, too!" I whispered back and kissed him again. It seemed the whole world shimmered at that moment. I figured it was my imagination because my love for Ash was so strong and I was feeling something similar to the essence thing. The ring felt warm on my finger. Not hot or uncomfortable, but a bit warmer than my body temperature.

After opening presents and cleaning up the paper mess, I took the puppy outside for a few minutes. After that, we sat around and talked while we looked at our Christmas tree. It was dark out and the tree was lit and really pretty.

"Do you have a name for your puppy?" Douglas asked me as we sat and watched him attack one of his raw hide toys.

"No. Not yet. Nothing seems to fit," I replied.

"How about Achak?" said Douglas. "It's Algonquin for 'spirit.' He seems like a spirited kind of guy."

"Achak," I said, trying it out. "I never heard that before. Sure, that sounds like a good name. I'll name him Achak." It didn't flow off of the tongue easily, but it was a cool name and having a large-breed pup that actually looked more wolf than its mother was as close to having a spirit guide as I would ever have.

The day just seemed to fly by. Before we knew it, it was getting late, and the humans were trying to suppress their yawns. Hawthorn and Olivia were the first to leave. Shortly afterward, Forrest and Douglas left. After a while, it was just Ben, Mom, Ash,, and me. Ben turned on the TV and Ash and Ben watched the late news while Mom and I cleaned up the dishes and put the leftovers away. Some of the food had been out too long and had to be thrown out, but there wasn't much waste. The puppy was sleeping on the middle of the living room floor, spread out like he belonged there.

After the cleanup, I curled up with Ash on the loveseat. "What's the significance of the ring? I noticed Hawthorn, Olivia and Forrest's reaction when they saw it." I asked softly so Mom and Ben wouldn't hear me. They were discussing the day and how well it turned out.

"It shows the wood nymph community that you're taken," he whispered and kissed my cheek. "It shows that I've bonded with you. I'll never take any other woman for a wife. I've claimed you as my future bride. It's kind of an engagement ring." He kissed me again. "You don't mind that idea, do you?" he asked.

"No, I don't mind at all," I replied feeling that warm glow surround me. An hour or so later, Ash left for home, and I took the puppy out for the last time. I had the puppy for over one whole day and he hadn't had an accident in the house yet. I put him in his kennel and went upstairs to clean up for bed. I had hoped it would be a good Christmas, and I had it almost right. It had been a great Christmas.

CHAPTER 23
WOLF MAN

I woke to my alarm and realized it was the day after Christmas. Christmas was over. I didn't have school today, but I did have to work. It seemed like half of the gifts people bought as gifts for Christmas Day were returned on the day after Christmas. I knew I was going to spend the day dealing with those returned items. I'd have to give a store credit or credit card credit, and then reshelf all those returned items. I wasn't looking forward to working today.

I got dressed and went to go let Achak out. When I got downstairs, I saw that Achak was lying on the living room floor chewing on a rawhide dog toy. "I got up early and let him out," Ben said to me. He was sitting at the dining room table drinking coffee with Mom. "Chuck must have heard me get up. I heard him whining in his kennel when I came to the kitchen. I didn't want him to have an accident so I let him out and fed him."

"Chuck?" I said as I went to get my breakfast.

"Achak's hard to remember. Chuck's simpler. I hope you don't mind me giving him a nickname," Ben replied, grinning at me while sipping at his coffee.

"I kind of like the name," I said.

"If he throws up, we can call him Up Chuck," Mom said laughing..

I rolled my eyes at both of them. "Oh, my God. You're both insane," I sighed. Just as I said that, I looked down at my puppy and he must have bitten off a piece of rawhide that was too big to swallow. He made some barf noises and vomited an unchewed chunk of rawhide onto the floor.

"See, Up Chuck," Mom said laughing. "Please clean that up, would you?" Mom and Ben were laughing their fool heads off.

"Don't make fun of my puppy. He's going to grow up and be a big dog some day," I said huffing off to the kitchen to get some carpet cleaner and paper towels. My cereal was getting soggy in my bowl on the table.

"Make sure you put that stuff in the burn barrel, okay?" Mom said wiping laugh tears from her eyes. "I don't want the house to smell like Chuck's upchuck."

"Yeah, whatever," I mumbled. I really loved her, but sometimes what she considered funny I found so *not* funny.

As I scrubbed the carpet, Achak came over and licked my face. "Eewww, puppy barf germs! Stop it Achak. You're so gross!"

222

I took the yucky paper towels and put them in the burn barrel garbage can in the corner of the kitchen. I'd take it outside to put in the real burn barrel later. Since we live in the north woods, we tried to recycle what we could and burned paper and other stuff to keep it from going into some landfill. I washed my face off in the sink, and Achak sat beside me wagging his tail. I looked down at him as I dried my face and said, "You should have had a drink of water before licking my face." Then I realized that I had to be to work in an hour.

"Dad, can you watch Achak for me while I work today? I only have six hours but I have to be there in an hour."

"Sure, honey. Chuck and I will be just fine," Ben replied, still laughing.

Mom got up from the table and said, "I have a couple of hours work waiting for me, too. The holidays can be pretty stressful. I have a couple of clients coming in this morning." She kissed Ben and me good-bye. She even reached over and patted Achak, saying, "Good-bye, Chuck," while giving me a big grin.

I went to eat my now soggy bowl of cereal, but the kitchen phone rang. I ran to get it. "Hello" I said almost out of breath, hoping it was Ash.

"Is this Laurel?" a voice I did not recognize asked. It was a deep, husky, sexy voice. It gave me goose pimples up both arms.

"Yes. Who is this?" I replied, leaning against the door frame.

"This is John Mingan. I'm a friend of Adam Whitestone. Adam told me to call you about a puppy you rescued," He replied. I loved Ash, but I couldn't help but be moved by this voice.

"Yeah, Adam told me he was going to ask someone to call me," I said.

"He told me that you had rescued a puppy. He said he told you that all of the people on our reservation are shape shifters. I shape shift to a wolf. Adam thought I might be able to help you with that puppy," he said in his deep, soft voice. While Ash and Douglas had voices like melted chocolate, this voice was a hot and smooth mocha.

"Huh. Cool. I have to go to work in an hour. But, I don't work tomorrow. Did you want to come here, or should I bring the puppy there?" I asked. I was kind of excited. I hadn't met a wolf shape shifter yet.

"I'll come tomorrow with Adam," he replied slowly. Did he realize what his voice sounded like to women? At least to me?

"Sure, tomorrow would be great. Early afternoon?" I asked. I leaned against the wall in the kitchen. I imagined this huge, good looking man coming over tomorrow. I just knew he wasn't going to be a small man. He sounded big and powerful. I felt my face getting hot just talking to him. What was wrong with me? Why was I fantasizing about a stranger? Wasn't I in love with Ash?

"Tomorrow, it is," he replied and hung up. He didn't say good bye.

"Huh," I said out loud and then turned to Ben. "Adam's coming over tomorrow with some guy named John Mingan that shape shifts into a wolf. He thinks he can help us with Achak." I hoped I sounded casual. I did not need him asking me questions about why I was red in the face.

"That might be good," Ben said. "Oh, oh. Chuck's sniffing around again. I'll let him out." Ben picked up Achak to take him out the sliding door.

"It's Achak, dad!" I called after him, finally sitting down to eat my now seriously soggy cereal.

When Ben brought Achak back in, he said he was going out into his workshop. "Don't worry about a thing, honey. Chuck and I will be fine today." I watched him carry Achak out with him to the garage.

I felt a little jealous about the bond Ben and Achak seemed to be developing, but I had to go to work. The truth was, it was better that they got along. It would've been worse if Ben hated Achak. I couldn't care for him when I went to work. I poked my head in to the workshop to say good-bye when I went into the garage to get into my Jeep to go to work. Ben was puttering with something on his work bench and Achak was asleep on a folded up blanket in a corner. Ben waved good-bye to me.

"See you later!" I said, reaching down to scratch the puppy's ears. The puppy didn't wake up.

"Have a good day at work!" Ben called to me as I left.

It was a long day. The customers were fairly nice, but the lines were long at both check out stations and at the table we set up to handle the returned items. I was more then ready to leave when my shift was up. I was exhausted as I drove home.

When I pulled into the yard, I saw Ash's car in the driveway. That made me feel better. I saw Mom's car in the garage when I parked my car, and I ran into the house, forgetting all about how exhausted I was.

"Hello!" I called as I opened the door. I took off my boots and hung my coat.

"Hi!" Mom called from the kitchen. "Ben and Ash are on the river side of the house with Chuck."

"His name's Achak, Mom," I said automatically, grabbing my coat and boots to join Ben and Ash. I went out the sliding door.

"What's going on?" I asked as I walked up to Ash and Ben. Achak was sniffing around. In deep pockets of snow, he would jump through the snow. Most of the snow was over his head.

"Not much. Chuck and I had a good day," Ben said. "We worked on fixing the name sign for the driveway."

We had a sign at the end of the driveway with "Redmond" on it with an arrow pointing down the driveway. During the snow storm of a few weeks ago, it had fallen off of the tree it had been attached to and the hanging hook had been ruined. Ben had apparently nailed in a new hook.

"Chuck?" Ash asked giving me a lopsided grin. Achak was by our feet and shaking the snow off of his coat.

"That's what Mom and Dad call Achak," I said in mock disgust.

"I kind of like it. It's such a human name." Ash grinned at me. He reached down to pet Achak and the puppy nibbled on his gloves.

"Yeah, but Achak isn't a human. He is a dog," I glowered back at him.

"Whatever. I think I like it," Ash said, grinning.

I looked at Ben. He was grinning, too. If calling my puppy Chuck was going to help Ben and Ash get along, I wasn't going to argue. I rolled my eyes again and shook my head. "Whatever." I mumbled.

Achak was apparently done with whatever business they'd brought him out to do. We circled the house back to the garage. As we walked in through the overhead door, Ben turned to look at us. "Do you have any plans for New Year's?" he asked us.

We went into the workshop and I sat on a bar stool next to Ash. A wood-burning stove Ben had lit earlier in the day kept the room quite warm and comfortable. Ben also had a refrigerator that he stocked with beer and soft drinks. Ben got himself a beer and offered us a soda. I took a Coke, but Ash took a bottled water.

"Not that I know of," I said. "Why?" I hadn't thought about New Year's Eve. Did wood nymphs do anything special for the last day of the year? "Do we?" I asked Ash.

Ash shrugged and said, "No, the last day of December is a human celebration. It's not a day we note. I guess I hadn't thought of doing anything special. What is usually done on New Year's?."

Ben looked at me and said, "Your mom and I are invited to a party in Merrill. I'd like us to go. Will you kids be okay on your own for New Year's Eve?"

I looked at Ash and wondered if he was thinking what I was thinking. Our first New Year's Eve, and we were going to be able to spend it together, alone. I saw his eyes light up. He *was* thinking the same thing. I'm glad Ben was fiddling with something on his work bench and didn't see the look we gave each other. A surge of heat went through my body just at the idea of being all alone with Ash for a whole evening. I figured I should change the subject before I said something stupid.

"Dad, I think we'll just watch TV or rent a video or something. Is that okay?" I said to Ben and then turned to ask Ash. He nodded.

I then said, "Ash, did dad tell you that some guy named John Mingan is coming from the reservation tomorrow with Adam? I guess he is a wolf shape shifter."

I tried to act casual. I was thinking way too hard about Ash and being alone on New Year's. It made me feel all hot inside. I also thought about John Mingan's sexy voice that had made me feel even hotter. What was wrong with me? I was in love with Ash! The ring Ash had given me was still warm against my hand, even though my hands felt like they were cold. I wondered if it had some magical properties.

"That might be interesting," Ash replied. "What time are they coming?"

I took a large drink of my Coke to cool myself off. "Early afternoon, I think," I said. "He knows canines. He might have some ideas on what we can do with Chuck."

Ben laughed. "Chuck?" He gave me a big grin.

Achak was a cool name, but Chuck was easier to say and remember. I didn't like names like "Killer" or "Spike." Chuck was a comfortable name. As I looked down at my puppy, all I could see was . . . Chuck.

Ash and I spent the rest of the evening with my parents. We taught Ash how to play Monopoly. When he won, Ben told him that he was a natural capitalist. Then Ben had to explain what a capitalist was and what capitalism was. That was fun.

The next morning, I went downstairs to find that, again, Ben had beaten me in letting Chuck out. I gave the puppy a pat on his head while he ate his breakfast and went to get my own. Mom and Ben were at the dining room table looking out at the snow on the river.

"How much snow did we get last night? It looks like a winter wonderland out there," I said looking out the kitchen window.

It really was beautiful. Snow lay heavy on the drooping pines and sparkled in the morning sunshine as if filled with diamonds. Everything had a new coating of white.

"It snowed about six inches last night, and now it is bitterly cold, about zero degrees out there. It's funny. When the sun is the brightest in the winter, the weather is the coldest. Good thing this house is so well insulated." Ben sipped his coffee.

I nodded my agreement. I loved having a modern house. We had no drafts. I was warm and comfortable walking around in my stocking feet.

"Thanks for letting Chuck out," I said as I sat down next to Ben. I poured milk on my cereal.

"Sure, no problem." Ben then turned to me. "What are your plans for today?"

"That guy from the reservation is coming over this afternoon with Adam," I replied and started eating my cereal.

"Oh, yeah, that's right," Ben said taking a sip of coffee.

"What are your plans today?" I asked.

"I'm going to work in my shop. Tools need to be put away and a few boxes need to be unpacked," Ben replied.

"What's your day like, Mom?" I asked.

"I thought I'd like to go to Wausau and check the after-Christmas sales. I'd have asked if you wanted to go with, but I doubt I'll be back by early afternoon. I better get going if I'm going to have a chance at any good bargains, too. I took some steaks out of the freezer. Ben, could you please get the grill out of the shed? It'd be nice to have charcoal grilled steaks. Oh, and Laurel, I took out an extra one for Ash."

Ben and I replied, "Okay," at exactly the same time and laughed. Mom shook her head at us as she got ready to leave.

"I think I'll do some research about wolves before they get here this afternoon," I said finishing my breakfast.

"That's probably a good idea," Ben said and got up from the table. "I'll take Chuck out in the garage with me. That way, if he does have an accident, it'll be on a concrete floor and not on the carpeting."

"Okay," I said and went back upstairs. I turned on my computer, went to Wikipedia and looked up gray wolves. They were also called timber wolves. Most wolves grew to be eighty pounds, but there were occasionally larger ones. From the tip of the nose to the tip of the tail they could be four and a half to six and a half feet in length. Wolves could trot at around six miles per hour for hours, but could reach speeds of forty miles per hour when hunting prey.

I'd never been particularly fond of research before moving to Wisconsin. Now, I found myself researching all kinds of things and liking it. I'd looked up Hodag on the Internet. While considered a hoax or a mythical creature, at least a few websites considered the Hodag a live creature. Yeah, I knew it was. I could still remember exactly what it sounded like. It made me shiver just to remember that sound.

While I sat there thinking about the Hodag, the doorbell rang. I shut the laptop and ran downstairs to answer the door. It was Ash.

"Hi!" I said when I opened the door. "Did you jet here?"

"Yeah, I figured if we had to go anywhere, we could take your Jeep," he said looking around. He put his arms around me and kissed me.

I felt little electrical pulses shooting throughout my body as he kissed me. I got that warm feeling that seemed to spread from the inside of my body to my extremities. Parts of me I didn't even know existed seemed to come alive when he kissed me. I felt my legs get weak. Each time he kissed me I remembered all over again how powerful his kisses were. I was convinced that there was magic in them. Nothing made me feel more alive than his kisses. They seemed to remove me from this world and put me in a whole new dimension, elevating me to a different plane of existence. Time seemed to stand still in his arms.

I don't know how long we were locked in our embrace before I felt a semblance of reality return. Maybe it was the bitter cold against my skin. We were standing in the doorway with the door open. I put my hands between us to gently push him away. When he realized what I wanted, he blinked his eyes as if recovering from a trance.

"We need to get in the house and shut the door," I said simply, pulling him into the house. He took his coat off and I hung it up in the closet.

"Every time I kiss you, I seem to lose more and more of myself to you," he said seriously as we walked into the living room.

"Yeah, I feel the same way. I can't get enough of you," I replied. I took his hand, and we went to go sit on the couch.

"I really do love you," he said, taking my face in his hands and leaning forward to kiss me again. Just then, I heard the front door open and jerked back.

"Laurel?" I heard Ben call and stamp the snow off his boots by the front door. "Can you come here for a minute?"

"Yeah, sure," I said, and Ash and I got up from the couch.

"Oh, hi Ash. I'm glad you're here. I'm trying to hang a couple of shelves and am having a dickens of a time getting them level. Can you guys come and help me a minute? I didn't see your car. You must have jetted here, right?" Ben asked. Ash nodded.

"Sure, let me get my boots and our coats," I said. We went out and spent the next couple of hours hanging various shelves in Ben's workroom. We were just finishing up when I heard a car pull up. It had a throaty, powerful engine.

"That's not Mom's car. It must be Adam and John Mingan," I said heading out of the garage. A sleek black sports car I hadn't seen before was parked by the house.

"Hi, Laurel!" I heard Adam call. He was climbing out of the passenger side of the car and gave me a huge hug when I reached the car. I gave him a half hearted hug back, looking at the man getting out of the driver's seat. He was easily the best looking Native American man I'd ever seen. He had perfect, strong facial features, dark hair, and intense golden eyes. He wore a short leather jacket and tight jeans that showed off the muscles in his legs. He was a little bit taller than Ash or Ben. He had dark black hair and looked like he was Douglas's age. When I looked into his eyes, it felt like my soul was being sucked up. I'd never seen eyes that color. They looked like they glowed in the sunlight. It took Ash squeezing my fingers for me break the eye contact.

"Ow!" I said pulling my hand from Ash's grip. I looked at Ash, and he was looking at whom I assumed was John Mingan with a really cold hatred. Ash's face looked like thunderclouds, his emotions a mixture of anger, fear, frustration, and awe.

John had what I could only describe as a predatory look on his face. He gave me a slow smile, like I looked really good to him. It made me uncomfortable. He looked hungry but not for food. He didn't even look at Ash or Ben. His emotions were interest, dark humor, and something that felt dangerous.

"Hi, everyone, this is John Mingan," said Adam. "John, this is the girl I told you about. Ash is her neighbor, and Ben's her dad." Adam was smiling, unaware of the energy flowing around the car. At the introduction, John Mingan finally looked away from me to nod at Ben and Ash.

I gave a quick glance at Ben for his reaction. Ben didn't look on guard, but his emotions were up. Had he seen the look John Mingan gave me? Ben smiled and looked casual, but I knew he wasn't completely relaxed and at ease.

I seemed to have been frozen in place with Ash beside me. He had taken my hand back into his. My feet didn't want to move, like my unconscious mind knew John Mingan was a predator and dangerous, and self-preservation was trying to keep me away from him. John walked around the car and held out his hand as if to shake mine. He moved like a predator, balanced, ready, cautious. His hand was really big. His fingernails were well manicured, but his hands looked rough and calloused.

"Hello, Laurel," he said slowly in that really sexy voice. It was even sexier in person than on the phone. It was velvet, if velvet had a sound.

I slowly put my hand in his, but he didn't shake it. While looking into my eyes, he raised my hand slowly to his lips and he kissed the back of my fingers. He took his fingertips and moved them slowly along the palm of my hand at the same time. I felt a shock at the touch, like all of the heat in my body ignited in an instant. I felt as if I was drowning in those golden eyes.

Ash squeezed my other hand again, until I felt my fingers getting pinched. I wondered if John had some kind of hypnotic ability with his eyes. Or was it something to do with his hand on mine?

I pulled my hand out of John's hand, and I yanked my eyes away from his and glared at Ash. "Ouch! Quit hurting my hand!"

As John released me, he looked at Ash and said, "Ah, the wood nymph thinks that he has a prior claim. Keep in mind that she's at least part Ojibwa. I may stake my own claim on her."

Ash looked at him and said angrily, "That'll never happen. She's mine for life."

"Maybe . . . maybe not," John Mingan replied with a sardonic grin. John then looked at the puppy.

As he turned away from me and Ash, Ash whispered, "Sorry. I didn't mean to hurt you." He'd loosened his grip on my hand, but he didn't let go. I could feel his emotions clearly. He was seething with anger. At me? Could he feel the emotional roller coaster I was on? Could he feel I was attracted to John Mingan? I didn't want to be attracted to him. It was like there was a force about John Mingan that drew me in like a moth to a flame. I forced myself to focus on my surroundings, to take my mind off of John.

I looked back at this handsome stranger, who was looking at Chuck. I could still feel his pull on me, but it wasn't as strong.

"Here's the puppy," Ben said reaching down to pick up Chuck to put him in John's hands.

I looked at Ash, and he was staring into my eyes. "We'll talk later," he whispered. I nodded and then turned back to see John with Chuck. I wondered if the Ojibwa had other powers other than shape shifting.

"I named him Achak," I said, "but my parents nicknamed him Chuck. They said it is easier to say."

John set the pup on the ground and squatted down to his level. He held his hand out to him. Chuck came to stand in front of me, facing John. His baby fur bristled. He growled at John Mingan. After a moment or so, he calmed down and came to sniff his hand.

"He's part timber wolf," John said while petting Chuck on his head. "His dam probably wasn't from what Adam described to me, but I bet his sire was. He'll be a big animal when he's grown. He has a good spirit. He'll be a good guardian for you, Laurel. I have never seen a wolf this young get protective of a human before. Perhaps it is because of his dog background or because you are more than human and he senses that you're special. Adam told me about you."

John looked at Ash and asked him, "Have you ever had wolves or any other creature get protective of your people?"

"Not that I know of," Ash replied curtly.

"I'd like to know what he is thinking, but I can only do that in my wolf form." The next thing, he had stripped down to his loin cloth right there in the driveway. I saw the dazzling flash of a million sparklers as he changed into a wolf. I looked over at Ben to see his reaction.

Ben hadn't move a muscle. He stared, incredulous, at the shape shifter. I looked back at John the timber wolf. He was a huge wolf. Wikipedia had said the largest timber wolf on record weighed in at around 170 pounds. I figured John had to be more than that. When I had seen him almost naked just seconds before, I had seen a man who was solid muscle. Weight-lifter muscle. As a wolf, he was the scariest thing I'd ever seen. George as a bear, hadn't instill fear in me the way this huge gray wolf did.

I looked at Adam, and he smiled. The shape shifter and the puppy were nose to nose. When John first changed, the puppy had yelped and backed into my legs. After

John changed, he stood still with his muzzle low. After a minute, Chuck walked slowly over to John and put his muzzle to John's nose. They sniffed at each other for a minute and then walked over to the edge of the driveway. The puppy squatted and John lifted his leg. They walked the perimeter of the parking area, urinating every few feet. We just watched them walk around. I wondered out loud why they were doing that.

"Why are they marking territory?" Ash whispered. Ben heard also, as he had come to stand beside us.

"I don't get that," Ben said.

Adam was close enough to hear Ash and Ben. "The young one will be Laurel's protector. John, as the alpha wolf, is teaching him the ways of marking the territory he is to guard."

The wolf and puppy had just made a circle around the house and driveway and came back to us. John nudged the puppy with his nose to stand in front of me. When the puppy sat down, John walked over to the car. I had to shield my eyes from the brightness of the change. John seemed to take his time getting dressed. He looked over at me and grinned. I turned away from him and saw both Ash and Ben frowning at him.

Once John was dressed, he walked back over to us. John turned to me. "This is a smart puppy. He understands he is to watch over you. It is fine for you to keep him in the house until he has grown, but he'll want to be outside at night to patrol. This is his territory now. He'll do his best to protect you. I showed him how to mark territory. I marked with him so that he knows I'm the alpha wolf if I'm in the area. He'll obey my orders. I've told him to protect you. I'll come back in a couple of weeks to see how he's doing. Maybe I'll get to know you better, too." John looked deep into my eyes for what felt like an eternity but was probably a few seconds. He gave me a wolfish grin, then turned to Adam. "Are you ready to go?"

Adam looked at me and shrugged. "Yeah, I guess so. Call you later, Laurel."

I nodded, and they got into the car and turned it around. As the car turned, John looked at me with those intense golden eyes and gave me a slow smile. I felt mesmerized. The next thing I knew John and Adam were driving away down the driveway.

Chuck watched the car drive away, not leaving his position by my feet. "What the hell was that all about?" Ben stated as the tail lights disappeared around the bend.

"I think Laurel has a new admirer," Ash said softly. I looked at his face. He was furious. He held my hand with his ring and kissed my finger. "That guy seemed like he was really into you, Laurel. He makes me nervous."

"Oh, you have nothing to worry about. I think he's just a bit . . . wild. Maybe it's because of his wolf characteristics, but he was a little scary." I I felt a shiver go down my spine.

Ben added, "He may be a good shape shifter and a good member of his tribe, but there's something strange about him. He's a very scary guy, and not a lot of things scare me. I wouldn't want to be on his bad side. Plus, I think he's a wolf even when not shape-shifted."

Chuck whimpered. Even though I had no idea what the whimper meant, I said, "Yeah, Chuck, he makes me nervous, too."

I said, "I'll have to call Adam and see what John said about us." The three of us and Chuck went into the house.

"Do you think that's a good idea?" Ash said. "Do you want to draw more of his attention?"

"Well, no. I really don't want *his* attention. I'm more interested in his motives. I mean, maybe this Mingan guy said stuff on the way back to the reservation I should know." Was that what I wanted? His scariness was kind of attractive. What would it be like to control a man like that? Did I want to control a man? I looked at Ash. He was perfect. And I'd never think of Ash as scary and I didn't want to contol him at all.

We were all a little nervous after meeting John. "Some of the things I've learned since I returned from Iraq have been neat and exciting," Ben said, his voice soft and cautious. "Some stuff's been weird. This John Mingan makes me flat-out uncomfortable. Now I'm concerned I have to go back to Iraq."

"I promise you, sir," Ash said earnestly as we went into the living room. "I'll take care of Laurel. I can get anywhere in almost an instant. Laurel has the call, and I'll alsways respond." Ash squeezed my hand and gave me a serious look.

Ben watched Ash's face, then said, "I believe you. But, what if it isn't enough?"

I let out an exasperated hiss. "Hey! Like, I'm right here! I'm not exactly helpless, you know. I can read emotions, and I have a guard wolf. Even though he's small now, he won't be for long," I said confidently. *Really!* I thought, *I'm not stupid.* My mother had raised me to be independent and to be able to think for myself.

"Laurel, I'm just worried about you," Ben said giving me a hug. "I want you to do your best to stay away from that guy. If you can't, try to make sure Ash or someone is with you when he is around, okay?"

"Yeah, sure," I said.

"Hey, I know," Ben said. "Let's go cross-country skiing!"

Ben always liked turning stress into exercise. Maybe it was a military thing. I also felt I needed to do something physical. Cross-country skiing would be a good way to burn off excessive energy and stress. John had left me feeling apprehensive.

"Yeah, that'd be fun! I haven't done any cross-country skiing, this whole winter! Ash, do you ski? Do you have skis?" I asked. It was something we'd never done together.

"Sure, let me run home and get them. I'll be right back." Ash gave me a kiss on the cheek and left.

By the time Ben and I got our skis and boots out of the closet and were putting them on while sitting on the front steps, Ash drove his car back into our parking area.

We spent the rest of the afternoon skiing through clearings and up the driveway. Mostly we would ski single file. Ben led the way, with me in the middle, Chuck running in the ski tracks behind me and Ash bringing up the rear. We saw deer beds in the snow. The heat from their bodies had melted the snow and strands of deer fur in the melted areas. Chuck growled. There were also plenty of deer tracks.

We skied until the sun was low. We got back to the house just as the sun dipped over the horizon. The garage door was open and Mom's car was inside. The garage lights were on and so were the lights in the house. Mom had even plugged in the outside Christmas lights. We took our skis off and stood them upright in the garage against the wall. When we went into the house, we smelled food cooking. I hadn't realized that I was hungry until I caught the whiff of the food coming from the kitchen.

Mom heard us come in. "As soon as the steaks are cooked, dinner will be ready," she called. "I made a pie and some side dishes. Plus, I brought home a couple of DVDs I thought we could watch tonight."

Ben went out to light the grill. Ash and I put the dishes on the table and talked to Mom while she put the salads together.

"John Mingan, a wolf shape shifter Adam knows came," I said.

"I remember you saying Adam was bringing him. What was he like? Did he shift into a wolf in front of you?" Mom put the vegetables into serving dishes.

"Yeah, he did," I replied. "He had a fancy sports car, too."

Ash gave a disgusted sigh and said, "It was fancy all right, but you don't drive a car like that in the dead of winter."

"Okay. It wasn't a four-wheel drive or anything, but it was a cool car. You have to admit that," I said to Ash, crossing my arms over my chest.

Ash put his hands up. "Okay, okay, it's a cool car, not appropriate, but cool."

I sighed. "Whatever. It got to our house just fine. Anyway," I said to Mom, "he is a big guy and a really big wolf. He has these yellow eyes that seemed to look right through me. He even made Ben nervous."

Mom turned to look at me. "Really, some guy made Ben nervous?"

"Well, I don't know if *nervous* is the right word, but he sure made all of us uncomfortable," I replied.

"He is a wolf even in human form," Ash said. "I have no doubt he could be a killer. I also think he was a little too interested in Laurel."

"Really? Should I be concerned?" Mom said while wiping her hands on her apron.

I heaved a sigh. "No, Mom. He wasn't inappropriate." Was the look he gave me innocent? Was the way he touched the palm of my hand accident or intentional?

"There's something about that guy that makes me uncomfortable. I don't trust him," Ash said straightening the napkins.

Ben came in to get the steaks to put on the grill, and he said, "Yeah, I don't either. He didn't say anything wrong exactly. It was more like a look about him."

I changed the topic of conversation to our cross country skiing, telling Mom about the deer beds and other signs of wildlife we had seen. Before I knew it, Ben came in with the grilled steaks. We ate dinner with no more talk about shape shifters or wolves. Chuck was asleep on the floor by his food dish.

I helped my mom clean up the dinner dishes. After the dishwasher started running, we watched a couple of new releases Mom had brought home.

It was not late when Ash got up to go home after the second movie. Ben and I were trying to suppress our yawns. Ash didn't look tired at all, but he knew I was. He held me close for a moment by the front door and gave me a soft kiss just before he left. "I love you." he said to me as he walked out the door.

"I love you, too," I said and closed the door. I went upstairs and cleaned up for bed. As I went to sleep, I started dreaming about golden eyes.

CHAPTER 24
NEW YEAR

I was curious about John Mingan when I got up the next day. I wondered if he would call to check on the puppy's progress. I called Adam to see if I could find out some more information about the wolf shape shifter.

"Hi, Adam. It's Laurel. I was really glad to see you yesterday. Too bad you couldn't have stayed longer. Your friend John Mingan is a lot bigger as a man and a wolf than I had expected." I tried to sound calm and collected. I leaned against the kitchen wall.

"Hey, Laurel! Yeah, I'm sorry we couldn't stay yesterday. I would've liked to have visited longer, but since I was riding with John . . . I guess I could have changed into the eagle form and flew home. Didn't think of that at the time. Anyway, you're right. John's a big guy. His whole family's built like that, and none of them are fat."

"Did John say anything about yesterday? What did he say about Chuck?" I asked, still working at a neutral tone. *Or did he ask about me?* I didn't say that.

"He thinks the pup'll get quite large, that it's got some malamute or St. Bernard in it maybe. He's pretty sure it's daddy was a wolf, too. John says it's really intelligent, and, baby that it is, it still understood everything he told it. The puppy was already feeling protective of you for rescuing it. As it grows, it probably won't want to let you out of its sight." After a pause Adam added, "John also seemed really interested in you."

"What do you mean, really interested in me?" He had my curiosity now. Did my voice sound too excited? Without meaning to, I was gripping the phone hard.

"Maybe it was just me, but . . . he seemed to almost eat you with his eyes. I've never seen him kiss any girl's hand before, not like that. But that's kind of weird. He has a girlfriend named Hurit."

"Hurit? What kind of name is that?" I asked. "Is it Ojibwe?"

"Hurit means beautiful. It's kind of weird, but her spirit guide's a badger. Go figure. She's unbelievably beautiful, but sometimes her temperament can match her spirit guide. Badgers can be quite vicious and stubborn when provoked and so can Hurit. She'd be really pissed if she knew John even *looked* at you. She's the jealous type. Think the evil queen in *Snow White*. Me, I try to avoid her. She's the dictionary example of beauty being only skin deep. No amount of prettiness can clear her evil core away." Adam snorted in disgust.

I would have asked a few more questions, but Adam said abruptly, "Sorry, I gotta go. I promised to help Uncle George with some stuff, and he's honking his horn outside. Call you soon!" I heard the phone click.

I sat there holding the phone for a minute after Adam had hung up. Then I got ready to go to work. I thought about John Mingan and his golden eyes all of the way to work. I wondered about his girlfriend. Exactly how jealous was she? Was she a nutcase? After I got to work, I was so busy I didn't think about John or his girlfriend for the rest of the day. Any time I caught myself thinking about him or his golden eyes and sexy voice, I'd picture a cartoon evil queen chasing me.

After work that day and every day for the rest of the week, Ash came over. We would have dinner together at my house and either play board games with Mom and Ben or watch TV. The next thing I knew it was New Year's Eve day.

I got up that morning realizing that tonight, Ash and I were going to be all alone for the first time for a whole evening. Mom and Ben were going to spend their New Year's Eve with some friends in Merrill, about half an hour away from our house.

I used to feel bad if I stayed home alone on New Year's Eve. It was a day to go out and celebrate the end of the old year and the beginning of the next. When no one would call me to do anything I'd feel bad and left out. This year however, I wanted to stay home because I wouldn't be alone. Ash would be with me. I didn't think about golden eyes anymore. I thought about green eyes like mine.

Mom made a light dinner of a mixed-green salad with grilled fish on top for all of us before getting herself ready to go out. When Mom came downstairs after dressing for the party, she looked beautiful in her black cocktail dress. Since living on a more or less wood nymph diet, she had lost weight and looked fantastic. Ben gave her a wolf whistle as she came down the stairs.

"I have lost twenty pounds in the last three months!" Mom said turning around so that we could appreciate all angles of the dress.

"You have always looked good to me, but you look exceptional tonight," Ben said giving Mom a hug and a kiss on her cheek.

"You really do look great, Mom!" I said as I went to get her dress coat for her. Ben already had his dress coat on.

"You both look great," Ash said. "Have a great time at your party."

"Have a great time!" I echoed as they walked out the front door. We walked out with them to let Chuck out. We waved as they drove off.

We stood by the front door as we watched Mom's Liberty disappear down the driveway. When the taillights made the turn in the driveway, I looked at Ash and said, "Well, we're all alone. What do you want to do?"

"I want to kiss you," Ash replied and took my hand.

We walked back into the house with Chuck. I gave him a chew toy to entertain him while I sat on the couch with Ash.

Ash put his hands on each side of my face and slowly kissed me. I kept my eyes open as I wanted to watch the expression on his face as his lips met mine. As his lips touched mine, I couldn't help it, I closed my eyes and lost myself in the kiss, feeling the heat build up inside in me. I really felt hot at my core. When Ash tentatively put his tongue into my mouth, I instinctively sucked on it. I felt his body quiver, and he put his arms around me tighter. After a small eternity, our kiss ended. We were both breathing hard.

"I want to try something. Can you hold still for me?" I asked. Ash had on a flannel shirt and I started to unbutton it. "Don't move," I whispered. Ash's entire body was trembling. When I looked in his eyes, I saw that he was watching me intensely. He put his hands down by his sides. I wanted to feel his bare chest. This was about to be my first sexual experience, and I didn't want to rush things and get scared. I didn't know how far we were going to go tonight, but I didn't want us just groping at each other. I loved his body, and this was my chance to experience it in my own way. I was sure if I did something that made Ash uncomfortable, he would let me know.

"Will I get a turn at this, too?" Ash asked breathlessly.

"Probably. Let's just see how this goes," I said, reaching over to lick his chest. I smelled something that I hadn't noticed before, a sort of musky cologne. "What's this cologne?" I asked leaning forward to kiss his chin and face. I smelled the musky cologne all over him now. It smelled really good and made me hotter.

"Ah, no," Ash said huskily. "Wood nymphs have glands in the skin that release a scent that's supposed to be attractive during . . . sex." His voice was quavering. "Laurel, I don't know how long I can hold still like this."

"I've never smelled anything so attractive as you are right now," I said and then kissed him and leaned my body up against his. Ash wrapped his arms around me. The next thing I knew, I was lying on the floor next to the couch and Ash was kissing my face and my neck and running his hand over my backside and legs. I wanted to get closer to him. He pulled away slightly and started to unbutton my shirt. He was kissing my neck and now my bare shoulder.

Then the doorbell rang.

"What's that?" Ash said, falling backwards away from me. Chuck started whining and barking.

"It's the damn doorbell!" I growled, quickly buttoning up my shirt.

"Do you have to answer it?" Ash hissed smoothing his hair and buttoning up his own shirt.

"What if Ben and Mom were in an accident? I have to answer it," I said trying to stand up on wobbly legs that didn't seem to want to hold me up.

The doorbell rang two more times by the time I got there. I knew my face was flushed, and I wondered if my hair was a mess. I ran my fingers through it on the way to the door. Olivia was standing there. "Oh. Hi, Olivia. What are you doing here?" I said, trying not to sound breathless or rude.

"I saw you with Ash. I don't think you're ready for that, yet," Olivia said seriously and walked past me into the house.

All of a sudden I saw some drawbacks to wood nymph gifts. "What do you mean, not ready? What exactly did you see? You have to realize, I'm probably the oldest virgin I know." I wasn't sure if I should be pissed off, surprised or what?

"Yes, I got a vision of you two on the living room floor," she said. "I don't ask for these visions, you know that. They just happen. But something bad was going to happen. I figured if I came here, I could stop the future from continuing into what I saw." Olivia hung her jacket over the back of a chair.

"What exactly did you see?" Ash asked, coming up to stand by me.

"Let's go into the living room," Olivia said and led the way.

Once we were all seated, she said, "I wasn't the only one watching you. A lot of people, shall we say, are very interested in Laurel and her ancestry. She is part Ojibwa, so, even if she isn't a shape shifter now, she could be one later. This could happen as a latent ability or her children could be shape shifters. She's half wood nymph, and we all know the range of abilities that we have. The water sprites are even interested in Laurel. I didn't let the vision get that far, but, let's just say you could have been more rudely interrupted than my ringing your doorbell. I saw the two of you undressing each other . . ."

I interrupted Olivia with a shocked, "Hey!" I didn't need a blow by blow on what I was doing. I knew what we were doing, and I hadn't wanted it to stop.

Olivia gave me an understanding look, but then continued, "Once the two of you were undressed, you would continue your sexual exploration to the natural conclusion. But as you were about to go into the completion phase of this sexual experience, that window would have blown in." She pointed at Mom's favorite picture window overlooking the river. "It would have shattered glass all over the two of you. I saw a lot of blood. Someone or something does not want you to lose your virginity, Laurel. At least, not right now."

Then she said, "I hoped if I got here before it got that far, I'd be able to prevent such an occurrence. Since the window hasn't been destroyed, I think I've been successful. I didn't see who or what destroyed the window."

"How do you know if Ash and my having sex had anything to do with the glass being shattered?" I asked Olivia.

"I guess it was just the intense feeling I got. Laurel, you're very important to a lot of people because you're the first of your kind. I wondered if the Stonehenge Wood Nymphs had found out about you, and if they were the ones to come crashing in, but no. I believe they would've still made their presence known."

"The Stonehenge Wood Nymphs? What are they to me?" I asked.

Ash said, "The Stonehengers are the world authority clan. Each wood nymph clan has its own rules. Each deals with humans in their own way. It's not unheard of, but definitely frowned upon to have humans fully know and understand wood nymphs. In other words, if some clan were to get completely out of line about this or some other point of law, the Stonehengers come and make the peace or do their own kind of damage control. Some of it can be . . . drastic. All of the most powerful and most talented wood nymphs are recruited to the Stonehengers."

"How come I've never heard of them before?" I asked, feeling a little alarmed.

Olivia shrugged. "I guess since we have almost nothing to do with them, it never came up in conversation. Also, it seems when they're talked about, they tend to show up."

She reached over and patted my knee. "Maybe we should have told you. You would definitely be interesting to them if they knew about you. As far as we know, you're the first hybrid human and wood nymph in history. They'd want to know all about you. We should try to keep that from happening," she said leaning back.

I pressed my eyes shut, trying to understand. "Okay, so we know someone or something was going to break our window. And maybe whoever it was saw you show up at the house and that scared them away. Maybe it had nothing to do with our private life or what we were doing."

"I guess that's possible, but why would I get the vision?" Olivia asked us.

"I don't know. Maybe we'll never know, but at least the window didn't get shattered or worse things happen. Hey, don't you have plans for New Year's Eve?" I asked.

"Nope. We don't celebrate New Year's Eve. Do you mind having additional company for New Year's Eve?" Olivia asked with a smile. I knew she was going to keep me and Ash apart. At least in the physical aspect.

I hated that Olivia barged in when she did, but what if she was right? What if there was someone out there that was watching me? That was a creepy thought.

All of the sexual feelings that I had with Ash before Olivia came over were gone. If Olivia left, Ash and I could try to get back into the mood. But if there was something lurking outside, it was better to have her here. I looked at Ash, and he smiled at me. "No, we don't mind having you here. How about a game of Monopoly?"

"What's that?" Olivia asked.

"I'll explain as I set up the board," I said standing up to go and get the game.

"It's a human game about capitalism." Ash replied getting up from the couch. "It's a board game. We need the dining room table to set up the pieces."

Olivia followed him and took a seat next to him. "Really?" Olivia looked amused.

"Yeah, kind of," I said putting the box on the table and setting up the game. I explained the game and we played until just before midnight. We decided that Ash had won, as he had most of the properties, and we moved to the living room to watch the ball drop in Times Square at the stroke of midnight.

"Actually, the ball dropped an hour ago in New York. They're just replaying it again for us in the Central Time Zone. I suppose they'll do it for Mountain and Pacific, too."

"How odd," Olivia observed.

"I don't know how many years they've been doing the ball drop, but it's kind of a tradition to say good-bye to the old year and hello to the new by watching the ball drop." I said trying to hold back a yawn. "I like to think of all the things I've been thankful for during the past year and things I'd like to change in the coming year as the ball drops."

"That seems nice," Ash said to me. "I'm glad that you are here." He kissed me in front of Olivia.

"I agree," said Olivia. "I'm glad you're in my life, too."

Olivia and Ash stayed with me until Ben and my mom came home.

CHAPTER 25
SPRING AND MY BIRTHDAY

I n no time at all, the three weeks of Ben's leave were over. We were all sad on the morning Mom took him to the airport. I had been back at school for about a week. I got up the morning that Ben had to leave and had to drag myself down the stairs. I was trying to postpone saying good-bye. Ben had to catch a flight out of Milwaukee, and it was a four-hour drive. Mom and Ben were leaving for the airport at the same time that I was leaving for school.

In the last week before Ben left, he had built a dog house for Chuck. We could leave him outside for long periods if the weather wasn't too cold, and he was fine outside. Chuck did not wander away from the house. Ben had also built a dog door into the garage for him. It was big enough for him to get into the garage, but a large wolf and Chuck when he was grown would not fit into the opening. Chuck was growing quickly on his diet of puppy kibble. His feet were very big. His mixed heritage was going to make him larger than an average wolf his age. John was right. He'd be huge.

I gave a big sigh that last morning, and then went downstairs. Mom and Ben were at the dining room table holding hands. They didn't notice me. Mom was crying, and Ben was wiping her tears away. I felt a lump in my throat. I had to clear my throat to talk as I walked up to the table. "Hi. I guess I should say good morning, but it doesn't feel like a good morning to me. I don't want to say good-bye." I wiped tears from my eyes.

"Oh, honey, it will be okay. I'll be back in June," Ben said getting up from the table to come around and give me a hug.

As I hugged him, I put my face in his neck to breath in his scent. I had always loved the clean smell of Ben. As a small child I would snuggle on his lap and go to sleep. I had photos and his smell to remember him by while he was gone. For some reason, I was having a harder time with Ben leaving this time, then when he left last June. I hugged him as tightly as I could. "You make sure you come home safe and sound. Promise me you will!" I pleaded. Chuck came over to me and placed his head against my leg and whined.

"I'll do my best. I don't want anything to happen to me, either!" he said into my hair. He took a deep breath and took his arms off me. He kissed my forehead and looked at my mother. "It is time to go. I can't miss my flight." He released me and I felt cold. It wasn't the room that was cold, it was like my soul was accepting the fact that he was leaving.

In all of the ways that mattered, Ben was my dad. I loved him. I couldn't stand it if something bad happened to him. Bad things happened in wars. Bad things were happening in Iraq. Almost every week, I heard about people getting killed in Iraq. I couldn't wait for the war to end and for all Americans to come home, especially Ben.

Mom gave me a brave smile as she got up from the table. I noticed Ben's luggage by the front door. "I should be home by the time you get out of work tonight," Mom said as she went to the closet to get her coat.

Ben hugged Chuck. "Take care of our Laurel, buddy. I'm counting on you!"

Chuck looked at Ben with his golden eyes as if he understood every word.

Ben stood up. "I love you, Laurel. Don't ever forget that!" he said as he gave me one last hug with his coat on just before he grabbed his luggage. I watched him go through the front door with my mom.

I stood in the front door and watched as Ben put his luggage in the back of Mom's Jeep. I watched as my mom backed out of the garage and turned to go down the driveway. My heart felt heavy as I watched them drive away. The last thing I saw of Ben was a blurry wave to me as my mom turned down the bend. I could hardly see through the tears. I waved weakly and cried. When they were gone, I went into the bathroom and blew my nose and wiped my face. I looked at the clock. If I didn't hurry, I'd be late for school.

I downed a tasteless bowl of cereal, wiping my tears at times, then got my coat and left for school. Ash was not picking me up today since I had to go to work after school. Chuck walked out with me.

"Chuck, you're going to be here all by yourself. You have food, water, and a bed in the garage, and you have a house here in the yard. Wait for me. I'll be home when I can."

As I drove my car out of the garage, I saw Chuck go into his house in the yard. He was lying in his house with his head on his paws watching me drive away. I didn't know if Chuck understood me or not, but even though I half expected him to chase me down the driveway, he didn't. He just watched me drive away.

By the time I got to school, I had control of my crying. My eyes and nose were still red though. When I got out of the car, I grabbed a handful of snow to put against my eyes and nose to reduce the swelling and the redness. I heard the warning bell for class, so I threw down the snow and ran to the school. I barely made it in time for class.

Ash was waiting by my first-hour class when I got there. "Are you okay?" he asked me when he saw my face.

"I'll be fine. It was just really hard to watch Ben leave this morning," I said, trying to give Ash a smile as I walked into class. "You better go. You're going to be late for class!" I said as I passed him.

Ash gave a shrug and said, "I'll see you next hour!"

I watched him jog down the hall until my teacher told me to take a seat. I took notes during the class, but without looking at them I had no memory of what I wrote. I was relieved when the class ended. As I walked out, Ash was walking toward me.

"You still look pretty rough," he said, taking my hand on the way to Physics.

"Thanks. It's not like I don't feel bad enough already," I mumbled back at him.

"I'm sorry. I mean, it's not like Ben's going to be gone forever. He'll be back in June, right? My dad leaves for work trips all of the time. Sometimes he is in Iraq, too."

"Yeah, well, your dad isn't in the military! It's not like he intentionally goes into dangerous countries every day! Soldiers die over there! Don't you hear the news? While there are civilian casualties, there are not as many as soldiers. Plus, your dad has a choice on whether he wants to go to Iraq or not. My dad doesn't. The Army tells him where to go, and that's it. No choice!" I was trying to keep my voice low, but people were staring at me. I rolled my eyes and sighed. I didn't want to get mad at Ash, but he didn't get it. Families that didn't have military members going into a war zone just didn't get it. I could try to explain until I was blue in the face, but he would never get it.

Ash gave me a helpless looking shrug and said, "I'm trying to sympathize with you. I know this's hard for you. I'm just saying that Ben won't be gone forever. He'll come home in about six months."

"Yeah, okay. I don't want to talk about Ben anymore. I just have to believe that nothing bad will happen to him." I took a deep breath and forced a smile. I said, "Come on. Let's sit down and get bored in Physics."

Ash smiled at me and we went into the classroom. I was able to maintain my composure through the rest of the day. I didn't mention Ben again and neither did Ash. I didn't want to hear a bunch of sympathetic words that would set me to crying again. After school, Ash walked me to my Jeep and kissed me good-bye. I told him I'd call him when I got off work.

Thankfully, we were really busy in the store that evening. We'd received a large shipment of spring planting equipment, and everyone was busy with the customers and with arranging the new spring items.

I was exhausted when I left for home. It was a clear, cold night. When I pulled up to my house, I saw that the house lights were on and Mom's car was in the garage. Mom was sitting at the dining room table when I walked in the door.

"Hi, Mom! What are you doing?" I asked after I had hung up my coat. She was sitting at the dining room table doing nothing. She wasn't reading a book or watching the television. She was just sitting there. "Are you okay?" I asked worriedly. Chuck was on the floor by her feet.

Mom looked at me and tried to suppress a big sigh. "Yeah, I'm fine. It sure was hard driving to the airport and then driving home. Is it just me, or did his leaving this time seem harder than when he left last summer?"

"I've felt that, too. I was distracted all day. But, once I got to work I was really busy," I said and then after a moment, I asked softly, "Ben is going to be okay, right? I mean, he's going to come home in June alive, right?"

Mom thought for a second and then said, "We have to believe that he will. We'll drive ourselves crazy if we worry too much. While soldiers die in Iraq, the majority of them come home safe and sound. We have to hold the thought that he'll be one of them."

We sat side by side looking into the darkness outside. Chuck gave off a soft whine as if he understood and sympathized with us.

The next morning, I felt a little better. It was bitter cold when I let Chuck out. He didn't need to be in his kennel in the basement anymore. He was fully housetrained and didn't chew on anything he wasn't supposed to. He had the run of the house when one of us was home, and spent the rest of the time outside or in the garage.

I didn't have to go to work that night. Ash picked me up for school. "You look better today. Do you feel better?" he asked as I got into his car.

"Yeah, I guess I do. I've accepted that Ben had to go back to Iraq, but I also believe he'll come back in one piece. I have to believe that or I'll go crazy."

"That makes sense," he said as he drove down the driveway.

We were quiet for a while, and then I asked, "How are things at your house? How are you doing with your dad?"

Ash took a deep breath and said, "Well, he still hasn't accepted that I have bonded with you. He hopes that because you're only half wood nymph that it won't stick."

I smiled. "We have bonded, haven't we? I mean, while humans fall in love, they can fall out of love. It isn't as if they're connected like this. I feel that if you were to leave me, my heart would just stop beating. I would die. It's like, well, it was really hard when Ben left, and it hurts to think about it. But when I think of you—I couldn't stand it if you left me. If anything did happen to you, I'd never get over it. I don't think I could live without you now." I realized I meant every word. It wasn't drama; it was the truth. Even though I was only seventeen years old, I had found my soul mate. My life would never be the same without Ash in it.

"You're a part of me now. There's no life without you in it," he said as he glanced at me and reached over to squeeze my hand. "I felt so bad that you were hurting yesterday. I felt your pain. If I could prevent that from ever happening again, I would. But, I can't. I can only love you and comfort you when you are feeling pain."

I had caused Ash pain! With my own selfish longing, I had caused Ash to feel pain! It was bad enough that I had to feel the loss, but because of Ash's connection to me, he had to feel it too! "I'm sorry I put you through that! I don't want you to hurt because of me!"

Then I thought about Ash's dad and his refusal to accept me. I knew that Ash and I were going to be together for life, but it wasn't going to be as happy a life as it could have been had Ash's dad accepted me. It was just something that we were going to have to deal with.

Ash and I spent every moment we could together. We got into a pattern. Every day I didn't work, we had dinner at my house. Then we would watch DVDs or TV or sometimes play a video game. Our homework took up most of many evenings. Mom didn't mind that we were spending all our free time at the house. I think she enjoyed the company. She did her own things. Most of the time after dinner, she would go up to her room and watch TV or read. I think she was just happy to have us in the house. She knew I was safe and she wasn't alone.

As the winter wore into spring, Chuck got bigger and bigger fast. If he wasn't such a friendly animal, he could have been frightening. When his adult teeth came in, they were huge. Olivia had the vet come to check on his progress. He said again that this was going to be a very big dog.

Sometimes as I watched Chuck, I'd wonder if John Mingan was ever going to come over again. He'd said in December that he'd come over in a few weeks. It was now April and I hadn't seen or heard from him at all. A few times Ash and I drove to the reservation to see Adam and the gang, or Adam flew down to see us, but we didn't talk about or see John Mingan.

I had been thinking about my birthday for weeks. I wondered what my mom and Ash were going to give me. I wondered if I would hear from Olivia and Forrest.

I woke up on my birthday actually forgetting it was the day. I got up and got dressed and went downstairs. There were helium balloons all over the place.

"Happy birthday, Laurel!" Mom called from the kitchen. "I'm just putting your cake in the oven."

"Oh, Mom. Thanks!" I said as I went into the kitchen to give her a hug. "Are we going to Silver Bird for dinner tonight?" I asked.

"Well, actually, I was hoping you wouldn't mind a little party here for your birthday," Mom said, wiping her hands on her apron. "Forrest called and asked if he could stop by, and then Olivia called. I thought it might be nice to have a birthday party with family for once. What do you think? If you really want to go out to eat, we can go tomorrow, okay?"

"A birthday party?" I said, feeling excitement growing quickly. "Sure, that'd be great! I have to work a couple of hours at the store today, but my shift ends at four. What time are they coming?" I got my usual cereal breakfast.

"I have to call them with an actual time. How about six? That'll give you time to clean up after work. Should I call George and Adam? I know it's last minute, but maybe they'll come. It's a Saturday." Mom got a cup of coffee and sat across from me at the kitchen table.

"Yeah, that'd be great!" I said between bites of my cereal. A birthday party with real family and friends. How cool was that? I finished my breakfast and went to get ready for work.

I was restless all through the work day. Jane had told everyone that it was my birthday and hung a helium birthday balloon at my checkout register. I got congratulations and happy birthdays from friends and strangers the entire shift. While it was a little embarrassing to get all that attention, it was also kind of fun.

At the end of my shift, I took my balloon with me when I brought my cash drawer to the office. As Mr. Reichert took my cash drawer, he said, "Happy birthday, Laurel! You are eighteen now, aren't you?"

"Yes, Mr. Reichert. See you next week!" I said as I walked out of his office.

When I got home, Mom and Olivia were in the kitchen preparing food for my party. "Hi, honey! You have two hours before people start arriving. Why don't you go rest awhile?" Mom called to me from the kitchen when I walked in the door.

"Yeah, okay," I said and headed for the stairs. I thought I'd write a nice email to Ben. I was more excited than tired, but I think Mom just wanted me out of the way while she made preparations.

I booted up my computer and wrote to Ben. I told him how much I missed him. I told him I wished he was here for my birthday. I was lucky that my birthday fell on a Saturday this year. I told him I didn't feel any different being eighteen than I did at seventeen.

My body had changed a bit since my seventeenth birthday. My face was thinner, my waist narrower. I was a little taller and overall, I thought I looked more mature. I thought about all of the changes that had taken place since last April. We had moved to Wisconsin, I found out I was only half human and that my father's people should be on the endangered species list. I'd found out that fairies were real. That Hodags and water sprites were real. Such an amazing year, and I was graduating from high school.

I wrote a lot of this to Ben as I reflected on the last year of my life. I looked at the clock and saw that it was almost time for people to start arriving. I heard the doorbell ring as I went downstairs after changing my clothes.

Adam, Jason, Jeremy, and Melody from the reservation were the first to arrive. Just as I was greeting them, George showed up. As I was saying hello to him, I saw Forrest appear in my driveway. After I had greeted Forrest and he went into the house, and I wondered where Ash was. Then his car came up the driveway. Last to arrive was Hawthorn.

Olivia and Mom had made a variety of appetizers put strategically on the tables and counters. We had to bring in chairs from the screen room for everyone to have a seat. We talked for a while, and then I opened my presents. Adam had given me a dream catcher. He said he made it himself. Jeremy and Melody gave me a necklace made of Indian beads. Melody had made it. She liked making jewelry. George gave me a sweatshirt with a black bear on the front of it. It made me laugh. Olivia and Hawthorn gave me a pair of diamond-stud earrings, and Forrest gave me a diamond pendant necklace. I got a diamond bracelet from Mom and Ben. I could tell that Mom, Forrest and Olivia had coordinated gifts as they were obviously a complete set. Each piece was very expensive.

"Thank you all so very much!" I said, overwhelmed. "This has been the best birthday ever!"

"Not so fast. You haven't received my gift yet," Ash said as he slowly walked over to me with a small gift that looked suspiciously like a little jewelry box.

I tore the wrapper off. Yup, a little black jewelers box. Just as I was about to open it, Ash put his hand over mine and said, "I followed wood nymph custom at Christmas, and maybe you didn't understand the importance of accepting that gift. This gift is the human equivalent." Then he kneeled next to me as I opened the box.

Inside was a stunning diamond solitaire ring. It was round and big. I looked up at Ash, tears in my eyes, and he said, "Yes, Laurel. It's an engagement ring. The ring I gave you at Christmas was also a promise ring. This ring shows the human world that you are mine. I know we have to go to college first, but once we graduate, will you marry me?"

The room was so quiet that I could hear the refrigerator running, and it was a quiet refrigerator. Everyone seemed to be holding their breath, watching for my reaction. I took a deep breath and said, "Yes, Ash. Every day I love you more. My life would be unbearable if you weren't in it. We've bonded, and you're the only one for me." I lifted the ring out of the box.

Ash took the ring from my hand and put it on my left hand ring finger. It was a perfect fit. Just that morning I had put the ring I had received at Christmas on my right hand. I reached over and hugged him, and he kissed me. I knew he wanted more than just a gentle kiss but there were people all around us.

"Oh, my!" my mother said with a sigh. "I really don't fully understand everything related to wood nymphs, but I understand this bonding thing. I know you're very happy with Ash, and you are both very mature for your ages. While I wish this hadn't happened quite this quickly, it is not unexpected. Ben and I have talked about it. Congratulations to you both!"

Even Forrest looked happy for us, but there was some sad expression on his face. I could feel sadness, too. "What is it Forrest? What's bothering you?" I asked him.

"I want you two to be happy. It bothers me that Ash's dad hasn't accepted you. Wood nymphs are generally pretty close knit. I've seldom seen it that all parties involved weren't completely happy with a match." He looked at Olivia and Hawthorn. Olivia patted his hand. "I guess I'm concerned Elm will try to ruin your happiness." Forrest said sadly. Then he forced a smile and said. "We're happy for you. We know you two are meant to be together. If there's anything I can do to make your lives more perfect, just let me know."

Olivia gave me a hug and said. "Hawthorn and I want you two to be happy, too. We'll do what we can to assist you in any way possible." Hawthorn, now very comfortable with me, stood next to her and nodded.

Mom, tears in her eyes, said, "Oh, honey, you're growing up so fast. I might have liked things to go differently, but this seems to be what's best for you. I love you."

Mom then went into the kitchen and brought out a bottle of champagne. "I was saving this for when Ben came home, and I know I shouldn't be contributing to the delinquency of minors, but I don't think a sip of wine will hurt anyone." By the time she poured out the bottle of wine to everyone there, we each only got about a shot glass of wine. "To Laurel and Ash!" she toasted. We all raised our glasses.

"I can drink a lot more than that!" Jason said, and we laughed.

Mom said, "Even that little bit was illegal. I'd appreciate your not mentioning it."

We spent the next couple of hours discussing colleges and weddings. I think everyone had a great time. It was after ten before people started leaving. By eleven, only Mom, Ash, and I were left.

We cleaned up the wrapping paper and put the leftovers away. After we were finished, Ash put some wood in the fireplace, and we sat in the living room and relaxed. "Would it be so bad if we got married before college?" I asked my mom.

She sighed. "I don't know. I guess if you were married before or during college, you could stay together in an apartment," she said thoughtfully. "Let's not talk about it today. We have plenty of time to talk about weddings."

I cuddled with Ash on the couch. I loved feeling his body next to mine. "This's been the best birthday I have ever had. I wish Ben could have been here," I said softly.

"Me, too," Mom replied. She yawned and said, "I'm pretty tired. I'm going to bed. Good night! Laurel, this was a pretty fantastic birthday party." She came and gave me a hug. "I'm glad you liked your gifts. And just for the record, Wow! I've never seen anyone receive so many diamonds in one day!"

"Thanks, Mom! Thanks for everything. And thanks for making us move to Wisconsin before Ben got back from Iraq. You made this day very special." I hugged her back. "Good night!"

Ash and I watched her go upstairs. We sat back on the couch. The fire was just glowing coals by then. "This really was the best birthday I ever had," I whispered in his ear. His natural cologne suddenly filled my nose, and I closed my eyes.

"It's time for me to go," he said. "If I stay longer . . ." Ash said getting up from the couch. I knew exactly what he meant.

"Okay," I said and walked him to the door. We let Chuck out while we said our good-byes at the door. When Ash kissed me, it was a soul deep kiss I could feel deep into the very heart of my existence. My life was perfect with him in it. With him, I felt like a perfect completion of something wonderful. I felt whole.

I let Chuck in and waved good-bye as Ash got into his car. Wow, what a birthday. I looked at the rings on both hands. The ring on the right hand felt warm, but the ring on my left hand felt just right. It belonged there. As I went to bed, I couldn't remember being so happy, and I had been happy a lot lately.

One Saturday in the beginning of May, I was outside with Chuck. I had just gotten up and looked at the thermometer. It was in the mid sixties. I put on a sweater after breakfast and took Chuck for a walk along the river. The snow was gone and spring was budding everywhere. Spring flowers were in full bloom. The air was fresh and clean. As we were walking back to my house, the fur on Chuck's shoulders stood up on end. He emitted a low growl and crouched. I didn't know what to do. We were almost at the house. Mom had had early clients and had left for work. Chuck and I were alone. Chuck, crawling in a crouch, inched his way past the pier and into our yard. I kept up with him, feeling cautious. As we creeped around the house, I saw a black sports car in the driveway and a huge gray wolf standing next to it. John Mingan was back.

When John saw that Chuck was crouched with bared teeth, he crouched and snarled back at him. Chuck stalked toward the wolf that was John with bared teeth. John Mingan stood up as tall as he could on four feet with his shoulder hair and tail raised and snarled at Chuck. Chuck approached slowly, then sniffed at John and seemed to recognize him. Suddenly he was a wriggly puppy again, rolling on his back and licking at John's mouth. John snapped near his face as if to remind Chuck who was the alpha in this group. John sniffed Chuck. When he seemed satisfied with his review, he stepped away from Chuck. I had to shield my eyes from the bright flash of light that told me that John Mingan was changing into his human form. At the same time, Chuck rolled over onto his feet and came to sit in front of me. I didn't fail to notice that he placed himself between me and John.

"Hello, Laurel." John said in that sexy, velvet voice. Hs loin cloth barely covered him. The photos I had seen of early 1900s Native Americans with loin cloths had more of their bodies covered than what John had. He seemed to almost strut as he came to stand in front of me. He knew he looked good.

Somehow, though, he wasn't as attractive to me as he had been five months ago. I mean, he looked hot, but I didn't have the same reaction as I had when I saw him the first time. I wondered if it was because my love for Ash had grown, and I realized I had bonded with him or because I knew John Mingan had a jealous girlfriend. Either way, once John Mingan realized I wasn't mesmerized by his good looks, his eyes narrowed, as if unhappy I wasn't drooling over his magnificence.

"Did you miss me?" he asked slowly, gauging my response. "I missed you."

"Um, while I was curious about what happened to you, I didn't actually miss you, no," I replied. The truth was, I now found him kind of creepy. I couldn't figure out what I saw in him before. Maybe it was just the newness of seeing a man change into a wolf, or his sexy voice. "You said you'd be back in a few weeks. It has been a five months."

"So you did miss me!" he said with a big smile. He walked up to me—way too much into my personal space. I took a step backward. "Are you afraid of me, little girl?" he asked, his teeth glinting in the morning light.

"No, I'm not afraid of you. You're just getting too close to me. You're in my space," I replied taking another step back. The truth was, he did scare me. I was alone with him. My protective dog wouldn't protect me from John Mingan.

"So, why are you here? Where's Adam?" I asked, my arms crossed over my chest. I tried to look strong and unafraid.

"Adam? I don't need Adam to come and see a beautiful girl. It's just lucky for me you're here alone! Lucky me!" He took another step toward me.

I took another step back. "Aren't you here to see Chuck?" The pup was letting John approach. I really was getting scared. If he tried anything, would my call get me help in time? How long did it take for help to come after a call? I had no memory of how long it took for Adam and George to find me in the snow bank.

"Saw the pup," he said, glancing at Chuck, who was doing nothing but watching him. "Pup's fine. Getting big. I see he's protective of you. That's a good thing. But I'm the alpha, so he wouldn't stop me from getting near you. You want me to get near you, don't you? Don't I look good to you?" He was almost purring as he took another step forward, and I took another one back.

"Don't you have a girlfriend?" I asked. Now I was getting angry. I didn't want to be afraid of this guy. But there was an evilness about him. He had no right to assume I was into him in any kind of way.

He laughed, enjoying my fear, and then he said in an evil voice. "Yeah, I guess I have one girlfriend, but I wouldn't mind having two. I'd like to have one girlfriend that is light and one that is dark. It'd be fun to have one girlfriend for daytime and one for nighttime. You could be my light-skinned nighttime girlfriend."

His intentions were clear, and they weren't honorable. I'd backed up far enough. I was in danger. I was about to scream for all I was worth, when Ash jetted into the clearing. He knew I wasn't happy. Maybe with our bonding thing, he could feel my fear and anger. He ran to my side. "What are you doing here, Mingan?" he asked brusquely. Ash put his arm around my shoulder. I wasn't sure if he was showing ownership or trying to comfort me, but I was glad to have his arm around me.

"Hey, little wood nymph!" John said to Ash, "you think she is yours, do you? Maybe I should just remove you from the situation. Yeah, I saw the wood nymph ring and a human engagement ring. Wow, such overkill. Why? She not sure? Maybe I'll just get rid of you." John Mingan took a threatening step toward Ash.

Then, Olivia and Forrest jetted into the yard. Forrest looked mad as hell. Olivia didn't look any happier. "What the hell do you think you are doing?" Forrest yelled at Mingan. "You have no right to threaten Ash or Laurel. You're not welcome here!" Forrest thundered. "I should just tell Hurit you're harassing another girl. That'd serve you right to have that angry badger after you."

John Mingan glared at Forrest for a moment and then looked at me. "You haven't seen the last of me." He looked back at Forrest and Olivia and stalked to his car. He spun his tires as he drove out of the driveway.

I leaned heavily against Ash and heaved a huge sigh of relief. "I was almost going to scream for all that I was worth when you came," I whispered.

Ash held me up against him. "I couldn't let him hurt you," he said fervently.

"Are you okay?" asked Olivia. "It appears that we came in the nick of time."

Forrest looked like he wanted to kill something. "Idiot shape shifter. Who does he think he is? Someone really should tell Hurit he was here. I'd do it, but he'd convince her you tricked him to come. She can be gullible as well as mean. If she thought you were trying to take him away from her, she'd be vicious."

Forrest wrapped an arm around me and kissed the top of my head. "I'm glad Olivia has the sight and you have the call. Olivia saw you were in danger and jetted to me. We may or may not have gotten here in time if you gave the call. I would like to think we'd have made it here before anything bad happened to you. I just wish I could be sure, if it came to giving the call, that someone closer would get to you first."

"I was going to come here soon anyway," Olivia said as we walked into the house. "I have been dreaming about the Stonehengers. While I haven't had an actual vision of them, I keep dreaming about them. In my dream they seem to be packing for a long journey. I've never heard of the Stonehengers leaving their underground kingdom. It makes me nervous to dream about them at all, and more nervous that I'm dreaming about their making a journey. I've never dreamed about them before, and it's very vivid. I can see the king clearly. I'm not certain, but I think they may be coming here." Olivia looked really nervous.

"Would that be a bad thing?" I asked as we sat in the living room.

"I don't know," she said. "Keep in mind, Laurel, there's never been a human-wood nymph hybrid before. You're the first. I think they would be curious about you if they knew about you," Olivia said softly, "and I'm more and more convinced they do. I get nervous just talking about them. I've never met them. From what I have heard, I really don't want to. They only get involved with someone if they want to take over their life. Take me for instance. I have the sight, but it isn't always reliable. I mean, I can't force a vision just because I want one. I've been lucky to have seen what I have. If they knew about my visions, they could force me to go to England with them. They conscript gifted wood nymphs. They make it sound like it's an honor to serve them, but the truth is, they remove the wood nymph's choice about it. If they want you, they take you. Period." Olivia was almost wringing her hands.

Forrest put his arm around her. "Olivia, you're thirty years old, and they have never tried to take you. I don't think they'd come for you now," he said reassuringly.

Olivia looked from Forrest to the rest of us and replied, "It isn't me I'm worried about. It's Laurel. What if they want her? We couldn't stop them!" She looked panicky.

"Olivia, I'm eighteen. Wouldn't they have came for me before now? I think we can relax about these Stonehenger people." I said with a smile.

"I do hope you're right," Olivia said softly.

"Enough of the negativity!" said Ash with a forced smile. I could feel he was just as nervous as Olivia, but he didn't want anyone to know. "And, hey, with any luck, we've seen the last of Mingan. I'm glad you showed up when you did!" he said to Olivia and Forrest. "I don't know if I could have jetted fast enough with Laurel to get away from him. I have never tried to jet while carrying another person."

"I have," said Forrest. "It can be done, but you have to stay focused and the person you're carrying has to hold very still."

"I would be afraid of hurting her." Ash said softly as he took my hand in his.

"Then don't do it," Forrest replied.

I could feel everyone starting to relax. "Is anyone hungry? Should I make lunch?"

"Lunch is a good idea," said Forrest. "Why don't we take your new car into town, and I'll buy us lunch at the diner? They have good food there," Forrest said.

We all agreed to this plan. I don't think any of us forgot about the Stonehengers or John Mingan. I had no doubt he'd come back sometime. But, if what Adam had told me about Hurit was true, and John took Forrest's threat seriously, maybe I wasn't worth the wrath of a badger. With luck, he'd just stay away.

When we went outside, I drew in a deep breath. I loved Wisconsin, loved the north woods. I had thought summer was beautiful last July with its warm days and cool evenings. Fall was magnificent with the changing colors and cool, crisp evenings and the subtle smell of the wood burning fireplaces gently heralding that winter was coming. Winter was gorgeous with the snow-covered pines and the sharp smell of balsam. I had experienced all of the seasons except spring. Today was spring, and it was just as wonderful as the other seasons but in its own delightful way. The spring flowers and buds were unlike any I had experienced any place else. I felt at home in Wisconsin in a way I had never felt anywhere else.

CHAPTER 26

PROM

started getting impatient by the end of May. Ben was coming home in less than month, and I was worried that something might happen to him at the last minute. I was hard to be around. Everything pissed me off. On Saturday morning I asked Mom, "Is it normal for me to be so angry all of the time? I'm so worried about Ben that everything makes me mad. Do you feel that way, too?"

Mom looked at me a long moment, then said, "Sort of. I feel edgy all the time, too. It is so close to when he'll be home for good that I worry something bad will happen at the last minute. I can't wait for this wait to be over. But, while I'm upset on the inside, I can't let that control my days. I have to function . . . and just wait."

"Uh, huh," I said. "I'm having a hard time holding my feelings in. Ash's afraid to be around me. I snap at him about everything. Then I feel guilty and apologize, but I just keep doing it! How do I stop?" I whined as I sat down with my breakfast.

"Knowing that you're being unreasonable is a good start. Most people take out their frustrations on the people closest to them. It's not right or fair, but it happens. People don't realize that they're doing it. At least you know you are," Mom said softly.

We sat in silence for a while, and then Mom said, "The best thing is to keep yourself busy. When your mind's occupied, you're less likely to worry."

"Yeah, easier said than done," I replied with a frustrated sigh.

We sat there in quiet for another few minutes. Then Mom got up from the table and said, "This, too, shall pass. I'm going into Wausau shopping. Wanna come? I was hoping to leave in a few minutes."

"Yeah, that might make me feel better," I said as I put my dishes in the dishwasher. "I need to change. I'll be down in a minute." I ran upstairs and changed into some jeans and a sweatshirt. I called Ash to say I was going shopping with Mom. He said to have fun.

While we were shopping, Mom asked if I knew what kind of dress I wanted for prom. Prom was coming up, and I hadn't even thought about a dress! I was so pathetic. We went to a specialty shop, and I tried on several formals. I actually found one that was perfect—long, floor-length in a light teal. It was satin and chiffon with spaghetti straps. The dress perfectly complemented my hair and skin color. As I walked around like a model at a fashion show, Mom said, "Yup, that's the perfect one!"

It was expensive. "Mom, I love the dress—the shoes, too—but did you see the price tag?" I said looking in the mirrors and saw that the dress fit me from all angles.

"Don't worry about it. My treat. You're only a senior in high school once, and you're my only daughter. Prom last year doesn't count. This is *your* prom! You should look your best. And that dress is perfect." Mom pulled out her credit card.

When we left the shop, we went to the Liberty and I put the shoes on the backseat and I carefully hung the dress on the hanging hook. We stopped at Applebee's for lunch and continued shopping. We bought jeans and shoes for daily wear. Mom bought a couple of suits for work. By the time we got home that night, we were exhausted and my feet hurt. The good thing—I hadn't had time to worry about Ben all day.

When June arrived, I was pretty much done worrying about grades and finals. Ash and I spent all of our free time quizzing each other about physics, English and our other classes. We both knew the material well.

By the end of the school year, Ash had become a track star. He did what he said he was going to do, just barely finishing first. After the first race, the coach asked him how he felt about winning. He said he was surprised he could run that fast. I had just taken a sip from my soda when I heard this and choked. Ash glared at me and I shrugged. When the coach asked him how he could run so far without breaking a sweat, Ash replied that he ran on his own a lot of the time and was used to it. I'm not sure the coach believed that, but he'd never guess the real reason.

Ash and I both knew we were both going to graduate with high grades. I had been in the running for Valedictorian, but Mary Clarkson got the honor. On the day of prom, I told Ash that I needed all day to get ready.

My hair appointment was at 1:00 p.m. The beautician was just a couple of years older than I was. "Such beautiful, thick hair!" she said as she got out the hot rollers.

"Aren't you going to wash my hair first?" I asked when the beautician guided me to her chair. I'd never been to the beauty parlor except for haircuts.

"No, honey. The hair holds a curl better if it is slightly dirty. Your hair is so thick and straight it'll take a whole lot of pins and a full can of spray to keep your hair up. Are you sure you want an up-do? With the weight of this hair on the top of your head, you could get a headache," she told me.

"For once I want a lot of curls with an up-do. I have long, straight hair every day. I want something different for prom," I responded as I leaned back in the chair.

"Okay. This is going to take some time. It's a good thing you booked your appointment early in the afternoon." She got out her potions, combs, pins, and brushes.

She was right. I was in that chair for a good couple of hours. I was grateful that the weather was clear and calm. I'd have hated to have had to fight a windy day. My head was full of curls, but a lot of them trailed down my back. The style wasn't a real high up-do. It reminded me of the Victorian styles a little bit. Still, I liked it.

When I got home, Mom called, "Hi! I'm in the kitchen!" Chuck came up and sniffed me. I must have smelled different with all of the spray and lotions the beautician put in my hair.

I went into the kitchen. Mom was ladling out beef stew into bowls. "You need to eat. I bet you haven't eaten hardly anything all day. Prom lasts a long time! They won't feed you until really late." She had me sit at the kitchen table.

Mom sat across from me. As we blew on our stew to cool it off, she said to me. "I really like your hair. It's different seeing you with all of those curls. It's really cute! I never thought you would get an up-do!"

"Yeah, I wanted something completely different. You want an ice cube to cool off your stew? I'm getting one. I still need to put on makeup. Ash will be here in a couple of hours." I got up from the table.

"No, I'll just let my stew cool by itself. I'm not going anywhere tonight. What time is Ash coming?" she asked as I sat back down.

"Seven," I replied plunking a couple of ice cubes into my stew. After that, we ate in silence. I was trying to eat as quickly as possible. I didn't wear a lot of makeup and I wasn't sure how to put it on. Mom didn't wear much either. Just as I put my bowl in the dishwasher, the doorbell rang.

"It can't be Ash! It's way too early!" I said as I ran to the door to tell Ash to come back in a couple of hours. It wasn't Ash at the door. It was Olivia.

"Hi!" she said with her usual brightness. "I remembered tonight was your prom. I thought you might like some help with makeup. I brought some with me." Olivia came in with what looked like a doctor's bag.

"Cool! I was a little concerned about doing my makeup. Neither me or Mom wear much, and I don't have a lot." I hung up her lightweight jacket.

"Hi, Olivia!" Mom said coming out of the kitchen. "I would have volunteered to help, but I probably know less about makeup than Laurel! Thanks for coming."

"Hey, no problem. I'm glad to help. Do you have a camera?" Olivia asked as she started up the stairs with her makeup case.

"Oh! Good idea! I think I would have forgotten to take pictures!" Mom said following me and Olivia up the stairs. "I have a digital one. I'll make sure the battery's charged up. It's in the office upstairs."

At the top of the stairs, my mom went in one direction, and Olivia and I went into my room. I sat at my vanity table and asked Olivia. "What do you want me to do?"

"Just sit there, and I'll make you more beautiful than you can imagine," Olivia said smiling at me and opening her bag.

An hour later, she let me look in the mirror. I stared at the image looking back at me. I was unbelievably beautiful. While I thought I was pretty, I looked even more like Olivia with all of my beauty enhanced with her cosmetics. "Oh, Olivia, is that really me?" I asked. Then I smiled. When I smiled, I was shocked at how perfect I looked. No wood nymphs I'd ever seen, including Olivia, was more beautiful than I was at that moment.

"Help me get my dress on. I want to see what I look like as a finished product!" I said having to force myself away from my mirror.

Olivia carefully helped me get my dress on without messing up my hair. I put on pantyhose, and then my heels. I have a full length mirror on the back of my room door. I turned to see my full reflection. I knew I was going to look good when I saw what Olivia had done to my face, but with my perfectly fitting dress highlighting my hair and skin color, I was drop dead gorgeous and knew it. I have never in my life felt this beautiful.

"Mom! Come and see what I look like!" I called to Mom.

When she got to my room, my door was closed. She knocked on the door. "I'm here, honey. Let me see."

Olivia opened the door and my mom saw me standing in the middle of my room. "Oh, my God! You're so beautiful! Tonight you're breathtaking!" Mom said as she came into my room and sat on my bed.

"Do you think Ash will like the way I look?" I asked as I turned in a circle so Mom could see all of me.

"He'd have to be blind not to," Mom replied softly.

Mom took a couple of photos of me from different angles and went into the office to download them to send to Ben.

I was afraid to sit down. I didn't want to wrinkle my dress. I was just starting to wonder when Ash was going to show up when I heard the doorbell ring. Mom and Olivia went downstairs to answer it. Mom wanted to take a picture of Ash's face when he saw me for the first time. Mom stood next to the stairs to get the best shot of Ash's expression.

I heard the door and Mom and Olivia greet Ash. Olivia asked to take his coat. When I was sure enough time had passed so Ash was looking toward the stairs, I slowly walked down, as slowly and gracefully as I could—a movie star making an entrance.

I saw the flash of Mom's camera catching Ash's expression. He looked to be in awe as he stared at me. He gaped at me. I smiled.

As I walked up to him, I smelled that wonderful scent from New Year's Eve. Olivia must have smelled it too, because she smiled and gave a knowing look to Ash, but Ash didn't see it. He didn't see anything but me.

"There's nothing in this world more beautiful than you," he whispered as I went up to him. I smiled a bigger smile.

"Oh, Ash, you are so handsome tonight!" Mom said. "Come over by the fireplace so I can get some good pictures of the two of you."

Ash reached for my hand and kissed the back of it. He was still staring at me.

I laughted. "Ash, you can blink now. Come on, Mom wants pictures," I said while leading him toward the fireplace. "Look at Mom! I think she has enough pictures of you staring at me. I think she'd like a few photos of us looking in her direction."

Ash slowly turned to look at my mom as if he was in a dream. Mom took a few more photos while telling Ash to smile. "You look like you're in a trance. Pretend you're having fun!" Mom said as she snapped pictures.

"You had better go or you will be late." Olivia said from behind my mom. "I want a full report of the prom later!"

Mom came to hug each of us. She was very careful not to wrinkle my dress. Olivia had given me some perfume to wear. It was a light and fresh scent. Mom knew what it smelled like from when she was taking photos upstairs. However, she looked at Ash and asked, "Ash, what an unusual cologne you have on. What is it called?"

Ash blushed and mumbled something like, "I'm sorry, I don't know."

Olivia and I laughed. We knew what it was. It was wood nymph male hormones raging. But, my mom didn't know that and found our laughter confusing. Before she could ask any questions, I went to the closet and grabbed my wrap and Ash's jacket. "Gotta go, Mom! See you when I get home!" I kissed her cheek. Ash and I walked out of the front door. Olivia and my mom waved at us as we drove away from the house.

"I like your cologne," I said teasingly as I laughed.

"Uh, huh. You know it is not a cologne," he grumbled. Then looked over at me and started staring again.

"Watch the road, or we'll crash!" I said, physically turning his face to the road.

As he watched the road, he reached over to hold my hand. "If I hadn't already bonded with you, I certainly would tonight. You're the most beautiful thing I've ever seen in my life, human or wood nymph," he whispered.

When we got to the hall where the prom was being held, Ash held my door for me as I got out of his car. Rodney had asked Mary Clarkson to be his date for the prom. They were arriving at the same time Ash and I were getting out of Ash's car.

"Oh, Laurel, you're so beautiful! I always thought that you were the prettiest girl in school, but tonight, you're stunning!" Rodney said as he came up to us.

"You really are going to be the most beautiful girl at the prom. No one else will even come close," Mary said softly. She didn't sound jealous exactly, more like she too, was in awe of how I looked. "Ash, you're the most handsome guy at the prom. The two of you are stunning!" Mary said when she turned to look at Ash.

"Thanks, Mary," Ash said with a smile. "Let's go in before we get cold." Ash held out his arm and I held on to it as we walked into the hall. I held on tight because while I looked graceful, I had to pay attention to my walking in heels.

We got inside, and the theme of the prom was the Victorian age. There was lace and lights that were made to look like old candle chandeliers. The decorations were beautiful. There were also crepe paper streamers that weren't exactly Victorian, but they did seem to look appropriate here.

When we walked into the ballroom, it seemed like everyone turned to look at us. All night long I felt I was being stared at. During the evening, Noreen Jensen came up to talk to us and told me how beautiful I looked. She looked stunning in her deep-blue evening gown. Her date didn't say anything, but he stared at me. We also talked to Bob Hansen who congratulated Ash for lettering in track, but stared at me the whole time. We saw Sam Anderson about halfway through the evening with his date. We heard his date say as they walked away. "That is one beautiful white girl. I hate her."

There was a DJ who played a variety of music. I didn't want to dance the fast dances with my heels. I also didn't want to shake my curls out. Ash and I did dance every slow dance though. At midnight, a buffet was set out for us.

It was dawn when Ash took me home. We were both exhausted. The outside light was on as we drove up to my house. "I had a really good time tonight. You're amazing," Ash said as we got out of the car.

"You're pretty amazing yourself. I had a great time, too. This was a much better prom compared to last year." I had told Ash about my first boyfriend and my first prom experience.

"I love you," he said after we walked into the house. He pulled me to him to kiss me good night. I could smell his hormones again. Between his words, his beauty, and his scent, I fell into his embrace. I was lost in his kiss when I heard Mom come into the room.

"Ahem," she said, and we stepped apart. "Did you have a good time?"

"It was great!" I said.

"Laurel was the most beautiful girl there. She's the most beautiful girl in the world!" Ash said looking at me. "Good-bye, Laurel. I'll call you in a few hours. Good-bye, Mrs. Redmond." Ash started backing out the front door. He kissed my hand before he left.

"That was some kiss," Mom said as we watched him drive away.

"This has been some night," I replied.

"I'm glad you had a good time. Do you need help getting out of that dress?"

"No, I think I can do it. I'll call you if I need help," I said as I started up the stairs. "Good night, Mom! Thanks again for the dress. I don't think I'll ever feel as beautiful as I did tonight."

"I think you will. Good night, honey." Mom shut off the downstairs lights and followed me up the stairs.

It took me half an hour to get all of the pins out of my hair. My hair was stiff and crackly, and I took a shower to wash all of the hairspray out of it. I was really exhausted by the time I dried my hair and went to bed. As I went to sleep, I thought about Ash's beautiful face and how wonderful we both looked tonight. The very last thought I had was of his wonderful, natural male wood nymph hormone scent.

CHAPTER 27
GRADUATION DAY AND BEN COMES HOME

The next week flew by. Every day at school I had exams. I got my yearbook and was busy between classes getting my friends to write in it. Each day after school I would review what people had written. Most people wrote things like, "Good luck in the future," or "It was nice to know you." Some people wrote about prom and how Ash and I made a perfect couple. No one wrote anything stupid.

Then it was Saturday. Graduation day. The ceremony started at 1:00 p.m. When I went downstairs that morning, I called, "Mom! Hey, Mom! Where are you?" I couldn't find her. Chuck came over and put his nose into my leg and whined. I let him out through the screen room. I sat on one of the screen room chairs and looked at the river as Chuck sniffed around. When he was finished with his business, I let him back in the house. Where was Mom? I went to the refrigerator to see if she left me a message. She had. It read, "Laurel, I had an early appointment today. I'll meet you at graduation. Don't wait for me. I won't miss it, I promise!"

Huh, I thought. I'd planned to drive over with Ash anyway as the graduating seniors had to be there an hour and a half before everyone else to practice going across the stage. "Well, Chuck, it is just you and me this morning," I said as I scratched Chuck under his chin. I laughed as I thought of the salesman who had made the mistake of coming to our house to sell us brushes a month ago. He had pulled up in front of the house. I didn't hear the car, but Chuck did and he let out an impressively throaty growl. I wondered what was bothering him, when I heard the doorbell ring. I went to answer it. As I opened the storm door, Chuck scooted around to be in front of me and his fur was raised on his shoulders as he gave the most ferocious growl I'd ever heard. The poor man was scared out of his skull. I didn't open the screen door as I was afraid of what Chuck would do. The salesman looked at me and then at Chuck and started backing to his car. He rattled off some dot com address if we wanted his brushes.

I just waved. "Come on, Chuck. Let's close the door." Chuck looked at me, his tongue lolling, as if he was smiling. I sighed and patted his head. "You shouldn't scare everyone away, but I guess I didn't want to say no a hundred times to a salesman. They just never get it. So, thanks for sending him away." Chuck wagged his tail.

I thought about Chuck and then thought, hey, today is graduation day. Wow. I did it. We did it. Ash and I were on our way to graduation. Next was college. Did I want to get married before college? It'd make things easier in finding an apartment. Ash and I were going to be together forever anyway, right? Why should we wait until we graduate from college to get married?

I went upstairs and got dressed in a black pantsuit that would look good with my cap and gown. I knew that my ankles and feet would show up in the graduation pictures and I wanted to make sure that what I was wearing wouldn't stand out in the photograph. I put on my diamond earrings, necklace, and bracelet. I put on my black heels and looked in the mirror. "Ben, I wish you could see this!" I said to my reflection. We'd gotten word that he was expected home at the end of the month. I was disappointed. That meant another whole month of danger for him.

I had some time to kill before Ash showed up. I got on the Internet and lost myself in the web site for UW Madison, looking up housing. I knew I wasn't going to be in a dorm. Ash and I were going to be living together whether we were married or not. I didn't want to live with a stranger when I could live with him. I looked at the clock, and was surprised that Ash was expected in five minutes. I hurriedly shut off the computer and grabbed my cap and gown. I did a last minute check to make sure I had everything. Oh! I almost forgot my tassle. I was graduating! Finally! Wow! I grabbed that and went downstairs just as I heard Ash's car pull up in front.

I gently laid my gown on Ash's back seat to keep it from getting wrinkled. "This is it! How do you feel?" I asked Ash as I got into the front seat.

"Great! I have you with me. I can handle anything!" he said. I laughed and gave him a kiss. "You better stop that or we will be late!" He pulled away from me with his hand on my cheek.

"I was looking up housing and apartments in Madison," I said as we drove toward school. "Do you want an apartment or a house?"

"I don't care, as long as I'm with you." He replied kissing my hand.

"Okay," I said as we pulled into the school parking lot. There were a lot of cars already there. We spent the next hour or so getting into our caps and gowns. I had brought bobby pins to hold my cap secure. Some girls hadn't brought pins and were having a hard time keeping their caps on. I handed out the pins. Then we were lined up, and the next thing I knew, it was time for the graduation ceremony. We went up one by one across the stage to receive our diplomas from the principal. He looked really happy to be able to hand out the diplomas. I thought that was cool.

Mary Clarkson gave a long and sort of interesting commencement speech as valedictorian. She talked about how we, as the next adult generation needed to try to work with nature and eliminate pollution. I thought the wood nymphs and water sprites would agree with her. I looked around for Mom but I couldn't see her. I was getting a little upset. She was missing my graduation. What could be more important for her than being here? Right now?

After graduation was over, we all paraded into the gym to meet and greet our families who had attended the ceremony. I had almost given up on finding Mom in the crowd when I finally saw her face. She wasn't alone! Ben was with her! I dragged Ash over to them and hugged Ben really hard.

"Congratulations, honey!" he said. "I'm so glad that I was here to watch you walk across the stage."

"Oh, Dad! I'm so glad that you're here! I thought you weren't coming until the end of the month!" I said as I looked up at him.

He smiled at me and said. "We got lucky. The Army Command that was supposed to replace us got there early, so we were able to leave. Mom and I have known for a few days. I wanted to surprise you. Are you surprised?"

"Oh, yeah! This is the best surprise!" I said giving him another hug.

"Hey, don't you have something else to show me?" Ben asked reaching for my left hand.

"Oh, yeah! Ash and I are engaged. Are you happy for me?" I asked Ben showing him my hand.

"Well, I guess I couldn't keep you my little girl for as long as I wanted. Ash is obviously head over heels over you, and you obviously love him. I'm not going to stand in the way of true love. When do you plan to get married?" Ben asked as we stood in the crowd of people in the gym.

"Dad, let's talk about it later," I said laughing at him. I was so happy! Olivia, Hawthorn and Forrest came up to congratulate me and Ash. I couldn't imagine being happier than I had been during the reception after the play, but today I was! I felt my joy increasing as my extended family came to congratulate me.

After we had all gotten punch and a cookie, I saw Ash's parents walking toward us. I nudged Ash and pointed in their direction. I felt Ash stiffen. My great mood evaporated in an instant because of Ash's discomfort. His father hated Ben and hated me. Ash let go of my hand and went to meet them. I felt empty as he walked away. I turned to Mom and Ben. They were watching Ash.

"I'm sorry, honey. I don't know what to tell you. In a perfect world, everyone would get along and respect each other. But, this isn't a perfect world," Mom said softly as she watched Ash greet his parents.

Ash hugged his mother and shook his father's hand. None of them looked really happy. Ash's parents were ruining a perfect day. After a minute or so, they looked over at us, and then they turned and left. They didn't say anything. They just walked away.

"Well, I guess we should be grateful that they came to see Ash graduate. It's a shame that our families do not get along, though," Ben said with a sigh.

Ash came back over to us and just shrugged. Then he looked at me and smiled. "I'm okay. Like Ben said, at least they showed up. They didn't create a scene, but then they wouldn't. They'd avoid a human scene at all costs."

Forrest watched Ash's parents leave and then said, "Let's celebrate! How would you like to go to the Silver Bird for dinner? My treat!"

Ben cupped one earring with his hand. "You're the only teenager I can think of that has this many diamonds. They're lovely. Which ones did your mom and I get you?"

"Oh, you and mom got me the bracelet. See?" I showed him the bracelet under my gown sleeve.

"You're so beautiful. You don't need diamonds. But, I have to say, diamonds do look good on you. You deserve them." Ben kissed me on the forehead.

Mom was grinning at us. I heard Olivia laugh. I was working on being happy again. I sighed. My life would have been perfect if we could have all gotten along and went to dinner together. I tried to shake off my feelings of sadness and concentrate on the happiness of graduation day.

We drove in separate cars to the Silver Bird. Forrest had made reservations. It was just 4:00 p.m. when we got there. They had just opened. We were seated immediately at a large table. After we sat down, we all ordered drinks and our food. While we were waiting for our food to arrive, I saw that Forrest and Ben were talking together. Olivia and Hawthorn were laughing and talking together. I was glad that everyone looked so happy. I looked at Mom and said, "Did you ever expect to see this day?"

"Of course! I just didn't expect it this soon. I'm just having a hard time watching you grow up. What were you talking about with Ben at the school? Do you have a date for the wedding picked out?" Mom said as she looked at Ash and I.

Everyone at the table must have heard Mom's question because everyone stopped talking and looked at me and Ash. I felt myself grow a little red. Ash looked at me and gave me a smile. He squeezed my hand and said to everyone, but looking at my mom, "We were thinking of getting married in August. That way we can live together in an apartment at college."

"So soon?" Mom said. "You just graduated from high school! What about children? Just your undergrad degree will take four years!" Mom sipped her scotch.

"I don't think we should worry about children," Olivia said. "It takes us a longer to have them and with each new generation."

"Yeah, but it only took one time for me to get pregnant," Mom said with a worried look.

"But you're completely human," Olivia whispered back. "Laurel's mixed. She may not get pregnant at all."

"Oh, now that's a sad thought! I want grandchildren," Mom said.

"Hey, let's worry about that later," Ben said. "Right now, we are here to celebrate their graduation. However, I can see Ash's point. Since they've bonded, there's no real reason to wait. I like the idea that they wouldn't be living in sin in Madison." Ben kissed Mom on her cheek.

"I'm not ready to give up my baby!" Mom said in a soft, but intense, voice.

"I'm not a baby, Mom," I said, reaching over the table to hold her hand. "I'm all grown up. This will make me happy."

"I guess that's the most important thing. I want you to be happy." Mom took her napkin and dabbed at her eyes. She looked at Ash. "I'm glad to know how much you love her. I don't think I could have handled this as well with a regular young man." We knew she meant human. Wood nymphs bonded for life. There'd never be a divorce.

"Wow! Such a special day! A graduation with wedding plans," Douglas said as he walked up to our table.

"Hey! Douglas!" I got up and gave him a hug. "How long have you been within hearing distance?"

"Long enough to hear there are going to be wedding bells this summer!" Douglas said as he pulled up a chair to sit at our table with us.

"Wedding bells? Laurel and Ash are getting married this summer?" Chris, the owner of the Silver Bird said as she came up to the table.

"Hi, Chris! Yeah, we want to get married in August before we get to college." I said showing Chris my ring.

"Well! Congratulations! I would have thought you'd wait, but I guess when it is true love, well, why wait?" Chris said as she reached down to hug me.

"A round of drinks on the house!" Chris said to our server. Then she turned to look at us. "You could have the wedding here, depending on the number of people you invited. Plus, since it is an August wedding, there will be the whole deck if you want to have your reception here."

"That is a great idea!" I said smiling. Then I frowned. I wondered if Ash's parents and family would show up for our wedding. I shook off the sad thoughts and smiled at Chris. "We'll get with you about prices and details later, okay?"

"Sounds like a plan. You two really seem to suit each other. You even look alike. Oh, here are your salads. Enjoy your dinner!" she said as the server arrived.

Everything was going to be perfect, wasn't it? Was there any way we could ever bridge the gap with Ash's family? I looked at Ash. He was smiling at me. I looked around our table and saw everyone smiling and laughing. Olivia was talking to my mom. I know she was trying to help her accept the idea of my getting married at eighteen. I saw Mom smile at something Olivia said. I reached out to her with my senses and found Mom relaxing. Good! Whatever Olivia was saying was making her feel better.

We spent a couple of hours at the Silver Bird. Even when we were finished with our meal, no one wanted to leave. Everyone relaxed and made marriage jokes, and everyone had a good time. I felt a little bad when we all had to go home.

Ash drove me home. It wasn't really late, but I was really tired. I hadn't slept very well last night. I was too excited about graduation. I yawned.

"Why don't I just drop you off, and you go get some sleep? I'll see you tomorrow, okay?" he said to me as we pulled up in front of my house.

"I guess I am pretty tired. I love you!" I said reaching over to kiss him.

"I know. I love you, too. Forever," he replied and kissed me back. We kissed until my back ached. I was leaning over the center counsel of Ash's SUV.

"I'll see you tomorrow," I said as I got out of the car and blew him a kiss.

I saw him smile at me and then he drove down the driveway. Mom and Ben were already home. I went into the house.

"Welcome home, Ben!" I said as I walked into the house.

"Thank you! I never have to leave again. I finished all of my out-processing. I'm on terminal leave until the end of the month and then I'm finished with the Army. Retirement, here I come!" he said and laughed.

"It's a good thing you're home. Mom's going to need you when I get married and go off to college," I said, giving him a hug.

"I'll keep your mom busy, I promise," he said wiggling his eyebrows at me.

"La la la la! Too much information!" I said covering my ears. I assumed he was talking about sex. Ewwww. Parental sex. Gross.

"No, honey, really. We have a lot of things to do around here. We plan to travel. I promise you, I'll do my best to keep her entertained. Keep your mind out of the gutter," Ben admonished me as we walked into the living room.

"I'll miss you terribly. But, this is the natural order of things. I just didn't expect it to happen this soon," Mom said. "Did you enjoy your graduation day?"

"Oh, mom, it was a great day! I just wish Ash's parents could have enjoyed it with us. It really bugs me that he hates us." I said as I leaned back on the loveseat.

Ben put his arm around my mom and said to me, "We can only do what we can do. We can't control other people. We can only respect their land and stay off of it. Maybe in time, they'll see that humans aren't so bad. They have to respect us, too. Diversity goes both ways."

I gave a big yawn that I covered with my hand. I got up from the loveseat and said, "I'm really tired. I'm going to bed."

"'Night, honey. Hey, do you want to go for a walk with me tomorrow morning? I want to check out the acreage and see if there are any fallen trees that need to be cut up," Ben said as he and mom stood to kiss me good night.

"Sure. Wake me when you get up. Good night!" I said, hugging each of them.

"Good night, my beautiful daughter. I'm very proud of you," Mom said as I headed toward the stairs.

"I love you, too, Mom! Dad, too!" I said as I went up the stairs.

As I lay in bed waiting for sleep to come, I thought of the look on Ash's dad's face at the graduation. He didn't look happy. This was his only son's graduation from high school, and he almost ruined it for Ash. He could have greeted us. The fact that Ash's parents just came for the ceremony was lame. I would have thought that they would have wanted to spend more time with their son. It took me awhile to get to sleep.

CHAPTER 28
TORNADO!

Ben woke me up at six in the morning. I quickly got up and dressed. I put on long jeans and hiking boots. The wood ticks were bad at this time of year and I didn't want to go hiking in the woods and find a tick on me when I got back home. I also put on a sweat shirt as it was still cool in the morning.

Ben had already finished his breakfast and was sitting at the kitchen high top table drinking coffee. "As soon as you finish eating, we can head out. This'll also give us a chance to catch up on things."

"Okay," I said as I got out my cereal and milk. It didn't take me long to finish. "Is Mom still in bed?" I asked as I put my bowl in the dishwasher.

"Yup. We'll let her sleep in. She had to get up early yesterday morning to pick me up from the airport. I slept on the plane." Ben grinned and grabbed each of us a light-weight jacket. "It'll be cooler in the woods." Ben picked up a pair of pruning shears from by the front door.

"I think I'll trim overhanging bushes as we walk. I'm going to buy a four-wheeler for Mom and me, and I want to be able to get through this path," Ben said as we headed out the front door.

There was a deer path that wound through the trees away from the river and ran kind of parallel to our driveway. We walked it. Our driveway was a mile long, and we owned acreage on either side of it. Every so often, Ben would cut a branch hanging over the path.

"Ben, how did you end up with all this land? In school I hear about land short-ages all over the world." Ben was almost as sure footed as Ash. I still tripped on roots.

"My dad bought this property in the 1940s," Ben said. "A fire had leveled most of the woods in this area. The land was ugly. Dad was able to buy it at a low price. When he died, I inherited it. It is kind of sad, though. He always wanted to build something on it, but he never did. I kind of think of our house is a tribute to his fore-sight in purchasing the land when he did."

We had been walking for at least an hour when I noticed that the sky was getting darker. "Um, Ben. Maybe we should head back." I said pointing at the sky.

The clouds were rolling in fast and black. The sky turned a funny green. "This is tornado weather," Ben said with caution. "Feel the shift in the temperature? See the color of the sky? I think you are right. We need to head back now, and we probably should hurry."

We were deep in the woods, a good couple of miles from the house and the deer path wasn't very level. I kept tripping over roots and stones. We reached a small clearing. I looked up at the sky and screamed. "Ben! What is that!?!"

Ben stopped. "Oh, Laurel, that is a tornado and we are in its path. It is too wide for us to escape it. The only thing we can do is try to find a low point in the ground and lie in it and hope the tornado goes over us. It has to be a quarter to a half of a mile wide!" Ben started looking around the clearing for a low point. I stared at the swirling black cloud that was coming straight for us. I was mesmerized at the thought of Ben and I dying. Poor Ben, he survived Iraq just to get killed in a tornado the day after he gets home.

I screamed at the top of my lungs, "HELP US!!!!" I was in complete panic mode. I was supposed to get married. Ben had just gotten home! Frozen, I just stood there and watched the wall of swirling gray debris head right for us.

"Laurel, lie down on the ground! It's our only chance!" Ben yelled at me. He ran up to me. The clearing was about 100 yards across, and I could see the tornado tearing up the trees in its path. It would be on us in seconds. I could already feel the wind.

Ben grabbed me and started to force me to lay down, when I felt something go around me from behind and yank me away from Ben. I screamed. Ben reached for me but I saw Ash's father grab him and say, "We're going to jet you out of here. Don't fight me! We don't have the time!"

I heard Ash's voice in my ear, "I got you, Laurel. Turn and hold on to me. I haven't done this before, and we only have one chance. If we don't make it, I would rather die with you than to live without you! Hold still!"

The next thing I noticed was that I didn't feel the wild wind whipping about my face. I was in the in between place I had felt when Forrest had jetted with me to the essence ceremony. In the time it took me to take a couple of breaths, we stopped. Ash was panting like he had run the race of his life. I looked around. I had no idea where we were. The first thing I did was to look for the tornado. It was about a mile away and heading away from us. I looked around and I saw Ben standing next to Elm. Elm was acting like it was no big deal to jet with a man the size of Ben.

"Are you okay?" Ash asked me when he could breathe without panting. He leaned on my shoulder like he was having trouble holding himself up.

"I'm fine! You saved us!" I said hugging Ash as hard as I could. "Thank you!"

"We heard your call, and my dad and I took off. We didn't discuss it, we just jetted. We were working in the shed on a boat my dad is refinishing. I heard the sheer panic in the call and wondered if we would be on time when I saw the tornado." He was still a little out of breath, although he was recovering quickly. He gave me a weak smile.

that she is just as much a wood nymph as a human, maybe even more so. I want my son to be happy, and he is happy with Laurel. They've bonded, and my family's going to accept it. I'd like there to be peace between us. I hold out my hand in friendship." Elm held out his hand to Mom.

At first, my mom shook his hand, and then she hugged Elm. "Thank you for saving my family. I want peace between our families, too."

While mom was hugging Elm, Forrest and Olivia jetted into our driveway. Forrest ran over to us. "Are you okay?" he said to me, checking me out from top to bottom. "We heard the call, and by the time we got to where the call originated, we saw that the tornado was just passing over that spot. We thought you were killed. Oh, thank goodness you're all right!" Forrest said with a heartfelt sigh.

"I was panicking when we got to where you were and saw the tornado was there. I too, thought that we had lost you." Olivia said feeling my arms to assure herself I was fine.

"Thank you for saving my family," Forrest said to Ash and Elm. He figured it out that they had saved me and Ben. "They mean a lot to us."

"I can see that they do. Let's plan a wedding!" Elm said, and we all laughed. "I'll call my wife and ask her to come over. Is that all right?"

"Of course it is. I'll make some coffee," Mom said with a bright smile. "Come in and use our phone!"

As we were laughing and walking up to the house, I heard a vehicle approaching. I heard the crunching on the gravel of the driveway. I turned to look down the driveway and saw two big black stretch-limousines coming toward the house. A very tall, black and very dignified man got out of the drivers side and opened the back door. Out of the back door stepped a majestic looking man. He had on a crown and a king's robe. He looked like a Victorian era monarch. He was followed by a beautiful woman in a gown that would have fit right in at a Victorian royal court. Immediately, Ash, Elm, Olivia, and Forrest bowed to them. Mom, Ben, and I just stared. Who were these people that would cause the wood nymphs to humble themselves in front of? I realized that they must be wood nymphs. Very important wood nymphs.

Various other wood nymphs came out of the other limousine. I assumed that they were the royal attendants. Two very huge and mean looking black wood nymphs came out of each car. I guessed that they were the body guards.

"I'm Cornelius Stonehenge. I'm the king of the wood nymphs. I rule over all wood nymphs in the world. While I do not leave England very often, my rule stands unopposed. This is my wife, Delphine." He said in a commanding voice.

I looked at Olivia, and she appeared to be trembling.

He then turned toward Ash, Elm, Olivia, and Forrest. "Rise, my children. It's with good tidings we have come. We hear that the first human-wood nymph child has been born. This is wonderful news, amazing, and very, very special."

And he looked at me. That look penetrated me in a way that felt ominous, even if his words sounded happy. Olivia pressed against me, and I could feel her tremble even harder, and her mind was a swirl of fear and anxiety. Ash had gone pale and crowded against me on the other side. Olivia, Forrest, Ash, and Elm registered shock, surprise, awe, and more than one of them was afraid. But, afraid of what exactly?

King Cornelius Stonehenge walked up to me and, without touching me, looked me over like buyer appraising a prize race horse. It wasn't a nice feeling. "You are this child I've heard about. Ah, yes, I can sense the wood nymph *and* human in you. I hear you have the call and possibly other gifts. What an interesting girl! Let us enter your domicile and get to know one another." With that, he hooked his arm around my elbow and led me toward the house. There was force in his touch. Ash and Olivia were forced aside.

I looked over my shoulder at Ash, who radiated panic and tension. The tension was even more intense in Olivia and Forrest. Poor Olivia was shaking badly now. Elm seemed to be feeling more awe and curiosity than anything else. Mom and Ben were just confused but edging into alarm.

The whole entourage followed the king and queen before my parents, Ash, Forrest, and Olivia could follow.

When everyone was standing in the living room, I pulled my arm away from the king, trying to be respectful but clear I didn't like his touch. I turned and took a step away from him, bumping into someone in the process. I saw that the two huge guards had moved to stand right behind me. Each planted a firm palm on my shoulder, and firm grips circled my wrists.

Panic flooded me, but the king's people formed a cordon around me, the king and his guards. I could barely catch a glimpse of Ash or Olivia or Forest or Mom and Dad. I could feel their emotions, though and they had all gone from alarm to terror. I could hear them struggling near the door, trying to get to me. I wanted to go to them, but the guards held me fast.

Then the king, looking now very instense and with no pretense of being joyful or even kind, said, "You *will* be coming with us."

THE END

"My son is in love with your daughter," Elm said to Ben. "While it's not what I would have wanted, I've decided to accept it. Ash kind of gave me a bit of grief yesterday about not accepting the inevitable. He told me that he and Laurel were getting married in August. If Laurel would have died, something in my son would have died. If you had died, Laurel would never have been the same. We came to save you, and I've decided to make peace with you since we're going to be in-laws."

"Thank you for saving us," Ben said. "I especially thank you for saving Laurel. I have lived a lot of my life, but her life is just beginning. She's just beginning her new life as an adult." Ben held out his hand to Elm.

Elm looked at the hand for a moment and then shook it. Just as Ben and Elm shook hands, the sun broke through the clouds. The tornado dissipated, and we were in the middle of a field on a sunny day.

"If my sense of direction is correct, that tornado missed both of our houses, right? How far are we from either of our houses?" Ben asked Elm.

We are about half a mile away from your house. I'll walk with you to show you the way," Elm said as he turned toward a path I hadn't noticed earlier.

Ben looked over at me. "Are you sure you're okay?" He was shaking a little bit, but trying to hide it. I could feel his terror fading away.

"I'm fine! Thanks to Ash and his dad, we're both fine," I said going up to Ben and giving him a hug. "Let's go home! I bet Mom's worried."

"I'll bet she is, too. Okay. We'll follow you, Elm. Lead on," Ben said as he walked behind Elm. I walked behind Ben, and Ash brought up the rear. The path was too narrow to do more than single file.

It took us less than half an hour to get back to the house. There was no damage at all, not even leaves torn down. The tornado had been half a mile away from our house at its closest point. When we got through the trees, Mom was standing on the front steps holding the cordless phone.

"Oh, Ben! Laurel!" she called and ran to us crying. "I was so worried! I saw the sky get green, and I saw the tornado. I knew you had walked in that way. Oh, God, I am so glad to see you!" She then saw Elm and Ash and raised an eyebrow to me.

"Okay, Mom. I'm going to tell you the truth, but you can't freak out. Ben and I were in the tornado's path, and I screamed, and it went out as a call, and Ash and his dad came and jetted us out of the tornado's path." I gave her a hug. "We're fine, thanks to Ash and his dad."

"Why? I mean, I'm not complaining, but, how did this happen?" Mom asked.

Elm said kindly, "I've been a fool to think that once a wood nymph has bonded that I could break the bond if it was with a human. Laurel has shown in many ways